He forgot he was a duke; he forgot she was a Wynchester. They were just a man and a woman, trapped in each other's gaze, the kiss he had almost taken inevitable rather than narrowly escaped.

Why did he allow himself so close to temptation?

He told himself that if Miss Wynchester ran amok, making a cake of herself at society events, showing up at his gala could cause quite the stir.

Lawrence *hated* causing stirs. That was true and best kept in the forefront of his mind. The way to deflect future gossip was to avoid complicating the situation he found himself in now.

Starting with not kissing Chloe Wynchester under any circumstances. No matter how soft her skin or how plump and juicy her berry-pink lips. Her mouth was not his to taste, her kisses not his to steal.

He had a plan, and she could never be part of it.

the rest of the world fell away

THE DUKE HEIST

BOOKS BY ERICA RIDLEY

The Dukes of War

The Viscount's Tempting Minx
The Earl's Defiant Wallflower
The Captain's Bluestocking
Mistress
The Major's Faux Fiancée
The Brigadier's Runaway Bride
The Pirate's Tempting Stowaway
The Duke's Accidental Wife

The 12 Dukes of Christmas

Once Upon a Duke
Kiss of a Duke
Wish Upon a Duke
Never Say Duke
Dukes, Actually
The Duke's Bride
The Duke's Embrace
The Duke's Desire
Dawn with a Duke
One Night with a Duke
Ten Days with a Duke
Forever Your Duke

Rogues to Riches

Lord of Chance
Lord of Pleasure
Lord of Night
Lord of Temptation
Lord of Secrets
Lord of Vice

Gothic Love Stories

Too Wicked to Kiss
Too Sinful to Deny
Too Tempting to Resist
Too Wanton to Wed
Too Brazen to Bite

Magic & Mayhem

Kissed by Magic
Must Love Magic
Smitten by Magic

THE
DUKE
HEIST

ERICA RIDLEY

FOREVER
New York Boston

Copyright © 2021 by Erica Ridley

Cover design by name Daniela Medina
Cover illustration by Paul Stinson
Cover photography © Shirley Green Photography
Cover copyright © 2021 by Hachette Book Group, Inc.

Forever
Hachette Book Group
1290 Avenue of the Americas, New York, NY 10104
read-forever.com
twitter.com/readforeverpub

First edition: February 2021

Forever is an imprint of Grand Central Publishing. The Forever name and logo are trademarks of Hachette Book Group, Inc.

The publisher is not responsible for websites (or their content) that are not owned by the publisher.

The Hachette Speakers Bureau provides a wide range of authors for speaking events. To find out more, go to www.hachettespeakersbureau.com or call (866) 376-6591.

ISBNs: 978-1-5387-1952-7 (mass market), 978-1-5387-1950-3 (ebook)

Printed in the United States of America

CW

10 9 8 7 6 5 4 3 2 1

*To anyone who has ever hoped
for a place to belong*

And to Roy, for everything

ACKNOWLEDGMENTS

This book would not exist without the invaluable support of so many incredible people: Lauren Abramo, my brilliant agent, for all of the wisdom and encouragement. Leah Hultenschmidt, my fabulous editor, who started the ball rolling and is phenomenal. The entire team at Forever, from art to promo to edits: you are fantastic.

Huge thanks to Rose Lerner, whose knowledgeable and thoughtful suggestions are incomparable. Intrepid assistant Laura Stout, who has been assisting me since birth (Hi, Mom!) and handles the mailing of prizes and all other tasks I cannot do from Costa Rica. My fabulous beta readers: Erica Monroe and Emma Locke, plus my awesome early reader crew. Thank you all so much!

I wouldn't have made it through the past year without the unflagging support and encouragement from too many people to name, but I'll try: Bernardita, Caro, Darc, Heidi, Jean, Julie, Karen, Lace, Lenore, Mary, Rachel, Susan, my Jewel sisters, and the Elite 8, whose Zoom happy hours are an absolute delight.

Muchísimas gracias and all of my love goes out to my personal romance hero, Roy Prendas, who not only came up with the idea for our Regency-themed wedding but also helps in countless ways to enable me to spend as much time as possible writing the next chapter. *¡Te adoro!* You give me Happy Ever After every single day.

Lastly, I want to thank my amazing, wonderful readers. You're all so fun and funny and smart. I love your emails and adore chatting books together in the newsletter VIP List, on social media, and in our Historical Romance Book Club group on Facebook. Your enthusiasm makes the romance happen.

Thank you for everything!

THE DUKE HEIST

1

March 1817
London, England

*M*iss Chloe Wynchester burst through the door of her family's sprawling residence in semi-fashionable Islington, followed closely behind by her sister Thomasina. Chloe's pulse raced with excitement. His Arrogance, the Duke of Frosty Disapproval, didn't have a chance.

Unable to keep her exuberance to herself, she yelled out, "I have news about the painting!"

In a more respectable household, a young lady might expect censure for being so vulgar as to shout, even within the confines of one's own home. Such a young lady might also be rebuked for donning trousers and strolling about Westminster under an assumed identity.

Chloe was grateful every single day not to have such limitations.

Her roguish brother Graham appeared at the top of the marble stairs, delight and disbelief writ across his handsome face. He was used to being the one with shocking news to share. "Don't stand about. Come up to the Planning Parlor at once! I'll ring for tea."

Exchanging grins, Chloe and Tommy dashed up the marble stairs, their gray cotton trousers allowing them to take the steps two at a time. In seconds they joined Graham in the Planning Parlor, the communal private sitting room the six siblings used for plotting their stratagems.

Chloe and Tommy tossed their matching beaver hats onto the long walnut-and-burl table in the center of the sound-dampened room.

Tommy rubbed a hand over her short brown hair, causing it to spring up at all angles. Graham moved a pile of scandal sheets from the table to the map case to make room for refreshments. Tommy and Graham launched themselves into their favorite needlepoint armchairs, between two large windows outfitted with heavy calico curtains of ruby and gold.

Chloe was far too excited to sit. Instead, she paced the black slate floor, which still contained traces of chalk from the last planning session. She paused before the unlit fireplace and lifted her chin.

For as long as she could remember, two paintings had always hung above the white marble mantel. One of them had been missing for the last eight months.

But it wouldn't remain missing for much longer.

"The Planning Parlor feels doubly empty without our Puck," Graham said gruffly.

"Not just the Parlor," Tommy corrected. "Our entire house." *Our lives.*

No one said the words out loud, but they all knew it to be true. The house had belonged to Baron Vanderbean, but the beloved painting belonged to all of them.

Bean had rescued his motley brood of orphans over the course of a single summer. Six proud, frightened children between the ages of eight and eleven: Chloe, Tommy, Graham, Jacob, Marjorie, and Elizabeth. Life had taught them to be mistrustful and careful. Coming together as a family had been the most pivotal moment in their lives.

Chloe lifted her gaze to the portrait above the left side of the mantel. Bean's fatherly visage bore a grin that crinkled the edges of his bright blue eyes. It was not at all the thing to smile in one's portrait, which was probably why Bean had done so. Chloe was glad he did. His smile always made her feel loved.

A maid entered the room and began arranging the tea. Chloe tugged her cravat free, so as not to fill it with crumbs.

Tommy wiggled with excitement. "I can't wait to hear your plan, Chloe. Once Puck comes home, it will feel like having a part of Bean back. Like being whole again."

Chloe's heart pounded in agreement. All six of the siblings would do anything in their power to bring *Puck & Family* home where it belonged.

Before they'd found each other, most of the siblings had never had anyone they could rely on or possessions to call their own. They'd learned the hard way not to develop emotional attachments to people or things.

Bean had offered permanence. A place to belong. A home. He told them they were the children he'd always wanted but never had. From the moment each had arrived on the doorstep, they'd felt loved and cherished in a way they had never known. The oil painting was their first purchase as a family. Their first *decision* as a family. For most of them, it was the first time their voices mattered.

The artist's uncommon skill wasn't why they'd chosen the unusual painting. It was the subject. A forest scene, featuring Robin Goodfellow—the mischievous demon-fairy sometimes known in folktales as Puck—and six fellow sprites of all sizes and hues, dancing about a fire with absolute freedom and joy.

It was the visual representation of what they'd found in each other. Happiness. Unconditional love. The ability to be oneself and to be *bigger* than oneself—to be a team, and a family. That was the most magical part of all. That painting was their soul on canvas.

To the Wynchesters, the painting was a family portrait . . . and their most cherished possession. It belonged to all of them. It *was* all of them.

"Once Puck comes home, we can get rid of that cherub."

All three gazes swung to the fireplace. An angel-shaped vase stood on the mantel, right beneath the faded rectangle where *Puck & Family* should have been.

A blank spot that matched the empty space in their lives where Bean used to be.

Chloe swallowed hard at the injustice. Nineteen years earlier the prior Duke of Faircliffe had sold them the painting to pay one of his many gaming debts. Then, eight months ago, when he suddenly wanted it back, the family refused. Instead of honoring the original transaction, the duke stole the painting and left an ugly vase behind in its stead, as though that could possibly make up for their loss.

Neither they nor the old duke anticipated a carriage accident interrupting his journey home—or that he'd succumb to his injuries.

When Bean visited the heir to politely request the return of their painting, the newly crowned Duke of Faircliffe refused to see him.

Rebuff Baron Vanderbean! Chloe's blood boiled. But that was hardly the first of the new duke's endless slights and rejections. He'd always been too lofty and self-important to notice anyone of lesser rank, no matter the justification.

Later, when Bean caught smallpox, he refused to allow the children into his sickroom lest he expose them to the disease. They threw themselves into retrieving the painting, and cursed Faircliffe when Bean slowly slipped away, without the safe return of their heirloom. Then or now, the Wynchester family couldn't command a single second of the new duke's time. She ground her teeth.

According to the society papers, the Wynchester children were nothing more than a dead baron's charity orphans—someone you might toss a coin to out of pity but never deign to speak to on purpose.

She didn't care what Faircliffe thought of her. Chloe was *glad* to be a Wynchester. She wouldn't trade a single moment for the boring, buttoned-up life of the beau monde.

Chloe was used to being invisible. It was her greatest talent and often the reason for the success of their clandestine missions. It had begun as a game.

When the six siblings were children, Bean taught them to play Three Impossible Things to give them skills and confidence. They gathered information, breached barriers, and performed feats of daring.

Later, their team became the specialists to turn to when the justice system failed those in need. The Wynchesters snuck food and medicine into prisons, exposed workhouses and orphanages with draconian practices, tracked down libertines who despoiled for sport, rescued women and children from abusers, delivered aid and supplies to those who needed it most. Bean had taught them nothing was impossible. Everyone deserved their best life.

Their missions gave them purpose and adventure. Chloe loved slipping about unseen, doing good works beneath people's noses. But being overlooked on purpose was one thing. Being dismissed out of cruelty was far worse.

"We no longer have to beg," Chloe announced. "We can steal it back from Faircliffe, just as his father did to us."

Graham added another tea cake to his plate. "How will we infiltrate the duke's terraced fortress? That town house is as tightly locked down as His Loftiness himself. Do we even know where he's keeping the painting?"

Chloe grinned at him. "We don't have to. I know where it's going to *be*."

He set down his cake. "Where? How?"

She leaned back. "I sometimes watch parliamentary proceedings from the peephole in the attic—"

"Sometimes?" Graham rolled his eyes. "When have you missed one? And what does your obsession with politics have to do with getting Puck back?"

"Well, if you would let me finish." Chloe pilfered her brother's tea cake and took a bite from the corner, chewing with exaggerated slowness before swallowing. "As I was saying, today Tommy disguised us as journalists and we sneaked into the Strangers' Gallery, where we sat behind Mr. York—"

"Wait," Graham interrupted, his brown eyes gleaming. "Mr. York, the MP whose daughter is rumored to have caught the Duke of Faircliffe's eye?"

"It's more than a rumor," Chloe said sourly. "We overheard Faircliffe say he intends to give *Puck & Family* to Mr. York's daughter Philippa as a courting gift."

Graham's face purpled. "Give away *our* painting? That *knave*. It's not his to give!"

"That's the bad news," Chloe agreed. She affected an innocent expression. "The good news is that my 'Jane Brown' alias has an invitation to Miss York's weekly ladies' reading circle. I met her when I was on that mission at the dreadful school for girls. Philippa was visiting with a charity group and—you know what? It doesn't matter. The important part is, I have access to the home where the painting will *be*. It's our chance!"

Her brother pinned her with his too-perceptive gaze. "You accidentally bumped into the Duke of Faircliffe's future intended and now have a standing invitation into her household? That's a bit of good fortune."

"Er...yes." Chloe became suddenly enthralled by her tea. "A very lucky, completely random coincidence."

It was definitely not because she read the same gossip columns as her brother and wanted to see for herself what kind of woman attracted the Duke of Faircliffe's attention.

Chloe had passed by him any number of times—not that he noticed. He didn't even acknowledge her when she'd placed herself in his direct path to demand the return of her family portrait. Barely a syllable had escaped her lips before he strode right past her toward something or someone he actually cared about.

Blackguard.

"Now that we know when and where to act, we can play the game and get the painting." Chloe counted the Impossible Things on her fingers. "First, ingratiate myself with the reading circle. Achieved. Second, retrieve *Puck & Family* once Faircliffe delivers it. Third, replace it with a forgery so no one suspects a thing. It all happens on Thursday."

Graham frowned. "Why would Faircliffe wish to interrupt a reading circle?"

"He doesn't know he's going to." Chloe smirked. "The Yorks are surprisingly crafty."

"Even a stiff, scowling duke like Faircliffe is a catch worth bragging about," Tommy explained. "Mrs. York will want witnesses."

"*We* don't want witnesses," Graham pointed out. "Wouldn't

it be safer to bump into Faircliffe on the street and 'accidentally' swap his rolled canvas for ours?"

"It would indeed," Chloe agreed, "if Faircliffe happened to stroll through Grosvenor Square with a rolled-up canvas. But the painting is framed, and the duke will arrive in a carriage where the York butler will be watching."

Graham lifted his tea. "There aren't a lighter set of fingers in all of London, so I've no doubt you can nick the canvas. And we'll ask Marjorie to create the forgery."

All six Wynchester siblings were talented in their own ways. Marjorie was an extraordinary painter who could replicate any artwork to match the original.

Chloe smiled. "Marjorie finished ages ago. I just needed an opportunity to exchange canvases. And some way to smuggle it out without anyone noticing."

She swapped Graham's spoon with Tommy's fork as she thought. Coins and keys were easy objects to palm, but a rolled-up canvas was much too big.

"Could you strap a tube to your leg?" Tommy asked.

"Perhaps if I walked very carefully..." Chloe mused, then shook her head. "I would have to lift up my skirts to strap on the tube, and being caught like that would be worse. What I need is—"

"Kittens." Their rugged elder brother Jacob strolled into the Planning Parlor with a lopsided basket in his strong arms. "Most ladies love kittens almost as much as a good book. If you were showing off a new pet..."

Chloe tensed. Although hints of fur clung to Jacob's ripped and patched waistcoat, she'd learned to be wary. The last time her brother had entered a room with a basket, he was trying his hand at snake charming. If she hadn't been wearing her sturdiest boots... "Do you really have a kitten in there?"

"Ferrets," he admitted, his dark brown eyes sparkling. "But

I have the perfect solution out in the barn. Tiglet is the best of all the messenger kittens."

"Messenger...kittens?" she echoed faintly.

"Like pigeons, but terrestrial," Jacob explained earnestly. "More fur, less filth. The perfect cover. He can find his way home from anywhere. He'll be a splendid distraction. Because where there's chaos—"

"There's opportunity," Tommy finished, eyes gleaming.

Chloe held up a finger. "First rule of Three Impossible Things: No plan without a contingency."

Graham brightened. "May I suggest—"

"Your acrobatic skills are awe inspiring, brother, but unnecessary in this instance."

Graham's shoulders caved. "When will it be my turn?"

"Whilst I don't anticipate the need for trick riding on the back of a racing stallion," Chloe assured him, "a *driver* would not be amiss. Just in case I must flee in too much haste to flag down a hackney."

"No hack required." Graham straightened. "We can't risk one of our carriages being recognized, so I'll drive a substitute that cannot be traced to the family."

Tommy cocked her head. "If there is a queue of carriages awaiting their literary-minded mistresses, how will Chloe know which coach is the right one?"

"Mine will have red curtains...and a conspicuously displayed glove for good measure." Graham's eyes lit up. "Better yet, I will not only be the first carriage you come to. I'll be in the coachman's perch. You shan't miss me."

"No plan without a contingency." Jacob's curly black hair dipped as he peeked into the basket of ferrets. "What if the Yorks' staff insist you move the carriage?"

Tommy clapped her hands. "Elizabeth will distract them."

When Elizabeth threw her voice, no one could tell where it

was coming from. Their sister could emulate an entire crowd of distractions. She was also handy with a sword stick. Either skill would do the trick.

Graham turned to Chloe, his eyes serious. "If we get separated for any reason, go somewhere safe. I'll find you."

She grinned back at him, exhilarated by the upcoming adventure. Puck was finally coming home. "The reading circle will have a wonderful afternoon. Other than a wee interlude with Tiglet, the most memorable event will be Miss York charming the Duke of Haughtiness."

Graham lifted a broadsheet. "Their alliance will be the talk of the scandal columns. No one will remember anything else. Which is too bad, because I rather enjoy their wild conjecture about us. One of my favorite columns claims: 'Such a large, isolated house could contain dozens of them!'"

Chloe wrinkled her nose. "Those gossips make us sound like *bats*."

"I like bats." Jacob scratched beneath the chin of one of the ferrets. "Bats are fascinating. They have navels like humans and clean themselves like cats. I have thirteen of them out in the barn."

"Please keep them there," Tommy murmured.

"Or give them to His Iciness," Chloe suggested.

"Faircliffe deserves as much." Graham moved the broadsheets in search of his spoon. "No doubt the duke's interest in Philippa York is monetary. Although she has no title, she does possess the largest dowry on the marriage mart. I've been keeping a tally."

"Poor Philippa." Tommy's mouth tightened. "She deserves better."

Chloe agreed. Faircliffe single-handedly lowered the temperature in every room he entered. The man was all sharp cheekbones and cutting remarks. That is, to everyone but her.

She was invisible when right in front of him. Even when she was *trying* to be seen.

Graham made a face. "Can you imagine being wed to that block of ice?"

Chloe pushed her teacup away. "I cannot fathom a worse fate."

2

*L*awrence Gosling, eighth Duke of Faircliffe, was on the verge of achieving what had once seemed impossible: replenishing the dukedom's empty coffers and restoring its tattered reputation.

His father had lived a charmed life on credit he had been unable to repay. And now, with the failure of their country estate's crops, the situation was becoming dire. If Lawrence did not secure a bride with a significant dowry before the end of the season, he would have to send the last of his loyal servants to the streets.

He would not repay them so shabbily.

Lawrence leaned forward in his rented coach and opened the curtain to be able to address his driver. As with all of his father's grievous missteps, each of Lawrence's attempts to restore respect and prosperity had been won at great personal cost.

The sacrifice was worth it.

Lawrence's reputation was spotless, his performance in Parliament impeccable. This season, marriage-minded mamas would have him at the top of their lists. For as long as Lawrence lived, the Gosling name and Faircliffe title would never again be spoken with derision. No heir of *his* would be dismissed, forced to shoulder ridicule and isolation.

Of course, that was because no one realized his shiny reputation hid a very empty pocketbook. The dukedom didn't need *a* dowry. The dukedom needed *the* dowry to end all dowries. A sum so staggering, Lawrence could restore the half-abandoned entailed country estate, repay the last of his father's debts, and have a respectable chunk left over to invest in a stable future.

The dukedom needed Miss Philippa York.

"The terrace house at the corner," Lawrence instructed the driver. "The one with yellow rosebushes."

"As you please, Your Grace."

Using a coach to travel from one end of Grosvenor Square to the other was a shameless display of pretension and excess...and the reason Miss York's parents looked favorably on a courtship between Lawrence and their daughter.

Although he'd sold his last remaining carriage that morning—right down to his prized greys—Lawrence had rented this hack to keep up appearances.

Mr. York was one of the most powerful MPs in the House of Commons. Mrs. York was bosom friends with a patroness of Almack's. They had wealth, status, everything they could ever want—except a title.

After the wedding, the Yorks' daughter would be a duchess, their grandson a future duke. To them, such a jaw-dropping coup would be more than worth any dowry required.

For him it meant a new leaf. The Earl of Southerby was seeking partners for an investment opportunity with very attractive interest rates—*if* Lawrence came up with his portion before the earl quit London at the end of the season. It was not a flashy wager, like the sort his father had made at his gentlemen's clubs, but the steady interest and future profit would provide a strong foundation for years to come.

To Lawrence, marriage to respectable Miss York meant far more than financial stability. His children could be *children*, without fear of mockery or poverty. It would give his sons and daughters the chance—no, the *right*—to be happy.

Everyone deserved as much, including his new bride. Lawrence could not afford to woo Miss York for an entire season, but he could give her a week or two to get to know him before the betrothal.

He reached for the framed canvas on the seat opposite. "Once the traffic clears, I'll alight at the last house. I shan't be more than half an hour."

But the carriages crowding the Yorks' side of the square did not move. The queue appeared to be idly awaiting passengers. One of the Yorks' neighbors must be hosting a tea. He grimaced.

Lawrence hated tea. He would rather drink water from the Thames.

"Stop here." He reached for the door. "Find your way to the front of the queue so I know where to find you when I return."

The driver nodded and allowed the curtain to fall closed.

Despite residing on opposite sides of Grosvenor Square, this was Lawrence's first call at the York residence. The warm red brick and painted white columns of the impeccable terrace house were bright and clean. Every window glistened in the sunlight, reflecting the azure spring sky or the trim green grass in the square.

Jaw clenched, he strode down the pavement toward their front walk as elegantly as one could with a heavy, brown-paper-wrapped, framed painting clutched beneath one's arm.

Lawrence *could* have brought his last remaining footman

along to carry the painting, but he hoped a show of personal effort would add an extra touch of romance to his unusual gift. It was not what he would have picked, but the important thing was giving his future betrothed something *she* liked.

The finality of marriage prickled his skin with equal parts nervousness and excitement. A fortnight from now, when the contract was signed, he and Miss York would be saddled with each other. His palms felt clammy. Was it foolish to hope their union might be a pleasant one? He drew himself taller.

As with all duties, one did as one must.

The door was answered as soon as he touched the knocker. Lawrence presented his card at once.

"Your Grace," said the butler. "Do come in. Shall I ring for someone to take your package?"

"I'll deliver it." Lawrence stepped over the threshold to wait for his hosts.

He and Mr. York had met in the House of Commons and enjoyed spirited debates for most of a decade. Last year, after the premature death of Lawrence's father, he had moved from the House of Commons to the House of Lords. A partnership with Mr. York would ensure vital allies across the two Houses.

All he had to do was remain sparklingly unobjectionable until the banns were read. Once Miss York married him, her dowry would save the dukedom and secure a better future for his family and his tenants.

The plan *had* to work. It was Lawrence's only shot.

Mrs. York bounded up to him, her hands clasped to her chest as if physically restraining a squeal of excitement. "Your Grace, such a pleasure, I do say!"

The unmistakable sound of female voices trickled from an open door halfway down the corridor straight ahead.

Lawrence's skin went cold. This was supposed to be a

private meeting. He hated surprises and was inept at impromptu conversations. He excelled in Parliament because he prepared his speeches in advance—just as he had done for today's visit with Miss York and her parents.

Interacting with an unexpected crowd would ensure he made a hash out of his well-rehearsed lines. He stepped no farther.

"Did I mistake the date?" he inquired carefully.

"No, no. Right on time, as always." Mr. York strode up to join his wife. "You're a man who cleaves to duty. A fine trait, I daresay. Very little in common with your father."

"Er...thank you. I should hope I'm nothing like him."

"Quite right, quite right. Your parliamentary speeches could rival Fox and Pitt. Your father, on the other hand, rarely left his club—or his cups. Indeed, there are many who say—" Mr. York coughed and gave Lawrence a jovial clap on the shoulder. "'Tis no time for gossip, is it, my boy?"

Lawrence affected an affable smile. At least, he hoped that was what his face was doing. He was conscious every day that the Gosling name teetered on the edge of respectability. Mr. York's unfinished intimation had been clear: there were still those who said Faircliffe dukes were a blight on society.

Duke or not, nothing was certain until the contract was signed.

"It is our *honor*, Your Grace," Mrs. York gushed as she fluttered her hands in excitement and impatience. "Is that the special gift for Philippa? Come, you must present it to her at once."

"I admit I can't fathom what beauty she sees in that painting," Mr. York murmured.

Lawrence held the frame a little harder. Dancing hobgoblins *were* an unusual subject. He did not understand why anyone would want it.

What if, upon second inspection, the young lady realized her error in having expressed admiration for such questionable "art" and laughed in his face when he presented it as a gift? Being able to give an item he already possessed had seemed like serendipity. Now he feared the omen might not be positive. His veins hummed with panic.

"It sounds as though Miss York is entertaining guests." He gripped the frame. "I should return when I'm not interrupting."

"Stuff and nonsense." Mrs. York looped her hand about the crook of Lawrence's elbow and all but dragged him down the corridor. "It's just a few of her bluestocking friends. I'm certain they'll all find it amusing to see what you've brought Philippa."

Yes. Exactly what he was afraid of.

But there was no backing out now. His father's word wasn't worth the breath it floated on, but Lawrence had kept every vow for two and thirty years. Miss York liked the painting; he'd promised to give it to her. On this day. At this time. Nowhere to go but forward.

Besides, "a few bluestockings" was hardly a lion's den...was it?

"Philippa, my dear, look who's arrived!" Mrs. York sang out as they entered a grand parlor.

The room was enormous, with seats for over two dozen guests, and every chair was full.

Lawrence could *feel* the weight of too many gazes landing on him at once.

Half of them, he did not recognize—perhaps those were the "bluestockings"—but the other half were familiar faces from polite society. He swallowed hard. He didn't merely need to impress Miss York and her parents; he needed to charm an entire room.

If only influencing a parlor full of women were as easy as debating customs and excise reform at Westminster with a few hundred of his peers. Quoting the latest committee findings was unlikely to gain him any points here.

He wouldn't acknowledge any of them, Lawrence decided. The situation was too fraught and the chance for error too high. Missteps like smiling at or snubbing the wrong young lady. He would place all of his attention on Miss York. That could be interpreted as romantic, could it not? Here he was with a courting gift, a knight bearing a tapestry of dancing demons for his fair maiden.

Miss York, for her part, was enshrouded in her usual yards of voluminous lace. Only her pink cheeks and dimpled hands protruded from the delicate froth, lending her the appearance of a life-sized doll.

Her eternally blank expression made the resemblance uncanny.

"Miss York," Lawrence began, then paused. He could not kiss her hand with a painting in his arms, and setting it on the ground risked damage. Bowing would be just as unwieldy. He would have to skip the niceties and rush straight to the romance. "I've brought you a humble token of my admiration."

"Ohhh," gasped one of her friends. "What could it be?"

"A painting my mother informed him I might enjoy." Miss York gestured toward a blank spot on the wall. "She intends to put it there."

So. She was not impressed with his courtship gift. Lawrence forced himself to smile anyway.

Miss York didn't smile back.

The rest of the room was alive with whispers.

"Is it a love match?"

"Why else would he wed beneath him? *My* father is a marquess."

"What, did you think he was bringing the gift to you?"

"Do you think she loves him?"

"Who can ever tell what she's thinking? I cannot wait to see the artwork he brought her."

The back of Lawrence's neck flushed with heat.

Yes, Miss York was marrying him for his title. Yes, he needed her dowry. But that didn't have to be all they shared. Even a marriage of convenience could work with a modicum of effort.

But first he had to get rid of this bloody painting.

"Could someone ring for a pair of shears?" he asked politely.

"Here!" Mrs. York trilled.

Two wigged footmen, identical in height and elegant livery, glided into the room and relieved Lawrence of the canvas.

Now was his chance to kiss Miss York's hand. Before he could do so, a maid handed her a sharp pair of metal shears.

Miss York rose to her feet in a rustle of lace.

A wave of whispers once again rushed through the parlor. Lawrence risked a subtle glance over his shoulder.

Every gaze was transfixed on Miss York...except for one. One woman's dark brown eyes arrested him.

She did not seem curious about the gift. Her disconcertingly intense expression was shrewd, as if she could see through the brown paper package, see through his meticulously tailored layers of fashionable apparel, see through *him* to the nervousness and desperation beneath. But she did not look away. Her gaze only sharpened, as if she had stripped him bare and still wanted more.

His throat grew dry. He tried to swallow. An odd prickling sensation traveled up his spine as though the tips of her fingers had brushed against his skin.

He quickly turned back to Miss York. The delivery of the

gift had stretched on long enough. If she didn't cut through the paper soon, Lawrence would rip it apart with his bare hands, make his bow, and escape to his waiting carriage before he was forced to follow this performance with tea and small talk.

"If you'd be so kind?" he murmured.

Miss York sliced through the brown paper as though she had little interest in safekeeping the art beneath.

The paper fell away. The painting was exposed. A gasp rippled through the crowd. Whether at the romance of the gesture or because the subject featured a family of mischievous sprites, Lawrence could not say.

"Thank you," Miss York said. "You are most kind."

Was she smitten? Bored? She did not appear to be upset or in any danger of swooning. He gave a gift. She received the gift. *Fin.*

The back of his neck heated anew. He appreciated her extreme lack of drama, Lawrence told himself. After her dowry, her predictability was his favorite trait. A woman like Miss York would never muddy the Faircliffe title with scandal. She was exactly what he needed: no scrapes, no surprises.

Mrs. York burst into loud applause. "Huzzah!"

Everyone in the room followed suit. Everyone, that was, except Miss York and the oddly intense young woman with the mocking half smile.

Her gaze continued to track him, as though she could hear each overloud heartbeat and sense each shallow breath from across the room. He did not like the sensation at all. Despite the roomful of strangers, her regard felt strangely intimate and far too perceptive.

"As soon as the painting is hung," Mrs. York chirped, "we shall all remove to the dining room for a nice, leisurely tea."

Good God, anything but that. Besides his distaste for tea,

Lawrence could not court anyone properly while dodging the unsettling gaze of the woman with the pretty brown eyes. Even now, he was thinking of her instead of concentrating on Miss York. It would not do. Once the painting was hung, Lawrence would bolt out the door and into the sanctity of his carriage.

His driver had better be ready to fly.

3

Chloe folded her hands in her lap and did her best not to glare a hole right through the handsome, haughty Duke of Faircliffe.

All of this would have been much easier if Faircliffe would simply *return* the painting. But addressing His Arrogance directly did not work. Chloe and her siblings had pleaded for months, in countless letters sent to his home and dozens of humiliating attempts in person.

His Infuriating Loftiness was far too superior to see reason...or commoners like the Wynchester siblings.

His frigid blue gaze looked right at Chloe—and slid away just as quickly, having glimpsed nothing to attract his interest.

How many times had she and Faircliffe crossed paths? Hyde Park, Berkeley Square, Westminster. Every disdainful glance in her direction was as indifferent as the last. She lifted her chin. Bean had taught her that, to the right person, she would be visible and memorable. Faircliffe was clearly the wrong person.

Not that she *wanted* him to notice her, Chloe reminded herself. The continued success of "Jane Brown" hinged on her uncanny ability to be wholly unremarkable under any circumstances. She gripped the soft muslin of her skirt. Tommy might be an unparalleled genius with disguises, but Chloe needn't do anything at all to blend in and be forgettable.

She possessed one of those faces that was at once familiar yet too ordinary to pick out from a crowd. She was neither tall nor short, ugly nor pretty. Nothing about her stood out.

Her skin wasn't palest alabaster like Philippa York's or golden bronze like her brother Graham's. She was not thin and willowy like Tommy or pleasingly plump like Elizabeth. Her limp brown hair wasn't spun flax like Marjorie's, or blessed with glossy black curls like Jacob's. Chloe was neutral and dull, with nary even a freckle to add a spot of interest.

She was just...*there*, like a dust mote in a shaft of light.

Her perpetual insignificance had helped her through scrape after scrape. Chloe would never admit how much she wished, just once, to see a flicker of recognition reflected back at her.

Not that her expectations of Faircliffe were high. What type of conceited, coldhearted knave blithely gave away *a painting he did not own* as a courtship gift?

A villain like that could not be trusted or reasoned with. He'd had his chance to deal honorably. Chloe wouldn't beg him for the painting even if she could. At this point, the duplicitous, arrogant blackguard *deserved* to have it whisked out of his hands.

She forced her tense fingers to unclench and folded them in her lap. *Soon.*

"Thank you ever so much for your charming gift," Mrs. York cooed loud enough for the entire party to hear, and likely the neighbors as well. "Philippa is overjoyed."

Philippa did not appear to be overjoyed. Or even middling-level joyful. She bore the same *I am here because I must be* expression she wore at every social function, save the brief occasions when her mother left her side and the reading circle could actually talk about books. Chloe imagined her far more interested in the duke's famed library than in the man himself.

Not that Faircliffe seemed particularly infatuated. A man in love would have dreamed up a gift better suited to his bride.

"My gratitude," Philippa murmured.

The duke looked self-congratulatory. "My pleasure."

Chloe glared at him on behalf of women everywhere who longed for more than token gestures of false affection.

But Faircliffe's kind didn't waste time on matters of the heart. Lords and ladies—or those who aspired to become them—selected their unions with cold practicality. Their minds were muddied not with emotion but with visions of titles and dowries and estates and social connections.

Chloe was *delighted* not to belong to a world like that.

Mrs. York clapped her hands together. "And now...a celebratory tea!"

The duke's face displayed a comical look of alarm. "I don't think—"

"You must join us!" Mrs. York's hands flapped like frightened birds. "The ladies were about to have oatcakes and cucumber sandwiches—"

"We were about to discuss epistolary structure in eighteenth-century French novels," Philippa murmured.

"I never meant to interrupt," Faircliffe said with haste. "I mustn't stay, and in fact—"

"Nonsense! Come, come, all of you." Mrs. York waved her arms about the room, driving her guests into the dining room like a shepherd herding sheep.

Chloe and Faircliffe were both caught in the flow.

Once they passed through the doorway, however, Chloe stepped to one side. She could not take a seat at the table or she would be stuck there for the next hour.

While everyone else was occupied, this was her chance to liberate her beloved Puck. But first, she needed an excuse to disappear. An adorable, furry reason.

She released Tiglet from the large wicker basket. The calico kitten darted between boots and beneath petticoats with a formidable *rawr*.

Mrs. York gave a dramatic shriek in response.

Tiglet scaled several curtains in search of an open window before darting out of the dining room and flying off down the corridor as though his tail were afire.

Chloe gasped as if shocked that her homing kitten was attempting to dash home. "How embarrassing! I'll run and find the naughty little scamp at once. Please don't wait for me."

Philippa glanced up from her place at the table. "I could help—"

"Sit *down*," her mother hissed. "The duke is here."

Philippa sighed. "We could at least ring for a maid or footman—"

"It's really no trouble," Chloe assured her. "Please serve the tea."

With a meaningful glance to Mrs. York, Chloe made several unsubtle tilts of her head toward the Duke of Faircliffe, who was tarrying noticeably, as if reluctant to take his place at the table.

"Oh!" Mrs. York said loudly. "You're absolutely right. Go on, dear. Take your time. Over here, Your Grace. Come and sit by Philippa. We've saved you the best seat."

"Have you met the others?" Philippa gestured at each young lady as she took a chair at the table. "To my left is…"

Chloe slipped from the room at the sound of Mrs. York chastising her daughter for performing introductions out of the order of precedence. Chloe could be gone an hour before anyone would notice.

She wouldn't need but five minutes.

With her basket hanging from her arm, she ducked into the parlor and closed the door behind her. A broken hairpin in the keyhole would not only prevent anyone from entering behind her but would also make it obvious a crime was under way. She would simply work fast.

There was no sense looking for the kitten. Strands of calico fur and unfortunate paw prints on a velvet curtain indicated Tiglet had already found an open window and was well on his way home.

Chloe hurried to lift her family painting from the wall and carried it behind a chinoiserie folding screen in the corner. Cutting the canvas free was not an option. The replacement must look identical to the original, and besides, she would never damage an object that meant this much. Quickly she lay the frame facedown and removed her tools from the basket.

Marjorie had drilled Chloe on mounting and unmounting canvases until her fingers were callused and she could perform the maneuver in her sleep. Up came the grips, off came the backing, out came *Puck & Family*. She rolled it into a scroll the size of her forearm and tucked it into the basket before stretching the forgery over the wooden frame.

This was the tricky part. There was no way to attach the painting without hammering the grips in place. She must do so in silence. If she placed only one grip on each side, and lined each one perfectly with the holes it had come from...There! She hurriedly returned it to the wall.

As long as it stayed there, no one would notice the imperfect craftsmanship. And if one day someone did notice, well, that was none of Chloe's concern. Faircliffe would be the one who had to explain the shoddy frame.

She did not feel sorry for him at all. This was not his painting to give away. For that alone she could never forgive him.

She ran to open the parlor door before anyone noticed it had been shut, and strode past the dining room to the front door without taking her leave from the guests. By now Faircliffe and Philippa were exchanging romantic words, with all of the other ladies hanging on every utterance.

Would anyone realize she had failed to return? Doubtful. If anything, the ladies would assume Jane Brown had slunk off in mortification.

Her throat prickled. She would never know what the other ladies thought of the current novel, but Chloe didn't need reading circles. She was a Wynchester. They had each other, which was more than enough.

Keeping her face down, she headed along the front walk toward the first carriage in the queue. Only when she glimpsed red curtains and a pair of leather gloves on the box did she lift her head toward the driver's perch.

It was empty.

Her lungs caught. Where was Graham?

Distant shouts reached her ears, and her tight muscles relaxed. Something unexpected must have occurred, and her siblings' planned distraction was in progress.

This was her cue to flee.

Chloe pushed the basket onto the perch, unhooked the carriage from its post, and leapt onto the coachman's seat. Female drivers weren't unheard-of, but all the same, she was glad she never went outside without garbing herself in the plainest, dullest, dowdiest clothes in her wardrobe. No one who glanced her way would bother looking for long.

She set the horses on a swift path out of Mayfair.

Only when Grosvenor Square was no longer visible behind her did she allow herself a small smile of victory.

Their cherished family portrait was coming home. Once she walked in that door with their painting held high—

"Did we escape?" came a low, velvet voice from within the carriage.

Chloe's skin went cold. Who was *that*? Graham wouldn't be hiding in the back of the carriage. A stranger was in the coach! She twisted about and wrenched the privacy curtain to one side.

A handsome face with soft brown hair and sculpted cheekbones stared back at her, glacial blue eyes wide with surprise.

"*Faircliffe*?" she blurted in disbelief.

"Miss...er...*you*?" he spluttered when he found his voice. "What the devil are you doing driving my carriage?"

4

Chloe swung the privacy curtain shut in Faircliffe's shocked face and spun back toward the horses.

No, no, no. This could not be happening. She had come *so close* to completing a perfect mission with no one the wiser until she...accidentally abducted a duke in the process? Her blood pounded loud in her ears. What the dickens was she supposed to do *now*?

Faircliffe jerked the curtain back open.

She did not turn around.

"Stop the carriage!" His Grace's imperious tone sent shivers up her spine.

Chloe urged the horses faster.

And to think she'd bragged to her siblings that the next time she saw Faircliffe, she'd give *him* the cut direct. Instead she was carting him across town like a gin-crazed hackney driver.

They were out of Mayfair, at least; that was something. But they had to get off the road before someone noticed the House of Lords' prized orator hanging his head out of the front window like a puppy, with some nondescript chit at the reins.

"I demand you stop this coach at once!" the duke thundered.

She made a sharp left into a narrow alley. One of the inns her family used as a safe harbor was a few miles from there. The proprietress was paid well not to ask questions. Chloe could jump from the carriage and slip through the kitchen and out through the laundry door before the duke scrambled out of the coach.

Not that a duke would *scramble*. At least, not a dignified nob like Faircliffe. He moved with stiff, austere precision— a godlike statue come to life. He was as clever as Apollo, as forbidden as Bacchus, as dangerous as Ares.

No matter where she glimpsed him, he managed to look utterly majestic and extremely uncomfortable in his own skin at the same time—as though a great prophecy had been bestowed upon him and he did not relish what the future had in store.

But today Chloe held the reins. She alone determined her path.

The rapid beating of her heart was due to the surprise of finding him behind her, not from his closeness or the way she could feel the energy radiating from his body along her spine and the back of her neck. He was a problem, and she would deal with it.

"I am warning you," Faircliffe began, "you haven't just stolen my coach; you've made off with my entire person! Do you know what happens to... Wait a minute." His words were slow and increasingly certain. "This isn't a proper theft at all, is it? I see your game. You don't wish to kidnap me. You wish to *compromise* me. You're a common social climber hoping to obtain an advantageous marriage by nefarious means!"

His smug certainty at his own hilariously inaccurate conclusion made Chloe wish Tiglet were still in the basket so she could toss him back at Faircliffe.

In Parliament, the duke seemed accustomed to being the

cleverest person in the room. This gave him the obnoxious tendency to assume others could not keep up with him. But in this case, his arrogance was a boon. If he wished to believe her some silly debutante scheming to land a duke "by any means necessary," so be it.

"H-how did you figure me out?" she stammered, injecting a measure of mortification into her voice.

Now that she'd stolen her painting and replaced it with a forgery, she couldn't let him suspect she was fleeing the scene. Absconding with an eligible bachelor was a far better alibi.

He snorted. "The only reason any respectable young lady would orchestrate a private encounter with a lord is to force him to the altar. What else could this be?"

What else, indeed! Chloe steered the horses down another back alley. She was more grateful than ever that she hadn't been born to aristocracy, if their marriage mart was this cutthroat.

"Well?" His velveteen voice was right behind her. "Aren't you going to tell me your name?"

"I'm..." *Jane Brown.*

But she didn't need that alias anymore. That was *her* painting in the basket beside her, which would have been returned ages ago if the almighty Duke of Faircliffe had deigned to answer her family's entreaties or acknowledge them when they attempted to seek an audience.

Now that she never again needed to humiliate herself by throwing herself into his path only to be brushed aside, she didn't care if he knew her real name. Better yet, she *wanted* him to know it. Despite his best efforts to avoid them, he was stuck in a carriage with a Wynchester. *Ha! Take that, Your Grace!*

She did not bother to hide her smirk. "I'm Chloe Wynchester."

The sharp inhalation of absolute horror squeaking from Faircliffe's throat should have been amusing. Instead, it was insult and injury. She clutched the reins and concentrated on getting to the Puss & Goose coaching inn as quickly as possible. Once she rid herself of the duke, she and His High-and-Mightiness need never cross paths again.

"Chloe *Wynchester*," he whispered, as if by not giving his full voice to her name perhaps it wouldn't be true. His moan grated. "Why couldn't it at least have been Miss Honoria?"

Oh, difficult to say. Perhaps because Baron Vanderbean's alleged daughter Honoria was another lie.

To provide the wards he considered family a lasting connection to the beau monde, the baron had created a fictional heir and heiress who existed only on paper. No one peered too closely at wealthy lords from far-off nations. The house and most of the fortune now belonged to "Horace Wynchester," an eccentric recluse like his father, who preferred to conduct all business via the post. Every single one of the siblings could pen the new baron's "signature" perfectly.

One of many secrets she would never share with the Duke of Faircliffe.

"My apologies for not being my *better* sister," Chloe snapped.

A mortified pause. "I'm sorry. I did not mean—"

"You *did* mean," she said bitterly.

And for that, Faircliffe *deserved* to be betrothed to a figment of the ton's collective imagination. After all, His Grace didn't give two buttons about what *person* he married. All that mattered was good blood, a fine dowry, superior social connections.

To him, those elements made Honoria leagues better than Chloe, sight unseen, regardless of intelligence or character. Honoria was highborn and legitimate. Chloe was a

Whitechapel foundling. In Faircliffe's eyes, a castoff like her wouldn't belong in a reading circle, much less hobnobbing with the ton. Although Bean had ensured his fostered children had their debuts, he couldn't force high society to accept them.

"We're here." She pulled the horses to a stop.

A crease lined Faircliffe's perfect brow. "We're where?"

At an inn the duke and his ilk would never frequent.

Rather than answer, Chloe leapt from the driver's perch, basket in hand, and tossed the reins over a post.

"Wait," he called in obvious alarm. "Where are you going?"

"To repent the naïveté that led me to this moment," she replied with a straight face. "My deepest apologies, Your Grace. You were right, as you are in all things. Compromise is a poor way to secure a husband. I see my error, and you are free to return home unbetrothed." She waved. "With luck, we shall never see each other again. I bid you adieu."

"Miss Wynchester—"

But she was walking, running—*flying*—up the steps and into the front door of the Puss & Goose. She would escape through the back door with the precious canvas while he drove himself back to fashionable Mayfair—

"Why did you come here?" His voice came from right behind her.

She stopped and spun around in shock. Was he *daft*?

Faircliffe was not fleeing as expected. He was standing in the reception room of the Puss & Goose looking imperial... and utterly confused.

"Are you renting rooms?" He glanced about the humble inn with obvious distaste. "I thought you lived at Baron Vanderbean's estate. Has something happened? Are you in trouble?"

God save her from the good intentions of overly helpful men!

Mrs. Halberstam, the proprietress of the inn, swept into the reception area.

"Oh!" Her eyes lit up. "Is that—"

"One room, please," Chloe interrupted, before Mrs. Halberstam could ask questions that were better left unanswered. "For a single woman, no guests."

No guests was code to mean anyone she was with could not be trusted.

"Of course, miss." Mrs. Halberstam provided Chloe a pencil for the guest book as if this were nothing more than a routine transaction. "Sign here, please. Do you prefer a window facing the east or the west?"

East meant all was well. *West* meant a note should be dispatched at once to Chloe's family.

She gave a bland smile. "West, please."

Mrs. Halberstam handed her a key and whispered, "Number four."

Perfect. Chloe closed her fingers about the key. All she had to do was climb a single flight of stairs, lock herself in the safe room, and wait to be rescued. By now Graham would have realized what had happened. He was likely to arrive here before the note found its way home.

She turned back to Faircliffe with her best expression of abject embarrassment. "I apologize ever so much for having misappropriated your time. I shan't waste a single minute more."

Before he could respond, she hurried up the stairs to the first floor and freedom.

He was right behind her the moment she opened the door to the room.

"Pardon the observation," she said politely, "but if you were worried that our being together in a carriage on a public street might lead to compromise, might I point out that voluntarily entering a private sleeping room in the unchaperoned presence of a Wynchester—"

"I am sorry I insulted you." His soulful eyes even looked as if he meant it, damn him. "Let me summon you a hack."

She held up the room key. "No, thank you. I have an untenable megrim and cannot rest at home because our house is under repairs. I shall lie down *alone* for an hour or two and leave once I am recovered."

"Then I shall send you a maid as chaperone," he said firmly, "and a footman to escort you. Your actions were rash and imprudent, but I want you to arrive home safely."

She bit back a retort. The only reason he wasn't bringing her up on charges was because he believed her a naïve little duckling unable to think through her actions. She would have to let him keep on believing it.

"You are all that is kind. I do not require your help." A scuffed dressing table stood beside a rickety wardrobe. Chloe slid the basket with the hidden painting under the table and sat gingerly on the worn stool, pretending to check her hair in the looking glass. "Have a good evening, Your Grace."

That was his cue to leave.

He took off his hat and sat on the windowsill instead.

A crack of air above the pane ruffled a few strands of his dark hair, lending him a sense of motion even while sitting still. It was as if, underneath his relaxed pose, every muscle were coiled and ready to pounce.

His blue eyes filled with sympathy. "It must be frightful to be without prospects. I do have compassion for those who are desperate."

"Do *not* feel sorry for me," she ground out through clenched teeth. To her surprise and misfortune, being visible was even worse than being invisible.

Poor Chloe Wynchester: so far beneath a duke. Ha! *He* was the one *she* should feel sorry for.

Many lords and ladies limited themselves to the thousand or so aristocrats matching their own class and station, relegating them to loveless marriages between debutantes and roués, first cousins, total strangers, sworn enemies. Whereas Chloe's pool of potential future spouses was *the entire rest of England*.

No one cared if she married a butcher or a bookseller, an apothecary or a highwayman. *She* was free to do as she pleased.

That was, if she ever escaped this interminable conversation.

Why was he ignoring her less-than-subtle verbal dismissals? Was he so used to being scraped to and fawned over that he genuinely wouldn't recognize *good-bye* unless she drove him home herself?

"It's safe to say we started off on the wrong foot." He gave her a sympathetic smile, which infuriated her all the more by making him even handsomer. Did the Ice King of Parliament truly possess a *dimple*? Good God. Right there in the hollow above his chiseled jaw.

No wonder the blasted man took being abducted in stride. A smile like that could melt petticoats. And inhibitions.

His gaze was earnest. "Although we shan't see each other again, and all we know of each other is the drivel printed in the society columns—"

That and the dozen other times they'd crossed paths, but who was counting?

He cleared his throat. "—before I go, I want you to know that—"

A door slammed beneath their feet. "*Where is she?*"

Chloe affected an alarmed expression. Rescue had arrived! Now what was she supposed to do with the duke?

5

When Lawrence saw the dismayed expression on Miss Wynchester's pretty face, he leapt to his feet in alarm. Some families could withstand a brush with gossip. His was not one of them.

"Someone is here for you?"

"My brother." She glanced over his shoulder toward the door. "He must have come to take me home."

Bloody hell, she'd been right. Lawrence should never have followed her up the stairs, no matter how unlikely it had seemed for someone to stumble across them in such a seedy establishment.

"Your brother cannot find us together." He darted a horrified gaze toward the open doorway. How on earth had the man found them so quickly? How had he even known his sister was missing? "Didn't you just reserve this room a few moments ago?"

"I told you," she said. "Our house in Islington is being repaired. Because it is too far to travel with a megrim, I told my family I would rest here if I suffered another attack."

Islington. Of course the Wynchesters wouldn't live in fashionable Mayfair. He wondered if she truly had enough money to rent a room or hire a hack. It was good for her that her family had come, but terrible for Lawrence.

"Where is she?" a loud male voice called from the foot of the stairs.

"Graham grows combative when he's distraught," she whispered. "He's extremely overprotective, even for an older brother. I don't know what he'll do when he finds a *man* alone with me..."

Panic itched beneath Lawrence's skin. Who cared why Miss Wynchester rented a bedchamber? All that mattered was not being caught alone with her inside of it.

"Climb into the wardrobe," she whispered. "Hurry."

He gawped at her. "What?"

"You don't want to marry me? I shan't make you." Miss Wynchester flung open the wardrobe door and jabbed a finger toward a dust ball in the back. "Get inside. You can return the favor later."

He hesitated. Hiding inside a wardrobe would make him look even guiltier...if he were caught. Was she really offering him a way out? Or had he misjudged her entirely and was now walking into a trap?

Footsteps thundered up the stairs.

Miss Wynchester arched her delicate brows. "Unless you prefer—"

"Don't let him find me. I'll owe you any favor you please." Lawrence stepped past her and scrunched himself into the narrow wardrobe. "Er, not money, that is. Or objects. And no—"

She shut the door in his face.

He fought the urge to sneeze. Or yell. Or break through the wooden panels and hurl himself out the open window and drive away high in the coachman's seat for everyone to see, as long as it took him far, far from the Wynchester clan.

Everything had been at sixes and sevens since the moment he'd arrived at the Yorks' town house. Lawrence *hated* not being in control.

"There you are," came a muffled male voice. Miss Wynchester's brother was right on the other side of the wardrobe door. "Are you alone?"

The moment of truth. Lawrence held his breath.

As much as he hadn't meant to insult her when he discovered her identity, even a platonic relationship with a Wynchester would be disastrous. The last thing a man guarding his reputation needed was an association with a walking scandal related to a dozen other walking scandals.

For Lawrence to restore lost respectability, he couldn't just *act* "better than thou." He had to *be* it.

Beginning with not being caught hiding inside the furniture of a shabby coaching inn with an incomprehensible spinster.

His breath came shallow and uneven. Time seemed to slow.

"It's all right," he heard her say. "I'm safe. I'm alone."

Lawrence would have sagged against the wardrobe's thin interior wall in relief if he trusted it not to fall apart with his weight.

"Can we go home now?" came Miss Wynchester's tired voice.

"Of course."

When the footsteps faded, Lawrence counted to four hundred before easing open the door to the wardrobe. His heart jumped. He'd left his *hat* on the windowsill? Thank God her brother hadn't seen it. Lawrence might be a skilled statesman, but no amount of talking would satisfactorily explain hiding inside a wardrobe.

He returned his hat to his head and hurried down the stairs, tossing a crown he could ill afford to part with to the proprietress for her discretion. After looking both ways, Lawrence returned to his rented carriage and untied the reins from the post.

With luck, that would be the last he'd see of the Wyn-chesters.

6

〰️

*C*hloe's home!"

The cry rang out the moment she and Graham walked through the front door. Her family surrounded her when she was barely up the stairs to the Planning Parlor.

"Do you have it?"

"What went wrong?"

"Nothing went wrong. It's Chloe!"

"She released Tiglet, didn't she? *Something* must have happened."

"I told you," Elizabeth said. "When the stable boys made a fuss about Graham's coach being first in the queue, I distracted them by calling them back to the mews in their own voices. Except Faircliffe's driver insisted on muscling his carriage to the front, so Graham—"

"Never mind the traffic quarrels," Tommy said, and turned to Chloe. "Is Puck back home?"

Laughing, Chloe swung her woven basket up and onto the walnut table. "Oh, you must mean this family portrait I liberated from some heiress's wall." She pulled the roll of canvas out from the interior compartment with a grin.

Her siblings cheered.

"Puck is home! Our family is complete again!"

"I told you Chloe could do anything," Tommy whispered to Elizabeth.

"And," Chloe admitted, "I may have also…inadvertently… slightly abducted the Duke of Faircliffe in the process."

"What?" Four shocked faces turned her way at once.

"Had him stuffed in a wardrobe by the time I got there," Graham confirmed with a grin. "Left his beaver on the windowsill, plain as day. I was half-tempted to swing open the door and expose him, just to see the look on his face."

"'Tis a good thing you refrained," Chloe scolded him. "As it stands, His Loftiness believes he owes me a favor."

Elizabeth's mouth fell open. "For *kidnapping* him?"

"For not crying 'Compromise!' and forcing him to the altar."

Tommy gave an exaggerated shudder. "Can you imagine?"

Chloe could imagine far better than she wished. Try as she might, she hadn't been able to rid the image of Faircliffe's strong shoulders and dimpled smile from her mind. Or the way his dark hair had fluttered in the breeze as if tousled by a lover's hand.

She wondered what it would have felt like to touch him, to toy with the softness of his hair, to feel the deceptive strength of his taut muscles beneath his gentlemanly exterior.

"Who needs an icehouse when you've got me?" came a perfect rendition of the Duke of Faircliffe from somewhere near the fireplace. Elizabeth throwing her voice again.

Everyone burst out laughing.

Everyone but Chloe. A few hours earlier she would have agreed with the sentiment wholeheartedly. But after witnessing the duke put her well-being above his own, following her into the Puss & Goose to ensure her safety, and offering to pay for a hack, she could not help but think there was perhaps more to him than met the eye.

Thank heavens she never had to see him again. People with hidden depths made the worst culls to target.

She shook her head. "Who cares about dukes? We've a family portrait to hang!"

"Thank you, children," came a perfect rendition of Bean's voice from his portrait above the mantel. Elizabeth affected a fatherly expression. "I knew my Wynchesters would never let me down."

"*Never*," Graham agreed.

Chloe blinked a sudden sheen from her eyes and knew several of her siblings were doing the same. Hearing Bean's voice again was something they all longed for. Its warmth felt like a blanket, like a welcoming hug, like a promise that the future could only get better. He had done everything in his power for them, and they would do the same for him.

The family's cherished painting was finally home.

Graham and Tommy cleared the table, replacing its various items in myriad secret compartments. As soon as she could, Chloe rolled out the canvas faceup. Elizabeth handed Marjorie small stones from a hidden drawer to weigh down the corners. Jacob kept Tiglet from leaping into the center, claws first.

The entire family was there, Puck and all six mischievous sprites cavorting merrily about a dancing fire with their arms wide and their heads tilted back in joy.

Tommy gave a happy sigh. "Perfect."

"Chloe, I cannot thank you enough," Elizabeth said in her own voice. "Our lives have felt so fractured. This puts us back together."

"I can breathe again," Tommy said fervently.

Jacob tried to extract Tiglet from his cravat. "All we have to do now is mount Puck on a new frame."

"Almost all," Chloe reminded him. "There's the small matter of an angel vase."

Tommy perked up. "Can we smash it?"

All six pairs of eyes swung to the mantel, where a cherubic porcelain angel hugged a slender crystal receptacle just large enough to hold a single rose.

"We cannot smash it," Chloe said firmly. "Even though it was against Bean's will, old Faircliffe entrusted it to us as collateral."

"Can we send it via post?" Elizabeth asked hopefully.

"We can leave it in the duke's stables. I happen to possess an exact copy of the Faircliffe livery." Tommy's eyes sparkled. "The next time His Grace enters the mews...*boom!* Saccharine angel, right where he least expects it."

Graham shook his finger. "You're wicked. I like it."

"Where's his smile?" came Marjorie's loud voice. It was the first time she'd spoken since Chloe's arrival. Some days she didn't speak at all, but when she did, the Wynchesters had learned to listen.

"Whose smile?" Chloe asked.

Marjorie pointed at Puck frolicking in the middle.

Chloe stepped closer.

Marjorie's finger shook. "Bean always smiles."

The other siblings crowded about the table.

"She's right," Jacob said in disbelief. "What happened to his smile?"

Marjorie frowned. "The brushstrokes are different, too."

Chloe's throat went dry. "It's the wrong *painting*?"

"It can't be," Elizabeth protested. "It came from Faircliffe. Both times!"

Jacob set down the kitten. "Never trust a duke. They're slipperier than snail slime."

"I can't believe there are two copies." Chloe covered her face with her hands. "And I stole the wrong one."

"Well, we'll just have to find the *right* one." Tommy narrowed her eyes. "No dukes shall get in our way."

Jacob stood tall. "We do this for Bean."

The siblings touched their hands to their hearts and lifted their fingers to the sky. "For Bean!"

Bean grinned back at them from over the mantel as if he knew they would succeed.

"He would be proud to know the new Duke of Faircliffe has finally acknowledged our existence," Elizabeth said. "Well, Chloe's, anyway."

Jacob brightened. "And he owes her a favor! If he still has our painting, you can demand it back, and this time he must comply."

Chloe made an aggrieved noise. "His Eternal Disagreeableness made a point to specify 'no money' and 'no objects.' He tried to say no to something else, but I slammed the door in his face."

"What kind of 'favor' is that?" Tommy said in outrage. "Why can't Faircliffe just be reasonable?"

"He's self-righteous," Graham replied, "like his father. Some aristocrats believe their wants are the only ones that matter. All they care about is themselves."

"Even if he hadn't put limitations on his 'favor,' Faircliffe cannot be trusted," Elizabeth reminded them. "We purchased that painting and the old duke stole it. That's not honorable."

"He's a cad," Tommy agreed. "He cannot be reasoned with."

"We don't need Faircliffe to be reasonable." Jacob's light brown eyes twinkled with mischief. "That's no fun anyway. We tried the respectable way for months, and it didn't work." He cracked his knuckles. "Now we do it our way."

Tommy grinned. "We find the real Puck and steal him back."

Elizabeth drummed her fingers on the sword stick she used as a cane. "If Faircliffe didn't give our portrait to Miss York, then it may still be on the duke's property. The tricky part will be snooping through every inch of his town house undetected."

Graham nodded. "If it's still there, we bring it home for good. And by 'we' I mean..."

All eyes turned to Chloe.

"Me?" she squeaked.

Tommy gave Chloe an arch look. "His Grace owes you a favor, does he not?"

Elizabeth's smile was wicked. "It's time for you to collect it."

7

⚜

The following morning, Chloe's stomach still churned.

The reason for the frantic flutters in her bosom was because this time, if all went to plan, Chloe would be presented to society as...

Herself.

"Who am I?" she whispered, her nerves clattering.

Chloe's invisibility curse was bittersweet. A lifetime of being overlooked brought its own share of pain. Every time she reintroduced herself with a new name to the same people and no one so much as blinked or remembered her was one more tiny cut on her soul.

If never standing out made her restless, well, she had her little ways to deal with that, didn't she?

She flung open her wardrobe doors.

Sumptuous fabrics in a breathtaking array of gorgeous colors towered before her.

She had never worn any of it outside of this room.

This was her dream wardrobe. The one secret she kept, even from her siblings.

These clothes symbolized the person she wished she could be. Proof she was still the same wistful girl she'd always been.

When she realized her parents were never coming back for her, she often slipped unnoticed through the streets, prowling for something special. To *be* something special. Once, when she nicked a rusty locket inscribed "To my Love," she immediately tied it about her neck and strutted about as though she were loved.

The items in her wardrobe came not from a lover, but rather from Chloe's own earnings. Bean had bequeathed a respectable sum to each of his children, but Chloe's collection had started long before. She had hoarded every coin she could until she had enough for a purchase.

Mittens, when she was eight. Fine ones of warm red wool, like a mother might acquire for her daughter. Chloe kept them safe in a cloth bag hidden beneath her clothes, never wearing the mittens or withdrawing them from their hiding place if another orphan might see.

She could not bear to have them mock her for pretending she had a mother, for believing she deserved nice things. As long as no one else knew, she could clutch the perfect red mittens to her chest, right next to the broken *To my Love* locket, and believe, with her eyes closed tight, that someone out there thought she was special and deserving of love.

"I *am* loved," she reminded herself.

She had five incredible siblings who all thought her special. Chloe the Chameleon, disappearing seamlessly into the background.

The strict Wynchester code of honor meant no sibling would ever snoop or pry into another's private affairs. They did not know her secret wish to one day be more than a blank canvas. To be *unmissable*.

Throat thick, she slammed the doors shut on her opulent wardrobe.

She moved to the smaller wardrobe. There, the fabrics were simple, the colors nondescript: gray, brown, wheat, porridge.

She picked one at random. It didn't matter. Faircliffe wouldn't remember what she looked like, in any event.

Even her looking glass was bored with her reflection. She glanced to the right of the fireplace, where a pair of curling tongs nestled in an iron basket.

Chloe had practiced every *Belle Assemblée* hairstyle so many times, she could play lady's maid to Queen Charlotte.

But before she left her room, she always straightened every perfect curl and scraped the whole back into a simple, uninspiring twist.

Even without a "favor" to collect, she was the best-suited Wynchester for this mission.

Chloe was the one who had borne witness to much of Faircliffe's political life. She could recite several of his views and had even quoted him in a few of her pamphlets encouraging reform.

If anyone could conduct suitably absorbing conversation to distract him from their true purpose, it was Chloe.

She wished the idea of delivering herself to him weren't so unsettling.

It wasn't just Faircliffe's wide lips and piercing blue gaze. It was the fear of being eye-catching and bold. She longed for it even as the thought terrified her. Today she would be walking into temptation.

She summoned the least conspicuous carriage from the mews. It was the perfect conveyance to take an unassuming miss over to the Duke of Faircliffe's grand terrace house. The Wynchesters' tiger Isaiah could accompany her without his usual livery.

Once she was no longer amongst the ton, she'd disappear from its collective memory, and life would go on as it always had. Today's "Chloe Wynchester" disguise was as disposable as any other.

But her fingers shook when she clanged the brass knocker.

The duke's butler swung open the door. Arthur Hastings, aged four and fifty, married, no children, sweet tooth, tender hip on the left side, lover of striped mufflers, irrational fear of small dogs. Chloe pretended Graham had told her none of that.

She held out a calling card. "Is His Grace receiving?"

Mr. Hastings squinted at the card. His eyes widened, but he did not toss her out on her ear. Butlers this rarefied preferred to eviscerate with a single look.

"I'll inquire." He motioned her out of the brisk spring afternoon and into a lavish entryway. "Wait here."

I would be delighted.

The moment Mr. Hastings took his leave, Chloe extracted a notebook from her omnipresent basket of tricks and began measuring the perimeter in paces. The decorative tiles covering the floor would amplify sound, so soft soles would be necessary for any maneuver requiring stealth. Her pencil flew faster. Locations and sizes of entrances and exits, including the windows. No squeak to the door, no loose clasps at the sill.

By the time Mr. Hastings returned, she was back in her original position beside the front door, her basket dangling innocently from her elbow.

"If you'll come with me, miss."

She followed Mr. Hastings to an elegant parlor nine and a half paces down the corridor. Perhaps this was a room where they brought guests they hoped would not stay long and who had no reason to set foot any deeper in Faircliffe territory.

"His Grace will be here shortly," Mr. Hastings informed her, and departed.

Chloe's fingers itched for her pencil. Did she have time to pace the parlor?

"Worth the risk," she muttered, and pulled the notebook from her basket.

She was completing a bird's-eye sketch of the room when a floorboard squeaked in the corridor. It had not squeaked for her and the butler, which might mean this footstep had come from the opposite direction. She shoved the notebook back into her basket just as the Duke of Faircliffe strode into the parlor.

His dark brown hair tumbled over his forehead, drawing one's gaze directly to the icy intensity in his blue eyes. His wide, full mouth was pressed into a tight line, as though displeased to find that Chloe had breached the butler-guarded perimeter and was now inside his ducal parlor. She fought the urge to pirouette, just because it would rankle him.

His jaw was tight and clean-shaven—touchably smooth despite the hard angles. The folds of his cravat were sharp enough to lacerate, spilling from his throat in a profusion of white linen blades.

This was how he looked in Parliament. Regal and ruthless, armed for battle. He was not afraid there, and he was not afraid of her. His mistake. Just because her spikes were not visible did not make her any less dangerous. Not all ammunition was meant to wound. Her weapons were her wits—and a feline coconspirator.

This fun was only beginning.

"It's Miss Wynchester, Your Grace," Chloe said helpfully. She dipped a curtsey, then lifted the lid of her basket in case the duke needed help remembering.

Up popped two pointy ears, one gold and one black, then bright inquisitive eyes, then a tiny pink nose with soft white whiskers protruding from either side.

Faircliffe's eyes lit up and he stepped forward before remembering himself and clearing his throat disapprovingly.

"Is that the calico cat-demon that caused so much chaos at the Yorks' residence?"

Chloe rubbed between Tiglet's furry ears. "The very one."

"Why," Faircliffe asked carefully, "would you bring him?"

"In case you didn't recognize me," she explained. "Most people remember Tiglet."

"I imagine they do." He sent a pointed look toward the open basket. "I shall thank you to leave the lid in place."

And I shall thank you *for leading me to my painting.*

She closed the lid.

Taking Tiglet along had been a calculated risk. She needed Faircliffe to remember both her and their pact, yes, but she also needed to appear inept when it came to mixing with high society. She was a damsel in distress, here to collect on an IOU. Chloe was going to enjoy the game.

"How may I help you?" Faircliffe did not look as though he wished to be of any service at all. "Remember: no money, no objects. And I shan't pretend to court you."

Ah, so that was the third condition. Luckily for him, Chloe didn't want that, either. She smiled up at him and tried to look as benign as possible.

"I need your help." This was true. Chloe let him see the sincerity in her eyes.

He didn't uncross his arms. "Help with what?"

"Fitting into society." That was believable enough.

He looked appalled.

"You needn't dance with me or feign particular interest," she assured him. "I am a romantic"—she was not—"and will only marry someone who wishes to marry *me*."

"What does any of that have to do with me?" he sputtered.

She lowered her gaze as if shy. "I wouldn't imagine someone as fashionable as yourself to know much about wallflowers, but it is impossible to marry well—or at all—from the fringes."

"I was right," the duke said in disgust. "You wish to ensnare some other sap in your social-climbing web."

But he didn't say no.

Got you.

"Someone with a fine house," she continued. "And at least four thousand a year."

"Those are the qualities with which a wallflower might 'fall in love'?" Faircliffe valiantly refrained from rolling his ducal eyes.

Chloe couldn't be more pleased. His indignation at her presumptuous aspirations meant he didn't question her motives. How could he? They were not dissimilar from his own.

"According to the papers, the Faircliffe dukes host a grand gala at the end of every season," she continued.

He closed his eyes as if begging her not to complete her request.

"I want an invitation," she finished. "And to be introduced to a few prospects beforehand."

He said nothing for a long moment, allowing his gaze to rake over her with humiliating thoroughness.

Half boots, as plain and ordinary as the rest of her outfit. Gown the color of old ash and just as uninviting. Bodice modest and covered but suddenly tight, as though the air she sucked into her lungs no longer quite fit. Pulse fluttering visibly at the base of her throat.

Lips dry, so she moistened them with her tongue, only to be caught in the act.

Faircliffe's eyes were no longer icy but glittered sharply, as though a dormant fire had been stoked deep within. Her tongue quickly retreated from view. Chloe's halfhearted bun with its strands of flyaway hair no longer felt frumpish but oddly sensual, as though she'd been caught in a state of undress by a lover.

Having completed his assessment, his eyes returned to hers. "Have you a decent dowry?"

"None at all," she replied, ignoring his implication that wealth would be the primary thing to recommend her. She injected her voice with false cheer. "But lack of fortune shouldn't matter. A duke can introduce an acquaintance to anyone he likes, can he not? A ball here, a dinner party there…"

He ground his teeth, his crossed arms tightening.

"You should invite Miss York's entire reading circle to your party," she suggested. "Then it won't be a special favor to me but a romantic gesture to your future bride. In fact, we can both attend her Blankets for Babes charity tea, if you'd like to invite everyone at once."

A muscle twitched at the duke's temple. He let out a breath and dropped his arms to his sides. "Very well. And then our slate is clean?"

"I shan't bother you after the gala," she promised. It was two months away. Chloe would be done with him long before that.

Everything was going perfectly. She didn't want Faircliffe to do his task *well*. She just required a pretext to ensure access to his residence until she uncovered the stolen painting.

"When is Miss York's charity tea?" The tortured expression on the duke's face indicated he would rather attend anything else.

Chloe smiled sweetly. "Tomorrow."

8

⚜

omorrow?" Lawrence stepped backward, aghast.

She not only wished him to acknowledge her publicly; she expected him to act as her *sponsor*? The unmitigated impertinence—

No. He clenched his jaw. *He* was the one in error. One might not expect better of a Wynchester than impertinence— and from the moment she'd pilfered his carriage, on this score Miss Wynchester had certainly delivered—but a *lord* should conduct himself with dignity in all circumstances.

That he had pursued a brazen thief would raise no eyebrows. Taking pity on a young woman of lesser status: charity. Offering to hire a hack to return her to her home: noble. Following her upstairs to an unchaperoned bedchamber: the absolute height of idiocy. What the devil had got into him?

She had. Miss Chloe Bloody Wynchester.

How did she manage to scatter his thoughts so easily? His veins pulsed. She infiltrated his senses like the fragrant smoke of spiced incense. Jasmine. The barest hint. He didn't know if the intoxicating scent was in her hair or on her skin or in the secret recesses of his mind, but he could barely think from the consuming desire to breathe her in.

She was not close enough to touch, and yet her presence

fluttered against his skin, slipping beneath his clothes to the heat of his flesh like the whisper of a promise.

He wanted to overwhelm her to make it stop. To cover her with his scent, his body, his power. He had faced mightier foes than soft curves and a knowing gaze.

"If I can secure an invitation to the tea," her Cupid's-bow mouth was saying now, "we needn't arrive together as though you were my escort."

"I would never—" He fought the impulse to rub his hand over his face in frustration. Three decades dealing with his father had taught Lawrence the importance of hiding strong emotion. Such admissions were easy for the duke to use against his son.

Miss Wynchester smiled at him as if not at all discomfited. Yet she held herself unnaturally still, the muscles in her face tight. Lawrence could not help but suspect that she was hiding her emotions, too.

That was what had spurred his damnable burst of forgiveness when she abducted him. He understood desperation. He fought against that drowning current every single day.

And he was *so close* to breaking free. Perfect-in-almost-every-way Miss Philippa York would replenish the family coffers *and* restore the fractured Faircliffe reputation. He could allow nothing to impede the plan.

Chloe Wynchester was more than a disruption. She was a whirlpool, dragging him further from his path. But what was his newly restored family name worth if Lawrence did not honor his word?

She was right, blast her. Inviting the entire reading circle to his gala would be a romantic gesture. It might even speed up the courtship.

"After you've put in your appearance at my gala, we're finished," he reminded her, each word hard and flinty.

She beamed at him. "You needn't even speak to me. I'll make a brilliant match and be on my way."

Lawrence glared down his nose at her warm brown eyes and long dark lashes.

She *might* be a success. An hour ago he would have doubted it, but now that he stood right before her and was almost but not quite certain that the faint scent of jasmine was indeed coming from her hair...He would not be the only man tempted to plunge his fingers into its depths and bury his nose in the soft tresses to capture a fraction of her essence.

But summoning baser urges was not the same as attracting a husband. She required help if she wished to rub elbows with the beau monde. And if he were the one to assist her, he risked his own standing in the process.

She knew this, and she asked it of him anyway. It was shameless manipulation. A woman of good breeding would not have asked him to do so. But he was the one who had agreed to owe a favor.

"Very well," he said coldly.

He would instruct his butler to allow visits and correspondence until this debt was paid.

Her lips curved. "Thank you."

Miss Wynchester should consider herself fortunate to have risen as much as she had. Although she was not Baron Vanderbean's daughter by blood, she had enjoyed and continued to enjoy his home and his generosity.

Lawrence's chest gave a familiar little hiccup at the tempting image of a big family. He was not jealous of Miss Wynchester—the thought was absurd—but after a fever had taken his mother, growing up all alone in a house like this one had been very lonely, indeed.

He never wanted his heir, or any child, to feel as adrift as he had. If Miss York wished to relinquish the child rearing to nursemaids and tutors, that was her prerogative. But Lawrence would ensure his children never doubted their father's love. Nor would they want for anything.

But first he had to be done with Chloe Wynchester.

He gave her his harshest glare. "If there's nothing else?"

She lifted a large woven basket. "Do you want to see Tiglet before I go?"

He did. "I do not."

She wrinkled her nose. "Do you dislike pets?"

"We are not friends, Miss Wynchester. My feelings on the matter are inconsequential to you."

His feelings were intense. Lawrence not only hoped to fill his home with children *and* animals, he intended to let each child pick out his or her own pet. None of which was Miss Wynchester's concern.

She tilted her head. "I think you'd like Tiglet."

"Alas, we shall never know." He gestured for her to precede him from the parlor.

She glanced at the unadorned walls instead. "Do you dislike art?"

Lawrence *loved* art.

This house had once been filled with it. For generations the Dukes of Faircliffe had added masterpiece after masterpiece to the family collection.

And then came his father.

The duke had been great fun—and unrepentantly frivolous. How Lawrence had looked up to the gregarious man who had far too many friends to show favor to any one in particular, including his starry-eyed son. Not when there were parties to attend and wagers to be made.

One by one the portraits that had kept Lawrence company when he had no one to talk to, the landscapes he'd escaped into when he could go nowhere else, had vanished from the walls to pay his father's increasing debts.

Lads at school mocked him for his father's excesses and embarrassing scandals. Everything Lawrence cared about was ripped away.

The parlor was bare. Although his father was no longer here to wrest the last scraps away, Lawrence could not help but hoard the little he had left. He had collected twenty-three dusty paintings from the failing Faircliffe country seat and gathered them in the town house library, which he now kept under lock and key. Its beauty was his refuge. Only his housekeeper was allowed inside.

"*I* enjoy art," Miss Wynchester continued, as though Lawrence had not rudely ignored her question.

A quicksilver, seductive impulse tempted him to show her his collection. Just to see how she reacted. To see if she could appreciate his collection even a fraction as much as he did.

He tamped down the desire. Impulsiveness was how his father had ruined himself and his family. The damnable trait was also the reason Lawrence was in his current scrape with Miss Wynchester.

"Good afternoon," he told her firmly. "Hastings will see you out."

She dipped a curtsey.

"Oh," Lawrence said, "do not take your disruptive baby jaguar back to the Yorks'."

Miss Wynchester's wide eyes met his. "I've no choice. Crowds cause me anxiety, and Tiglet is the only creature capable of giving me comfort."

With that, she was gone.

Traces of jasmine remained in the empty place where she had stood.

He stepped into it despite himself, as though he would be

able to feel her if he placed his body where hers had been. The long legs beneath her skirt, the swell of her bosom. What would it be like to kiss that fleeting smirk from her lips?

Hastings swept into the parlor. "It is a pleasure to see you entertaining callers, Your Grace. What a unique young lady."

Lawrence stepped away from Miss Wynchester's ghost. "She cannot mean to drag that beast all over society, can she? Good God, just imagine it loose here during my gala."

Hastings arched gray brows. "You adore animals. If I recall correctly, there once was a time when you begged your father for—"

Lawrence cut him off with a frosty glare.

Hastings returned his gaze with faux innocence.

Of course the blasted man "recalled correctly." Hastings had been butler since before Lawrence's birth. He could recall any number of memories Lawrence had worked very hard to forget.

Such as the dark days after the funeral, when Lawrence had come to realize the full extent of his father's debts. After years of being resentful every time another of his ancestors' treasures vanished from the wall, Lawrence realized he would be forced to do the same…and that the sacrifice would not be enough.

He reduced staff to a minimum in both the London town house and the entailed country seat, then sold any items that held no sentimental value—and several that did. He settled long-overdue accounts with tradesmen before addressing his father's gambling debts because hatters and cobblers and haberdashers did not have the benefits of titles to protect them.

As a peer, Father could not be sent to debtors' prison no matter how profligate he became. The working class was not so lucky. Lawrence would not put their lives in jeopardy just because "gentlemen" prioritized debts of honor to their peers.

His lip curled. There was no honor in living lavishly on credit one could not repay and allowing the less fortunate to bear the brunt of one's selfishness.

By selling heirlooms and being frugal, there was just enough money for one final season. He *must* wed an heiress before Parliament ended in mid-June or he would not be able to provide for his tenants, repair the failing estate, and pay his loyal staff's wages.

Destitute, Lawrence would no longer be able to fight for reforms in the House of Lords, because he would not be able to afford a town house or *any* rooms for rent, much less possess any extra money to make investments that might help him out of this mess.

Miss York's dowry could not arrive fast enough.

"I'll be in the library," he informed Hastings, then strode down the corridor to his sanctuary.

Lawrence unlocked the door, stepped into the large room, and let himself breathe.

He adored the rich scent of books, of old paper and worn leather. The comforting crackle of a cozy fire drew the eye toward a plush sofa and two worn leather chairs, arranged invitingly near the warm blaze.

The walls did not boast nearly the quantity of books they'd once held, but the thin spaces above and between the shelves were now filled with paintings. He had brought them all here to the one remaining place where his heart felt full instead of empty.

As always, he started to the left of the doorway, making his unhurried way canvas by canvas. He knew every brushstroke, every play of light against darkness. It was here that Lawrence could let himself think, and be, and feel.

He liked to imagine himself in the shoes of the artists who had lived before him. Would he have chosen this color, this canvas, this style, this subject? Might he have added a flying horse for whimsy? Or painted the trees purple instead of green? Would his imagination mirror the real world at all?

His peers believed Lawrence spent every spare moment in his library out of an overabundance of studiousness. It would shock them to know how much time he spent daydreaming about learning to paint so he could add a creation of his own to these walls.

Many gentlemen had hobbies. Once his pockets were flush again, there would be an opportunity to hire an art tutor when Parliament was not in session.

An opportunity he would not take.

Money was not enough. The perfect wife was not enough. *Lawrence* also had to be perfect. If he were to make the attempt and discover all the tutors in the world weren't enough to coax passable art from talentless fingers...No. It did not bear considering.

If Lawrence could not be the best, he would not do it at all.

He was respected in Parliament because of long hours and hard work. Sleepless nights writing and rewriting every sentence of every speech.

It was also why he eschewed society events whenever possible. The only time he received callers was at the end-of-season gala that he controlled.

Lawrence kept others out not because he believed himself superior but because, if they knew the real him, they would no longer be interested—or, worse, he would be mocked.

He was not *good* at doing and saying the right things unless he'd had time to craft the perfect response.

The smell of fresh coffee reached his nose and he turned to see his housekeeper, Mrs. Root, enter the library. She arranged the contents of a silver tray on the small table next to his favorite chair.

Her blue eyes normally sparkled, but today they were filled with concern.

"What is it?" he demanded.

Her hands shook. "My niece."

Mrs. Root had four nieces, but there was no need to inquire which one. Betsy, the youngest, had always been sickly. Now she was expecting a child.

"What does the doctor say?" he asked, his voice gruff. There was nothing worse than losing a loved one.

"That a month of confinement remains and Betsy should spend it in bed." Mrs. Root twisted her hands. "My next holiday isn't for a fortnight, but would you mind if I took a day or two—"

"Go." Lawrence held up his palm. "Take as much time as you need."

Betsy was a washerwoman. A month of no wages, the cost of medicines and doctors, weeks to recover with the baby...Lawrence scanned the thinning shelves until his gaze lit upon a volume that might earn a reasonable amount. He would send a donation on the morrow.

"Thank you." Mrs. Root curtseyed.

"You can depart now if you like. I'll ring for someone else to collect the tray."

She made no move to leave.

He frowned. "Was there something else?"

Her eyes softened. "Hastings says you're to acquire a kitten."

Deuced meddlesome butler!

"Hastings is mistaken," Lawrence said coldly.

Mrs. Root looked as though she wanted to pinch his cheek. "It's a wonderful idea."

"I am not in the market for a kitten," he enunciated.

"A puppy, was it?" Her smile widened. "I thought Hastings had misunderstood. How you used to long for a dog! 'He'd be the best friend a lad could have,' you told your father. One must lay newspaper for a puppy, of course, so I'll have a word with Peggy and Dinah before I go—"

He exaggerated each syllable. "No. Pets."

Mrs. Root appeared crestfallen.

"I knew it was too pleasant a thought." Her gaze brightened. "What if…what if you didn't purchase an animal from a breeder but rescued one off the street? If you haven't the time or dislike it, you can always give her to someone else."

He narrowed his eyes. "You think if I let it in, I'll never give it away."

"I would never call you sentimental, Your Grace." She placed a hand to her bosom and backed away toward the door. "Hastings, on the other hand…"

"I am not sentimental!"

It was already too late. Mrs. Root had left him in the center of a library stuffed with family portraits and every scrap of art he could scrounge from the Faircliffe estate.

"Not *that* sentimental."

But his feet led him to an empty pedestal where he intended to place the one item of beauty Father had ever valued. A gift for his wife.

Lawrence had been perhaps six years old when he realized his mother was increasing in size. He could still remember how happy he'd been at the knowledge he'd soon have a sister or brother to love and play with.

He'd yearned for a huge family, full of love and laughter and adventure. A sibling was a dream come true. In the afternoons he would sneak into the drawing room where his mother embroidered by the fire, watching for the smile that played at her lips and the way she would touch her belly whenever she received a kick. He counted down the days.

The baby was stillborn.

There had been no more smiles in his household after that. Mother was inconsolable. Father commissioned an exquisite crystal vase clutched in the plump hands of a beautiful cherub. An angel, just like Lawrence's sister who had not lived. Every morning Father replaced the flower in the vase with one from their garden. Eventually, Mother emerged from her darkness. The angel accompanied her to the dining room, to the drawing room, to her bedside.

The following year, when a fever sent Mother to heaven with her daughter, the vase disappeared from her sickroom. Father had placed the angel in his study, where it never held flowers again.

Sometimes, Lawrence would sneak into the duke's study and hide in a corner, arms wrapped about his knees, to watch his father work and to catch glimpses of the vase, still as delicate and painfully beautiful as Lawrence recalled.

Every time his father caught him, there was a dreadful row. Nannies were sacked. Father would shake him and toss him into the corridor. He began to lock the study even while inside the room. The duke guarded that angel as jealously as a dragon protected its treasure.

It was the one thing Father still cared about.

Lawrence swallowed the old hurts. It was past time to give his mother's vase its rightful place of honor here in the library, amongst things of beauty.

He rose unsteadily to his feet. He would not be cowed by his father's ghost any longer.

After the old man's death six months before, a footman had entered the duke's study in order to relocate the papers and journals to Lawrence's study. The closed door still seemed cold and forbidding, but Lawrence was no longer the boy he had once been.

He did not need to fear the study and the rejection it symbolized. It was empty now. He had a key. Father was gone, but the angel could live here in the library with Lawrence.

He strode to his father's study, ignoring the way his breath accelerated and his muscles tensed as if preparing for the inevitable blow. It took three tries to fit the key into the lock, but this time there were no angry shouts when he pushed open the door.

The room was dark. It seemed much smaller without his father. The air was stale. It filled Lawrence's lungs like brackish water, making it difficult to breathe. There was no need to tie back the curtains. This would be quick.

He shoved open the door until it banged against the interior wall. A small act of defiance he would never have dared if his father were alive. Dim light from the corridor brightened the gloom just enough for Lawrence to glimpse the angel's glass case.

The vase was gone.

Lawrence jerked back against the doorjamb, the blood roaring through his veins and his mind awhirl.

Stolen.

Father would never have parted with his angel willingly. It must have been taken by one of the servants Lawrence had been forced to let go once he'd realized how close he was to financial ruin.

His muscles twitched with rage. By now his mother's vase could have changed hands any number of times. Strangers' hands. His mother's angel reduced to a cheap monetary transaction, nothing more meaningful than the exchange of a few coins.

Lawrence would find that vase and prosecute its theft to

the fullest extent of the law. He would sell every book and every painting for reward money if that was what it took to bring the angel home. He turned from the study and headed for the front door.

It was time to visit the Bow Street Runners.

9

Chloe attacked the crown of ringlets she'd spent all morning perfecting with a wet brush until her hair hung about her face in uneven, limp chunks. Excellent. She shoved every strand behind her head in a knot—competent enough to indicate she'd tried, bland enough not to garner a second glance—and then returned her pearl drop earrings to the mahogany drawer with all of the other baubles.

She carefully removed her white crepe frock with its cerulean-striped puffed sleeves and matching sarcenet slip. Like the rest of her fashionable attire, this gown would never be worn outside the privacy of her dressing room.

It still felt strange to keep a secret from her siblings—especially Tommy, whose cot had been near Chloe's at the orphanage. Before Bean, there had been no practical means to have privacy.

If a tiny part of Chloe couldn't stop wondering what Faircliffe might think when he saw her in an hour, well, that was just silly. He wouldn't be looking at her. He was to wed Miss York.

Nor was Chloe the least bit interested in the duke's vaunted opinions!

Her objective was to gain enough of Faircliffe's confidence

to find out where he'd hidden the painting that belonged to her family—or ledgers to indicate where he'd sold it.

Nothing more.

Once she was down to shift and stays, Chloe hunted through the smaller wardrobe for something appropriate to wear to a Blankets for Babes charity tea. Brown? Sand? Ash? She settled for a lackluster gray-violet.

There. Chloe couldn't look in the mirror without wanting to snore. She grabbed her most unflattering pelisse and strode from her bedchamber.

Before heading downstairs, she paused at the open doorway to the empty Planning Parlor. Bean's face smiled down at her from his frame above the mantel.

"I wish I'd been your daughter by blood," she whispered, "so I would have been born with rank."

Bean's oil-on-canvas smile did not reply.

It didn't matter. She'd confessed her desire to be his "real" daughter hundreds of times while he was still alive. Sometimes his loss was so big, it threatened to burst from her chest and rend her to pieces. But she was strong. All of the Wynchesters were.

Bean always said the stars had brought them together. He loved her as she was. What could be more real than that?

The family depended on her to do her part. She would never let them down.

She stepped out of the Planning Parlor in time to catch Jacob frowning in the corridor, sniffing the air with confusion on his handsome face.

"Someone ought to check the flues," he told her when he caught her quizzical expression. "One of the fireplaces smells like burnt hair."

Er, that would be Chloe's room, courtesy of her curling tongs.

"I'm sure it's nothing," she assured him, and hurried down the marble steps before he could ask any questions.

Graham sat alone in the dining room, surrounded by empty tea plates and stacks of society papers, some trapped by a vase of daffodils. He looked up as Chloe entered the room.

"What do you think?" He was adding to one of his hand-written journals. "Is Princess Caraboo actual royalty?"

Chloe switched his fork for a flower while he wasn't looking. "Nobody ever is who they say they are. I don't know why you read this rubbish."

But she picked up one of the pages anyway. Lord D— injured in a duel. Heiress K—caught in the arms of a notorious rake.

It was silly to envy these people's plights. Finding one's name in the scandal sheets often spelled disaster for a re-spectable lord or lady. A permanent tumble from social grace. Chloe was grateful she had no further to fall.

"There's your basket." Graham motioned to the opposite side of the table.

Chloe peeked beneath the wicker lid. "Where's Tiglet?"

"I banished him to Balcovia."

As Balcovia was the small principality in the Low Coun-tries where Bean had been born, this turn of events seemed unlikely.

"You've no idea where Tiglet is." Chloe shook her head fondly. "A rhinoceros could charge from the teakettle whilst you read your papers and you wouldn't even notice."

He grinned unrepentantly. "I'm trying to fathom out how I can become Prince Caraboo. Wouldn't it be a lark if people believed me to be royalty?"

And now she was jealous at the thought of her brother being fawned over and written about when Graham was only jesting. Wasn't he? Chloe tried to picture him as royalty. She imagined he would make a striking prince...if he set down his society papers long enough to overtake a castle.

It was Chloe who was always in the midst of it all. Like the scuffed brown parquet of a dance floor: omnipresent and invisible, useful and unnoticed. Witness to everyone else's fun.

A flicker of calico fur flashed between the curtains.

She scooped Tiglet up, tucked him into the basket next to the blankets, and hurried out to the waiting carriage.

As the wheels inched forward with the queue of eager attendees, Chloe arranged her gown and her basket as neatly as possible. She shouldn't care about her appearance, and she especially ought not to care what sort of impression she made on Faircliffe—if he even came. She definitely shouldn't care how she compared to Philippa York.

Until recently, Chloe hadn't given Philippa much thought. She was a typical young lady inasmuch as any beautiful, spoiled daughter of a powerful MP could be considered typical.

If Chloe was the dance floor, Philippa and her ilk were sparkling chandeliers. Chloe had spent the same amount of time trying to get to know her as one might spend conversing with a candle.

But the next few weeks would be different. For this ploy to work, she must attend the Blankets for Babes charity tea not as Jane Brown, but as Chloe Wynchester. Every inch of her body was on edge.

It had nothing to do with the Duke of Faircliffe's probable presence, she reminded herself. Nor his interest in wooing Miss York. This unusual attack of nerves was solely due to not having a pseudonym to hide behind. What if they recognized her? What if they didn't?

When it was Chloe's turn to alight from her carriage,

she took a deep breath before striding up the path to the open door.

As on previous visits, Mrs. York bounced beside the butler, excitably welcoming guests through the door and into her home.

Beside her stood Philippa, draped from head to toe in frills and lace, her peaches-and-cream face a perfect mask of ennui. She looked like a bored but beautiful doily.

"Did you bring a blanket...er...Miss?" Mrs. York asked Chloe, despite being obviously unable to place her name. As hostess, she would not want to admit her failure.

"I brought two." Chloe pulled them from the basket and surreptitiously flicked off a few stray Tiglet hairs before handing the blankets over.

All six Wynchester siblings had gamely spent the night quilting. Chloe had brought the two most middling attempts—hers and Graham's—and would donate the other four separately during her weekly visit to the orphanage where she'd once lived.

"Thank you, thank you," Mrs. York gushed, handing Chloe off to her daughter to greet the next guest. "Oh, Gracie, how marvelous to see you! Never say you made this ravishing blanket yourself."

Just like that: forgotten.

Excellent. Chloe straightened her spine. That made things easier.

"Miss York," she said to Philippa in hushed tones, leading her off to one side. "This is distressingly awkward, but I do hope you can help me. At the last reading circle, a guest called me by the wrong name. I didn't correct her because I didn't want her to feel poorly, but I thought you might remind the others privately in case anyone else is confused?"

"Of…course." Miss York's halting tone suggested she could not place the name, either. "What did they call you?"

"'Jane Brown,' if you can believe it." Chloe gave a light, trilling laugh as if the mix-up was just so amusing. "'Brown' couldn't be further from 'Wynchester,' of course, but 'Jane' is a fair guess, being such a common name. I'd likely try the same thing, were I ever in those shoes."

"*Wynchester*?" It was the quietest screech Chloe had ever heard, and it came from the shocked face of Mrs. York, who had apparently tiptoed behind them to eavesdrop. "Philippa, darling, you cannot possibly have invited a Wynchester into our home. If tomorrow's papers contain a caricature of *my* parlor—"

"Mind the door, Mother," Miss York interrupted without changing expression. She looked as bored now as she had when Chloe had first entered the room. "Here comes Lady Eunice with a blanket."

Mrs. York let out an indignant squeak but rushed back to her post next to the butler.

Chloe took a longer look at Philippa. She'd handled her panicking mother with practiced skill, as if some random Wynchester elbowing into her charity tea uninvited was the least interesting thing to happen all day.

"Don't mind her," Philippa said. "Her cousin is a caricaturist, and he's never found anything Mother does to be interesting enough to sketch. Or me, for that matter. My reading circle isn't the least bit respectable, and we get on fine."

Chloe hid a smile. Perhaps it had been a mistake for the floor not to speak to the chandelier. Philippa seemed someone Chloe might like.

Before they could speak further, Mrs. York's pale hand flashed out to grab her daughter by the arm and tug her ignominiously to one side.

"He's here," Mrs. York hissed, in a whisper that surely carried to every witness in the entranceway. "Pinch your cheeks for color."

Philippa ignored this advice and successfully dodged her mother's attempts to do it for her.

However, Chloe glimpsed several other unwed young ladies furtively pinching their cheeks and adjusting their bodices before pushing forward.

She was outraged on Philippa's behalf—weren't these "ladies" angling for Philippa's duke supposed to be her friends?—but also intrigued by the idea nothing was final until the marriage contract made it so.

Banns had not been read; Faircliffe had not yet asked official permission from Philippa's father. Until then, Chloe supposed every young lady was well within her rights to do as best she could for her future. Of course, she had no wayward temptation to pinch her own cheeks for color.

She gripped the handle of her basket in both hands as the duke approached.

The sunlight cast his eyes in shadow, but she knew their blueness by heart. As endless as the sky, and as sharp as fine crystal. Cold enough to send shivers of gooseflesh along her skin and sometimes hot enough to do the same.

She could see nothing of him but his eyes and still feel dwarfed in his presence. The sensation should discomfort her, anger her. She was not used to feeling trapped by nothing stronger than a heated gaze. Instead, it was strangely thrilling. Her muscles thrummed with anticipation for the moment the shadows would fall away and his eyes would be visible to hers.

He cut a fine figure beneath the brilliant sun. A perfectly tailored frock coat hugged his wide shoulders. A hint of emerald-green waistcoat shimmered beneath the elegant cutaway. Fawn breeches molded to the muscles of his legs. His coal-black boots reflected the light, no doubt champagne-shined for impact.

If he intended to make an impression, he had achieved his aim. The entranceway fairly vibrated from the effort to contain so many racing pulses at once.

"Your Grace," Mrs. York cooed. "How splendid for you to join us. And with a blanket for the children! What did you have embroidered on yours?"

"Embroidered?" he echoed blankly.

Oh dear, had Chloe failed to mention the finer details? Perhaps he shouldn't have swept her out of the house like so much rubbish. She hid a smile behind her fist and feigned a dainty cough.

"When we donate to Blankets for Babes, we embroider the softest cotton with our favorite Bible verses or inspiring axioms, to create cheer and hope in the lives of orphans," Mrs. York continued earnestly. "The little dears have nothing else to look forward to, you know."

Without a word, Faircliffe handed Mrs. York a folded square of beautiful material that would be welcome anywhere, lack of embroidered platitudes notwithstanding.

He sent his flat gaze over Mrs. York's shoulder, past her daughter and her friends, right to Chloe. There were his eyes, cerulean and sharp.

Her amusement faltered. She knew the duke had sent her a meaningful look because he hadn't known to embroider his blanket, but others would think he had singled her out because she was a foundling who had grown up in an orphanage, just like the pitiable "babes" they'd embroidered Bible verses for.

Chloe lifted her nose high. She was not ashamed of who and what she was or where she had come from.

Mrs. York poked at Faircliffe's offering. "Heavens, this won't match the others at all. We've spent the past week embroidering—"

"Mother, it's a blanket," Philippa pointed out dryly. "And babies can't read."

Faircliffe's eyes met Chloe's again. From their fire it was clear he was not thinking about charity. He did not seem to be thinking about blankets at all. He was staring at Chloe as if he wished to peel her plainness away like petals on a dahlia to expose whatever secrets hid inside.

She shivered and forced herself to look away.

Realizing her daughter did not command the duke's full attention, Mrs. York turned to see who had presumed to distract him.

She paled when her gaze landed on Chloe.

Chloe fought the urge to wiggle her fingers.

Mrs. York waded through the river of pink-cheeked ladies leaping to greet the duke and grabbed Chloe by the arm.

"You must go at once," she hissed, "and never return."

"I don't want him," Chloe assured her just as quietly, "if that's your concern."

Mrs. York was unswayed. "My concern is the presence of a *Wynchester* in what, until this day, has been a respectable household."

Chloe refrained from mentioning that she'd been present before.

When she'd initially infiltrated the reading circle using her Jane Brown identity, she expected to amuse her siblings with tales of idle gossip. Instead, she was fascinated by the selection of books and the insightful commentary. The weekly meetings became a favored part of her routine.

Mrs. York's face flushed and she lowered her voice to a hiss. "I will not allow the stain of your presence to jeopardize

Philippa receiving the marriage offer she very much deserves. If you're not gone within the next—"

"Good afternoon, Miss Wynchester." Faircliffe's deep voice resonated throughout the hall. "Shall I presume Tiglet is in that basket?"

Chloe dipped a princess-perfect curtsey. "Good afternoon, Your Grace. And indeed he is."

She lifted the lid. Up popped soft pointed ears and long white whiskers as the kitten peeked out.

"Keep the little rascal inside this time." A ghost of a smile curved Faircliffe's lips before he turned to greet the next guest.

Mrs. York's jaw fell open. "You... He..."

Chloe's spinning head felt much the same way.

The Duke of Faircliffe had acknowledged her publicly. He had not cut her, ignored her, or failed to notice her altogether. He'd *remembered* her and greeted her with a familiarity that cast no doubt they shared a friendly acquaintance.

Her. Chloe Wynchester!

She hadn't realized until this moment how much she'd doubted he would go through with it. That today would be one more embarrassing disappointment in a lifetime of going unnoticed.

"*Philippa.*" Mrs. York tapped her daughter's lace-encircled wrist. "His Grace is on speaking terms with *Miss Wynchester*. You must invite her to your next event. Until you're wed, you cannot be rude to anyone he's friendly with, no matter how distasteful. At least, not in front of him."

There was the douse of water Chloe needed. She was useful to a point, but once the betrothal was announced, she was to be cut forevermore.

Oh, she could return if she wished to. She could be Anne Smith one day and Mary Jones the next, and Mrs. York would be too busy preening at Faircliffe to know the difference.

This time, however, the thought of doing so felt less like revenge and more...dreary.

"Lady Quarrington is hosting a soirée on Friday," Philippa said to Chloe. "You must attend."

Mrs. York swatted at her daughter, aghast. "You cannot invite a Wynchester to other people's soirées! Besides, I thought you refused to attend your cousin's fêtes."

Philippa's porcelain face was hard as marble. "I'll go if Miss Wynchester goes."

Mrs. York flashed Chloe a furious smile. "Then we'll make certain she receives an invitation."

Somehow Chloe kept her mouth from falling open. Easy as that? *Oh, well, I suppose we shall grant her entrée because two people failed to cut her as expected.* A word from Faircliffe and another from Philippa, and suddenly Chloe Wynchester had *worth*?

Fingers of doubt crept up her spine. Perhaps she'd underestimated how much influence a man like Faircliffe wielded. After all, she hadn't selected him because he was likely to be an easy mark. She hadn't selected him at all.

"Come along, everyone." Mrs. York urged her guests down a corridor. "Off we go to the dining room, where we'll have room to display our blankets...and enjoy tea!"

Chloe let the river of excited, chattering guests pass her by. Maybe Philippa wasn't as narrow-minded as her peers. Chloe hadn't been able to send an apology for the Tiglet catastrophe because she'd been operating under an assumed name. Now that *that* tiny detail had been cleared up, maybe she and Philippa could even be...friends.

"Are you coming?" asked a familiar velvet voice.

Startled, she glanced up to see Faircliffe's handsome face lined with concern.

Why was he doing this? The magic of his attention had

already borne fruit. He needn't *keep* talking to her. It wasn't part of their agreement.

He stepped far too close beside her. "I'll walk with you."

The other unmarried ladies were almost as vexed by this turn of events as Chloe was. The only thing she wanted from Faircliffe was the location of her family's painting.

She tried to make meaningful eyes at Philippa to come and enchant her soon-to-be betrothed.

Philippa stared back at her blankly, then disappeared down the hall as if the most pressing matter was sampling the tea cakes.

How could she be so sanguine? Did Philippa not care who Faircliffe escorted because she had already won? Or after five years on the marriage mart, was she tired of playing the game? Why, oh, why couldn't she be a possessive, screeching harpy?

Faircliffe showed no signs of abandoning Chloe's side.

She tried not to find his solicitousness charming. It was an act, just like everything else the beau monde did or said in front of each other. He wasn't kind to her by choice.

Philippa could have him. The last thing Chloe needed was the insincere attentions of some titled nob. She'd rather go back to being invisible.

"Take any seat you wish." Mrs. York clapped her hands. "There are more cakes coming."

Faircliffe touched his hand to the back of a gracefully curved bergère facing a decorative looking glass and two candelabra. "How about this one?"

"*No.*" Chloe's revulsion was too visceral to hide.

His surprise was obvious. "Does it look uncomfortable?"

"It looks..." She was too rattled by his continued solicitousness to invent a lie. "I know artfully placed mirrors are customary to increase a room's light, but I cannot spend the next hour and a half dodging my reflection in the looking glass."

She *hated* her reflection. Not always; sometimes she was almost pretty. But only in the privacy of her bedchamber. If she sat across from a mirror in this house, she would be forced to acknowledge how ill-matched she was to the others. How much plainer, how dull and irrelevant.

She would rather be tossed into the Serpentine.

"I spy a better location," Faircliffe said, without asking further questions. "Come and see if this vantage point is superior."

It was the chair nearest the door—half in shadow, because it made little sense to reflect light toward the hallway. Farthest from Philippa and her mother, with the view obscured by the towering tea trays.

It was perfect.

"Thank you," Chloe said, and meant it.

"*Your Grace*," Mrs. York simpered, "I saved you the best seat, over here next to my Philippa."

"Thank you," the duke replied, but did not sound pleased.

Chloe grinned up at him and bounced her fingers good-bye.

"In case I haven't a chance to speak to you after the tea…" Faircliffe cleared his throat. A hint of color touched his cheeks. "This lilac color brings out your eyes much better than the ecru did."

With that, he was gone. He must have taken Chloe's breath with him, because she found herself without air. She sat down hard on her chair and tried to weather her vertigo. Her pulse fluttered so rapidly at her throat, it felt like it was trying to break free. She touched her fingers to the spot to quell it and could not. She stared after him.

Faircliffe wasn't just pretending to see her today. He *saw* her. He'd seen her last time, too. He remembered what she wore, and he liked...this...soul-sucking lavender-gray color better than the watered-down porridge of the other muslin. It brought out her *eyes*. Eyes no one but relatives had ever noticed.

Thank God she wasn't seated before a looking glass. She doubted she'd recognize the expression reflected back at her.

10

I always say there's a right and a wrong way for a kitchen to prepare a cucumber sandwich. Mine are the finest of all!"

Lawrence tried to concentrate on Mrs. York's animated chatter. She would soon be his mother-in-law, and she deserved his attention and respect. His thoughts were much too fractured to be coherent, but fortunately his reputation for icy ducal hauteur meant he was not expected to smile and prattle in return.

He was *supposed* to be thinking about Miss York. Instead, he was preoccupied with Miss Wynchester.

She had looked oddly defenseless when he told her the lilac brought out her eyes. Startled, perhaps, as if unused to hearing compliments. Or perhaps unused to society in general. That was why she had come to him, was it not? She didn't know what to do or what to expect.

She certainly didn't need to know what else he thought when he looked at her.

Her scent tickled his skin like feathers, sending a frisson of awareness along his flesh from the knowledge she was near. He could feel her, like the air just before a thunderstorm.

The lilac did bring out her eyes, but he would have noticed

them regardless. They were her best and worst feature—too arresting and perceptive for comfort. His blood quickened. Her clear gaze made his clothes feel too warm, the fabric rough when before it had been smooth. He wondered if she felt the same.

He wanted to touch her skin to see if it felt as soft as it looked. To slide his fingers into the hair at her nape and draw her close, enveloping her in his embrace the way her scent enveloped him. Magnetic and inescapable, washing over him like rain. A summer storm, hot and wet.

These were dangerous thoughts that he would never admit. Acknowledging her was risk enough. Acting on animal impulse would be ruinous. A wise man would keep his distance.

Miss Wynchester was interesting, surprising... and not meant for Lawrence. He must put her out of his mind and remember his duty to his title. This little favor meant nothing. Miss York was the quarry. With his proper, respectable new wife at his side, Lawrence wouldn't even notice Miss Wynchester's presence at his end-of-season gala.

He hoped.

"I am delighted to have you for tea," Mrs. York cooed. "Don't worry about the blanket."

Yes. Lawrence supposed Miss Wynchester was both to blame and to thank for that.

If it weren't for being honor-bound to fulfill their bargain, he would not have attended an event called Blankets for Babes. Lawrence was a champion for the poor, but in the House of Lords. He *hated* not being in control, and he was unquestionably out of his element at this inspirational needlework symposium.

Then again, strategy was everything. Miss Wynchester had given him the perfect opportunity to present himself as more than a hard, standoffish duke. Perhaps his presence here today would warm Miss York's affections.

Not that she glanced in his direction.

"You're all invited to my June gala," he announced.

Several of the young ladies cheered.

"Thank you," gushed Mrs. York. "You are everything that is gracious and kind."

Miss York did not stifle her yawn.

"I spied His Grace last week in his theatre box," whispered one of her friends.

"He never misses a performance," said another with great authority.

"He's always alone."

"I suppose someone in this room will be his first guest..." said another slyly.

Even before the passing of Lawrence's father, the Faircliffe private opera box had been exclusively Lawrence's domain. Father had never attended. Lawrence, as this impertinent chit had pointed out, could not keep away.

Attending a performance felt like stepping into one of his paintings, into a life full of music and daring and love. He couldn't afford the extravagance, but neither could he give it up. The private box was his haven. He didn't *want* anyone close enough to watch him grip the sides of his seat during reckless acrobatics onstage or see him swallow hard to hide his emotion during plaintive ballads of heartbreak.

The unmarried ladies of the ton had taken one look at an eligible duke seated all alone in a theatre box and determined the first female to be invited within those hallowed half walls would undoubtedly become his bride.

They were almost right.

Lawrence would never refuse his duchess her rightful

place... But he would not relinquish this innocent private pleasure until then.

Yet, the ladies made a fair point. If attendance by his side in a theatre box was tantamount to a public proposal, some level of *private* conversation with Miss York was long overdue.

He turned toward Mrs. York. "What interesting craftsmanship on that tall case clock across the room. Might I inspect it closer?"

"Straightaway. Philippa would *love* to escort you." She sent her daughter a speaking look. "Darling, please show His Grace our clock."

Miss York did not appear enthusiastic, but she inclined her head in assent. "As you please."

The back of Lawrence's neck crawled. What would Miss Wynchester think when he and Miss York engaged in a tête-à-tête on the other side of the tea cakes? As he rose to his feet, his gaze flicked in her direction.

She wasn't even looking. Tiglet had climbed up her bodice and was trying to lick her face. Miss Wynchester twisted this way and that, making droll faces as though the kitten's little tongue tickled. The effect was endearing. He could hardly look away.

And... perhaps the Duke of Faircliffe was paying too much attention to the wrong woman.

He immediately offered Miss York his arm and forced an awkward smile.

She took his arm but did not return the smile. They walked to the ornate Chippendale tall case clock in silence.

He *liked* silence, Lawrence told himself. His reputation for reticence was unfeigned. There was no reason to blather about nothing. A wife with whom he could share the occasional companionable silence would be a treasure.

If his moments in Miss York's company had thus far failed

to seem companionable...well, this was his opportunity to correct that.

"Do you want to look at the clock?" she asked. "Here it is. Shall I point out how numerical and clocklike it is?"

His lips tightened at her jibe. Perhaps she felt as uncomfortable as he did. Lawrence had never learned to be flirtatious and rakish. He'd been too busy studying to be a better man than his father. Moments like these weren't easy.

As a child, he'd been shunned for so long, solitude had become normal. He'd longed to connect meaningfully with others but hadn't known how. He still didn't know. He hoped his wife would be the person he could be genuine with, without judgment. He wanted a relationship based on mutual trust and respect. Safety and comfort. Not duty.

"I don't want you to do anything," he assured her.

Except that wasn't true, was it? He wanted her to *want* to marry him.

"That is," he clarified, "I don't want you to do anything you don't wish to. May I be frank?"

"As you wish, Your Grace."

"Shall we dispense with 'Your Grace'? You have my permission to call me Faircliffe."

Miss York studied the base of the clock without saying anything at all.

Lawrence tried not to be frustrated. This was no love match; therefore, he could not expect passion. He'd just hoped for...*more*.

Like him, Miss York was an only child. The only hope for a large, happy family would be to pray for many healthy children. Lawrence would be as devoted to them as he would be to his wife.

Was Miss York hesitant because he'd given her cause to doubt his intentions? His neck heated. He should not have allowed his gaze to wander toward Miss Wynchester. And he should do his best to dispel any fears that he'd fallen victim to any of the other guests' overeager charms.

"If you've noticed others making flirtatious comments to me, I want you know I am not interested in any of those young ladies."

"They're lovely young ladies." Miss York glared at him. "That's why they're my friends."

"Er…yes. I didn't mean…" Good God, this conversation was going worse than he'd feared. "Let me be honest, Miss York. Perhaps it is gauche to be forthcoming about my motives, but I dislike prevarication and cannot countenance any sort of relationship built on lies."

"Do we have any sort of relationship?"

"I am working on it." His spine was rigid. "I'm working on many things. I've spent a lifetime elevating my reputation above my father's. I keep a town house and an entailed country estate in the best condition my limited finances can provide. An investment opportunity in June will further secure the dukedom, if I have the means to take advantage of it. My greatest advantage is my rank, which I will share with my wife and pass along to future generations."

"It sounds like you have everything."

"I haven't a duchess." Making such a bald statement was a risk, but he needed her to understand what he was offering and asking. A dowry for a duchy, so to speak. "I hope that over the next few weeks you may wish to take that role."

Her brow creased. "Why wait weeks? All you need is a moment alone with my father. He's itching to sign a marriage contract."

"That may be." Indeed, Lawrence *hoped* it was true. "But I will not ask you or your father to agree to a union that goes against your will. If he signs a marriage contract, it must be because both you and I wish to wed."

She tilted her head. "You are an odd duke. I think I like you more than I thought I did."

Not quite the *Yes, yes, please let me be your duchess* a man of his status might expect, but a step in the right direction. He could certainly appreciate candor.

Perhaps one day it could blossom into something resembling love.

A movement on the opposite side of the crowded room caught his eye. Miss Wynchester cradled Tiglet in her lap and was stroking his soft fur. Anyone would purr to be touched as sweetly and as adoringly as that.

"A friend of yours?" Miss York asked.

"*No.*" He thought it over. Were they? "No, definitely not."

Miss York pursed her lips.

Clearly this required more explanation. Lawrence straightened. There was no reason to hide his association with Miss Wynchester; indeed, the terms of their agreement would make it public knowledge. Besides, if all went well, Miss York would be right there at Lawrence's side when he...

"I've promised to acknowledge her a few times this Season," he explained. "As a personal favor to improve her standing."

"Astonishing." Miss York's gaze was flat and her tone sardonic. "You will valiantly refrain from publicly humiliating a young lady with a direct cut, at least for the moment. How generous."

He shifted his weight. "Er..."

"Wait." Miss York tilted her head. "You *are* aware she's a Wynchester?"

"Were *you* aware?" he countered. "To be frank, I never dreamed your mother would open her doors to—"

"She did not." Miss York's smile was brittle. "Mother remains the pinnacle of respectability you dreamed she would be. There was apparently some confusion with the guest list."

"There's always confusion where the Wynchesters are concerned." His gaze flicked back across the room. "That's why I stay away."

"Hmm." She arched a brow.

Lawrence remembered her insinuation that he had been the one to behave poorly, not Miss Wynchester.

What must it be like to *have* to manipulate others into performing ordinary acts of kindness?

Miss York gestured at the clock. "Gaze upon the infinite vastness of time for as long as you please. I must return to my mother. Guests will soon be departing."

"I'll take you to her," he offered.

But he would not be so forward as to stand by her side as the guests took their leave. There would be plenty of time for that once they were duke and duchess.

Instead, he made his way toward Miss Wynchester.

What was this pull she had over him? His limbs were *his* to control, yet the only direction they turned in was hers. He felt taller, more powerful, and more exposed all at once.

She tucked Tiglet into her basket and rested her chin in her hand, her fingertips tapping lightly at her cheek. He wondered what she would taste like there, if he were to kiss the soft skin beneath her cheekbone, all the way to the sensitive crease at the lobe of her ear. He would run his finger along the edge of that perfect shell, then his tongue, then perhaps nip lightly before moving down to the pulse just beneath.

Ignoring her was impossible.

With their chins high and noses pinched, some said the Wynchesters were as common as flies. Lawrence rather suspected that if Miss Wynchester was wild and common, she was more like a dandelion. Strong and beautiful, able to spring back taller than before no matter how hard one tried to cut her down.

11

Although several peers and statesmen went straight from Parliament to Lady Quarrington's soirée, Lawrence was the only man who had been counting down the minutes because he could not cease worrying about a Wynchester.

There were many reasons her evening might not have gone as desired: for example, not knowing how to dress or comport herself, having never received such an invitation before.

Simply because one's name was Wynchester.

But Lawrence was not here for *her*, he assured himself as a footman whisked away his coat and hat. He had a future duchess to woo.

The butler accompanied him to the door of the ballroom and announced Lawrence's arrival.

As hundreds of faces tilted his way, he could not help but wonder what the reaction had been to Miss Wynchester's name.

Had she been allowed to cross the threshold? Was her cat peeking from a wicker basket? Had she found a more suitable gown? What if the prospect had proved too daunting, and she hadn't come at all?

He could not blame her if that was the case. He'd been born to this world, and it still overwhelmed him.

From the moment Lawrence's feet touched the ballroom floor, he greeted a never-ending current of acquaintances. Some calculating faces looked at him and saw an unclaimed title for their daughters. Some saw a potential vote in the House of Lords.

All that others saw was his father.

Soon there would be no more vowels to pay. The gossip could finally turn from the misdeeds of his father to the question of when Lawrence and his bride might expect an heir.

He would do everything in his power to ensure *his* children needn't cringe whenever someone mentioned their father.

"But enough about auld lang syne," droned the Marquess of Rosbotham, a well-respected statesman who had attended Eton with Lawrence's father. "What is the meaning of that speech you gave yesterday? You're as Tory as I am, of course you must be, but some of your wild ideas sound perilously close to the nonsense spouted by those liberal Whigs!"

"Nonsense" like social reform and caring for the plight of the common man, who had no entailed house to sleep in nor family treasures to fund his every desire.

"I believe in the sovereignty of king and church," Lawrence assured the marquess. "But if ladies can support their little charities, should not gentlemen perform good works using the superior resources we possess?"

"Mmm." Rosbotham's eyes were suspicious, but as Lawrence had framed his point as a question of manliness and rank, the marquess found himself without an easy retort.

This was why Miss York's father would be such a critical ally. They needed each other. Lawrence could sway votes in the House of Lords, and Mr. York was a favorite to be the next Speaker for the House of Commons.

"What about—" Rosbotham began, but Lawrence did not hear the rest of the marquess's question.

His eyes had locked on Miss Wynchester along the far wall.

For once she was not dressed in shades of gray but wore a gown the color of fresh cream with a bodice of seafoam green and embroidery to match along the hem. Her soft brown hair was swept up in a simple coil, drawing one's attention to her lively brown eyes and rosy lips. He wanted to taste the dip at the top, run his tongue along the seam until she allowed him access...

She did not seem at all the sort of woman who needed to ask to be kissed. He could imagine begging for the pleasure, the seductive feel of a victorious smile tugging at her lips even as she pressed them against his.

Miss Wynchester was no peacock of fashion, but she played her part with astonishing precision. She mixed well with wealthy, cultured wallflowers who had been coming to these events their entire lives. If the butler had not read her name too loudly, the current company would have no reason to suspect a Wynchester was in their midst.

Lawrence noticed every sparkle in her eye and stray curl of hair. He had the nape of her neck and the curve of her cheek memorized, yet watched her helplessly all the same. Miss Wynchester was like air. He could not help but breathe her in.

"What's caught your attention?" Lord Rosbotham asked.

The back of Lawrence's neck began to sweat. He could not possibly respond with *A Wynchester*.

Could he? She was here to make the best match she could. No one would believe he'd extended an invitation to his end-of-season gala if he didn't acknowledge he knew her.

Perhaps more to the point, she needn't *attend* his gala in search of leg shackles if she happened upon an interested gentleman beforehand. Anything Lawrence could do to speed things along would do them both a favor.

And the Marquess of Rosbotham had three unmarried sons.

"If I'm not mistaken," Lawrence said as casually as he could, "the pretty girl in the celery-hued gown is Miss Chloe Wynchester."

"Wynchester?" Rosbotham snorted in derision. "God save us all. Baron Vanderbean might have been allowed into less discerning households, but that is no reason for his collection of strays to be afforded the same luxury."

Lawrence's cold fingers curled into fists. Despite having felt much the same way less than a fortnight earlier, there was little more he wished to do now than plant the Marquess of Rosbotham a dizzying facer.

"Parentage is not one's only trait," he pointed out. "Besides, I can think of several by-blows who move quite freely in society."

"Whose by-blow is *she*?" Rosbotham spat. "Some harlot who discarded her own spawn? Why should we feel obligated to bow and scrape to the likes of—"

Lawrence did not wait to hear the rest of Lord Rosbotham's diatribe. He was not so foolish as to punch a marquess in a crowded ballroom; neither could Lawrence stand passively by while an innocent young lady was disparaged. Heritage was never a child's fault. One's actions, however—*those* defined the man.

Without begging his leave, he stepped around the marquess and headed straight toward Chloe Wynchester. At least she hadn't brought her cat or her basket—unless Tiglet had already escaped.

An elderly woman with wiry gray hair and sharp, narrowed eyes stopped him less than a foot away.

"Have you been properly introduced to my great-niece, young man?" Her thin voice quavered as she swayed unevenly to block his path.

"Yes, Aunt." Miss Wynchester gave the older woman's pale hand a reassuring pat. A thin ring encircled one of the aunt's narrow fingers. "That's no ne'er-do-well. That's the Duke of Faircliffe." Her brown eyes sparkled up at Lawrence. "Your Grace, my great-aunt Wynchester."

Her great-aunt stared at Lawrence with enough suspicion that he dipped an involuntary bow to prove himself harmless.

"A duke, you say?" Mrs. Wynchester sniffed with obvious resignation, as though she'd been holding out hope some unfettered king or prince would fall madly for her great-niece, and Lawrence stood in that royal hero's way. "Humph. I'll get the ratafia."

Ratafia. Lawrence despised the sickly-sweet cordial almost as much as tea.

Miss Wynchester shook her head. "I don't want ratafia, Aunt."

"It's not for you." Another harrumph.

Lawrence jerked back in alarm. "I don't require ratafia, either, madam."

"I'm afraid it's not for you, either," Miss Wynchester murmured as her great-aunt doddered away without a backward glance. "I wish you better first impressions next time."

He could not help but recall Lord Rosbotham's commentary. Baron Vanderbean was just important enough to be considered part of the beau monde, but Miss Wynchester would have had to fight for every scrap.

"You look like you belong," he offered, unsure if he was damning her with faint praise or if she would take the remark in the complimentary spirit in which he had meant it. "You're even prettier in light green than you were in lavender."

A touch of pink flushed her cheeks, and she glanced away. "You have a gaggle of admirers awaiting your attention."

He followed her gaze and wished he hadn't. A half dozen debutantes tittered back at him from behind painted fans.

This was one of many reasons he rarely attended society functions. First, accepting an invitation implied reciprocity, and he lacked the funds for more than a single annual gathering. Second, any unwed gentleman was presumed on the hunt for a wife. An unwed *lord*, on the other hand, was attacked on all sides by hopeful young ladies and social-climbing mamas alike.

Now that he was here, however, he might as well make the most of it. For his own sake—specifically, his pursuit of Miss Philippa York—his interests were not best served by idling about with Miss Chloe Wynchester.

Yet he might have done so all evening had Lord Bussington not chosen that moment to whisk him away.

"You must save me," young Bussington whispered to Lawrence, his tone urgent. "The next set is a country-dance, at which I'm obliged to stand up with my sister's nettlesome friend. But that means there's no one left for my sister. If I must suffer, so must you."

Lawrence tossed a helpless look at Miss Wynchester, but her blank gaze slid elsewhere, as if she'd already grown bored with the entire concept of a ball. Or had she simply failed to cause a stir and was salvaging her pride however she could?

"Good Lord," Bussington chided him as soon as they were out of earshot. "What's come over you, Faircliffe? My sister isn't here, and you're lucky for it. Mrs. York has been staring daggers at you for visiting wallflowers before greeting her daughter."

Miss York. How had Lawrence forgotten to dance attendance on Miss York?

"You aren't the sole unwed lord in England," Bussington continued. "If the rumors are true and you're after a wife, then fish in the best pond. To a man trying to swim upstream, even the best Wynchester is nothing more than an anchor."

12

Chloe was still gazing after the Duke of Faircliffe's attractive backside when her sister returned from the refreshment table.

"I see what you mean." Tommy handed her a glass of orgeat. "That overbearing lord absolutely reeks of arrogance. The awful way His Disdainfulness sensed your presence like a haughty bloodhound, plowing through his peers to contemptuously inform you that nothing disgusts him more than your pretty eyes—"

"That's not what he said," Chloe mumbled. "Besides, you weren't here. I thought you went after ratafia."

"The queue was too long. This is better."

Chloe wrinkled her nose. "Insipid orgeat is better than ratafia?"

"*Previously* insipid." Tommy lowered her voice. "I may have given ours a splash of gin."

Chloe gasped as if scandalized. "Great-Aunt Wynchester, you crafty old bird!"

Tommy's eyes crinkled all the way to her temples, thanks to tonight's extra wrinkles. "What else are chaperones for?"

"I feel like there *is* something else. Something important."

Chloe tapped her cheek as if in deep thought. "I can't put my finger on it."

"Now, now, dear. It is I who can't remember things. You concentrate on your duke." Tommy's temporarily liver-spotted hand clinked her glass of orgeat and gin against Chloe's. "I deduce that's no hardship?"

"He's vexingly handsome," Chloe admitted.

As the musicians prepared to play the next set, she could not help but watch him. The sharp angles of his jaw and cheekbones were stern and rigid, much like the man himself, but his lips were quick and mobile, giving the impression that kissing them would not be stiff and cold at all but rather a tender onslaught of wicked sensations.

Faircliffe's tall figure and raw power drew her like pollen attracted bees. Her blood buzzed with the yearning to rend his buttons from his well-tailored clothes and splay her fingers against the hot flesh beneath.

Her pulse jumped at every glimpse of him, as though recklessly leaping toward him despite her protective layers of silk and shift and stays. Her body's attraction was instinctual, and no amount of silent inner lectures could stop her from holding in a tiny little breath every time she glimpsed him through the crowd.

His eyes met hers as if he sensed her watching him. Although his expression did not change, the temperature in the ballroom increased from the intensity of his gaze. Her lungs caught. Every breath attuned to him and the tension crackling between them.

But when the music resumed, he turned and extended his arm to Philippa York.

Chloe tried not to feel the loss. She was not there for him. Who cared who he danced with? Yet she could not help but wish her sister Marjorie were present to read their lips.

Then again, perhaps it was better not to know what flirtatious compliments or words of love Faircliffe might murmur to Philippa. After all, *she* was the one he intended to make his bride.

The thought soured Chloe's stomach.

"Do you think he's courting her for her large...dowry?" Chloe tracked their progress about the dance floor. She wished she could like Philippa less.

After Chloe had sent a note of apology for the "misunderstanding" about her name, she was pleasantly surprised to receive forgiveness as well as a renewed invitation in return. Then again, perhaps Philippa's graciousness had more to do with Chloe's connection to Faircliffe than any desire to be friends.

Tommy shook her head, her gaze locked on Philippa. "Her dowry is far from the only attraction. Besides being kind and clever, she's always the loveliest young lady in the room."

"She dresses like a doll."

Tommy's voice was soft. "A *beautiful* doll with sky-blue eyes and soft, womanly curves..."

"I will dump this orgeat on your head," Chloe warned.

"You would never mistreat gin," Tommy countered. "Or your great-aunt Wynchester."

Chloe sniffed. "I don't care whom he dances with, or whether it's because of looks or money."

"Or both," Tommy added helpfully. "In Miss York's case."

Chloe bared her clenched teeth.

Tommy sipped her orgeat, unrepentant. "Good thing you're not interested."

"I'm not." Whom Faircliffe courted, or married, or danced with, had nothing at all to do with Chloe.

Yet she could not help but wish she were whirling in his arms, if only for a moment. Whether as Jane Brown or as herself, Chloe was relegated to the periphery, tucked so far away that even her fellow wallflowers failed to notice her.

That was her role, she reminded herself. Her responsibility. Melting into the background was how she contributed to her family. Was she really complaining because she had the talent to perform her position *well*?

"So many ostrich feathers." Tommy gazed out over the rim of her glass of orgeat at the dance floor. "It's like a chicken coop in a hurricane."

Chloe owned almost as many feathers as were present in this ballroom. Hers rarely left their hatboxes. How she longed to attend such an event swathed in her finest fripperies!

Instead, she was a pigeon amongst peacocks. Overshadowed even by Great-Aunt Wynchester.

"I love you, you know," she said to her sister.

Tommy was invisible in her own way. Even when she was the most flamboyant person in the room, it was always as someone else and never as herself.

"Don't be mawkish," Tommy scolded, but did not meet Chloe's eyes. "I only follow you around in the hopes that you will get your hands on another one of those halfpenny pies."

Chloe grinned to herself. Along with mittens, as a skinny child of eight or nine, pies were amongst the first things she'd spent her pickpocketing riches on. And Tommy, whose bed was the next cot over, was the first person she'd shared her bounty with.

"You always looked after me." Tommy smiled. "I dreamed of being as strong as you."

Chloe blinked in surprise. "As me?"

"You always had the answers or could find the way to get them. You saved so many of us. You found Bean." Tommy gave her a pointed look. "Why else do you suppose you're the leader?"

"*Me*?" Chloe squeaked. "*You* were the one who gave me a place to sleep when I lost mine."

"And you had a new plan by morning. You always did. I followed you and learned from you. Bean was brilliant, generous, and impossible, but you somehow managed him. You can manage Faircliffe, too"—Tommy wrinkled her nose—"even if your eyelashes aren't as long and pretty as Miss York's."

"For the love of..." Chloe buried her face in her hands. "Why did I share my pies?"

"You knew you'd need me one day. This is my time to shine. Great-Aunt Wynchester, eater of pies and drinker of gin, summa cum laude in World's Worst Chaperone." Tommy snickered. "Faircliffe hasn't got a chance."

Chloe narrowed her eyes. "You mean with our painting. We steal it back, he won't know the difference, and we never speak to him again."

"Yes, yes, that's what I meant. How absurd would it be for him to become overset with baser passions and throw himself at your feet? I won't know, because I'll be too busy being a terrible chaperone somewhere else. You must fill me in afterward." Tommy thought it over. "And no replacing his spoons with twigs."

Chloe pressed a hand to her bosom. "I've no idea how that keeps happening at the breakfast table."

Tommy gave a very Great-Aunt Wynchester harrumph.

"We don't see you do it," she said with a wink, "but we know it's you."

Chloe's cheeks heated. That *was* why she did it. Traded a spoon for a twig or a button for a fig. To make sure her siblings noticed her. That at home, at least, she wouldn't be invisible.

But Tommy was saying that Chloe had never been invisible. Even when they didn't see her, they knew she was there. They looked up to her. Chloe's throat pricked with emotion.

She wouldn't let them down.

"Tomorrow," she told Tommy. "We arrive at his door as Clueless Chloe and Great-Aunt Wynchester and start the search for our painting."

Tommy nodded. "I'm ready. You distract His Royal Aloofness and I'll totter forgetfully from room to room. If *Puck & Family* is in that town house, we'll find it well before the gala."

Chloe's gaze darted back to Faircliffe. He was not looking at her but Philippa. They made a striking couple. Elegance incarnate.

Yet it was not Philippa's pretty looks that Chloe envied but Philippa's hand in Faircliffe's.

Philippa knew what it felt like to dance close enough to feel the warmth of his body. She knew the weight of his fingers against the curve of her back. She knew what it was like to move with him rather than against him. To let him lead her not just around the ballroom but straight to the altar.

Faircliffe could tell by looking that Philippa was the woman he wanted.

No one ever looked at Chloe and entertained such a thought. They rarely looked at her at all.

The music ended. Faircliffe handed Philippa back to her mother. Now he was murmuring something that Mrs. York found gay and amusing. "Ha-ha, ho-ho"—such peals of laughter. The Duke of Faircliffe was the wittiest lord in the room. What's this, a waltz? And him standing right there? Surely this was a sign from the heavens that he was meant to whisk Beautiful Philippa back onto the dance floor.

Chloe didn't stay at the party to find out.

She drained the last of her orgeat and turned to her sister. "Meat pies?"

13

*Y*ou look delightfully decrepit," Chloe whispered to Tommy late the following afternoon as their carriage pulled to a stop before the Faircliffe residence.

"You look adorably forgettable," Tommy whispered back.

Only a sister could find Chloe's calculated tepidness adorable.

It was relentless, foolhardy optimism that had caused her to tuck a few extra items into her usual basket of tricks. She had never worn fashionable accessories outside of her dressing room—and certainly wouldn't do so at tonight's party—but knowing they were there comforted her. Other people needn't see inside her basket for its contents to bring her joy.

"Faircliffe thinks Wynchesters are embarrassing," she reminded her sister. "Don't let him down."

Tommy grinned back at her. "My pleasure."

Chloe rapped the knocker.

Mr. Hastings swept open the door, his pale face impassive.

Before Chloe could give him a winning smile, Tommy hobbled over the threshold, darting the butler myopic, suspicious glances.

"Are you *certain* this pile belongs to the Duke of Faircliffe?" she queried tremulously.

"Great-Aunt Wynchester, wait!" Chloe called, and slipped past the startled Mr. Hastings and into the grand hall.

"Halt right there," Mr. Hastings demanded, but he was obliged to lock the door before giving chase.

Tommy wandered into the adjoining room that Faircliffe had brought Chloe to the first time she'd appeared, uninvited.

"I'll wait here," Tommy announced, in full Great-Aunt Wynchester belligerence. "Go tell your duke there's an old lady in his parlor because her niece insists Faircliffe is the rare man who can be made useful."

"Now, Aunt," Chloe chided, "I never claimed anything of the sort. Oh, Mr. Hastings, there you are!" She pretended surprise at finding him red-faced in the doorway. "We are Miss and Mrs. Wynchester, here to see His Grace."

He reddened in consternation, likely torn between throwing her out on her ear and demanding to know how, precisely, she'd characterized his esteemed employer to her great-aunt.

"If the ladies Wynchester would *please* wait here." Mr. Hastings turned and stalked down the corridor.

"Was he handsome?" Tommy's trembling nasal voice was loud enough to be heard in the kitchens. "I love a handsome butler. Even more so than matched footmen. Did I tell you about the time—"

"Yes, Aunt," Chloe assured her, trying to disguise her laughter. "Many times. I fear it's for the best that your eyes aren't what they used to be. A man as important as His Grace must have very fine footmen."

"May I help you?" came a low, droll voice from the doorway.

"Yes," she said brightly. "That is, I hope so."

With a final pat on Great-Aunt Wynchester's supposedly frail shoulder, Chloe turned to face the duke. His striking blue gaze was aimed right at her.

The duke's dark hair looked as though he'd recently raked his fingers through it, and his chest moved as though he was still catching his breath.

The poor man must have sprinted from wherever he'd been occupied. Chloe and her "aunt" had been left alone less than five minutes.

She wanted to touch her fingertips to his lapels, to feel the rise and fall of his strong chest as he caught his breath. Perhaps then she could find her own. And her wits, which seemed to have scattered.

His lips curved in a smile so faint, it was easily missed, yet she was certain it had been meant for her alone.

Chloe was standing still, yet her heart thudded against her chest, pressing her bodice toward him with every heartbeat. He stood laughably far from her, but neither of them dared close the distance. Anything could happen if they were close enough to touch.

"Mrs. Wynchester, Miss Wynchester." He arched a brow. "How may I be of service?"

Chloe opened her mouth.

"You likely cannot," Tommy barked, then shook a scolding finger at Chloe. "My niece was raised by wolves."

"I will keep that in mind and do my best," Faircliffe said wryly. "Once I have any idea what we're talking about."

"Social ruin for this chit." Tommy waved a hand. "If she shows her face at the Apeworth parade."

"Ainsworth party, Aunt," Chloe corrected gently. "Please let me tell it." She looked up at Faircliffe and affected an expression of deep distress. "I've been invited to a society supper tonight, followed by dancing. It's a wonderful opportunity to meet my future husband...if I don't embarrass myself with all those spoons and forks and who sits where."

"Ainsworth party?" Faircliffe's forehead lined. "Tonight?"

"I won't take more than half an hour of your time," she said in a rush, "if you're able to part with that much. It's just...Wynchesters have never been given proper instruction in anything"—Bean had filled the house with tutors and drilled them on *everything*—"and if I make a poor showing tonight, there might *be* no further invitations until your end-of-season gala."

"You intend your comportment to be indistinguishable from that of a highborn lady in...half an hour?" Faircliffe glanced at the clock atop the mantel, then frowned at her. "The dinner won't start for hours."

"Waste of everyone's time," Tommy blustered with an exasperated shake of her head. "You're a lost cause, girl."

The duke let out a defeated sigh. "One hour. That's all I can give you."

"Thank you," Chloe gushed, doing her best to keep the laughter out of her voice. "Tonight I might meet my future intended."

A tendon pulsed in Faircliffe's neck. He turned to his butler, who had been hovering behind him. "Hastings, would you have the formal dining room set for a party of, say, twelve?"

"At once, Your Grace." But the butler slid Chloe an appraising look.

She smiled back at him blandly.

He disappeared to do his master's bidding.

"I suppose we should begin by pretending I'm your escort." The duke raised his elbow toward Chloe, then frowned over her shoulder. "Does your aunt require assistance?"

"I don't want your arm," Tommy quavered. "I'm old, not incapable. Now, if you've got a pair of handsome footmen to spare..."

"Ignore her," Chloe whispered. "She blusters to salve her pride."

"Pride? I don't know what I did with mine," he muttered. But he left his elbow proffered for her to take.

Her breath was unsteady as she slid her fingers around his upper arm. She was touching him just as she'd imagined doing. A shiver spread over her flesh, weakening her knees. She held tighter. Memorized the feel of him beneath each fingertip.

His arm was warm through the layers of shirt and jacket, and well-defined due to the musculature he'd earned doing... what? Did he swim or practice a sport like boxing?

Chloe tried not to imagine Faircliffe stripped to his shirtsleeves, dodging blows and throwing sweaty punches, before emerging from the ring triumphant and proud. Her pulse jumped at the idea of watching his muscles ripple, of pressing the soft tip of her tongue to his hard chest to taste the salt of his skin.

"Are we there yet?" Tommy barked.

Faircliffe glanced over his shoulder. "I'm taking the shortest path."

Chloe held on tight.

A tour of his town house would have saved them a bit of reconnaissance, but she and Tommy had both agreed it was best for the duke to believe them uninterested in the details of his residence. Besides, none of these terraced homes was particularly large.

Not that there appeared to be any reason to worry. Faircliffe had accepted Great-Aunt Wynchester's frightful lack of manners without question and believed that a woman of Chloe's age could grow up under the tutelage of a baron and somehow not know which fork to use with the fish. All because their last name was Wynchester.

It would be funny if it weren't so serious.

At the open door to the dining room, Faircliffe launched

into a long explanation of the order in which guests would enter and who would sit where.

She pasted on a wide-eyed *Oh dear, you're talking so fast, this is confusing me* expression, and nodded encouragingly at each tedious new tidbit.

He believed in her utter ignorance and complete incompetence so fully, it was difficult not to throw up her hands and scream. Perhaps invisible *was* better. She would rather keep believing she could fit in if given a chance than to have the idyllic fiction snatched away.

"All right," Faircliffe continued. "Because of my rank, I would be one of the first to enter and be seated, whereas you—"

"Would be dead last," she finished dryly.

Faircliffe rubbed his chin. "Let's pretend I'm a younger son of an ordinary, untitled man."

"The horror," Chloe murmured.

"In that case, we might sit next to each other. I would lead you to the table like this."

She locked her knees as they walked, allowing her wooden gait to make the short trip more awkward.

Tommy already sat at the head of the table and was inspecting her pristine glasses and cutlery for spots. A nervous footman stood just behind her.

Faircliffe joined Chloe in the middle, then motioned to the footman. "Jackson, if you'd pretend to serve..."

Tommy placed her hand on her stomach and gave a loud groan. "Ohhh, this pernickety gut. I cannot even glimpse an *empty* table without...Have you a water closet, young man?"

"'Your Grace,'" Chloe hissed. "Faircliffe is a duke."

"He just said he wasn't," Tommy pointed out belligerently. "He said if he *were* a duke, he'd have the best seat at the table, but instead he's over there by you."

"We're acting, Aunt." Chloe tossed Faircliffe a chagrined expression. "His Grace is still a duke. This is the only time he'll ever sit with me."

"Acting!" Tommy clutched both hands to her belly. "Well, does this theatre have a retiring room or not?"

"I'll take her," Chloe whispered.

Faircliffe nodded. "Down the hall, first left, second door."

"I heard the instructions." Tommy pushed to her feet. "And I don't need a chaperone. I *am* the chaperone. Don't you two get up to anything but spooning and forking until I return."

Chloe gave her a quelling look.

Tommy widened her eyes innocently and hobbled out the door.

Chloe turned back to Faircliffe. To buy Tommy time, Chloe needed to funnel all of the duke's attention into explaining how one ate supper at a supper table. Easy. Innocent. No spooning or forking. Just a nice, long, boring speech about proper etiquette and table manners.

"What comes next?" she prompted with excess zeal, as if she were deeply invested in how best to unfold one's serviette.

His attention was not on the place settings.

Faircliffe was staring at her as though what he'd most like to dine on was not dinner but Chloe. She could feel not just the heat of his gaze but the heat of his body.

Their chairs were placed too near. The folds of her skirt flirted with his ankle. They were close enough that their shoulders would touch if they were facing the table. Instead, they faced each other and breathed the electric air, feeling it crackle within their veins. He was much too close. Much, much too close.

"Fork," she stammered. "Spoons."

She wasn't making any sense. He didn't seem to notice. His gaze was on her parted lips, her flushed cheeks, her...hair?

"Most young ladies frame their entire faces with curls. You've just got the one. It should be unfashionable, but it suits you."

She'd left a *curl*?

Chloe swatted at her hair in horror. She'd spent the morning daydreaming in her dressing room as she always did, and she was *certain* she'd remembered to uncurl every single painstaking ringlet she'd arranged in her hair. . . .

"Here," Faircliffe said softly.

She froze, pinned in place like a trapped butterfly. She could not have moved if he paid her.

He reached up toward her ear. She could sense his hand long before she felt it. It was big, large enough to nestle her cheek into as he dragged his thumb across her lower lip or sank his fingers into her hair. She kept her neck as rigid as possible.

She felt the slight lift in pressure as her ringlet fell across his fingers. His gaze was not on the rebellious brown curl but on her mouth. She sank her teeth into her lower lip to keep it from parting in anticipation.

He tucked the curl behind her ear. That should have been all. But then his knuckles grazed her cheek once, twice. She became light-headed. It took all of her strength not to sway into his touch, just as she'd imagined.

"Your skin is so soft. I could—" Faircliffe seemed to collect himself and dropped his hands in his lap before clearing his throat. "I don't subscribe to *Ackermann's Repository*, but you might find it in a lending library for a better idea of the current style."

Chloe clenched her teeth to keep from retching. Of course she was not an irresistible siren. She was his *project*.

He was the overbearing, holier-than-thou nob who was helping.

She fiddled with her serviette and ignored the itch of embarrassment. This entire *Show me how spoons work* ruse depended on him continuing to believe her a lost little fawn, helpless without his guidance. She would flounder through every social encounter, eternally unsuccessful in her alleged matchmaking endeavor, until *Puck & Family* was home safe and sound. That was the plan. It was *working*.

So why did it make her want to overturn the table?

"The ton is governed by rules, just like the rest of England," Faircliffe was saying. "One needn't like these rules. One needn't even believe them good rules. But one *must* follow them."

Chloe contemplated him in silence.

She'd long believed the pomp and circumstance of which rank preceded which into a dining room, and who sat where, as blatant examples of the "betters" keeping the "lessers" in their place.

She hadn't considered that those same strictures might feel like a prison, even to the betters.

"Why must you follow the rules?" she asked, her voice quiet but curious. "Cannot even a duke do as he pleases?"

He gazed at her as if there were very many things he wished to have but could not.

"Very little that I do is to please myself. I must think first and foremost of my position. The estate, the staff, the tenants, the upkeep. And I must ensure everything passes on in the best condition I can make it."

She hesitated. "To . . . your son or to the next cousin in line? Do you want children?"

"I want dozens," he said passionately, then colored. "That is, I would settle for one or two, of course. My role is to beget an heir, not to populate a circus."

Chloe had a feeling he was repeating a quote someone else had oft cited.

"Let me guess," she teased. "Circuses are against the rules?"

He stared at her without responding.

She took pity on him. He might always know what to say when giving speeches in Parliament, but that did not mean he would know how to talk about personal matters...with her.

"I like circuses," she offered. "My brother used to live in one. Some say we still do."

"Dukes don't have circuses," he said at last. "But the fortunate ones might start a family."

The fortunate were *born* to a family, Chloe corrected in her head. Or welcomed into one with open arms. Waiting half one's lifetime in the hopes of one day having a family seemed...

Lonely.

She tried to imagine being constantly surrounded by syco-phants and the crème de la crème of high society without having a true connection with anyone—and then realized she didn't have to imagine. She slipped into his world whenever she pleased, as easily as pulling on a bonnet, but it was never *her* world, *her* friends, *her* place.

The orphanage had been worse. She would never forget the exquisite torture of yearning for somewhere to belong. No...of longing for *people* to belong to. Craving someone to claim *her*, to want her, to miss her, to need her.

It had never occurred to her that someone like Faircliffe might feel the same way.

"I shall cross my fingers for you to be the most fortunate duke in all of England."

His answering smile caused a strange flutter in her belly. "I wish as much good fortune to you."

"I *am* lucky," she said, "whether or not you believe it."

The ladies and misses and wallflowers Chloe pretended to be were bound by society's rules, just as Faircliffe was. But at the end of the day she could go home, toss the current alias aside, and just be Chloe.

The things Faircliffe pitied about her—lack of rank and her unusual family—were what gave her the most freedom. Bean's Balcovian barony was sufficient status to gain access to certain people and places, but not so lofty as to need to please the patronesses of Almack's.

Chloe didn't require a husband for any practical reason. She had a home, she had a family, and she had her own money. Unbeknownst to the public, Bean had created a legal trust for each of the siblings rather than provide dowries for the girls. He was clever like that.

Dowries were funds bestowed upon a future husband, not on the bride herself. Chloe and her sisters would have had no say in how it was spent, because the money would not belong to them.

A legal trust, on the other hand, was held in the name of the beneficiary. Chloe's money was *hers* to do with as she pleased. It would still be hers even if she married. Her husband would not be able to touch a single farthing.

Not that she would marry some fortune hunter who prized gold over love. She had a life she *liked* just as it was. She had *fun*.

Bean's infamous eccentricity, more than his wealth, allowed Chloe and her siblings to get away with nonsense like Great-Aunt Wynchester. When no one expected any better of you, either you went home and cried about it or you turned it to your advantage. You *let* people underestimate you, because their dismissal gave you power.

So why was she peeling back the mask, if only a little, with Faircliffe?

"I believe you." His words rasped oddly. "Lucky people always show it in their eyes."

Her blood rushed so loudly, it sounded like waves pounding ashore. "What do my eyes look like to you?"

"Happy." He reached up, not to hide her errant ringlet, as Chloe presumed, but to graze his thumb across the side of her cheek. This time he did cup her face, for no reason except that he wanted to. "Inviting."

Yes. She was definitely inviting him to look closer. All this waiting and wishing had every nerve alive and prickling with awareness. This touch was different than the ones before. This time something momentous was going to happen.

His gaze lowered to her mouth.

She could not help but lick her lips in response. His eyes were no longer ice, but rather as hot and dangerous as the flicker of blue at the center of a flame. She was the moth who could not help but fly closer to danger.

"You look..." Her voice was breathless, her pulse fluttery. "...hungry."

"Perhaps I am."

He still hadn't taken his hand from her cheek. His fingers curled gently behind her neck, supportive, possessive. He lowered his head until his breath tickled the corner of her lip, right where she could imagine his.

She tilted closer. "Hungry for what?"

He smiled as though they both knew the answer. "Hungry for—"

"Well, that's the last time I eat beans for breakfast," came Tommy's nasal shrill as she clomped back into the room.

Chloe and Faircliffe jerked apart and guiltily inspected opposite sides of the room.

"Or was it nuncheon?" Tommy blathered on. "Was it beans or was it broccoli? Niece, did you make me eat vegetables today, or was that yesterday?"

"We serve vegetables every day, Aunt," Chloe answered automatically. She could not bear to look at either of them.

Tommy leaned on Chloe's shoulder as though to catch her breath and dropped a folded square of foolscap into Chloe's lap.

"I don't know what kind of gentleman you're playing at," Tommy quavered at Faircliffe, "but is it the kind that helps an old woman into her chair?"

He leapt up at once and set about seeing to Tommy's comfort at the head of the table.

Chloe lowered her eyes to her lap and unfolded the message.

"Keys" was written at the top. Underlined three times. "Housekeeper on holiday. Can't get inside. Maid saw me. Has to be you."

Underneath was a rough map and a sketch of where the keys hung in the room.

She slid the missive into a hidden pocket and turned to Faircliffe, who was just finishing with Tommy.

Chloe resumed a look of naïveté. "Are there likely to be beans and broccoli at supper tonight?"

He nearly choked. "No, no. The Ainsworths have a prized French chef. What they'll likely serve..."

As he exhaustively explained the composition of the same dishes she and Tommy ate at home on any given Tuesday, Chloe went over the map again in her mind. Even if there was a servant strolling the corridor, palming the keys would be child's play.

All she needed now was an excuse to slip away.

14

Once Great-Aunt Wynchester had settled into Lawrence's rightful place at the table, he turned his attention back to her great-niece.

She was again wearing layers of pale brown—if one was feeling generous, one might go so far as to discern a wheat hue, with accents of...burnt biscuit? This mix of tannish chaff did not lend itself to waxing poetic, yet its very non-descriptness served to make her dark brown eyes stand out all the more.

When he looked in her eyes, the rest of the world fell away. He forgot he was a duke; he forgot she was a Wynchester. They were just a man and a woman, trapped in each other's gaze, the kiss he had almost taken inevitable rather than narrowly escaped.

Why did he allow himself so close to temptation?

He told himself that if Miss Wynchester ran amok, making a cake of herself at society events, her presence at his gala could cause quite the stir.

Lawrence *hated* causing stirs. That was true and best kept in the forefront of his mind. The way to deflect future gossip was to avoid complicating the situation he found himself in now.

Starting with not kissing Chloe Wynchester under any circumstances. No matter how soft her skin or how plump and juicy her berry-pink lips. Her mouth was not his to taste, her kisses not his to steal. There was a plan, and she was not part of it.

No matter what his aching loins might think.

"I need to rest my eyes," Great-Aunt Wynchester announced as she placed her spectacles on her dinner plate and closed her eyes. "But I can still hear you, children."

"Yes, Aunt," Miss Wynchester said calmingly.

Lawrence had remembered her dislike of reflective surfaces and selected her seat accordingly, but he doubted she'd fare so well at the Ainsworth party.

Should he attend? He definitely should not. What would his presence accomplish? He'd disrupt the seating, for one thing. Dinner parties were carefully calculated to feature an even number of men and women. If he showed up willy-nilly, he'd cause more problems than he could solve.

Of course, he could send a note over *now* to let the hostess know. An extra guest at the last moment was not ideal, but a *duke* at the last moment... well, his title counted for something, did it not? Adding another female to balance the numbers would be effortless.

"Jackson"—he glanced over his shoulder at his footman—"bring pen and paper."

Miss Wynchester's eyes widened. "Should I be taking notes?"

"No, dinner parties aren't that complicated." Although he supposed for her they might be.

It occurred to him how brave she was being: not just by admitting the obvious failures in her upbringing but by putting herself in situations again and again where she might be ridiculed or rejected outright.

Whatever her faults, Miss Wynchester was willing to *try*. Willing to be wrong as many times as necessary in order to become right.

"I'll attend the party with you," he explained. "Well, not *with* you, of course. I'll arrive on my own, and you with your aunt. But if you run into trouble, send a glance in my direction and I will do my best to guide you."

Her brow creased. "Won't your rank place you too far down the table for me to see?"

Well, that was surely an exaggeration. True, at such parties one tended to speak to one's immediate neighbors. And if they found themselves on the same side of the table, facing each other might be difficult. But that was no reason not to—

"Your pen and paper, Your Grace."

Lawrence accepted the materials from his footman and set about scratching a quick note to Lady Ainsworth, apprising her of his attendance, to give her time to juggle the seating arrangements.

He folded the paper, then added Lady Ainsworth's name before handing the letter to his footman. "See that this is delivered at once."

"As you wish, Your Grace."

Lawrence paused in sudden discomfort. A duke could decide at the last moment to do or attend whatever he pleased, but someone like Chloe Wynchester had to literally abduct him out of desperation to negotiate a handful of trifling invitations.

To her, they were not trivial and insignificant. For Miss Wynchester, an invitation meant the world.

He could help. His attraction to her was foolhardy and dangerous, but he could push that aside and concentrate on objective, concrete tasks like proper comportment and what new things she could expect. He enjoyed helping others. There wasn't any more to it than that.

"Guests will enter the dining room by rank, in the method I described," he explained to Miss Wynchester. "At supper parties the hostess will often alternate female guests with males. The intermittent pattern means one needn't cleave to a strict Debrett's hierarchy."

She tugged at her curl. The one he had touched. It made him long to reach out anew, stretch the soft ringlet in his fingers, then cradle her face with both hands and give her the kiss he would have stolen if her aunt had not returned at that moment.

"So we *will* be sitting together?" she asked. "Since one needn't cleave to hierarchy?"

"Probably not, as I'm still considerably—" He cleared his throat and looked around. The footman had just left the room. Great-Aunt Wynchester had started to snore. Lawrence lowered his voice all the same. "About what happened earlier..."

Miss Wynchester lifted her delicate brows. "Nothing happened earlier."

Fair enough. He tried again. "About what *almost* happened, then."

Miss Wynchester's return gaze was direct and unflinching. "What almost happened?"

She knew, he realized. She knew good and well and was trying to force him to say *I almost kissed you because I have lost all self-control and cannot trust myself whilst in your company.* A kiss would be just the beginning.

"Are you in love with Miss York?" she asked.

He drew backward. "Love is not relevant to business decisions."

"So Miss York is...good business?"

He clenched his jaw. She made it sound so cold! Which, he supposed, it was. But it was how things were done.

"Faircliffe was a highly respected title for generations," he explained. "My grandfather was arguably the most esteemed of the line, but an apoplexy caused my father to inherit at a young age. He spent the subsequent decades dismantling every advantage our predecessors had fought to attain."

Lawrence fought a wave of memories better left suppressed.

"If my father could undo two centuries of high regard with a series of poor choices, then it is my duty to restore our lost stature with a series of *correct* choices."

"And Miss York is the right choice?"

"She is," he said firmly. "For myself and for future generations."

"You'll have a circus together?"

Lawrence could not picture that at all. "We will not. But I'll be able to give my children a sterling reputation, financial security, and societal approval."

"Is that what children want?"

"It's what they *need*." He swallowed hard. "It's what any father who cared about his offspring would strive to give them."

"What about a better world outside of the home?" she asked. "Do children want that?"

"I strive for that as well." This was much safer ground. "It is my hope that Miss York's father and I will champion complementary issues in our respective chambers of Parliament. Indeed, one of my pet projects for reform is excluding children from workhouses and other means of exploitation, such as their use as chimney sweeps...."

Lawrence was deep into this familiar territory when he realized he'd been speaking for five minutes straight, and the usually inquisitive Miss Wynchester hadn't said a word.

Was he boring her? This was a topic he dared not bring up

outside of Westminster for a reason. It was hardly the stuff of flirtatious dinner parties.

He trailed off and made an apologetic face. "I beg your pardon. One cannot help becoming passionate about such subjects."

Miss Wynchester's eyes flashed. "Then please allow me to take a counter position."

He lifted his palm.

She gave a sharp smile that didn't reach her eyes. "Poverty is not limited to children. By generalizing the adult poor as rabble who eschew 'honest work,' you paint a picture wherein it is only *children* who do not deserve exploitation and unpaid labor—"

"Pardon me," he interrupted. "You do not understand how Parliament determines—"

"I've determined *you* don't understand." She pushed to her feet.

"Oh dear," Great-Aunt Wynchester murmured, no longer asleep. "Now you've done it."

"Miss Wynchester—" he began.

"I shall smarten myself up for the party." She scooped up her basket and stalked away from him without a backward glance. "I 'understand' your people value looks over brains."

He rubbed a hand over his face. How he wished he hadn't botched everything! He and Miss Wynchester both wanted the same things. But Parliament was a slow-grinding machine. He was the one in a position to do something about it.

"You're wrong," Great-Aunt Wynchester said flatly.

He glowered at her. "What did you say?"

"She knows more about Parliament than you do."

He straightened. "I scarcely think—"

"Obviously." Great-Aunt Wynchester glared at him. "My niece, on the other hand, rarely misses a session."

"I never miss the House of Lords," he informed her. "And I've never seen your niece at Westminster."

"Or anywhere, I wager. Not until you failed to mind your carriage and she ran off with you like a cat with a mouse."

"That's not how it happened!" That was essentially how it happened. "My driver was in his perch only seconds before, until he went to investigate a commotion caused by—"

"When does the dessert course start?" she interrupted. "I'm peckish."

He took a deep breath. "This isn't the real party. We're still acting. You'll visit the Ainsworth residence once your niece is back from the retiring room."

"You've an ugly carpet." Great-Aunt Wynchester pulled a face. "A duke should have an Axminster."

"It *is* an Axminster. All of the rugs—" Lawrence tilted his gaze heavenward.

What was he doing, arguing with an old woman about whether his grandfather had overpaid for the carpets?

And how "smartened" did Miss Wynchester believe she could get? A taupe underdress with a taupe overlay would blend straight into the Ainsworths' oak décor.

An odd protectiveness itched beneath his skin. He *liked* Miss Wynchester and wanted things to go the way she hoped they would. He wouldn't wish being mocked or mistreated on anyone.

At Eton, Lawrence had been both singled out and left all alone because of his father. Because of her family, Miss Wynchester was in a similar situation—only, in her case, it was much worse. Lawrence was a peer. No one could deny him his rightful place. Whereas Miss Wynchester...

She deserved a fair chance. There had to be a way. Perhaps he could help her find a talented modiste at a price she could afford. It was too late tonight, but if she commissioned a nicer gown, she might catch the eye of—

Miss Wynchester swept back into the room.

Lawrence's throat went dry and his mind emptied of rational thought.

Gone was the insipid blandness of tan on tan. Although she wore the same underdress, her curves were now draped in an elegant overdress of white-and-pink netting. The dark velvet trim on the light rose bodice matched the velvet Vandyke points decorating the bottom, just above two matching twists of white crepe encircling the hem. The gauzy romantic colors brought out the dark brown of her hair and the deep brown of her long-lashed eyes.

His body tightened, and it was all he could do not to reach for her, pull her against his chest, and claim the kisses that weren't his to take.

A smile flitted over her lips, as if she sensed the maelstrom she'd unleashed within him. Arm stiff, she held out her hand and dropped her basket to the floor.

Her kitten hadn't been inside; rather, it was an entirely new identity.

His lungs squeezed, making it difficult to speak. "You look magnificent."

"She looks like Chloe," Great-Aunt Wynchester barked.

He barely heard her. Lawrence's eyes were still drinking in Miss Wynchester, thinking her much too far away for his taste. That bodice would be displayed at its best pillowed against his chest, the perfect distance for a man to embark on a trail of kisses from her rosy lips, down the column of her throat, and into the swell of her bosom.

Tonight he would dream of nothing else.

Why hadn't she *begun* the evening dressed like this? If tearing his eyes from her had been next to impossible before, this...*this*...He couldn't believe others thought her plain. He had believed she dressed in her dowdy attire because she didn't own anything better. Yet she now appeared a worthy model for any fashion plate. It was almost as if—

It was almost as if she'd done so on purpose. Dressed not to impress but to be comfortable. To allow her personality, rather than a garnet tiara, to shine. She didn't want to catch everyone's eyes, only that of her future husband.

This evening she might well accomplish both.

"You look as marvelous on the outside as you are on the inside," he tried again.

She sent him a flat look. "You don't know me. And I'm a Wynchester."

He opened his mouth to explain that her scandalous family was perhaps not an *insurmountable* disadvantage, but was it true? All the fine clothing in the world wouldn't prevent members of the beau monde from lifting their collective noses and muttering *Wynchester* in disdain as she walked by.

Had she not absconded with him in his carriage, Lawrence would still be just as superior and condescending today. The realization made his stomach turn.

"My apologies," he said quietly. "Instead of assuming I knew best, I should have come to know you before making a judgment."

She let out a slow breath. "Perhaps I should say the same."

He blinked. Had she been appraising *him* from afar and found him lacking? He smiled grimly. Was the idea so fantastic?

Like her, he longed to be judged for who he was, not what he was. When people looked at her, they saw a Wynchester. When they looked at him, they used to see his dissolute father. Now they saw a duke, a title, in want of a wife.

He was trying to use their preconceptions to his advantage. He had made his case to Miss York as His Grace, an unwed duke in search of a duchess, rather than as Lawrence, a man with thoughts and feelings and secret dreams of his own. Perhaps he suspected those attributes wouldn't be enough.

Perhaps that was why offering a dukedom was so much safer than offering his heart.

Miss Wynchester took a step toward the table. The swing of her hips was sensual and confident. She was a Wynchester and a woman of flesh and blood. Not being a lady erased none of her power.

He leapt to his feet to help her into her chair.

She stopped her forward progress when she was less than an arm's length away from him. Close enough to touch. Close enough to *see*. Her eyes were the warmest shade of brown he had ever beheld. They were fathomless, penetrating. He wanted to see them flutter closed in pleasure and know that it was he who had brought her to that peak.

All he could offer were bland lessons in comportment. Such banality should have dampened his ardor, yet his blood quickened at the wickedness of his forbidden thoughts under the surface.

Lawrence could pretend there was nothing between them but a gentleman granting a simple favor for a little while longer. There was no cause to rush off to the Ainsworth party. The earliest guests wouldn't arrive for at least another hour.

He needn't share her yet.

"I find myself very pleased to meet you, Miss Wynchester."

"I fear I may be just as pleased to meet you, Your Grace." She gave him a pert look.

He grinned back. Miss Wynchester had no need to avoid her reflection. She was an impressive young woman, no matter what she was wearing.

"This kitchen is abominably slow." Great-Aunt Wynchester made a disgruntled sound. "We rang for tea an hour ago."

Miss Wynchester sank into her seat. "We did not ring for tea, Aunt. This isn't a real party. We are pretending."

"How will your pretending ease my parched throat?" Great-Aunt Wynchester made tiny coughs. "Every time I sip from my glass, it's *empty*."

"I'll ring for tea," Lawrence said. He had never previously done such a thing—he despised tea—but there was always plenty on hand for the staff. He motioned for a maid to bring the tea.

"I should smarten up as well." Great-Aunt Wynchester swayed to her feet, then lowered her mouth toward her niece. "I told this pup he has ugly carpets and that you practically live in the Palace of Westminster."

Miss Wynchester's eyes met his, and the corners of her mouth twitched. "One of those things is true."

Her great-aunt scooped up the basket and doddered out of the door.

Lawrence's eyes were only on Miss Wynchester. "You hate my carpets?"

"You have fine carpets."

He'd been afraid she would say that. How had he been so wrong yet again?

"You watch from the ventilation holes in the attic?" he stammered.

She lifted a shoulder. "It's not the best angle, and not everyone enunciates, but we make do."

"'We'?" he echoed faintly.

"My siblings sometimes, if I wheedle," she explained. "But I'm not the only woman interested in politics. A few of the statesmen's wives have attended in this fashion for as long as I have."

She was right, he realized. He *didn't* know her.

And now that he had begun to, he could not help but like her more each time.

"What are your thoughts so far this session?"

"The Highways Act was brilliant, the Hospitals Act overdue, and the East India Trade Act a nightmare," she replied without hesitation. "If you didn't spend so much time dithering over the Postage Act, perhaps you *could* address poverty and exploitation. If I have to hear one more speech about the post—"

"Boring, is it? The reason we're always on about postage—"

Thus began the liveliest discussion Lawrence had ever had outside of Parliament. Great-Aunt Wynchester was right: Her niece knew more about current issues than half of the peers. And she could boast significantly better attendance.

Even when he'd let his membership in his club lapse to save money, he'd continued to debate ideas at private homes and political dinners. But never had any of his compatriots alternately complemented and skewered his ideas with Miss Wynchester's surgical precision.

Perhaps because they were *like* him, he realized. An entire room of peers shouting sweeping generalizations based on a superficial understanding would either send her into paroxysms of laughter or tears.

How he would enjoy frequent heated discussions with Miss Wynchester. She was brilliant. Thrice already he'd reached for his pen to jot down a salient point he needed to consider or have investigated in a more comprehensive manner.

They were both startled by the arrival of the tea service.

Miss Wynchester reached for the pot. "Aunt prefers lukewarm tea, so I'll pour hers now. It'll be just how she likes it when she returns."

Lawrence suppressed a shudder. Lukewarm tea was worse than hot tea, and cold tea was an atrocity worse than that. He might actually attend the occasional tea party, if the teapot were make-believe.

Because he was paying more attention to the kissable curve of Miss Wynchester's cheek than what she did with her hands, she filled his cup with tea before he could stop her.

He recoiled from the steaming brown liquid in horror.

Bloody hell. He'd offended her more than enough for one day. He would have to drink the tea.

Perhaps if he wasted enough time preparing it, she and her aunt would finish before he was required to sip any. Cheered by the thought, he began sliding lumps of sugar into his cup one by one, making each brief journey from dish to tea last as long as possible.

Miss Wynchester watched him over the rim of her own cup. "Is this another *haut ton* profligacy ritual?"

He was so startled, he dropped his spoon. "What?"

"If you want to eat the sugar, eat the sugar. No sense turning perfectly good tea into marmalade to prove that you can. Sugar is expensive. You're a duke; you've got lots of it. I'm suitably impressed. Just drink your tea."

"I wasn't showing off my...excessive consumption." Except he supposed he had been, if inadvertently. Why did all of his attempts to make a positive impression end up having the opposite effect?

She pursed her lips. "Then what are you doing?"

He appraised the contents of his cup. *Was* it possible to turn tea into marmalade? A dash of lemon, four hundred and thirty-two lumps of sugar...

He pushed his saucer away. "Can you keep a secret?"

"When I want to." She lifted her brows. "Do you have a good one?"

"A terrible one," he admitted. "One I hoped to take to my grave. A duke must maintain a certain reputation. Especially when clawing out of his father's shadow and trying to avoid ridicule at all costs."

She set down her cup. "All right, I'm intrigued. I promise to keep your dirty secret."

He hoped so. "I hate tea."

She blinked. "What?"

"I hate tea." He shuddered. "It's as British as I am, but I cannot stand it. I add sugar to mask the flavor, but that only makes it horrid and syrupy instead of horrid and bitter." He swallowed. "No one knows but you."

She gazed at him.

He turned red.

She burst out laughing. "You...haven't heard many dramatic confessions, have you."

"It *is* dramatic," he protested. "Hating tea is my deepest shame."

"You must try to live a more interesting life. If you were a Wynchester..." She wiped tears from her eyes. "What is your *second*-deepest shame? Stirring in a circular motion instead of back and forth like a true gentleman?"

He crossed his arms. "You don't understand the pressures of my position."

"You're right," she confirmed. "I would be a *terrible* duke. And it would have nothing to do with my tea consumption at parties. Was that why you were hiding in your carriage? Or do you not even *like* society events?"

"I wasn't hiding...exactly." He leaned back. "What does 'liking' society have to do with anything?"

"Nothing? Everything?" She lifted a shoulder. "What is the point of being a duke if you cannot at least conduct your own life as you please?"

"That's not the point of a peerage. Privilege is not about oneself. It's an honor bestowed upon one's line and the solemn duty to—"

"Good God." She shuddered. "All of that may be true, but

you cannot believe 'responsibility' means no longer being oneself."

"Publicly," he clarified, lest she misunderstand the entire point. "Publicly I must be perfect in all things, but privately I have never seen this teapot before in my life."

Her head tilted to one side. "What else are you hiding?"

His muscles froze. "Nothing."

"Everyone hides something. What else are you stifling to be more palatable to your peers?"

Art.

The thought came to his head unbidden. Lawrence had always dreamed that if he hadn't been a duke, he would have been a painter. Not a Royal Academy artist, but something experimental. He might not become famous, but he'd be happy and carefree. He wouldn't have to be perfect.

And he wouldn't marry Miss York. Not just because her family would never condone a courtship with a common painter, but because there would be no need for political allies and strategic marital dynasties. Instead, he could pursue whomever he wished. He'd be perfectly free to lean forward and—

"*That.*" Miss Wynchester's voice was like warm honey. "Whatever you're thinking at this very moment. *That* is what you should be doing."

He'd been thinking of her. Of devouring her kiss by kiss, lick by lick, until she was limp and sated in his arms.

It was highly improper dinner party behavior.

His voice was hoarse. "I don't think you understand what I…"

"Don't I?" Her eyes were on his, her gaze intense and unwavering.

He tried to calm his runaway pulse, his carnal desires straining to be set free. She *meant* this. That he should be and do as he pleased.

But what he wanted would lead them both to ruin.

"My father..." His voice was too low, too rough. A rumble of thunder on a spring day. "Father was emotional and impulsive. It made him a laughingstock." It had made *Lawrence* a laughingstock. "I will not compound his mistakes."

Even if there was nothing he wanted more than to end this conversation by covering her mouth with his.

Her gaze searched his face. "What if it's not a mistake? How will you know, if you keep yourself gaoled inside your head?"

Gaol. That was exactly what he should do with the urge to take her, kiss her, taste her. Lock those libidinous urges behind bars and throw away the key. It was the only way he would be strong enough to resist temptation.

"I..." Had he leaned closer? Had *she*? Their forbidden kiss was a breath away.

Her eyes sparked with challenge. "What *would* you do, Your Grace? If you *were* the sort of craven rogue who indulged his every desire. What impulse are you trying to fight?"

He reached up to touch her cheek. He should not have. Its softness was his undoing.

With no gaoler to stop him, there was only one thing Lawrence wanted...and she was right in front of him. He was done fighting. For the moment he would allow desire to break free from its chains.

He grasped her face, his fingers delving into the softness of her hair, and brought her to him. Heaven. Hell. His lips upon hers were less a kiss and more two souls crashing into each other, shattering and melding at the same time.

She smelled like honeysuckle and tasted like fresh tea. Had he thought he hated the flavor? He adored it when it came from her lips. No amount of sugar could compare to the sweetness of her mouth, the fierce rush of her fingers twisting in his hair.

Something fluttered in his chest, an unfurling, a rebirth. He explored the contours of her mouth, mapping each hidden corner to remember later, to revisit in his mind when he could not have her in his hands.

Both palms now cupped her cheeks. Not to keep her in place but to stop himself from skimming his eager hands down the column of her neck, the hollow of her back, the flare of her hips.

If he touched her there, he'd be tempted to pull her closer. To leave no doubt that kissing her was no fleeting impulse but a gale-force temptation he barricaded himself against every time he thought her name or saw her face. *This* was what he had hungered for. Her. Beneath his fingers.

Kissing her was as inevitable as the rain falling from swollen clouds, and just as impossible to hold in one's hands forever.

He forced himself to wrench his mouth from hers, panting. He touched their foreheads together and tried to regain his breath. It was no use.

"Now you know." The words were a growl, a plea. "All I can give is a moment's passion. Do not ask me to uncage myself again, unless that is what you want."

15

❦

_C_hloe's pulse skittered unsteadily as her carriage ferried her toward the Ainsworth residence. Her lips were tender and still tasted of the Duke of Faircliffe's kiss. Her head swam every time she let herself remember the feel of his strong hands holding her face, the sensation of her own fingers rumpling his hair as though he were hers to dishevel.

"I 'accidentally' wandered into two different rooms," Tommy was saying, "and not only haven't I found our portrait, I have glimpsed _no_ art at all. Does Faircliffe despise creativity? He wouldn't have tossed our painting into the fire, would he?"

Ah, yes. This was what Chloe was supposed to be thinking about: pillaging the duke's estate, not offering him her body.

"Why would he burn it?" she mumbled.

"_I_ don't know. Because peers are madmen?" Tommy toyed with the stolen key ring, then shoved it back into the basket. "Maybe he didn't read our letters because he anticipated our logical request and could not possibly respond, 'Sorry, dropped your family heirloom into a fire. Saved the ashes in a nice tin, though.'"

"I really don't…" Chloe frowned. "Tommy, are you all right?"

"I'm frustrated," Tommy admitted. "I thought this would be easy—that the painting would be hanging on a wall. You'd distract him by whatever means necessary—clever touch with the kissing—and I'd filch the canvas. What if he's hidden it? Searching nooks and crannies will take forever, even with a set of keys."

Chloe's cheeks burned. She had heard only part of the explanation. "You saw us kiss?"

"I'm so sorry." Tommy patted her hand. "It must have been torture."

A wondrous, delicious, toe-curling torture. Chloe's skin heated at the memory. She would be replaying every moment to herself tonight, and the next night, and the next. Her skin still tingled where he had touched her.

"By the by, wherever did you find this stupendous over-dress? And these baubles!" Tommy admired the pearl comb in Chloe's hair. "I thought *I* was supposed to be the master of disguises, but you've outdone me by far."

It wasn't a disguise: these prized treasures from her secret collection were the closest to the real Chloe any family member had ever seen.

"Poor dear, you look miserable." Tommy added another pin to her white-haired-grandmother wig. "It might take an age to exhaustively search each room for hiding places, but I'm working as fast as I can. As soon as we find Puck, life will return to normal."

Huzzah?

Chloe clasped her hands in her lap. Before she could examine her complicated thoughts on the matter, the carriage pulled to a stop before the Ainsworths' house.

She took a deep breath and shoved her basket to the floor.

When the door swung open, it was not their tiger Isaiah ready to hand her down from the carriage, but the Duke of Faircliffe.

A chill breeze whipped his dark hair asunder, but his blue gaze was targeted on her. Knowing, now. Possessive. He had learned things about her she had never divulged to anyone. How her heart skipped when he touched her. How her mouth was his for the taking.

"Allow me." He offered his arm.

This time she knew how it would feel beneath her fingers. The warm contours of his muscles were no longer a mystery but a favorite memory. She had touched his shoulders, his face, his hair. Surely her fingertips could curve about his elbow.

Yet she hesitated. "Are you certain you should walk me to the front door at all?"

"My coach happened to arrive right before yours. I'm offering aid to a fellow guest, as any gentleman worth his salt ought." He lowered his voice. "Don't worry, no one will imagine the two of us arriving together on purpose."

Ah. Chloe lifted her chin. Tommy was right. The sooner things went back to normal, the better.

When they were ushered into a parlor, "Great-Aunt Wynchester" hovered protectively at Chloe's side while the fashionable attendees surrounded Faircliffe.

That was it, then. The last time they'd speak for the rest of the evening. She wouldn't have bothered attending the party had she not needed the excuse to drop by the duke's town house. Was it bad form to grab her sister and flee home the moment the dessert plates were cleared?

"I'm bored," Tommy whispered. "It must be stultifying to live like this."

"You're bored because no one is speaking to us," Chloe whispered back.

Good breeding required a formal introduction before gentlemen could speak to a young lady, but she doubted any such introductions were forthcoming. Once any reputable gentleman heard "Wynchester," he'd have the only detail about her he wished to know.

A familiar figure came their way.

"You did come." Philippa's smile looked as though she meant it. "I wasn't certain you would."

"How could I stay away from all this?" Chloe gestured toward Tommy. "My great-aunt Wynchester adores a dinner party. What were you saying about how lovely Philippa looks tonight, Aunt?"

A wordless gurgling sound came from Tommy's throat, followed by the slightest flush of her skin beneath her wrinkled-old-lady cosmetics.

"Oh dear, I have to go." Philippa made an aggrieved expression. "My mother just looked this way. Will you both be at the next reading circle?"

"We wouldn't miss it," Chloe promised. "I'll even leave Tiglet at home."

Philippa's eyes sparkled. "Please don't. He's the only reason you're invited."

Chloe grinned back at her. "Warn your mother: Tiglet has siblings."

"Let it be a surprise." Philippa winked and hurried off into the crowd.

"I like her," Chloe murmured.

Tommy cleared her throat. "Me too."

"She's the best of this crowd by far." Then again, Chloe supposed she didn't know anyone else in the beau monde well enough to judge.

Her eyes searched the room. As a child, she had wondered if her birth family shared her features. Perhaps they were also overlooked, wherever they were. Invisible to everyone's eyes but hers. They would recognize each other at once, according to the fantasy, and thus would fall into each other's arms with smiles and tears.

None of that had ever happened. Chloe was as out of place in society as she was in a rookery.

After Bean, her hope gradually turned to fear. She adored her new life. She was loved. The last thing she wanted was to stand out and risk having it all ripped away from her. Chloe's parents hadn't wanted her back then, and she did not want them now.

Being recognized would be a nightmare.

"Ah, here they are."

Startled, she glanced up to find the Duke of Faircliffe striding toward her in triumph, as if it had been a struggle to locate her and her sister hovering by themselves against the parlor wall.

He stood next to a handsome gentleman with exquisite tailoring and friendly gray eyes.

"Mrs. Wynchester, Miss Wynchester, may I present the Earl of Southerby? He is a rascal, but not half-bad at a country-dance. Southerby, if you spy Miss Wynchester with a basket, back away slowly. There might be a tiger inside."

Lord Southerby bowed. "How intriguing. I find tigers to be exhilarating animals."

Chloe curtsied in reply. "Why, that's just how I feel about rascals."

Faircliffe suddenly looked as if he wished he hadn't provided an introduction. His teeth were clenched, his eyes flashing, his muscles bunching alarmingly beneath his elegant jacket.

She tried to tamp down a strange new thrill in response. He was jealous. He did not want to be, but he was. And because of the rules they had set, he was forced to introduce her to eligible gentlemen who were not already promised to another.

Within an hour Faircliffe had presented her and Tommy to all of the other guests at the party.

Sometimes more than once.

Chloe was used to this reaction. Or non-reaction. She didn't stick in people's heads. They *saw* her, at least for the brief exchange of words during which she was right in front of their faces, but as soon as she stepped away, it was as though she tugged her memory from their minds in the process.

Faircliffe was not having it at all.

"*Wynchester*," he repeated forcefully to the Marquess of Rosbotham. "As you may recall from my introduction less than ten minutes ago."

Chloe kept her brittle smile in place. Even if someone didn't forget her naturally, they did so purposefully once they learned her name. That was, until recently. She peered up at Faircliffe. It was heady to have someone as important as a duke outraged on her behalf.

Lady Ainsworth chose that moment to welcome her guests into the formal dining room.

As he had predicted, Faircliffe sat too far down the long table for them to overhear snippets of each other's conversation, much less speak to one another.

As Chloe had both hoped and feared, he was still within sight.

She could not touch the contours of his lips, the hard lines of his jaw, but she knew how they felt, could not rid the memory from her mind.

Unfortunately, her imagination was as close as she could get. He was seated next to Philippa, with whom he intended to share meals for ever after. The unwanted reminder ruined what was left of Chloe's appetite. The wise thing to do was to keep her eyes on her plate. Nothing good could come of watching Faircliffe and Philippa in intimate conversation.

Chloe should definitely not spend the evening darting hungry glances toward the handsome duke.

Especially when she kept catching him gazing back at her.

Shivers of awareness tickled up and down her skin. Nobody knew he had kissed her. Perhaps nobody would believe it, even if she told them. But she knew. She remembered. She couldn't close her eyes without feeling the hardness of his muscles beneath her palms, the heat of his mouth slanting across hers.

And she couldn't lift her gaze to his face without wanting to do it all over again.

She had to get out of here before she gave herself away.

Somehow she survived all six courses. After the blancmange, she was ready to bolt, but then Lady Ainsworth clapped her hands and said, "Now for the dancing!"

A sharp burst of longing, white-hot and razor edged, sliced through her.

How she wanted to dance with Faircliffe—wanted to be fully in his embrace—but, more than that, wanted everyone else to see her as he saw her. Someone desirable, irresistible. Someone he could not prevent himself from kissing, no matter how valiantly he tried.

Not that he would admit to finding her kissable. Her throat grew thick. If his peers couldn't imagine him attending a social event with her on purpose, they wouldn't believe he'd want her in his arms.

She should go. She should *definitely* go. Watching him dance with everyone but her was a terrible idea.

But she stayed. Just in case.

There was one waltz. Faircliffe did not stand up for it with Chloe. He hadn't spoken to her since being seated for supper. The waltz was reserved for Miss Philippa York.

Chloe couldn't even hate her for it. Philippa was doing exactly what Chloe would do if Chloe were in Philippa's dancing slippers.

Well, almost everything. Philippa did not appear gratified to find herself the lucky object of the Duke of Faircliffe's attentions.

For years Chloe had fantasized she could burst from her dressing room and into a ballroom dressed as her real self, not her blending-with-the-wood-grain self. Not to show up the beau monde but rather to be bold because she *could*. To just once know what it felt like to strut into a place like this wearing, saying, and doing anything she pleased—and be accepted anyway. Not just to be herself, but to *belong*.

But she'd given up such dreams long, long ago.

When Lady Ainsworth announced that the second-to-last set of the evening would be a pair of country-dances, Chloe still sat along a forgotten wall with Tommy.

Until a gentleman stepped into her path.

"Is this dance spoken for?" It was Lord Southerby. The handsome rascal who found tigers exhilarating.

"Er..." Chloe said brightly.

She could dance; Bean had seen to that. The siblings occasionally danced with each other or at informal gatherings with middle-class friends. But she had never danced in a place like this. Never in front of *people* like this. She wished Marjorie were here to sketch the moment so Chloe could remember exactly how she'd looked, the time she was treated like a lady.

"Take her out of my sight," Tommy blustered in her guise as Great-Aunt Wynchester. "And keep her away from that Faircliffe fellow. He seems shifty."

"He's a duke, Aunt," Chloe murmured, her pulse ticking faster. "And he's coming this way."

"Dukes are the dodgiest," Tommy asserted with a dramatic sniff.

"I'm afraid I cannot be dodged at all this set," came Faircliffe's dry voice. "These figures require four partners."

Which meant...of course it did. Faircliffe's partner was Philippa York.

Chloe jerked her gaze back to Lord Southerby and allowed him to lead her onto the parquet.

Faircliffe couldn't dance with her any other way, she reminded herself. People might think it *meant* something.

Only a fool like her would want it to.

As the country-dance began, she forced herself to smile at the Earl of Southerby as she performed each step. He wasn't the enemy. He was a kind gentleman, willing to stand up with her when no one else would. Even if he was no more romantically interested in Chloe than the Duke of Faircliffe was.

Not that Faircliffe was a monster, either. His carefully cultivated hauteur wasn't the result of believing himself better than all others but of believing that if he wasn't as perfect as possible, he risked his title, his reputation, and the happiness of his future children.

Who could argue with a motive like that?

Chloe's birth parents hadn't been able to offer that to her, but the Wynchester family more than made up for it. They didn't have to try to be perfect. They loved each other just as they were.

She was a Wynchester, first and always. She would only give a second glance to a man willing to come into *her* fold rather than one whose precious reputation would rip her from those who loved her.

The country-dance switched figures, and she suddenly found herself partnering with Faircliffe instead of Southerby.

Chloe and Faircliffe had never touched publicly. Her fingers trembled as she looped her arm through his. His heat was familiar now, his taste, his scent. All of it seemed bigger than before, including him. He was somehow taller, his shoulders wider, his arm firmer beneath her touch.

It was impossible to be this close without remembering their kiss. The knowledge of it surely showed on her face.

She felt naked before so many witnesses, as if they could see through the innocent dance steps to the carnal way her body reacted to his proximity, his touch, the flexing of his muscles. Even though she could not keep him, he felt as though he belonged to her. His tongue had been in her mouth, tasting her. She had done the same to him.

"I owe you an explanation about why you and I cannot..." he murmured. "But this ballroom is not the place."

"Nowhere is."

She did not want his explanation. It would burst the warm memory like a pin piercing a bubble. What had once glimmered like a rainbow would be gone without a trace.

Chloe did not want words he did not mean or promises he could not keep. She wanted his arms about her, his heart next to hers, his mouth claiming her one last time. But in seconds, the pattern of the country-dance would rip him away, sending him back to the woman he chose to give his life to.

There was nothing to do but dance and pretend the music gave her joy.

His gaze rose from her lips to her eyes. "If things were different..."

She shook her head.

Things were *too* different. He was the Duke of Faircliffe. She was a Wynchester. He was a member of Parliament. She was a recovering pickpocket who still visited her old orphanage bearing gifts for children who didn't have a Bean of their own. Faircliffe's good works took place in the House of Lords. He knew nothing of Chloe's world, just as she did not belong in his.

"You don't have to explain," she said. "I understand."

The music changed and she was back with Southerby. She hoped he did not notice her painful gazes over his shoulder.

Faircliffe and Philippa were an excellent match—if not by Chloe and Tommy's preferences, then at least by the expectations of everyone else in this room.

Their union would mean more than titles and heirs. Faircliffe aligning himself with Philippa's important MP father would help both men be better able to enact the exact laws Chloe had been praying to see unfold beneath the stuffy Westminster attic. If anything, she should be the Faircliffe-York union's biggest champion.

In fact, she *would* be.

That was what an impartial observer who wanted the best outcome for the greatest number of individuals would do, wasn't it?

What did *feelings* have to do with anything?

When the music ended, Faircliffe and Southerby walked away together, their heads bent in conversation.

Chloe rolled back her shoulders and turned to Philippa. "You should marry him."

Philippa did not pretend to misunderstand; nor did she appear pleased with the unsolicited advice. "You know me well enough to know which specific person I should spend the rest of my life with?"

Chloe paused. Together as allies, Lawrence and Philippa's father could make great strides in the reforms Chloe had been fighting for. Doing it for the orphans and workhouses seemed more than enough reason to her, but perhaps not to the beau monde.

Philippa sighed. "If it will take the bee out of your bonnet, you may be pleased to know that my parents have threatened to burn my bookcases if I don't accept Faircliffe's suit."

"He offered?" The words came out as a whisper. The parquet seemed to tilt.

"Not yet." Philippa twisted her lips. "He seems to be waiting for me to give him a sign of encouragement first."

Chloe frowned. "Is that a bad trait?"

"It's an admirable trait. He's splendid, a dukedom would be splendid, the whole thing is splendid."

Philippa did not make any of it sound splendid.

"But I'll do it," she said dully. "Mother wants a title for her only child, Father wants more hooks in the House of Lords, and Faircliffe wants my dowry. He admitted as much."

Chloe winced. Although her spirits leapt at confirmation that the union was practical, rather than a love match, she would not wish anyone into a life of misery.

"What do *you* want?" she asked.

"To escape." Philippa's steady gaze met hers. "I suppose Faircliffe is my chance."

Chloe swallowed. She well remembered the panicked desperation to escape her old life—and the blessed relief of finding sanctuary at last.

She could not stand in the way.

16

⚜

*L*awrence stood off to the side with his butler as men from Christie's auction house carried the last of the expensive carpets out of the door. The spring weather had brought an overabundance of rain. Several of his tenants needed new roofs more than Lawrence needed his grandfather's carpets.

Once the men had gone, Hastings handed Lawrence his hat. "Off to woo a bride, Your Grace?"

Hastings knew perfectly well Lawrence was headed to Miss York's town house in hopes of catching the reading circle. The butler's wording seemed to imply there was some doubt about who the bride would be.

"I'm off to see Miss York," Lawrence said firmly.

His butler politely refrained from pointing out that if seeing Miss York was Lawrence's *only* aim, a private call without her reading circle present might be more romantic.

Very well, the company Lawrence yearned for was Miss Wynchester's.

After their practice supper, all he could think of was their kiss. After their brief moments together in the country-dance, all he wanted was her back in his arms.

He could not have her. Not her kisses, not her humor, not

their lively conversations. But he could glimpse her, secretly. Be closer in proximity, even if her body was not his to touch. He had the memory.

It would have to be enough.

After crossing the square, he strode down the Yorks' now-familiar corridor toward the sound of voices. When he entered the parlor, more than a dozen faces smiled up at him in surprise. Lawrence did not slow until he reached Miss Philippa York and could make the appropriate pleasantries.

Then, and only then, did he allow himself to dart a brief glance toward Miss Wynchester.

His chest clenched as if his heart had stalled, then picked back up at twice the tempo. His blood rushed far too fast. Looking at her made his mouth water, his fingers twitch to reach for her even though he knew he could not.

In her beige-on-beige lap, she wrung her soft hands. No one else might have noticed, but Lawrence's heightened senses were solely attuned to her. He had not missed the widening of her eyes at his entrance, the hitch in her breath as her gaze met his.

She clearly hadn't anticipated his presence here today. Nor would he admit to her that she was the reason he'd come.

He had *missed* her, damn it all. A few fleeting moments of interchanging partners in a country-dance was not enough.

Now that he'd witnessed how others in his social sphere treated Miss Wynchester—or, rather, now that he'd seen her and her aunt shamefully overlooked for the entirety of an evening—he worried the same might be true everywhere.

The thought had him ready to grab his shield and his sword and ride into battle.

Or into a reading circle.

He knew what it was like to want the acceptance of one's peers. Except Lawrence had a title to fall back on—one that outranked almost everyone else's. Miss Wynchester was not bon ton. She did not have "Lady Chloe" to use as both armor and weapon. She had no power, parents, or cachet.

But she did have Lawrence.

A fierce protectiveness rushed through him. She was doing all right, wasn't she?

The other ladies weren't talking to her, but neither were they *not* speaking to her. They were discussing goings-on at Almack's or had been, until he barreled into the room.

Miss York smoothed out a lace hem. "Will you join us for tea?"

"Tea sounds lovely," he forced himself to say.

It did not sound lovely. It sounded like torture. Except for the fact that tea would forever remind him of the kisses he'd shared with Miss Wynchester. No amount of sugar would ever taste as sweet.

He darted another secret glance at her. Was she thinking the same thing? Did she relive those moments again and again, as he did, or had she already forgotten their shared embrace?

Now was definitely not the moment to ask.

He offered his arm to Miss York and accompanied her into the adjoining room. Because this was a reading circle, rather than a formal dinner party, her guests were welcome to take any seat they pleased. His place, presumably, was at Miss York's side. But Miss Wynchester's place...

Quickly he scouted the table for the best seat. A comfortable chair, close enough to him to allow the exchange of words, but not so close as to raise suspicion, and positioned in such a way as to avoid the many elaborate gilt-framed mirrors decorating the York parlor.

He helped a few other guests into chairs that were *not* the seat he'd earmarked for Miss Wynchester, then motioned her to the safe one.

As she lowered herself into the chair, he could not tell whether she understood that he was protecting her as best he could in what he knew to be an uncomfortable situation for her. But whether she realized didn't matter. He wanted her to be comfortable.

At least one of them would be.

Footmen arrived with silver trays. The quartered sandwiches and little cakes looked scrumptious, but Lawrence couldn't tear his gaze from the delicate teapots.

For the past two and thirty years, he'd avoided any public situation in which he might be expected to choke down a few drops of tea.

Until today.

He filled his cup halfway with milk and stopped the maid before she poured tea to the brim. The moment called for sugar. Loads of it. But as Miss Wynchester had rightfully pointed out, sugar was dear. Lawrence would not make a favorable impression on Miss York or her mother by hoarding their supply for himself.

His trepidation rising with every passing moment, he waited until the ladies had taken their sugar before dropping one lonely lump into his cup.

He picked up his spoon as slowly as possible. If he wasted enough time dissolving the lump, perhaps he wouldn't have to drink the tea at all. He eased the silver spoon below the surface of the steaming liquid.

The spoon immediately stopped moving. Frowning, he gave it a little wiggle. A half dozen sugar lumps briefly broke the surface.

He stared at his cup. If a half dozen sugar lumps were visible, that half dozen must be resting atop *another* four or five lumps. If he stirred this much sugar into the mix, it would taste more like syrup than tea. With a squeeze or two of lemon instead of milk, it would practically become...

Marmalade.

He jerked his startled gaze toward Miss Wynchester.

The corners of her mouth twitched. She could not hide the wicked twinkle in her eyes.

"How?" he mouthed to her.

She lifted a dainty shoulder, then brought her teacup to her lips to hide a grin.

He narrowed his eyes.

She pursed her lips as if about to blow him a kiss, then covered her mouth with her teacup.

Impertinent minx.

Her actions were not materially different from his own quest for the chair she would hate to sit in the least. He'd been trying to make an unpleasant thing more palatable for her, and she had done the same for him.

But why must they suffer through distasteful things? Could he not provide something for her that she *liked*, without qualifications or compromise?

Of course he could. He was the Duke of Faircliffe. What good were all of his privileges if he could not use them to make someone happy?

Pensive, Lawrence stayed long enough to speak to Miss York and pay his respects to her mother. Ostensibly, that was why he'd come.

But the moment he could gracefully escape, he leapt into his coach and directed his driver to the best milliner in all of London.

He would have to sell a few more books, but bringing a smile to Miss Wynchester's face would be worth it.

If the milliner found the duke's shopping list curious—a dozen plain bonnets in varying styles, feathers of every shape and size, a rainbow of ribbons, handfuls of wax fruit and several fake birds—he was far too polite to comment.

Within the hour Lawrence had it all unpacked atop his dining room table. He and Miss Wynchester would part ways after the gala, but before then he would give her a moment they would both remember forever.

One of the maids passed through the dining room and skidded to a stop.

"Might I inquire," Peggy said, failing to hide her obvious amusement, "what Your Grace is doing?"

His voice dripped with icy haughtiness. "I am *trimming a bonnet.*"

They looked at the table, then at each other.

"Badly," he added.

They both burst into laughter.

"Ring for the others," he said with a sigh. "If I'm to make an utter fool of myself, I might as well do so *en famille*. We can all be mad as hatters."

In moments Lawrence and every remaining member of staff hunched over the dining room table, fighting over wax fruit and trading spindles of colored thread to match decorative ribbons.

Peggy and Dinah, the maids, proved the most competent with a needle. Mrs. Elkins, the cook, had a heavy hand when pasting adornments to the crown of her bonnet.

"It's not marzipan," Hastings chided her, his blue eyes sparkling with mischief.

Mrs. Elkins sniffed in disdain, but twin spots of color bloomed on her round cheeks.

"Miss Wynchester will love these, Your Grace," Dinah assured Lawrence.

Jackson, the footman, beheld his lopsided creation doubtfully. "Will she?"

"I didn't say this was a gift for anyone," Lawrence protested.

Nobody paid any attention.

"I'll pray she accepts it," Mrs. Elkins promised him.

A sharp pang slashed through Lawrence's chest.

How he wished this *were* a romantic gesture and not a platonic gift between friends. He didn't just want to make her smile; he wanted to taste the sweetness of her tongue, to explore every curve of her body with his hands and his mouth.

He didn't want to hide his glances in her direction. He wanted her to know what she did to him, to never doubt his ardor for a moment. But he could not indulge those desires.

A decorated bonnet was the most he could give.

17

⊷

The door to the Wynchester family coach was flung open and a blur of jangling brass soared inside.

Tommy caught the flying ring of keys with her left hand. "You did it?"

"Of course I did." Graham leapt inside the carriage and threw himself on the rear-facing seat next to Jacob and the short-tailed field vole in Jacob's lap. "Have I ever failed to deliver on a promise?"

Chloe cleared her throat. "I seem to recall a certain boiled pudding…"

"Culinary mishaps don't count!" He laced his fingers behind his neck and leaned back against the carriage wall. "Where to now?"

"Vauxhall? Isn't there a balloon launch today?" Elizabeth tapped her cane with its hidden blade against Chloe's basket. "If there's a blanket in here, we can make a picnic."

Tommy shook her head. "No blankets, just Great-Aunt Wynchester."

"Who should accompany me to the Faircliffe residence posthaste," Chloe said pointedly. "Now that we have our own copy of the keys, we ought to put the originals back in the housekeeper's chamber before she returns from holiday."

"Lucky for you, I enjoy being Great-Aunt Wynchester." Tommy stretched out. "Unluckily for you, the Ainsworth dinner was your last invitation. Until another arrives, you haven't a pretext for visiting Faircliffe."

That was indeed the tricky part.

Other than slipping sugar into his tea at Miss York's reading circle a few days ago, Chloe hadn't crossed Faircliffe's path in a week. The reading circle would reconvene again before too long, but that wouldn't help her to rescue Puck.

Graham leaned forward. "I'll do it."

Tommy arched a brow. "You'll be Great-Aunt Wynchester?"

"I'll be Icarus, the Flying Fool." Graham's brown eyes lit with excitement. "It's been ages since I put my acrobatics to good use. I won't need an excuse to knock on the door, because I'll slip in through an upper window instead."

"Icarus fell to the earth when his pride tempted him to go too high," Elizabeth reminded him.

"He flew, didn't he?" Graham gave an unrepentant shrug. "The Splendiferous Schmidts ran a circus, not an encyclopedia. It was a good name. And this is a good plan."

"It's a horrid plan. We can't risk you getting caught." Jacob returned his field vole to his lap. "Which is why we should use one of my trained pigeons."

Chloe covered her face with one hand. "Jacob..."

"Birds are cunning creatures," he assured her. "Watch this."

He leaned across Graham to crack open the door's window, cupped his hands to his mouth, let out a loud, strangling gurgle, then flopped back into his seat in satisfaction.

"What does that do?" Tommy asked. "Call the babies to the nest for a nap?"

All four siblings except Jacob jumped backward when a large hawk filled their view and cracked its beak angrily against the window.

"Pigeon." Elizabeth fanned her throat. "You said *pigeon*."

"This clever girl was closer." Jacob's brown hand nuzzled beneath the hawk's sharp beak. "I fear Hippogriff thinks my vole is dinner."

"No pigeons, no acrobats, and no feeding voles to hawks in my presence," Chloe said firmly. "Tommy and I have this under control. Don't we, Great-Aunt Wynchester?"

"We'll be under control by the time we arrive." Tommy pulled her wig out of the basket and started pinning it in place.

"The girls always have all the fun," Jacob groused.

Elizabeth rapped him with her sword stick. "*Women*."

"Women," he agreed with a sigh.

Tommy grinned at him. "You have no idea."

Chloe held out a looking glass so her sister could apply her wrinkles.

Jacob cocked his head at Chloe. "Ever since this Faircliffe operation began, all you do is gloom about."

"Can you blame her?" Graham pulled a face. "She's forced to feign interest in the most insufferable, arrogant, haughtier-than-thou duke in all of England, the poor thing. Chloe deserves a holiday once this is through."

"Or a medal," Elizabeth agreed. "You've had to put up with the Ice King of Parliament for an entire month. At least Tommy can escape when she combs through the town house. How will you distract him today?"

Tommy burst out laughing. "Easy. Faircliffe adores explaining *everything* to Chloe, no matter how obvious, and he takes five hours to do so."

"He's trying to help," Chloe muttered. She averted her gaze to hide an unwelcome twinge of guilt. The duke was naïve but meant well. "He hasn't any idea what regular people are like."

"Because he hasn't tried to meet any," Tommy said dryly.

"Ask him how mittens work," Jacob suggested. "There are five fingers and only two holes. It's so confusing!"

"No, ask him how to tie a garter about your stocking." Elizabeth's eyes twinkled. "Maybe you can trick him into showing you his shapely legs."

That was not a terrible idea. Perhaps she could then inquire how gentlemen removed their smallclothes and whether he possessed any knowledge of how to unlace a woman's pesky stays.

Chloe lowered her gaze so her siblings wouldn't guess her true feelings. She *liked* Faircliffe. He had stopped being arrogant and insufferable almost as soon as they came to know each other. And as for icy, she couldn't imagine hotter kisses than his. The feel of her fingers in his hair and his mouth on hers haunted her dreams. What she wanted most was a chance to do it all again.

The carriage wheels crunched to a stop.

Tommy glanced out of the window. "We're here."

"If you need Hippogriff, just make the call." Jacob leaned forward. "Do you want me to demonstrate again?"

Graham clutched his chest. "Do not demonstrate again. Ever."

The door swung open and their tiger Isaiah handed Tommy—er, Great-Aunt Wynchester—out of the coach.

"Niece!" Tommy shrilled. "Are you certain this is the right terrace? It looks uglier than last time."

Elizabeth grinned back at Chloe. "Go and distract a duke."

Chloe fell into step beside Tommy as they headed up the path toward Faircliffe's door.

"I wish Jacob hadn't repossessed Tiglet," she whispered. "I think the duke covets our kitten."

The butler swung open the door with an unusually observant expression.

"Er . . ." said Chloe.

"Right over here," replied Mr. Hastings.

She exchanged a startled glance with her sister as they were led not to the austere parlor adjoining the entrance but rather to a drawing room deeper inside the ducal residence that she'd seen only in Tommy's maps.

Still no paintings on the walls. Or art of any kind. There wasn't even a carpet on the floor.

"Wait here, please." Mr. Hastings lifted his palm. "His Grace will be with you shortly."

"How did His Grace know we were coming?" Tommy whispered in bafflement once the butler had left the room. "*We* didn't know we were coming. Wynchesters are unpredictable."

"Apparently, so is the Duke of Faircliffe." The thought filled Chloe's stomach with butterflies. He *was* one of the cleverest orators in Parliament. It would not do to underestimate him. She smoothed out her skirt with nervous hands.

Faircliffe stepped into the room. "You're here."

His eyes were on hers, as if theatrical Great-Aunt Wynchester were the wainscoting and Chloe bold and unmissable.

How was she supposed to gaze upon him without immediately longing to hurl herself into his embrace?

The angular lines of his cheekbones and the sharp cut of his coat might have seemed harsh, but Chloe had been in those strong arms. She had kissed those warm lips. Her entire body quivered with yearning to have his mouth upon her again.

"You left us sitting for too long." Tommy struggled to her feet. "Now I have to stretch this bad hip."

Rather than express disbelief or irritation at this patently outlandish claim—less than a minute had passed between their arrival and Faircliffe's—the duke appeared comically relieved to be rid of Great-Aunt Wynchester so quickly.

"Of course, of course." He leapt out of her way. "Please do whatever you need for your hip. Take your time."

Behind the duke's back, Tommy darted a quizzical glance over her shoulder at Chloe, then disappeared down the corridor.

Faircliffe took the chair opposite Chloe. "How are you?"

"I'm well," she drawled. "How are you?"

It did not seem that he was going to take advantage of a private moment for torrid kisses after all.

Pity.

He twisted his hands in his lap. "Can I make an indelicate observation without offending you?"

She crossed her arms. "Probably not."

He cleared his throat but then said nothing, as if torn between his desires and his better judgment.

She flapped her fingers in resignation. "Go forth and offend."

"It's just that I've been watching you," he blurted out. He ran a restless hand through his dark hair. "You may think nobody is, but *I* am, and I've come to think that *you* think no one sees you. You dress so they *can't* see you without expending a modicum of effort, hoping that someone will do so and thus be worthy of you in all your true glory. Except that no one does. Instead of showing your full colors, you favor plain dress so that the reason they're not seeing you isn't because *you're* not worthy but because you've chosen to be invisible."

Chloe's pulse trembled erratically, her lungs robbed of breath.

She wasn't offended.

She was stripped bare.

"That's all fine," the duke said swiftly. "You should dress however you like and for whatever reasons you please. But whilst you're here in my house...whenever it's just the two of us, together...I want you to know that you're free to be *you*, whatever that might look like."

Chloe couldn't respond. Her words tangled in her throat.

"I don't know if this will make it worse or better, but I thought...Wait here. I'll go and get them."

Faircliffe darted up from his chair and dashed to the corner of the room, where a large trunk stood next to a blank wall. He lifted the trunk by its leather handles and brought it to the bare floor between his chair and Chloe's.

And then he flipped open the lid.

She gaped in astonishment. A dozen ladies' bonnets, ranging from stylish to garish, piled one atop the other. Some boasted a profusion of ribbons or ostrich feathers or wax grapes or the occasional stuffed parrot. One of the bonnets bore no decoration at all.

She pointed at it. "What's that one?"

"A choice." He gave a self-conscious little laugh. "If you *like* plain, then by all means wear it. The only thing I'm trying to give you is the power to choose."

She touched her chest, her throat suddenly dry and her eyes stinging.

Wasn't this what she had longed for: the ability to decide whether others noticed her? To control what others saw when they looked at her?

The bonnets were all so different. Plain, fancy, tasteful, gaudy, symmetrical, unconventional. Faircliffe didn't see just one thing when he looked at her. He understood she was all of these things and none of these things, conflicted and complex, a whole person with changing humors and multiple needs and desires.

He didn't see a pseudonym or a mask or a blank slate. He saw Chloe. And he wanted her to see herself, to *be* herself. To have this room as a safe place. To have him as both her protector and partner in crime. Or rather, partner in silliness.

No one outside of family had ever seen her so clearly. She should feel naked and discomfited.

Instead, she felt inexplicably, completely at home.

"If you hate these options..." He transferred bonnets onto every surface until he exposed a cornucopia of motley accoutrements at the bottom of the trunk. "Most items are held on with pins," he explained earnestly. "If you want all of the birds on one bonnet, you can do so. Feel free to be as creative as you please."

He gazed uncertainly at her, visibly holding his breath. His shoulder twitched as if every muscle coiled with nervous energy.

How did he not realize just how perfect his gift was?

She reached for an oddly fascinating bonnet with the greatest number of adornments pinned at all angles and placed it on her head. The weight of a white-necked pheasant caused it to list precariously to one side. A hunk of blue ribbon uncoiled from the clump of flowers on the brim to dangle before her eyes.

"I'm sorry." His cheeks flushed pink. "I may have decorated that one."

"I adore it." She wanted to hug it to her chest. She wanted to hug *him* and squeeze him tight. "It's my favorite of them all. Is there a looking glass?"

"Yes. Yes, there is." He leapt from his seat and hurried out of the door.

It was then that Chloe realized that this drawing room no longer bore the light-reflecting mirrors indicated on Tommy's maps. Was that why she'd been brought here today: because Faircliffe had removed them in deference to *her*? To ensure that every seat in the chamber would be one she'd feel comfortable in? She touched a hand to her throat.

The duke rushed back into the parlor bearing a hand mirror. One that could easily be turned facedown on any surface if she decided she was no longer interested in glimpsing her reflection.

She lifted the handle high and angled the glass to face her. A startled laugh burbled out of her chest, delighted and joyful. She looked absolutely, positively ridiculous. A peacock would be ashamed to make such a display.

Chloe had never loved a hat more in all her life.

She turned to Faircliffe. "You know the laws, do you not? What are the rules regarding a woman marrying her favorite bonnet?"

Faircliffe's entire body relaxed in obvious relief. He affected a serious expression. "As long as no one objects during the reading of the banns, and the bonnet agrees to a ceremony in the Church of England..."

She couldn't contain her grin as she nudged the trunk in his direction. "Your turn, good sir. Which frippery is yours?"

"Which frippery, *Your Grace*," he corrected sternly before selecting an oversized bonnet sprouting flowers and feathers. He waved his fingers in the direction of his white neckcloth. "Does this match my cravat?"

"It does not," she informed him gravely.

He placed the bonnet on his head anyway. "Pity."

She supposed he should look preposterous, but she couldn't possibly be more charmed by his boyish smile and cheerful silliness.

This was who *he* really was, when he wasn't trying so hard to be a perfect duke: delightful, approachable, irresistible. She wanted to grab the ribbons of his outlandish bonnet and kiss him for days. She wanted to wear the one he'd made for her for the rest of her life.

She touched the brim of her hat with trembling fingers. "Did you really decorate this one yourself?"

"Isn't it obvious?" He gave a sheepish smile. "They're all yours. You can keep them here if you prefer, or you can stuff them into your basket with Tiglet. His claws cannot possibly make my designs any worse."

"Tiglet is a paragon of fashion," she admitted. "Let's leave them here so he doesn't outshine us."

"Tiglet outshines everyone, with or without bonnets," Faircliffe pointed out.

Chloe wasn't so certain.

The Duke of Faircliffe, with his wide shoulders and chiseled jaw and floppy flowered bonnet covered in wax cherries and a rainbow of silk rosebuds, outshone any other member of the beau monde Chloe had ever met.

He *saw* her. He didn't want anything from her. He wished to do things *for* her. He wanted her to be herself.

Could a woman ask for anything more?

"Thank you," she said softly. "I've been flippant because I am speechless."

The tips of his ears reddened. "Don't thank me. I had plenty of help. My staff and I spent the evening pinning these contraptions together and giggling like schoolchildren."

The picture he painted caused Chloe to giggle as well. And to rethink more of her assumptions about Faircliffe. He was a duke, yes, but he was also a man who would sit around a table piled with millinery, playing at handicrafts with his servants. Servants like...

"Mr. *Hastings* made one of these hats?" That explained the secret smile on the butler's face.

"He fashioned the bonnet on my head," Faircliffe confirmed. "There was a clump of wooden apples, but they kept falling off. Dinah and Peggy used them on a different headpiece."

Chloe's chest lightened. She was visible not just to Faircliffe but to his entire staff. Even those whom she had not met yet had worked together to surprise her with a gift they weren't certain she would want.

All so that here, with him, there would be no need to hide.

"One cannot be anyone but oneself," Faircliffe said with a crooked smile. "There's no point in fighting it."

Could that be true?

This week, she had gone to Philippa's reading circle not for any nefarious reason but because Chloe liked books. And Philippa. And highly, highly valued being invited as Chloe Wynchester rather than forced to infiltrate as Jane Brown. That alone had once seemed impossible. The idea that she could take that further and be as peculiar and quirky as she pleased with Faircliffe was heady indeed.

"I was wrong about you," she admitted.

His face fell. "I'm *not* the most dashing duke in the entire history of England?"

Definitely the most kissable.

"You're more than what you seem," she said. "Just like me."

He was as complex and as surprising as his bonnet. There was so much to admire. He was honorable, indefatigable in Parliament, loyal, caring, imaginative. His empathy was not reserved for speeches about the nameless, faceless masses but for every person individually. Her, specifically.

He liked her and was unashamed to have her know it.

Chloe held out her hand as if meeting a stranger for the first time. She had crossed paths with Faircliffe a dozen times in the past. Her fingers shook as she realized that he would never forget her again.

He didn't just remember her when he saw her. He thought about her even when she wasn't there. Maybe even as often as she thought about him.

"Good afternoon. I'm Chloe. And I'm thinking very seriously about living inside your millinery trunk."

He took her hand and gave the trunk a dubious glance. "There's not much oxygen in there. Experts recommend a dressing room with plenty of natural light."

"I've got one," she admitted. "And if you think *your* collection is eccentric..."

He pressed his lips to the back of her fingers. The gesture was not torrid but tender. As if she was a prize worth winning. "It is delightful to meet you, Chloe Wynchester. I'm Lawrence. I daresay you're perfect no matter what clothes you wear."

"I daresay I'd like to kiss you, Lawrence," she said before she lost her nerve.

His face slowly broke into a grin. "Prove it."

The brims of their bonnets mashed together as she threw herself into his embrace.

His mouth was familiar and forbidden, his heat a cocoon from which she never wished to break free.

Without dislodging his lips from hers, he rose from his chair, pulling her to her feet and closer to his chest. His heartbeat was as syncopated as hers. As her knees melted from the heat of his kisses, he cradled her to his body. Protecting her. Plundering her. Branding her with his kiss.

Bean had always said that, to the right person, she would be visible, memorable, worthy of love exactly as she was. His words had proven true only for members of their family. No one else had ever seen beyond the bland mask to the woman just behind it.

Until now. Until Faircliffe.

No—until *Lawrence*.

His hands glided down her spine, hungry, searching. He was learning her dips and curves just as he'd learned her lips and mouth.

He had wanted a pretext to see her again, she realized. He

had missed her. He had hoped she would return soon. He had spent his evening not at Almack's but hunched over his table, pinning silk flowers to hats for her.

She kissed him for every feather, every wax grape, every bloom, and every ribbon. She kissed him for the plain bonnet with nothing at all, because he hadn't wanted her to feel obliged to do anything she wasn't ready for.

He didn't realize she wanted everything he could give and everything he could not. She longed to spend the rest of the afternoon there in his arms, losing herself in each new sensation until she was dizzy with desire.

Her siblings hoped Tommy found their painting quickly, but Chloe prayed the hunt would last all the way until the end-of-season gala. Even if she could now ask Lawrence for the painting, she wouldn't do so unless she had to. She wasn't ready to lose him. To be invisible again.

Once the painting was in their hands, the game was over. No more bonnets. No more kisses.

No more Faircliffe.

18

~

$\mathcal{L}$ awrence reveled in Chloe's kiss. He was more addicted to her taste than an opium eater to laudanum. Each kiss was drugging, beckoning him deeper, filling his every sense with the warmth of her soft curves and the jasmine scent of her hair.

He hungered for the forbidden contours of her body. He promised himself that each kiss would be the last and proved himself a liar over and over again.

An infinity of kisses would not be enough.

The more he gave, the more he felt whole. He adored that she adored his silly hats. He adored that, out of all the fantastical options, she'd immediately chosen the one he'd created.

He felt disproportionately proud, as though he had not decorated a bonnet but climbed a mountain and brought her the moon. He wanted to give her so much more than silly hats and stolen kisses. He could not shower her with gold, but he could spoil her with pleasure.

His body grew hard at the thought. Her mouth was sweet and demanding, her curves supple and tempting. He would rather tear their clothes off than pile more adornments on. Kiss her all over, leaving no inch untouched by his mouth and tongue. He pressed her closer to him to resist the temptation.

No matter how much he longed to sink between her thighs and bring them both to pleasure, he could not indulge such desires.

Chloe's fingers slid into his hair, dislodging his bonnet from his head. As she stroked the hair at his nape, his entire body felt like purring in pleasure. It required all of his will-power not to pet her even more intimately in response. To show her just how sensual a touch could be. He wanted her to luxuriate in his kisses, to come apart in his hands.

But these were not gentlemanly thoughts. These were the craven yearnings of a man who took far more than he ought to have. To keep kissing her would risk offering more of his soul than he was prepared to give.

In an act of self-preservation, he wrenched his mouth from hers.

She blinked up at him, her eyes sleepy with passion, her lips plump and kissable, her hands still twined about his neck. If he did not find a chaste distraction quickly, he would tumble her onto the closest sofa and lose what little good sense remained.

He wracked his jumbled thoughts for an activity that might not lead to lovemaking.

"Come see my"—he floundered for a suitable word— "library."

The corners of her eyes crinkled. "All right."

And just like that, his rampant desire was washed out by an icy wave of dread.

He *never* allowed visitors into his library. It was locked for a reason. The last time anyone had glimpsed these paintings had been during the previous year's end-of-season gala. He'd thought Miss York would like the painting she'd compli-mented, but her response had been tepid at best. Nothing like Chloe's surprise and delight at his gift of bonnets.

He tucked her fingers about his arm and led her to his sanctuary. What would she think?

The shelves were not as full as they had once been. Their sparseness did not bother him. He came to the library not just to read but to gaze upon its walls. All that remained of the Faircliffe treasures hung in gilded frames. This, too, was a much thinner collection than it had once been. But, gathered together in one room, the art that remained appeared magnificent.

To Lawrence.

With trepidation, he turned to face Chloe. Her lips were parted, her eyes wide with wonder.

"It's like a museum," she breathed.

His knees almost buckled in relief. Museums were good. People flocked there. His chest swelled. She thought his library was fine. He thought she was wonderful.

"It's my favorite room," he admitted. The only blight was the empty pedestal where his mother's angel vase belonged. "Do you want to meet my ancestors?"

"Can I?"

He led her to the wall where he'd relocated what had once been the Hall of Portraits. "This is Loftus Gosling, the first Duke of Faircliffe."

"He has kind eyes," Chloe replied. "And a darling dog."

"That is a very serious man with a very serious companion, out and about on the very serious business of hunting."

"Mmm. If you say so."

"All the Faircliffe men have been renowned for their solemnity." He winced. "Except my father."

"Do you mean 'until' your father? What about the present Duke of Faircliffe?"

"I am very serious and solemn," he protested. "I have on multiple occasions been called as hard as a glacier."

"Mmm," she said again. "Perhaps because they haven't seen you in a bonnet."

"It was a very serious bonnet," he murmured. "The seriousest. If you found it silly, it is because *you* are silly. I'm at my most statesmanlike with several colorful woodland creatures pinned to my head."

"Aren't we all," she agreed, and set her bonnet at a rakish angle. "Who is this next gentleman?"

Lawrence took her through them one by one, introducing her to great-great-grandparents and recounting family legends. It had been his mother who had shared the old family stories with him, passing them down at night as bedtime stories. He cherished each and every one.

A series of portraits was not the same as having a large family, but it was as close as Lawrence could get. Standing there, picturing the old stories in his mind's eye, made him feel a little less alone.

He'd always planned on continuing the tradition with his own children one day. Yet this was the first time he'd thought to share those tales with a friend. Not just any friend— with Chloe.

"My favorite bit," she said, "was how your grandfather won your grandmother. My brother's favorite would be that he named his horse after his great-great-grandfather's."

Perhaps Lawrence's grandfather had gone to sleep listening to the same bedside tales.

"That does it," he said. "I'm renaming my horses after the ones in these paintings."

Chloe shook her head.

"Don't do that. Your children and grandchildren may want to name theirs in *your* honor."

The thought made a strange flutter in his stomach. He had fantasized about having a family of his own for so long, it had never occurred to him that future generations might fantasize about knowing *him*.

"I should've given my new nags better names than 'Elderberry' and 'Mango,'" he muttered.

She giggled. "If you need assistance with future livestock, my brother Jacob adores animals."

An odd sensation tickled his chest. How wonderful it must be to have siblings—to be able to offer one up as if he were an extension of oneself, as if Lawrence could call her brother a friend by proxy! *Good day. You don't know me, because I am a complete stranger, but I have a horse with no name. Have you any suggestions?*

If only it were that easy. Walk up to someone as though you were related and be immediately welcomed into the family. He suddenly wished more than anything that it were possible, that a large, loving family would one day open their arms and choose him.

"Your ancestors are as handsome as you are." Chloe turned to glance about the library. "What other treasures lurk around the corner?"

He hesitated. His family portraits were important but fairly pedestrian.

What would happen if he showed Chloe the handful of more experimental paintings that fascinated him? Would she like them, too? Or would she find his taste questionable and his art laughable, and perhaps rethink her opinion of him as well?

He was appalled to discover he feared Chloe's rejection as much as society's.

Lawrence did not seek her approbation but to forge a connection. To be understood by her in a way no other acquaintances sought to know him.

"Over here," he found himself saying. "My secret collection."

When they reached the corner, she regarded the panoply of styles with interest.

"I am no artist," she admitted, "but I am intrigued both by it and by you. Tell me what I am looking at."

He took a deep breath and did just that.

She asked insightful questions and listened intently to his replies, even when the answer was "I don't know. It felt like part of me when I saw it."

"Art fascinates me," he explained, "because it captures a moment in time that may or may not have existed. No matter how rich the detail, it can never tell the full story."

This was much the same way he felt every time he looked at Chloe. She was beauty, she was mystery, she was more than she revealed at first glance. He suspected he could gaze upon her for the rest of his life and never uncover all of her hidden depths.

He hesitated before confessing, "One of the best aspects of the theatre is the sets behind the actors."

"Is it?" She gave a startled laugh. "You would get on well with my sister Marjorie. She says the same thing."

"Does she?" He searched her eyes in wonder.

He had expected her to mock such a ridiculous fancy, not accept it without question and immediately offer yet another sibling whose taste apparently mirrored his own. It was intoxicating to realize Chloe didn't find his eccentricities strange but, rather, *normal*.

This time he could not deny the wave of envy running through him. He didn't want to belong to just any big, loving family.

He wanted one like the Wynchesters.

"Marjorie paints," she explained with obvious pride. "If I tell her you find the act of creating as valuable as the art itself, you will be her favorite person in the world."

He could not help but wish she *would* repeat it to her sister. His belly fluttered. Lawrence had never been anyone's favorite person before. Even as a jest.

"Do you have a favorite person?" he asked.

"I have many of them," she answered without hesitation. "Bean and my siblings. More, if you count Tiglet."

"I would never fail to count Tiglet," he replied solemnly.

Was it foolish of him to wish his own name on that list?

Once he pledged himself to Miss York, there would be no more passionate embraces with Chloe, but it did not mean they were obliged to return to being strangers.

What if he and Chloe could remain...friends? Openly, this time? The thought made him dizzy. What if he *could* meet Jacob and Marjorie and whoever else was in her family? Not portraits on a wall, but real people whose legends were still unfolding. The Wild Wynchesters...and the Goslings.

A throat cleared in the doorway. "Your Grace?"

He turned to see his butler bearing a folded missive on a tray. "Yes, Hastings?"

"I'm sorry to interrupt, Your Grace, but Lord Southerby—"

"Good God." Lawrence strode over and snatched up the letter, suddenly realizing that Southerby's footman had been awaiting his response for nearly an hour.

The earl's seaside development venture was almost fully financed, and he needed to know soon if Lawrence was able to be a founding partner. He had been about to respond when Chloe's unexpected arrival had caused him to forget everything but her.

"Please have the earl's footman relay the message that I am not yet ready but will be before the end of the season."

"As you please." Hastings bowed and left.

Lawrence turned to Chloe. "I'm so sorry. If it were up to me, I'd spend the rest of the evening showing you every piece in my collection, but I'm afraid I've a debate tomorrow in the House of Lords that I must prepare for."

She gnawed her lip as if biting back words, then said in a rush, "I could help... if you wished."

Her voice was so soft as to be barely audible, but the look in her eyes matched what must have been the expression on his own face when debating whether to risk showing her the library: hungry. Hopeful. Terrified of rejection.

"You don't have to let me," she said quickly. "I'm a woman—"

"And no doubt brilliant. I'm a man used to doing everything on my own, because that is how it has always been." His voice scratched. "Perhaps it needn't be so tonight."

Her shocked gaze held his. "That means... that means yes?"

He offered her his arm and tried not to think about how right she felt at his side. "Do you think your great-aunt can find us if we remove to my study?"

"She's probably asleep on a sofa." Chloe's eyes twinkled as she leaned in and lowered her voice. "She's a dreadful chaperone."

"I hadn't noticed," he replied dryly. There was nothing he was more grateful for than Great-Aunt Wynchester's ineptitude in that regard. "Shall I have a maid find her and deliver the news of where we've gone off to?"

The embers of the fire crackled. Or perhaps it was the air sizzling with possibility.

"That depends." Chloe ran a finger lightly down his chest. "Can you guarantee there will be no kissing?"

He placed his hand over his thudding heart. "On my honor, I can swear no such thing."

"Then we definitely shouldn't tell her." She gave a saucy wink. "Just in case."

19

As nonplussed as Chloe was that Lawrence had accepted her offer of help—and as determined as she was to prove herself useful—her feet slowed as she followed him out of the library.

This was the room. Puck was in here; she could feel him. As soon as she and her sister were together out of earshot, Chloe would tell Tommy to look closer at the library.

When Lawrence turned to lock the door before heading to his office, Chloe asked no questions. She wanted him to think her primary interest lay in Parliament, not in his art collection.

That it was kept under lock and key was no matter. Tommy had her own copy. From what she gathered during previous promenades, the housekeeper had not returned from holiday, and the other two maids were busier than usual, taking up the slack. Which meant Tommy could slip in and out of the library with no one the wiser.

The idea that *Puck & Family* might return home before the end of the season gave Chloe's stomach an odd twist. She shoved the unwelcome sense of sorrow away.

Lawrence led her into a warm, cozy study. Late afternoon

sun streamed through the windows. "You can take off your bonnet if you've tired of wearing it."

She would never tire of it. "I like my bonnet."

His dimple flashed. "Then by all means. Please take a seat."

A large, comfortable-looking, worn leather chair stood on the far side of a mahogany Pembroke table he appeared to be using as an escritoire. Two armchairs, presumably for guests, sat on the other side. Chloe chose the one with better light.

She wanted to burn every moment of this evening into her memory.

Rather than walk round to his chair, Lawrence sat down beside her and began rotating the piles of documents so that the text faced in their direction.

She tried to breathe. Lawrence wasn't just fulfilling her romantic desires; he was treating her like an equal. More so, in fact, than she imagined he would treat Lord Southerby if the earl were there.

"I've never shared my methods with anyone before," Lawrence said, negating the idea of even his peers being welcome in this space. "I have an exceptionally rough draft, but it reads longer than I like to speak and is missing half the points I want to make."

"Then let's start at the beginning." She motioned to the pages clutched in his hand, her pulse skipping.

How many times had she spied upon the House of Commons from the attic or infiltrated the Strangers' Gallery in disguise? This was more than having a statesman right in front of her. The Duke of Faircliffe was about to perform a speech for her alone.

He cleared his throat. "'As anyone who has ever driven past Whitechapel is well aware, the—'"

"No," Chloe interrupted. Perhaps she would be more useful than she'd thought.

His blue gaze shot to her, befuddled. "No?"

"The speeches you begin with a question garner markedly greater immediate interest than the others," she explained. "And your phrasing, however innocently meant, implies one of the most poverty-stricken rookeries is something one drives *past* rather than a poor but lively neighborhood in which one grows *up*, lives, works, and loves."

He leaned backward. "I can promise you that no one hearing my speech has spent a night in Whitechapel, much less grown up there."

"False." She jabbed a finger at her chest. "The orphanage that raised *me* is in Whitechapel. *I've* listened to a decade of your speeches. If you mean to say that those who live in a rookery do not have a voice in the House of Lords, then you are correct. That is why you must *be* their voice. To have compassion for the 'unfortunates,' first the ruling class must see them as people—not a dirty stain one drives past as quickly as possible."

His eyes held hers for a long moment. Then he picked up a pencil and struck through the first paragraph of his speech without argument.

"That's saved us fifteen seconds." He pushed the pages in front of her and placed the pencil on top. "Why don't you show me what else can be trimmed or reworded? We might be able to fit in all of the missing points after all."

They hunched over the pages together, debating the merits and pitfalls of every line.

Chloe was astounded by the breadth of his knowledge and his commitment to researching facts and educating his peers. She'd witnessed his speeches on countless occasions but had never fathomed how many drafts he had gone through, how many anecdotes and salient points discarded, in order to arrive at the version she saw him deliver.

Many legislative elements were worse than she had feared. Others were surprisingly better or jarringly complex. In all of it, she and Lawrence were united in their desire to work for the good of the people.

But they disagreed wildly on how best to achieve that aim.

He did not toss her from his office when she dared to contradict him. Instead, he welcomed her dissenting opinions. The House of Lords, he pointed out, would be full of them. That was why his drafts were so long: he tried to think of every argument against each assertion and include preemptive rebuttals.

The pile of discarded drafts grew as they whittled and honed, adding and trimming and rearranging for impact. When they both put their pencils down in triumph, the final revision practically glowed.

"That," Chloe informed him, "is going to be your best speech yet."

He grinned at her. "Thanks to your meddling."

Her cheeks heated.

He leaned back in his chair looking casual and powerful and kissable. "I realize it is you, not the other MPs, that I need to impress."

"You have impressed me," she admitted. "I've always admired your contributions to the debates, but I hadn't grasped how much *work* it was to make it look so easy."

"And there's so much I hadn't thought of." He gave her a long look. "You understand my political aims in a way few people do outside of Parliament, yet you argue from an angle I've never considered. You haven't just made this speech better. You've permanently improved my tactics going forward."

She gazed back at him, her bosom swelling with pride. She had *helped* him. She had value.

"I'd kiss you for it," he said, his intense gaze hot with something more carnal than gratitude, "but I suppose it's past time for me to give you back to your family. I'm out of excuses to keep you away any longer."

"Can you kiss me and *then* give me back?" she asked hopefully. Was she begging? It didn't matter, as long as she got her way.

"See?" His hand cupped her cheek. He lowered his lips to the shell of her ear. "You have the best counter-arguments."

"Prove it."

He slanted his mouth over hers, his tongue giving, demanding. She held on tight, as though to let go would cause him to disintegrate like ash on a breeze. He was a dream that she held in her hands only for a moment. They belonged to each other as long as their mouths touched and their bodies pressed together. If she let go even the slightest bit, reality would claw its way in.

A creak sounded in the hall. Tommy? A maid? The wind?

They dropped their hands and stepped apart.

As much as Chloe hadn't wished for their kiss to end, she was equally distraught at the idea of never again being as important, as necessary and esteemed, as she'd felt tonight.

"Anytime you need an ear," she said in a rush, "if you want to analyze a performance or need help with a future speech or want a sounding board for policies, or for how to take down your rivals...I'm good at those things."

She *was*, she realized. Invisibility wasn't the only gift that made her useful to her family. After nineteen years of being a Wynchester, she was well versed in strategy. How to argue, how to persuade, how to think critically, how to plan for contingencies, how to succeed at all costs. The Wynchesters were more than a team. They were invincible.

It was dizzying to think she and Lawrence could be, too.

"I enjoyed tonight very much," he said.

Ah. That was not the same as *Yes, I would love for you to help me plan my speeches*. It was *How kind but no, thank you*.

She handed him her hat. "Let me find my aunt and send for our carriage."

"Only one of those things is necessary." He bowed. "Allow me to send you home in mine."

She narrowed her eyes. "In a coach without your crest, of course."

His *rented* coach. Graham had discovered the ducal coach had been sold the morning of the reading circle, leading to the mix-up of carriages. Lawrence could offer his rented conveyance in place of a hack, because the two would be indistinguishable.

"Would it matter?" His blue gaze held her rapt.

Her skin warmed at the idea that he would not have been ashamed to see her in a coach bearing his family crest. She all but floated to the carriage.

With the Duke of Faircliffe's driver within hearing distance, Chloe could not confess any of the afternoon's discoveries to her sister. Instead, she was forced to sit in silence, replaying every word of their debate, every passionate moment and heated kiss, her stomach twisting at the knowledge it would soon come to an end.

When the coach drew up at her house, Graham and Jacob were outside in the garden.

"What funny horses! I adore them." Jacob pretended to chase after the retreating carriage. "Can I keep them?"

Elderberry and Mango, Chloe thought, and immediately wished she didn't know their names.

"Take the beasts," Graham told his brother, "but leave the coach to me. I'll drive it for a quick holiday to—"

"You can't have any of it," Chloe couldn't stop herself from saying. "It belongs to Law—to Faircliffe."

"Pah." Jacob wiggled his eyebrows. "Anyone who lives as far beyond their means as the Faircliffe dukes won't notice the absence of a horse or two."

"He *would* notice. He's more attentive and considerate than you think." Oh, for the love of figs, Chloe *knew* her brother was teasing. There was no need to defend Lawrence.

"He's his father's son," Jacob reminded her. "He likely sleeps on cushions stuffed with IOUs he'll never repay."

Graham made an exaggerated face. "Maybe *that* is what's been up his arse this whole time."

Tommy and Jacob laughed.

Chloe did not.

She had no high horse from which to judge her siblings, she reminded herself. She had said the same things. Vowed to steal Bean's painting out from under Faircliffe's nose as revenge. Relished the idea of someone so icy and arrogant receiving a taste of his own medicine.

And now it was Chloe who felt like she'd swallowed a bitter pill.

"He doesn't want to live on credit," she said, although she doubted her next words would change her siblings' opinions of him for the better. "That's why he plans to wed Philippa for her dowry."

Tommy's lips pressed into a thin line.

"Oh, Graham, look!" Jacob gestured toward the duke's elegant conveyance. "Perhaps you can keep the coach after all."

The carriage had turned around and headed back toward the Wynchesters. They watched in anticipation as the driver pulled to a stop in front of Chloe.

"Almost forgot." He reached for a large object under a

woolen blanket on his perch and placed it in her hands. "There you are, madam. Good day."

With that, he drove off.

Her siblings crowded around her. "What is it? What did he give you?"

Chloe knew exactly what she held in her hands.

It wàs a hatbox. With the world's gaudiest bonnet inside. But more than that, it was a private jest between her and the Duke of Faircliffe. Her entire body warmed.

Lawrence thought on too many levels for anything he did to be only what it seemed. The hatbox was a message: Be whoever she wished to be. He was literally putting the power—and the choice—into her hands.

She turned and walked to the house.

"Where are you going?" Tommy called, startled.

Chloe didn't slow. "I'll meet you in the Planning Parlor."

There was something she had to do.

Lawrence was right. If she could be her outlandish, magpie self with him, surely she could be as bold and confident with her siblings. There was no reason for her interest in fashion to stay hidden in her own home.

As soon as she reached her dressing room, she stripped her layers of relentless beige from her body and placed her curling tongs over the fire. Then she flung open the doors to her enormous wardrobe.

She feasted her eyes on the dazzling array of colors and fabrics before her. Now that she'd given herself permission to wear whatever she pleased, Chloe found herself spoiled for choice. She'd been hoarding fashionable gowns and accessories for years. How was she to decide?

It was impossible to choose the perfect ensemble, so she didn't. She put on her favorite gown and her favorite slippers and her favorite pelisse, even though none of it matched.

She curled every single hunk of her hair, rather than just the tendrils at her temples, and allowed the profusion of ringlets to bounce from her head in any direction they pleased.

She couldn't decide between her two favorite combs, so she put in both. Ostrich feathers? Three. And perhaps that frilly lace fichu...

There. She turned to face her looking glass and burst out laughing. Instead of her usual place in the shadows, she was a Vauxhall firework bright enough to light up the night sky.

Chloe Wynchester, shooting star.

If this went well, perhaps she would begin meeting with her modiste in person, instead of sending fashion illustrations scrawled with notes and measurements. It would be a joy not to have to hide this side of herself anymore. But first...

She rolled back her shoulders and opened her bedchamber door. Her legs were unsteady. What if her siblings laughed at her or accused her of trying to copy Tommy's skill with disguises?

What if they didn't *notice* her stunning change in appearance, because no matter how she dressed, she would never stand out?

She forced herself to stride into the parlor anyway, with her spine straight and her head of curls held high.

"Finally." Elizabeth affected an aloof expression. "Miss Chloe deigns to share her mysterious packages with the rest of us."

"I told you she wasn't collecting badgers," Graham whispered to Jacob.

"You didn't know," Jacob sniffed. "Badgers can be well behaved when they wish."

Tommy pulled off her white wig and scrubbed her fingers through her short brown hair. "Does this mean I can start raiding *your* wardrobe when putting together my disguises?"

Heat pricked Chloe's eyes as she grinned at her siblings. Of course they would accept her, just as they always had done. They didn't care if she wore diamonds or a burlap sack. She had never been invisible to them.

They were a family.

20

꒱

"I don't think a tiara would have *ruined* your appearance," Elizabeth said, gripping her sword stick as the carriage rolled over a particularly jarring patch.

Chloe shook her head. It was a thrill to dress as flamboyantly as she liked at home with her family, but nothing had changed in the world outside their walls.

"Tommy and I don't care about the York ball," she informed her sister firmly. "Rescuing Puck is our only priority. I'll distract the duke by pretending I need waltzing lessons, and Tommy will slip into the library to search for the painting."

"If it's there, he's hidden it well. I won't have much time to search." Tommy made a face. "Faircliffe has a ball to attend."

"According to Graham's reconnaissance, tonight Faircliffe will officially ask for Miss York's hand." Chloe's words were hoarse. "Mrs. York wants as many witnesses as possible to her daughter becoming a future duchess."

Speaking the words aloud was enough to make Chloe nauseated. Philippa would soon be Her Grace, the Duchess of Faircliffe.

And Chloe...would just be Chloe.

"Poor Philippa." Elizabeth fussed with Chloe's gown. "Isn't it time for you to consider employing a lady's maid?"

"Two lady's maids," Tommy agreed, her eyes twinkling. "One for each wardrobe."

"We can afford it," Elizabeth reminded her. "You could have a different lady's maid every day of the week if you wished."

Chloe didn't wish.

She had never bothered with a maid before, because she always left the house in ensembles so plain, she could go from her bath to being fully clothed in under five minutes.

That she spent the *rest* of her time dressing and undressing, curling and uncurling, adorning and de-feathering, was her secret indulgence. Her siblings aware of the truth did not mean she was ready for anyone else to see.

"Unnecessary." She smoothed out an invisible wrinkle. "When we bring home our Puck, life will return to normal. I'll be a nonentity again."

"Not to us," Elizabeth insisted staunchly.

"With or without ostrich feathers, Chloe is more than enough for anyone who matters," Tommy agreed. "Who cares about Faircliffe?"

Therein lay the crux of the matter.

Chloe leaned her elbows on her knees and rubbed her face with her hands. Who cared about Faircliffe? Chloe did. She could still glimpse him if she sneaked into Westminster in disguise, but it wouldn't be enough.

She would miss being important as much as his kisses.

"Here we are." Tommy handed Chloe her basket.

"Good luck," Elizabeth said as the carriage rolled to a stop. "I'm off to spy with Graham. Did he tell you the housekeeper returned to the town house late last night?"

Chloe nodded. "Mrs. Root."

With the housekeeper back home, the other maids would no longer be busy sharing extra work. It also meant another person would be roaming the same halls Tommy was. A person with the same ring of keys.

Tommy checked her wrinkles in a mirror. "It is neither fast nor easy to check every floorboard and potential hiding place whilst dodging two maids and a footman. I spend more time babbling as Great-Aunt Wynchester than I do searching."

"We have until the end-of-season gala," Chloe reminded her quickly. "It's best not to rush."

Anything to have one more month with Lawrence.

When Chloe and Tommy reached the front step, the butler was already swinging open the door. Mr. Hastings ushered them into the special mirror-less drawing room without delay.

Faircliffe arrived moments later. Not Faircliffe—Lawrence. The duke whose mouth she knew as well as her own.

"Good evening, *Lawrence*," she whispered, as if Great-Aunt Wynchester would be scandalized to discover them on a first-name basis. Tommy already knew. She thought it was part of the plan.

"Good evening, *Chloe*," he mouthed back, his eyes warm and sparkling, then turned to bow to Tommy. "You look well today, Mrs. Wynchester."

"What!" Tommy barked. "Speak up if you're talking to me, green buck." She shook her head. "Lads these days, with the mumble-mumble. Next time I come, I'm bringing an ear trumpet. You won't get anything by me then, I warn you now."

Lawrence arched raised brows toward Chloe.

She gave a *What can you do?* shrug and whispered, "Don't worry. She doesn't know about the kissing."

His cheeks flushed.

So did Chloe's. Tommy would definitely tease her about this later.

"Er..." Lawrence cleared his throat. "To what do I owe the pleasure?"

"I have an invitation to a ball tonight." She didn't mention the Yorks, although with the rest of society planning to be in attendance, she imagined there was little doubt. "I'm told the sets are to include waltzing. I hope to avoid treading upon toes, but I've never had formal instruction."

"You want me to teach you to waltz?" His stricken expression added a silent *With someone else?*

But they both knew neither had any claim upon the other. No matter what Chloe's traitorous heart might wish.

She nodded. "If it's no bother."

"No bother at all," he said quickly. "I, too, have an event this evening, but it will be my honor to play dancing master between now and then."

Touché. Tonight, they would both seek someone else's arms.

"I've the perfect room for dancing," he added, then turned to Tommy. "Great-Aunt Wynchester, might you play us a melody on the pianoforte?"

"With these knuckles?" Tommy shook her fist at the duke. "I daresay you don't know a thing about arthritis, young man. All I can do with a pianoforte is glare at the blasted thing. Thank you for reminding me."

"Er..." Lawrence sent Chloe a helpless glance.

She gave another little shrug in response. Tommy was a fine musician. Great-Aunt Wynchester, on the other hand...well, that old bird was unpredictable.

Lawrence made a considering expression. "If you're willing to try something that smells a bit...*off*, my butler swears there is no better remedy for arthritis than the poultice my housekeeper makes."

Tommy lurched to her feet.

"I'll beg her for a dollop at once." She clumped from the parlor without waiting for permission.

"How could she possibly find Mrs. Root?" Lawrence gave his head a disbelieving shake. "My staff is convinced your aunt can barely find her way down a straight corridor. Shall I send someone to assist her? Perhaps Hastings—"

"Leave your butler at his post," Chloe interrupted smoothly, before the duke could drum up a chaperone for her chaperone. "Great-Aunt Wynchester may be old, but she's more capable than people think. She likes to do things for herself. Besides, every chamber has a bellpull. If she needs help, she knows what to do."

He inclined his head. "In that case, we shall leave her to her own devices, and us to ours. Are you ready for dancing lessons?"

Chloe was not.

Her chest clenched with the longing to waltz with him at a real ball. Her mind knew all of this was make-believe, but her speeding pulse and shaky breath indicated the rest of her body believed the fiction all too real.

Every new stolen moment in his arms would only make their inevitable separation all the more heartbreaking.

"I'm ready." She curled her fingers about his arm as if they were no different than any couple about to dance. "Lead the way."

The way, it turned out, led to a large, airy chamber, its floor bare save for a pianoforte in one corner and a smattering of plush chairs along the wall opposite.

"Is this where you host your end-of-season fête?"

"It is indeed." His eyes were cloudy, as if the thought filled him with as much pain as pleasure. Then he smiled, and it was as though the sun bloomed overhead rather than an unlit chandelier. She could look nowhere but at him.

He lifted her palm in his and curved his other hand above her midsection. It was not quite the embrace she craved but more than enough to weaken her knees. She would not have to feign awkwardness after all.

His voice was gruff. "Until the gala, I'm afraid we must pretend to hear the orchestra playing."

She did not have to pretend. Her heart beat loud enough to keep time for both of them. Gently, carefully, she placed her free hand atop his shoulder.

"I'll go slowly," he said. "One-two-three, one-two-three. Just try to relax into my lead."

She was anything but relaxed. She hoped he forgave her when she trod inelegantly on his feet. Every limb felt overwarm and clumsy.

Rather, that was what she thought until Lawrence began to move. He waltzed like a dream come true, the blackguard. Of course he would. It was impossible not to glide about the empty ballroom in perfect harmony, with or without music to accompany him. Her body was his to command.

Their feet found their own melody. His eyes did not leave hers. Their bodies moved flawlessly together, as if all previous dances had been practice for this moment, here, with him. She wondered if it would be like this every time, or if it would become even better.

This was the only waltz they would ever share, she realized bleakly. The memory would have to sustain her. It wasn't enough. She wished she had something tangible, like her broken locket or the warm red mittens. Her gaze lit upon the perfectly pressed handkerchief in his pocket. Before she could stop herself, it vanished from his chest and disappeared into a hidden fold of her gown during their next sweeping turn.

"I've been hoping you would stop by," he murmured. His hand at her back was all that was proper, but his thumb stroked her body. The small caress burned through her gown and shift and imprinted itself on her skin. "Poor Hastings spends every moment of his day peering out of the window in the hopes of spotting the Wynchester coach."

Ah, it *was* possible to miss her step and tumble against his chest.

He caught her, and then they were dancing again.

"W-what?" she stuttered. Hoping she would stop by was not at all the same as paying a sentinel to stand watch, just in case.

He pulled her closer, his words rasping as if he had not meant to speak them aloud. "I missed you."

"I was here yesterday," she reminded him. It was she, not he, who had spent every moment apart thinking of their kiss. "You spent all night in Parliament."

She had watched him. He had been glorious.

"Part of the night," he agreed. The hand holding hers came to his lips for a kiss, then stopped just before contact. He lowered her fingers back to a safe distance with a tortured expression. "The rest of the night I spent wishing I were kissing you."

Damn him for saying so! As much as Chloe would like to believe his restless night was due to thoughts about her, she did not let herself believe such pretty balderdash. After tonight he would belong to Philippa. Chloe was merely a temporary diversion.

If he honestly missed her, he could ask her to visit. He now knew where she lived. He could have sent a carriage, or a note, or a messenger kitten. But he had not—and would not.

"You're not wearing your bonnet," he murmured.

She'd placed it under her bed, where she would not have to confront his memory by looking at it, but where it would remain close enough to slip into her dreams as she slept.

"If the fripperies in the bonnet trunk would be useful to you, I'd be happy to loan you anything you'd like for tonight's ball." He smiled. "A rakish feather, perhaps?"

"I don't want one." The words erupted from her mouth more harshly than she had intended. She did not soften their blow.

If gazing upon his handmade gift in solitude was too much for her aching chest, wearing it while she watched him court someone else would be impossible.

"All right." He asked no further questions.

She frowned. What happened to his twenty-minute explanations about everything?

"You won't try to convince me?"

"It's your hair and your life." His eyes held hers. "You're clever enough to know how you wish to live it."

If only it were that easy.

"Knowing is not the same as doing," she mumbled.

He stopped dancing and pulled her closer. "Did something happen?"

Everything had happened. Her entire childhood had been a constant barrage of knowing what she wanted and not being able to have it.

"It's nothing," she said.

His expression was open. "You can tell me."

She sighed. There was far too much. An entire lifetime he knew nothing about. But if she had to pick a single defining moment...

"You and your peers aren't the only ones who hurry past rookeries as though there aren't real people there. Within the poorest parts, there are still haves and have-nots. I was a have-not."

He winced. "Because of the orphanage?"

"The orphanage is the reason I'm alive. It was everything to me. I did not make the same impact on it." She gave a sad smile. "I was a plain child. You might think being ignored would make me misbehave, but I saw what happened to unruly children. Blending in was better than standing out. I didn't want to be cast away from the only home I ever knew. Not again."

He frowned. "Again?"

"I'm not an orphan." Or at least she hadn't been at the time. "I wasn't sent to live in an orphanage because there was no one else to take me; I was discarded because my family didn't want me—tucked into a basket with a note that said I was one mouth too many in a family that already had more than enough." Her throat tightened, as it always did. "My parents looked at all their children and decided the helpless baby was the one they wanted least. Me. The most useless of the lot."

She'd been the newest, the least loved, the least familiar. A blank little slate, indistinguishable from any other squalling infant. An expensive mistake that wasn't worth the cost.

"I'm sure they loved you," he said quickly. "I'm sure they planned to come get you as soon as things turned around."

"Is that what you think? It would have been a difficult task. They did not sign the note or leave a token or even mention my name. I had to borrow someone else's." The headmaster's mongrel had been called Chloe. It seemed to fit her, too. "The orphanage did not have enough funds to feed those mouths, either. Once I was old enough, I would slip out to beg for crumbs."

"That was how you got enough to eat?"

"No." She snorted. "People looked right through me. My only chance for a halfpenny was to scrounge through discarded rubbish at the side of the Thames or learn to pluck it directly from the pockets of those who never noticed my presence."

"Which path did you choose?"

"Both. I was six, seven, eight. There were rumbling bellies in every cot, and I shared whatever food I'd scavenged with the other children before tumbling exhausted into my own bed. And then one day..."

Her lungs seemed to close.

His hand covered hers protectively. "One day...?"

She fought the pricking in her throat. "One day, when I sneaked back through the dormitory window with an entire loaf of bread to share, my bed was full. The minders had given the cot to someone else. I had been gone for three hours, and already those in power had forgotten there had ever been a little girl to save it for."

Lawrence's face contorted with horror. Before he could respond, a footman appeared at the open doorway.

"Pardon the interruption, Your Grace. You'd asked me to remind you when it was time for your engagement."

Ah. Chloe blinked quickly. The York ball, of course. The sand had run out of the glass. Her shoulders crumpled. She'd kept the duke longer than she had a right to. His bride awaited. It was time to be replaced and forgotten.

Yet again.

21

Chloe plodded out of the Duke of Faircliffe's residence with a heavy heart. She flung herself up and into the family carriage and into her sister's arms.

"Are you all right?" Tommy cupped Chloe's face in alarm. "What did that scoundrel do to you?"

"Nothing." Chloe buried her face in her sister's shoulder and willed herself not to cry. "Absolutely nothing."

Tommy stroked her hair. "What did you *want* him to do?"

Everything.

Chloe hugged her close rather than answer. Lawrence hadn't even kissed her good-bye. He belonged to Philippa already.

The coach wheels started rolling.

Tommy slid open the panel to the driver. "Home, please. We shan't be going to the ball."

"*No.* We have to go." Chloe's stomach rebelled against the idea. "I don't *want* to watch him propose to Philippa, but I need to see it happen. I have to *know*."

Tommy gave her a tortured look and then nodded. "All right." She craned her head back toward the driver. "York residence, please."

Chloe sagged against the back of the carriage. "Tell me you found our Puck."

Tommy shook her head. "I looked over every inch of that library. I peeked under chairs and even inside books in case they'd been hollowed out to make hiding spaces. *Puck & Family* isn't there."

Chloe's skin turned cold. "Not *there*?"

"I looked everywhere I could think to look. *Twice*. The housekeeper almost caught me locking up after myself. I'm sorry, Chloe. It's somewhere else. We have to go back."

Back to the house but not back into Lawrence's arms.

The next time they came to call, he'd be spoken for, and might not be alone. Chloe's arrival could disrupt private time with his new betrothed.

She wasn't certain she could bear to witness him with someone else after all.

* * *

Lawrence retied his cravat for the third time and glared at his reflection.

Chloe had left just moments ago, and here he was primping for her, rather than for the young lady he hoped to make his bride.

Did he wish to wed Miss York? He turned away from his looking glass. He didn't *want* to marry for money, no matter how practical and commonplace it was. But one's wants did not signify when one must also consider tenants, staff, and a familial estate that would crumble before his eyes without timely renovations.

Even if he were willing to give up his hard-won respectability and accept the scandal and censure an alliance with the Wynchester clan would bring, Chloe still was not an option. She had no dowry.

The unfortunate truth was Lawrence needed an heiress.

Miss York did not seem particularly keen to wed *him*, but she needed a title. Neither would be getting what he or she *really* wanted, but beggars could not be choosers, much as he might wish that were the case.

When he reached the front door, Hastings handed him a letter.

"This came a few minutes ago. It seemed important."

Lawrence glanced at the seal and handwriting, and his stomach sank. It *was* important. Nor was it the first message he'd received from the bank that held the mortgage to the town house.

Father had apparently stopped making payments years before. To repay the debt, Lawrence deposited three months' worth at a time, with the proceeds from selling items of value from the estate.

The bank had allowed Lawrence to postpone the date by which all overdue funds must be fully repaid with interest, on condition that the exorbitant monthly sum would be received by the first of every month without fail. But there wasn't enough money. Not yet.

He slid a trembling finger beneath the wax and began to read.

It was the twenty-fifth of April. He had missed this month's payment and only provided half of the last month's sum. They were very sorry, but he would not be able to keep the town house through June after all. Unless he balanced his account within the week, the mortgage would be in foreclosure and he would be evicted at the end of May.

Not only would there be no end-of-season gala, there would be no end of season at all. No more House of Lords, no more London, no more Chloe.

Lawrence crumpled the letter in his palm. If the crops had not failed, he *would* have had the money. But last year had been the Year Without a Summer. Crops had failed all over England—all over Europe. Lawrence wasn't the only one whose income had suddenly shriveled to nothing.

Which was likely why the bank would allow no more postponements. They knew his fallow fields would not become fertile on the morrow. He had made good progress on his father's debts—fine progress, exceptional progress—but the balance remained overdue, with no way to pay it.

No way except to secure a healthy dowry as quickly as possible.

He would have to wed Miss York sooner rather than later.

Mrs. York would be pleased. She had strongly suggested to Lawrence that tonight would be a fine night for a proposal. He suspected she'd dropped hints into all of her friends' ears as well. His fingers dug into his palm, compressing the foreclosure notice into a jagged little pellet.

It was time for the show.

* * *

The Wynchester carriage rolled to a stop at the end of a long queue.

"I'm going to be ill," Chloe moaned.

"You'll have to wait until later." Tommy looked out of the window glumly. "We're here."

Chloe took an unsteady breath and reached for her basket of tricks.

Many years before, Graham had teased her for carrying a basket instead of a reticule. It wasn't all of the time, she had retorted hotly, and besides, she'd like to see him hide a change of clothing and a stolen paperweight inside a tiny silk reticule.

The truth was, baskets held special meaning for Chloe. Her

first interaction with one had been when she was abandoned at the orphanage, only a few days old. Since then, she had determined that the baskets in her life would contain items of value, of worth. If something was inside a basket, it was because it was *important*, and she wanted to be certain she could find it again. To keep it with her at all times.

Tonight her basket contained cosmetic baubles that would help her pretend the York ball could not hurt her. That she did not need the Duke of Faircliffe. That she was better off without him. He should be crumpling to the floor in tears because he was the one who was missing what had been right in front of him.

She reached inside and pulled out an exquisite diadem of amethyst and gold.

Was there such a thing as a revenge tiara? She slapped it on her head and affixed it angrily in place. There. She'd float through the door, sparkle beneath the chandeliers, and march back outside to her carriage as soon as her presence had been registered by the one and only person who might actually notice.

If he *didn't* notice...

No. She wouldn't think about that.

What was the alternative? She could admit she possessed a substantial sum of money. But she did not want to "win" Lawrence that way. It would be no victory. Besides, dowries were for husbands. Chloe's trust was designed to let her do as *she* pleased.

And what she wanted was to be chosen for *herself*, not her money.

Was that too much to ask?

She alighted from the carriage with her head held high and put each foot in front of the other all the way to the Yorks' front door.

The party was absolute madness.

"Mrs. York must be in heaven," she whispered to Tommy in reluctant awe. "Every one of Graham's scandal columns will dub this night the 'Crush of the Season.'"

"All other hostesses might as well surrender now," Tommy agreed. "Even Great-Aunt Wynchester couldn't make herself heard in this din."

"Try." Chloe nudged her sister forward. "If we have to be here, I'm at least going to eat some dessert."

Tommy perked up. "Dessert?"

As they inched their way through the teeming masses, the music grew louder. Every window in the bustling ballroom was open to allow in fresh air, although the crowd was too dense for much circulation.

Tommy stopped in her tracks, her face gray. "There's Philippa."

"Is Faircliffe with her?"

"Not yet."

"How does she look?" Chloe closed her eyes so as not to see. "Like someone who's about to marry England's most eligible duke, like it or not?"

That Philippa didn't even *want* to marry Lawrence twisted the knife all the worse—not just for Chloe but for Lawrence and Philippa. What kind of marriage would that be? It sounded even worse than being alone.

"She looks beautiful," Tommy whispered back, her voice strained. "She's wearing a purple and azure gown with Antwerp lace. I've never seen her look prettier. Anyone would want to marry her."

"Wonderful," Chloe groaned. "Exactly the report I was hoping for."

Tommy glanced at her sharply. "Do you wish her to be unwell?"

"No," Chloe admitted. "I like Philippa, and I suspect she's in misery. She may be the only person who wants this union less than we do. Oh, why must aristocrats be so complicated? I've known fishwives who married for love."

"Note to my future self," Tommy murmured. "Fall in love with a fishwife next time."

"Fish spinster," Chloe corrected. "If she's a fish*wife*, you're already too late. I've come to believe timing is the biggest predictor of success in matters of the heart."

"Fish spinster," Tommy echoed with a sharp nod. "Don't act surprised when it happens. I'll tell everyone it was your idea."

"Then your first mistake was taking my advice," Chloe said weakly. "Everything my heart tells me to do is a bad idea. For example"—her breath caught—"there's Faircliffe."

Tommy froze in place. "Is he heading toward Philippa?"

"He is not." Chloe frowned. "He's dancing with Lady Eunice."

"But this is a waltz." Tommy's brow creased. "There's rarely more than two in a night. What could it mean?"

"That he's delaying the inevitable," Chloe said. "Or…that the gossips are wrong. Lawrence is still on the marriage mart."

She tried to burst the joy that bubbled inside her at the thought. What if it was true? What if, even after this party, Lawrence remained the most eligible, extremely not-betrothed, very bachelor duke in all of England a little while longer?

For a fleeting moment she let herself pretend she was the one he wanted most.

Her bosom filled with wistfulness. Lawrence was the Duke of Faircliffe. He was visible and powerful, and his duchess would be, too. What would it be like to be remembered and respected amongst the beau monde?

You'll never find out, she reminded herself sharply. He would never choose a Wynchester, and she would reject the suit of anyone who did not accept her family, fully and publicly.

Faircliffe was not that man.

She was *glad* he had chosen Philippa. Glad, glad, glad. She would keep telling herself so until it came true.

Tommy grabbed her arm in excitement. "I think I found lemon cakes."

"Wait. The music stopped." Chloe took a deep, shuddering breath. "Now he'll go straight to Philippa."

Tommy glanced up over Chloe's shoulder and shook her head. "He's not looking at Philippa. I'd better get those cakes."

"But—"

Tommy vanished, leaving Faircliffe standing in her place as though the crowd had played the most cunning sleight of hand.

Lawrence gazed at her as though she were the most fascinating painting in his entire fine collection.

Had there ever been a man so handsome or so dangerous? He was freshly combed and pressed, a paper doll come to life—sharp edges and all.

She preferred his cravat crushed between them and his hair tousled by her fingers.

That would not happen ever again.

"I wish…" His eyes searched hers. "I cannot put off my duty to my estate and my title any longer."

Her stomach sank. She didn't ask what he meant.

He told her anyway. "Mr. and Mrs. York are hoping tonight's ball will feature a special announcement."

"I know." Her fingers curled into fists. "Everyone knows. Just do it."

"I'm working on it," he muttered. "I'm reminding myself of all the reasons I *must* do this."

"You told me yourself that she's what you want," Chloe said, her words sour. "A perfect highborn family to carry on the Faircliffe legacy, scandal-free."

None of which was anything Chloe could offer.

"I know." A muscle flexed at his jaw. His gaze was hot on hers. "*I know.*"

"Then go," she said quietly, before he could make things worse by hinting at the possibility of Chloe becoming his mistress.

The only thing worse than being replaced and forgotten was being tucked away in the darkness on purpose.

She would rather remain a proud Wynchester spinster than some man's secret shame.

22

Lord Southerby stepped into Lawrence's path before he could reach the Yorks.

Lawrence gritted his teeth. He was not in the mood to talk about Chloe—or business affairs. "I don't have my portion to invest yet, but I will before the end of the season."

"So you said." The earl gave a lazy shrug and nodded in the direction from which Lawrence had come. "Quite a lot of interest you've been showing in Miss Wynchester lately, hmm?"

Lawrence could barely even walk away without longing to sneak another glance at her over his shoulder. He'd just been at her side moments before, and yet every time he glimpsed her he felt as if he were standing at the helm of a ship. Her presence had *force*, like a strong wind buffeting him off his feet.

Except this time his sails carried him to a different shore.

"I've no claim on her," he forced himself to reply. "I . . . hope she makes a splendid match."

"Doubtless someone will bite." Southerby's lips stretched in a slow smile—the wolfish one mothers warned their daughters about. "I find her intriguing. She seems like the sort of woman one might like to know."

"She *is*," Lawrence agreed, before he could stop himself.

And why *should* he stop himself? Or the Earl of Southerby, rather? The raffish lord was a well-connected gentleman with no debts to pay and a promising development project that would increase his already considerable fortune. He was charming, intelligent, friendly... Dashing Lord Southerby was practically perfect in every way.

He made Lawrence's stomach roil.

"She has no dowry," he told Southerby. "The new heir is rich, but Miss Wynchester is not."

The earl looked as though Lawrence had sprouted horns. "What do *I* care about dowries?"

Bull's-eye. A perfect arrow. That was the difference between the two men. One must wed for money, and the other could pursue anyone he wished.

"And before you tell me she's from a scandalous family, I know that as well," Southerby added. "According to the gossip columns, I happen to be considered somewhat scandalous myself. Miss Wynchester might not wish to waltz with a 'shameless rakehell' like me." He cuffed Lawrence on the shoulder. "Relax, Faircliffe. All I'm looking for is someone interesting to dance with."

Lawrence clenched his fists.

The earl might only be thinking of a single dance, rather than a lifetime of marriage, but every moment in Chloe's company fanned Lawrence's desire for more. He had no doubt the earl would feel the same. Chloe could be the one to bring a "shameless rakehell" like Southerby up to scratch.

But he had no right to care whom she married. He was supposed to be chasing Miss York.

"If you'll excuse me." He sidestepped the earl.

Southerby might be about to whisk Chloe off her feet, but Lawrence didn't have to watch it happen. It was time to stand up with Miss York for their set.

Without looking back, he closed the final distance. "I believe this dance is mine?"

Miss York laid her hand on his forearm without comment, but her mother stepped forward to whisper into Lawrence's ear, "Is this the moment?"

"For my minuet with your daughter?" he asked, misunderstanding on purpose. "Yes, I'm quite certain. Miss York, if I may?"

"Good-bye, Mother," she said flatly.

"There's no 'good-bye,'" her mother spluttered. "I'll be watching. Give me a sign when—"

The opening chords drowned out whatever else Mrs. York meant to say.

Lawrence barely arranged himself and Miss York in position in time to begin the dance with the others.

Although he tried not to look, his gaze flicked over her shoulder toward Chloe.

She was not dancing with Southerby. Chloe and her great-aunt were ducking out before the song had ended. Disappearing without saying good-bye. His chest ached. It was as though a hole had opened within him.

When she left, Chloe took the air from his lungs with her.

He returned his gaze to Miss York, trying his damnedest for a pleasant smile. Perhaps Chloe's sudden absence would allow him to concentrate on fulfilling his duty, as he should have been doing all along.

Miss York gazed back at him, her expression level and her eyes blank as she completed each step of the minuet without fault.

She was a clever woman. Everyone said so, even if Miss York was disinclined to share her intellect with Lawrence. He would not force the matter. Animated conversation was not a prerequisite for the role of duchess. It wasn't as if a husband

and wife were expected to spend lazy afternoons discussing art or debating politics. Not as he'd done with Chloe.

Miss York would bear him an heir—and, if not, a daughter or two—and he and his wife would be as happy as . . . as . . .

All right, perhaps they wouldn't be easy company.

They'd be indifferent strangers.

Lawrence would be hard at work on parliamentary matters. And Miss York would be . . . reading, perhaps. He'd restore the ducal estate with her dowry, beget a few children, and then enjoy an extraordinarily dull, loveless marriage, like those of their class often did.

It was not what Lawrence wanted at all.

Anxiety crept beneath his skin like ants. He tried not to let his steps falter in the dance. This was the moment he'd been preparing for. He was Wellington, poised to win or die trying at Waterloo. Miss York was . . . Napoleon Bonaparte? What was happening with this metaphor? Marriage wasn't war. There was no reason for proposing to feel like being run through with a bayonet.

He was Lawrence Gosling, eighth Duke of Faircliffe, and he, like all but one of the previous holders of the title, would do what was right.

He performed the steps in silence to give a sharper look at Miss York. An unsettling sensation twisted in his stomach. Did she wish *she* could choose someone else?

Perhaps she'd been unenthusiastic about the prospect of becoming a powerful duchess married to a virtual stranger because she, too, had been hoping to find love.

Was that the man he had hoped to become? One who improved his own lot at the expense of others? He could not live with himself if he did right by his title only to do his bride terribly wrong.

"Do you want to marry me?" he asked suddenly.

She stumbled. "Are you asking me to marry you?"

"I'm asking you if you *want* to marry me."

"If you ask, I'll say yes."

"Because it's what you want?"

"Because it's my duty." Her eyes were tired. "Isn't it yours?"

Not like this. He was desperate, but not a monster.

"It is not my duty to beget children on someone who would prefer I not visit her bedchamber."

The words were crude and ungentlemanly, but neither of them deserved a future in which he must force himself upon her to do his duty, and that she must allow herself to be violated to do hers.

"I know my responsibility," she mumbled.

That did not sound promising at all.

"If you were not honor-bound to obey your parents," he asked, "how interested would you be in pursuing wedlock to me?"

She completed a few steps of the minuet in silence, her eyes never leaving his.

And then she sighed. "About as interested as I imagine you are in me. In that, at least, we are well matched."

He couldn't do it. Not to her and not to himself. He would not become the devil she feared in the night. Not even for a dukedom.

"Then let me ease your mind." He gave a tight smile. "I shall refrain from asking a question to which you would be forced to assent in opposition to your own wishes, thereby saving us several decades of misery. You're free, Miss York. At least, as free as I have the power to grant you."

An uneasy prickle slid down his spine. He pushed it aside. He would find a way to save his estate and his standing without hurting anyone else in the process.

Somehow.

"Thank you." Miss York's tight posture relaxed, and her steps resumed a steady rhythm. "Are congratulations due to Miss Wynchester?"

"No," he said with a sigh. No matter how passionate he felt. "Since you're familiar with duty, you understand why not."

"Mmm," was all Miss York said in reply.

Since he *couldn't* choose Chloe, it was bloody good fortune he wasn't in love with her or anything inopportune like that.

Miss York kept time with the music. "When will you take your painting back?"

Lawrence nearly tripped. "You don't want it?"

She smiled. "I was only interested in your library."

His neck flushed. "Until you noticed it contained fewer books every year?"

"No, that would be the best part: filling up the blank spaces with whatever I pleased." Her steps were light. "I could tell you cared more about the artwork than the gala."

He narrowed his eyes. "Is that why you said you liked the dancing hobgoblins?"

"Anyone liking it should have raised suspicion," she chided, her eyes twinkling playfully now that she needn't fear being burdened with Lawrence and his questionable taste in art. "I doubted anyone had complimented you on it before, so, to be kind, I thought I would. I never expected you to *give* it to me."

The only reason he'd been willing to part with that painting was because it *wasn't* special. His father had another just like it.

His skin itched with shame. "I thought it could make one of us happy."

"Now you know." Miss York's expression was wry. "I'll have it sent back posthaste."

Now that they'd officially called off their unofficial union, the finality of their decision made him light-headed with panic. "I'll tell your parents—"

"Allow me. I will say I refused, which is what I should have done from the beginning. You and I both knew we did not suit. It is time I did what was best for *me*." She glanced over his shoulder and winced. "Do you mind if we wait until tomorrow? I'll need to think of the best way to inform my parents of the new development, and I'd rather not ruin the party."

"Tomorrow is more than fine," he assured her. "There's no one else I must hurry off to propose to."

"Hmm." Miss York said nothing more, but her eyes were full of skepticism.

Very well, Lawrence *was* in a hurry. There were accounts to settle and wages to pay, and none of it would be possible without a large dowry.

But he also had to *live* with the decision he made. His bride would have to live with him, too. The brief courtship with Miss York had shown him that "forever" was far too long to be wed to someone who would rather not be.

Even if his future bride's motivation was just as mercenary as his—a dukedom in exchange for a dowry—as long as she was happy with the arrangement, and the money would be his on their wedding day, Lawrence would do as duty must.

Chloe must understand the predicament all too well. She was doing the same thing. When she'd come to collect her favor, she'd admitted frankly that she had no dowry and was on the hunt for a wealthy suitor.

That man wasn't Lawrence. He could no longer claim to be solvent. He was losing his town house.

But until he and Chloe both found what they were looking for, perhaps they could have each other.

If only for a few more stolen moments.

23

With dawn came the morning papers. Chloe couldn't bear to look. She didn't have to. Graham inhaled every word before breakfast.

There was no engagement announcement. Nor was there any gossip that the betrothal had been delayed. Other than a description of Philippa's gown and a faithful recounting of which sets she'd danced with Faircliffe, there was no further gossip about them whatsoever.

Chloe rubbed her temples. "What does it mean?"

"It means," Elizabeth said with a shrug, "it'll be in tomorrow's paper. These were likely on the printing press long before the dancing stopped."

"I'll hear before that," Graham assured Chloe. "When I make my rounds in an hour, I'll learn all about the betrothal and report back to you."

"Please don't," she said. "I do not want to hear any details at all."

Randall, the Wynchesters' butler, stepped into the dining room bearing a silver tray. "Letter for Miss Chloe."

"*Philippa.*" Chloe groaned.

Perhaps Philippa wished to spread the good news to her reading circle before the gossip columns did it for her.

The last thing Chloe felt like doing was congratulating her on her fine catch.

But the letter wasn't from Philippa.

The Duke of Faircliffe's seal was right there in the middle.

"I...I'll read this in my room." Chloe rose on shaky legs.

Tommy leapt to her feet. "I'll come with you."

As soon as they were alone in Chloe's chamber, she broke the wax seal and read the letter's contents.

> I miss you. Come over?
>
> ~L

He missed her.

She didn't know whether to laugh or cry, toss the letter into the fire or frame the words on her wall. How long had she waited in agony for such a sign? That he noticed when she was gone, that he wished she were there...that he *cared*.

And he'd chosen to send this the day after he betrothed himself to someone else?

Tommy's brow lined with concern. "What are you going to do?"

Chloe crumpled the letter in her fist, then just as quickly uncrumpled it, placing the wrinkled parchment atop her dressing table and running her trembling hand atop the ridges in an attempt to smooth it back to the way it had been before.

It didn't work.

"I don't know," she said, her voice raw and miserable.

Tommy leaned against the plain wardrobe. "Do you want to see him?"

"*Yes.*" Chloe stared bleakly at nothing. "*No.*"

She lowered her heavy forehead to the dressing table, pinning the wretched letter with the weight of her thoughts.

Of course she wanted to see Lawrence. The knowledge that she had lost him, that it was now final and official and over, was more than she could bear. Why drag out the inevitable good-bye?

But they *had* to go back, damn him. Whether he missed her or not. He still had their Puck. Chloe distracting him was her family's best chance to recover it. This was their opening.

She lifted her head. "What do I wear?"

Tommy opened both wardrobes. "What do you want to wear?"

Dully, Chloe scanned her choices. Bland beige again, since she had already lost? An extravagant evening gown, to show him what he was missing? Neither option was appealing. Both gave away too much of how she was feeling.

She selected a simple day dress of blush-colored muslin with long sleeves and a double flounce of figured lace at the bottom hem. Neither frumpish, nor flamboyant. The sort of walking dress an ordinary woman whose heart was in no way broken might wear on an ordinary outing to pay calls on ordinary acquaintances.

Chloe would not let on that anything was amiss.

"Go put on Great-Aunt Wynchester," she told Tommy. "Today we bring our painting home."

* * *

Lawrence valiantly strove to return his attention to the research for the next Exchequer bill.

It did not work.

Every distant creak of a floorboard: Was that his footman Jackson, returning with a note from Chloe? Every whistle of wind outside the window: Was that the Wynchester carriage rumbling up the street outside?

He checked the clock for the fiftieth time. She had received his letter by now. Jackson must be home. If she had sent a reply, Lawrence would already have it in his hand. She wasn't coming. She wasn't even responding. Perhaps Southerby had won her hand and she no longer had need for Lawrence or his increasingly unlikely gala.

If Chloe wanted nothing to do with him, it was no less than what he deserved. Regardless of what his heart might want, he was still on the hunt for an heiress.

Indulging in stolen moments knowing full well it could lead nowhere was not the comportment of a gentleman— especially not one who had promised to help Chloe marry someone else.

The thought hardened his stomach, and he shoved it away. He was not going to *deflower* her. He just wanted to see her. And perhaps steal one tiny little kiss.

He was strong enough not to ask for any more than that.

Hastings appeared in the doorway. "Your Grace?"

Lawrence jumped. "Yes?"

His butler's eyes were merry. "Mrs. and Miss Wynchester are in their parlor."

Their parlor. The one with no mirrors and a trunk full of ugly bonnets. They were here!

He leapt to his feet at once. "Send for tea. I'll be right there."

Hastings nodded and disappeared.

Giddy with relief and excitement, Lawrence ran a hand through his hair and straightened his neckcloth before making his way to the drawing room where Chloe and her aunt awaited.

When he entered, both of them were wearing silly bonnets from the trunk.

He bowed deeply to hide his grin. "Ladies. I am honored by your visit."

Great-Aunt Wynchester narrowed her eyes. "Chloe said there would be jam tartlets."

"I did not say 'tartlets,' Aunt," Chloe corrected quickly. "I said there might be tea."

"There will definitely be tea for the two of you."

He seated himself in the chair across from the ladies' chaise and gazed wordlessly at Chloe. She dazzled. This was the first time he'd seen her without the specter of a loveless union to someone else hanging over his head, and she seemed brighter, bolder, too pretty to be real.

Her hair looked soft and touchable, her lips pink and kissable, her curves set off to perfection beneath a deceptively modest high-necked day dress, whose rose-colored bodice accentuated the swell of her bosom. He would dream of this gown tonight. Peeling off every layer and pressing heated kisses to each new inch of flesh he revealed.

"Does he know staring is rude?" Great-Aunt Wynchester demanded from behind her cupped hand. "I thought you said he was a duke of good breeding."

"With *occasional* good behavior," Chloe murmured back. "Didn't we agree we both have a soft spot for rascals?"

Lawrence stiffened. His reputation was the opposite of rascally. He was the pinnacle of good behavior. If this was an insinuation that she'd fallen for that damnable Earl of Southerby—

"Faircliffe looks like he'd rather eat you than tea cakes," Great-Aunt Wynchester grumbled.

Truer than she knew. Chloe was a succulent summer fruit and he wanted to devour every morsel of her. Lawrence could not wait to get Chloe alone so he could kiss her.

Er, *talk*. So they could talk. In a calm, well-behaved fashion.

He was saved from making a fool of himself by the timely arrival of a footman bearing the tea tray.

"Ohhh..." Great-Aunt Wynchester clutched her stomach and let out a moan worthy of a green-gilled sailor. "It's too soon for more lemon cakes. I may have overindulged at the ball."

"Then these are for me." Chloe helped herself to a cake.

Lawrence did the same. "Did you sleep well last night?"

It was an innocent question. Or at least it was *meant* to be an innocent question. But when Chloe's dark eyes met his, he felt their heat sear every inch of his skin.

"No," she answered without breaking their gaze. "Did you?"

"No," he croaked.

Free from the specter of marriage to Miss York, Lawrence had spent a restless night thinking only of Chloe. Endless carnal dreams of their naked limbs wrapped around each other, her little gasps of pleasure as he drove into her again and again. He'd awoken with his cock hard and swollen. Relieving the pressure with his hand only allowed him to slip into another torrid dream.

The sudden hope that she'd had similar thoughts of him was enough to make his groin tighten all over again.

"I didn't sleep well, either." Great-Aunt Wynchester poked at her knees. "These old joints say it's going to rain."

"It's London, Aunt," Chloe murmured. "It rains every day."

Great-Aunt Wynchester narrowed her eyes. "You weren't this cheeky when you were a little girl."

Lawrence leaned forward with interest. "What was she like as a child?"

"Oh, the tales I could tell!" Great-Aunt Wynchester cackled.

Chloe sent her a look. "Do not tell them."

"Once," Great-Aunt Wynchester began, ignoring her niece, "she got lost deep in the forest and would have died of hunger had she and her brother not stumbled across a house made of gingerbread."

"That never happened," Chloe scolded her. "That's the plot of 'Hänsel und Gretel,' which was translated for us a few months ago in the reading circle."

"Another time," Great-Aunt Wynchester continued as if Chloe had not spoken, "she consumed a poisoned apple and *did* die. Only the kiss of a dashing but ill-bred undertaker could bring her back to life. I pretended to be dead, too. A woman of my age doesn't receive many kisses. And then there was the time we were trapped in a Gothic castle—"

"Please do not claim Death abducted me on horseback, like Lenore. Or that I enjoyed a rollicking career as a prostitute like Fanny Hill." Chloe shook her finger. "I should never have shown you that lending library."

"And then there was that pieman," Great-Aunt Wynchester said dreamily. "No matter what you'd saved your halfpenny for, in the worst days of winter you never could resist a hot, fresh pie."

Chloe's expression softened. "I always shared with you."

Her aunt's eyes shone with love. "I never tasted a meal half so good since."

"Even a night spent gorging on lemon cakes?" Chloe teased.

Great-Aunt Wynchester let out a groan and clutched at her stomach. "Don't remind me. It's aggravating my gout."

Chloe raised her brows. "You do not have gout."

"I can feel it starting," her aunt insisted. "I must lie down at once, and for many hours."

Lawrence hid his amusement. "Would you like me to ring for a maid to show you to a guest chamber?"

"See?" Great-Aunt Wynchester hissed. "Very fine gentleman. Not a scoundrel at all."

"She won't come back for hours," Chloe warned. "That's the last you'll see of her until well past nightfall."

"Impertinent chit." Great-Aunt Wynchester sniffed. "Wait until you're my age."

Lawrence's brain had seized on the words *well past night-fall*. Be alone with Chloe until then? He'd give Great-Aunt Wynchester anything she wanted.

He tugged the closest bellpull. "Peggy will be here shortly to show you to a chamber."

The moment the maid whisked Great-Aunt Wynchester off down the hall, Lawrence turned back to Chloe. He could not wait to have her in his arms, to bury his face in the sweet scent of her hair. He wanted to hold her closer than he'd ever held anything and kiss her until nothing else existed but their arms around each other and their lips locked tight.

"And what," he said, as suggestively as he could, "might I interest you in, my lady?"

Her gaze was unreadable. "I wasn't able to peruse all of your artwork. Perhaps you could show me what I've missed?"

Lawrence had been hoping to show her an hour or two of passionate kisses and was surprised to discover that this suggestion was just as attractive. Never before had anyone been interested enough in his obsession with unusual art to inquire about it, much less encourage him to share that side of himself openly.

He offered her his arm. "This way, if you please."

It would be easy to minimize most of the art collection as pieces left over from generations past with no more meaning than that. But with Chloe, he did not want to hide his peculiarities. He suspected she would like him better with every new oddity he revealed.

He led her to a nook no one ever browsed except him. "These are my favorites."

She tilted her head at the unusual perspectives and provocative portraits. "Why are they your favorites?"

"Because they fill me with questions and spark my imagination." He gestured at the painting before them. "Why her? Why him? Why this moment? Why this angle? What are they looking at, just off from the canvas? What caused those birds to take flight?"

"Oh, I see." She stepped forward to take a closer look. "There were many perspectives from which to paint this scene, but the artist chose this one for a reason."

His relief deepened into joy as they paused before each painting, asking probing questions and providing ever more outlandish possibilities each time.

"This is far more diverting than any visit I've paid to a museum." She peered up at him. "No wonder you adore this collection."

"I used to wish I didn't. My father always preferred his obsessions over his home and family, and I feared I was destined to follow in those footsteps."

"If art is your zany bonnet, then tie it on and wear it with pride." She gestured expansively. "Why purposely cut yourself off from something you love? If viewing paintings makes you happy, then do what gives you joy."

"I don't want to look and imagine." He cleared his throat. His muscles were rigid, his voice stilted. "I want to do it, to be it, to paint it."

He held his breath. The back of his neck prickled in trepidation.

Her eyes brightened with interest. "Then why don't you?"

His body relaxed. If only it were so easy. He reached out to touch her face. She turned at the last second, and his hand fell back to his side without making contact. His skin grew cold. He'd expected her to laugh at the notion of him as an artist, not to recoil from his touch. He shifted to hide his embarrassment.

"I cannot risk losing status. I've spent my entire life trying to avoid comparisons to my father. Being the serious and respectable Faircliffe. Avoiding gossip at all costs." He gave a self-deprecating snort. "I wouldn't know how to mix paints if I had any, and there's no money to employ tutors for frivolous hobbies. What if I'm no good at painting?"

Her brow furrowed. "How can there be funds for an end-of-season gala and yet not even a shilling for a moment or two with a tutor?"

"There aren't any funds for an end-of-season gala." His jaw hardened. "There would have been, if I'd offered for Miss York, as was my duty, but without her dowry, there's little chance of continuing a tradition my family has upheld for generations."

Her mouth fell open. "You didn't offer for Philippa?"

He cursed himself. Of course Chloe had not melted into his embrace. She had thought him promised to someone else.

"I did not," he said quickly. "I couldn't."

"But why?" she stammered. "I thought she was the answer to your prayers."

"All but one of them." Miss York wasn't Chloe. No one else could compare. "I could not consign us both to misery."

Her face tilted up toward his. "If not her, what do you hope to find?"

"I don't know what the future holds." His voice was husky as he reached for her. "But in this moment I have everything I desire."

A pleased, secret smile flirted at her rosy lips. "You desire me?"

"More than breath itself." But he had to be fully honest. He brushed his thumb against her cheek. "I'm yours for the moment, but this freedom is temporary. My intentions are not honorable."

"Who said mine were?" She glided a finger down his waistcoat. "You're available for anything I please? At this very moment?"

"Anything at all." The words rasped from his suddenly dry throat.

The tip of her tongue touched her lower lip. He wanted to taste it.

"Start with a kiss"—she rose up on her toes so that her mouth brushed against his—"and then tempt me."

He cupped her face in his hands and pressed his mouth to hers.

Power and vulnerability warred within him. Her kiss was everything he had hoped and feared it would be. Thrilling, drugging, devastating. It did not quench the fire within him. It fanned the flames hotter. Every kiss begat two, every two begged four more.

She had the upper hand, whether or not she realized it. He was greedy for as many kisses as she deigned to give. He would hoard them in his heart to savor for the rest of his life.

It was heady to realize he'd relinquished all control to someone else. Or perhaps she had wrested it from him just by looking in his direction.

Tonight he was hers to command.

24

He was no longer marrying Philippa!

Chloe slid her fingers into the Duke of Faircliffe's dark hair and tried to tell herself this news meant nothing, that his marital plans did not signify, because when it came to her, they had no future.

But with Lawrence a kiss was never *just a kiss*. It was earth-shattering, heartbreaking, sublime. From the moment she'd received his invitation to visit, she'd known the greatest challenge would be resisting the urge to throw herself into his arms and melt against him. And now there was nothing to resist!

He was hers, for a little longer. Hers to do anything she liked with. A thrill sizzled through her. Temporary she might be, but tonight she would also be memorable. He might leave her, but he would not forget her.

No one could forget kisses as hot as these.

With him, she was no scuffed parquet or so much faded wallpaper. With him, she was the candle, the torch, the chandelier: bright and dazzling, the pinnacle of the night, their passion a fiery comet. She would not let herself think about how it would feel to hit the ground.

Moments such as these were not to be squandered.

She unlaced her fingers from behind his neck and ran her palms over his shoulders, his arms, his chest, greedy to know every inch of him.

"What are you doing?" he asked between kisses. His breath tickled the corner of her mouth. "Stealing another handkerchief?"

She giggled despite herself. "You knew I took it?"

"Not until you admitted it just now." He covered his handkerchief protectively. "Minx. What did you do with it?"

"Burned it."

A lie. It was folded neatly in the tiny cedar box that contained the blue hair ribbon Bean had purchased for her when he realized she'd never had a pretty one. It was her box of things too perfect to touch.

The duke, however, was endearingly imperfect and an absolute delight to touch. She lifted her fingers to loosen his fastidiously starched cravat. Slowly. Deliberately. And then she pressed a kiss to the newly exposed flesh of his throat.

"Be careful what you start," he warned her. "I need every knot and every thread in place if I'm to keep my body away from yours."

She released the top button of his tailcoat without taking her eyes from his. "When on earth did I give you the impression that I wanted distance between us?"

A dark eyebrow arched. "When you asked me to help you find a wealthy suitor."

Oh, right. That little fib.

She shook her head and reached for the next button. "I don't need to save myself for—"

He twirled her to the door of the library as if to the tune of a private waltz playing just for them. He turned his key in the lock with one hand because his other arm was busy holding her close.

"There are many things one can do without ruining oneself"—he paused—"in the classic sense."

She slid a finger beneath the exposed collar of his linen shirt. "What if I want the classics and the non-classics?"

"Chloe." His gaze was tortured. "I can't offer you marriage. All I can offer is pleasure."

"That's all I want." She slid her arms about his bare neck. "Lots and lots of pleasure. Ruin me for all others, Your Grace. Wynchesters never were cut out to be respectable."

He covered her mouth with his as they swept backward through the library. Her knees buckled against the sofa and they came crashing down atop the cushions in each other's arms. Her pulse was jittery beneath her skin, but already her body was ripening, impatient for what was to come.

His eyes shone like blue fire. "Are you certain this is what you want?"

"Lying with you is what I've *wanted* to do ever since you made me those bonnets." She dragged her lower lip against the scratchy edge of his jaw. "I realized it was what I was *going* to do the moment you said 'Not betrothed.'"

He caught her lip between his teeth, gently, then licked where he had nibbled.

"In that case, I should have mentioned it sooner." He pressed openmouthed kisses down the side of her throat, tasting her, supping there at the base. "I've wanted you since you made me put in an appearance at the Blankets for Babes charity tea with the wrong kind of blanket."

"I didn't make you do anything," she protested, dipping her head to allow him more access. "A certain know-all decided to go off half-cocked without asking any questions."

But her insides warmed at the knowledge that he had been thinking of her even then, try as he might not to. She was not the one he needed, but she was definitely the one he wanted.

The feeling was mutual.

She knew better than to become romantically entangled with a cull. But along the way, he had stopped being a mark and started being Lawrence. The man whose seductive kisses and romantic murmurs melted her knees and who somehow kept a straight face when Tommy's "Great-Aunt Wynchester" was at her most outrageous. He did all of that for Chloe.

Her pulse rushed faster. Although she had not coupled with anyone before, her life had been far from sheltered. She knew what to expect and was glad it would be with Lawrence.

This was the memory she wanted to look back on when she remembered her first time. One perfect night. A fantasy come to life, before reality came to snatch it all away. This was their moment.

Chloe reached for him with eager hands. She could not divest him of his clothing until she got rid of his coat.

The buttons slipped free in a blur. "Aren't you hot under all these fashionable layers?"

"My entire body heats at the mention of your name," he growled, and reached for her. "The sight of you makes my trousers too tight."

She grinned and pushed his tailcoat off his shoulders.

"Poor darling." She ran a finger down his chest. Finally she could undo his waistcoat. "How terrible it must be to suffer inside such binding breeches! We must get you out of them at once."

He allowed his waistcoat to fall to the floor, but he did not let her reach for his waistband. Instead, he caught her wrists in his hands and pressed a kiss to each pulse point. Her blood ran faster, carrying the kiss to every secret place she hoped he'd find.

He dropped her wrists and sank between her knees to the carpet to begin untying her half boots. She could see only the top of his head. As he loosened each lace, he buried his face beneath her skirts to kiss the top of her thigh or the inside of her knee. She felt each touch of his tongue on her flesh all the way to her core.

She was boneless by the time he slipped the boots from her feet, her limbs trembling with anticipation. They were going to make love. She was about to feel him inside of her.

But he did not immediately rise to cover her body with his. He stayed on his knees between her parted legs. Slowly he slid the pads of his thumbs beneath the hem of her skirts to skim the thin silk of her stockings.

"I've been told," he said, his voice deep and gravelly, his gaze burning, "that I look at you as though I'd like to eat you."

It sounded wicked and wonderful. She swallowed hard. "Is that what you want?"

"Trust me." His arrogant smile had never looked so arousing. "It's what *you* want."

He ducked his head to where her stocking covered her calf. As he slid her hem higher, he feathered little kisses first to one sensitive patch of skin, then the other. He made thrilling dark promises with his mouth and tongue as he exposed her inch by inch.

When her hem reached her hips, she gasped—not at the sudden contact with the library's cool air, but at the heat from his mouth as he kissed the secret spot between her legs where only she had touched before. It had never felt like this. Wanton and overwhelming.

Her eyes fluttered shut, blocking out everything but the sensation of his talented tongue, teasing her and tasting her. Pressure built within her, sharp and luxurious. Her legs trembled and her body pulsed with need. She was almost at her peak.

"I want…" she panted. Her fingers dug into the cushions of the sofa. "I need…"

Without lifting his tongue from the little nub, he slid his hand between her legs and filled the ache with his fingers. Her body responded at once, the twin pleasures radiating through her. She came apart against his mouth and fingers, exploding like a distant star in the heavens.

Only once the tremors ceased did he climb atop the sofa to nestle her to his chest.

"What are you doing?" she whispered, once she found her voice.

He brushed a damp tendril from her forehead. "Cuddling with you."

"Stop it at once," she demanded. "We aren't finished."

His eyes were dark with desire. He stroked her hair, her cheek. "You've no idea how deeply I yearn to bury myself between your thighs. You may not care about your reputation, but I shall not defile you."

She wiggled beneath him, coaxing their hips to align. There was no sense saving one's virginity for a prince who would never arrive. She had never planned to marry. A wise woman took what she could when she had the means to do so. The man she wanted was in her arms. There was nothing to stop them.

"I want you to make love to me." Her voice was husky, unrecognizable with desire. She trailed a fingernail down his back. "I know what I'm asking and what it means. This moment is about taking what we want, not what others think we should have. You're worth it. So am I."

He propped himself up on one elbow, his eyes glinting.

He did not look convinced, but he was close. The wildness in his eyes made him look as though he wanted to pounce upon her, rend her gown from her flesh, and show her exactly what *ravish* meant. He was holding himself back by a thread. A single, solitary, gossamer thread.

She could snap it with one touch...

"You once told me not to uncage you unless that was what I wanted." She ran her hands up his strong arms. "It's what I want."

He brushed his knuckles against the underside of her bosom. Her breasts tightened, the peaks hardening. His lips parted as though he wanted to taste them just as he'd devoured her below.

"Besides"—she tugged his shirt free from his waistband—"it's not 'defiling' if I'm begging you to finish what you start. It's an act of mercy." She skimmed her fingertips across the hard planes of his stomach and felt the muscles jump. "A true gentleman would not hesitate to bring pleasure to us both."

His breath caught, his eyes hot and his voice raw. "If my very honor depends upon finding release with you..."

"It does," she assured him. She slid a finger down the seam of his fall. "I shall be quite piqued if we walk away now."

"Well, I cannot have you piqued with me," he murmured, and slid his hand to where his fingers and tongue had been moments earlier, this time keeping his gaze locked on hers to see just how deeply he affected her.

She could hide nothing. Her body was still slick and sensitive, more than ready for his touch. She moaned as the welcome teasing sensation quickly spun the pressure inside her higher and higher.

A sense of power filled her. He was no more capable of walking away than she was. He craved her just as she craved him, had feasted upon her and still hungered for more. In seconds he would have her back at the edge of need, teetering on the precipice.

"*No.*" She reached for the buttons of his fall. "Not without you this time."

Eyes glittering, he flung his linen shirt from his chest in a single movement.

She had not realized the sight would be so erotic. His skin was hot and inviting, the hard muscles twitching beneath the light pressure of her fingertips as though her touch brought both pleasure and pain.

He caught her hands and pinned them to the cushion as he covered her mouth with his. She should feel trapped and helpless, but instead her body quickened with exhilaration, relishing the promise of his possession, eager to join as one. She let her legs fall apart in invitation.

When his hands released her wrists from their sensual prison, she immediately sank her fingers into his hair, marking him as he had marked her. His hair was disheveled because of her hands, her thighs. His gorgeous perfection mussed from feasting on *her*.

Her body clenched deliciously in remembrance.

"Hurry," she begged.

His smile was wicked. "No."

As he reached between their bodies to unbutton his fall, his knuckles brushed against her slick core.

Her body pulsed with need. Now he would claim her with the most intimate part of himself. Her breath was ragged. She'd loved his mouth, his tongue, his fingers, and was ready for—

His thick shaft pressed hot and heavy against her belly. It felt impossibly big and unspeakably tempting. If a single finger could push her over the edge, how much more pleasure would all of him bring? She writhed against him.

"Patience," he murmured against her lips. His shaft pulsed between them.

"Don't make me wait." She barely recognized the smoky need in her voice. "Please."

He lowered himself until he slid perfectly against her, but nudged nothing more than the tip inside. It was decadent, potent, teasing her with promise. She wanted more. She wanted all of him. If only for tonight.

She lifted her hips to coax him inside. Every new inch stretched her, bound them closer. He was not just on top of her but inside of her. The realization made her dizzy.

"Chloe," he said, his voice strained. "This is going to..."

They gasped together as he entered her fully.

A sharp pain pierced her and disappeared as fast as it had come.

She clenched her muscles around him, testing the strength of this new invasion.

He sucked in a ragged breath.

"You felt that?" she whispered.

"It almost broke me." His words were rough, his gaze hot with need. "You have no idea how much I've longed to be inside of you. I can barely think."

She could not stop her lips from curving into a naughty grin. "Now that you're here, what are we going to do?"

He began to move his hips. Slowly, tantalizingly, his hard shaft surged within her. The feel of him inside her, the sight of his strong shoulders from this strange new angle, almost undid her.

She wrapped her legs about him, at first matching his rhythm, then goading him faster, deeper. Each stroke fed the increasing pressure like kindling to a fire. Soon it would consume her.

Kissing her hungrily, he cupped his hand to her breast. His fingers teased the pert nipple the way he had played between her legs. Little sounds escaped her throat, sounds she did not recognize. The pressure rose and rose until it was difficult to breathe and all she could do was feel. It was happening again, this time with him inside of her.

He would feel it, too.

She grasped his shoulders. "I'm going to—"

It was too late for a warning. The peak was already upon her, lifting her, squeezing him, fracturing her into a thousand prisms of light and taking him with her. Sweat lined his brow.

"Thank God," he muttered, pumping his hips rapidly in short succession before jerking free to grip himself with his handkerchief and allowing it to tumble to the floor. He collapsed beside her, sated and exhausted.

She had done this to him. No—even better. They had done it to each other.

He pulled her against him possessively. "Any other favors?"

She nestled against his warm chest, reveling in the sound of his heart beating as fast as hers. "Do it again?"

"Give me five minutes," he mumbled, and lay his cheek against her hair.

They nodded off for a few moments, awakening when the chill in the air permeated their sated embrace.

Lawrence tugged her hem back down to her ankles, then arranged his breeches and slipped his shirt back over his head. Much as Chloe was loath to cover him back up, she enjoyed being the one who could do so.

She helped with his waistcoat and his cravat, not because he needed it but because she wished to. Adjusting the folds of a neckcloth and rebuttoning the jacket they'd tossed aside somehow felt just as intimate as everything they'd done moments before—perhaps more. It was different now. No longer a mystery. They knew what they could have together.

He kissed her forehead. "Shall we tour the rest of the library?"

It took her embarrassingly long to fathom what on earth he was talking about.

Art.

The reason Chloe was allegedly here. In his house, in this room. Thank goodness Lawrence was keeping things on track.

"Yes," she managed. "The tour would be fascinating."

He laced his fingers with hers and led her to a different section of the library from the last. Instead of paintings on the walls, there were waist-high fluted columns topped with busts and sculptures.

All except for a single column with nothing on it.

She pointed. "What belongs there?"

The casual joy disappeared from his eyes.

"A vase. My father's most prized possession, and mine as well." A tendon flexed in his neck. "When I find the black-guard who stole it..."

"A vase?" she repeated.

"A fine one. It looks like a cherub or an angel."

She knew the vase quite well indeed. It was sitting back home in the Planning Parlor. But she hadn't known the vase was *missing*. Old Faircliffe had given it to Bean voluntarily, as compensation for stealing a family heirloom. Then again, Bean had not agreed to the trade. The vase had been imposed on him against his will.

"You're certain it's been stolen?" she asked carefully.

"I've been through every inch of this property," Lawrence said darkly. "It was here before the accident and gone after Father died. Someone took it while the house was at its most vulnerable."

While *Lawrence* was at his most vulnerable.

Chloe gulped. "Er, perhaps it's not what you think."

He wasn't listening. "The Bow Street Runners are investi-gating as we speak."

Her stomach dropped. "They are?"

"Between their best investigators and the reward money, I'll have the culprit before the magistrate in no time." His eyes were hard. "And then I'll make him pay."

Oh, no. Oh, no, no, no...

If only the prideful man hadn't been too lofty to acknowledge a Wynchester from the start! They had *tried* to exchange their fathers' possessions. They'd sent countless offers to purchase back the painting, for ever-increasing sums of money.

Chloe had intercepted Lawrence on half a dozen occasions to broker a trade—outside Parliament, in Hyde Park, at Berkeley Square—only to be rebuffed before she could get a word out. Ignored, unacknowledged, time and again.

He'd never truly seen her until the day she stole his carriage. The debt of a favor—no money, no objects—this ruse had been her one chance to ensure he wouldn't brush her away yet again.

Everything had changed since then. *He* had changed. She couldn't risk her siblings' freedom, should one of the Runners take an interest in the wild Wynchesters. There was no choice but to try.

He wouldn't listen to her in the past, but perhaps he would now.

"I..." She cleared her throat. "I might know where to find your father's vase."

He dropped her hand. "What?"

This was the right thing to do. The *only* thing to do. Even if it destroyed whatever connection she and Lawrence had forged between them, at least the truth would give him peace and Puck could finally come home.

"Your father gave the vase to mine—" she began.

"He would never," Lawrence said fiercely.

"He did. He left it behind in exchange for the one piece of art my family cherishes above all others. A lively portrait of mischievous fairies."

He blinked in surprise. "The one I gave Miss York?"

"No, that was a copy." Which she had replaced with an equally erroneous forgery, none of which was important at the moment. She was the one in the dragon's lair. She would not implicate her siblings. "Where is the original?"

His face flushed. "Is that why you're so 'interested' in my library? Our little 'tours'? You're hoping I'll lead you to an ugly painting?"

"I adore your library," she said, "and I *do* want my family heirloom back, more than anything. We can trade, just as our fathers wished. That is, if you still have it."

He stepped backward.

"That's what you've been after all this time." Each word was a blade of ice. "Not me, but a painting? Bloody convenient to have this streak of honesty now, once I've mentioned the Runners, rather than coming to me right from the start—"

"Right from the start?" she choked out in disbelief. Every muscle trembled at the unfairness of his accusation. "That painting is *ours*. We came to your father and then we came to you. I knocked on your door, my sister knocked on your door, my brother knocked on your door...We sent dozens of letters. They all came back unopened!"

"*I* have a reputation to protect," he snarled. "Calls and correspondence are only accepted from respectable parties. Anyone not on the list is rejected out of hand. I only lifted the prohibition on Wynchesters because I owed you that favor." His eyes flashed. "I see I was right to distance myself from your duplicitous family."

She recoiled as if struck.

"You were *right*?" Her throat went dry, her limbs shaking with anger. "You wish we came to you from the start. We did, and you ignored us. You needed money. We tried to pay you—for an item that was rightfully ours. The only reason you acknowledged me this time was because I stole a carriage with you in it."

His lip curled. "I should have known then what kind of person you'd turn out to be."

"As should I," she retorted, jabbing an unsteady finger at his chest. "If I hadn't tricked you into allowing me across your precious threshold, you would have no idea where to find your father's vase because *you* can't be bothered to acknowledge the existence of your 'lessers.' So, explain to me, Your Grace, which one of us has a right to be offended by the callousness of the other."

"I ignored you. I did not lie to you," he said, his tone frigid. "Take me to my father's vase at once or I shall take *you* to visit the Bow Street Runners."

25

⚘

Chloe climbed up through a fog of dread and into the Duke of Faircliffe's waiting coach.

What had she done?

This had been the most wonderful and terrible afternoon imaginable. And now, taking him home to meet her family, under conditions such as these... What would they think of him? What would *he* think of *them*? Once they traded the Faircliffe vase for the Wynchester portrait, would she ever see Lawrence again?

Would he return the painting? He hadn't confirmed it was still in his possession. Had her unfortunate honesty ruined everything for nothing?

Up came Tommy, who took the seat opposite until Chloe grabbed her by the arm and tugged her into the squab at Chloe's side.

Tommy sent her a sharp frown. "What's happening?"

Before Chloe could answer, the duke bounded into the carriage and took the rear-facing seat Tommy had vacated to glare at them, stone-faced.

"Er," said Tommy. "Was it the lemon cakes? They looked delectable. I just thought it would be better if this old stomach refrained from turning inside out onto your settee."

"It's not the lemon cakes." He rapped on the wall facing the driver, and the horses burst into motion. "I've learned that the real reason your niece has been coming round is because she intended to steal a painting—and is also in possession of my father's vase."

Tommy's mouth fell open, and she jerked her shocked gaze at Chloe. "You *told* him?"

The duke gaped at her. "You *knew*?"

"I knew about the vase and the painting." Tommy's nostrils flared. "I did not know my niece was a ninnyhammer."

Chloe clenched her teeth together and made a smile as brittle as her soul.

"You might say," she bit out, "things did not go as expected."

What she really wanted to do was to toss Lawrence from his carriage and then throw herself straight into her sister's arms.

Tommy's frustration melted at once and she slid her hand over Chloe's.

Chloe squeezed back, grateful beyond words for a sisterly anchor in the midst of the storm.

"I demand the return of my vase," the duke commanded.

She ground her teeth. Moments before, they had been equals. Now he was back to being superior, treating her as though she weren't a person in her own right. As though his needs and wants were the only ones that mattered. As though his heirloom were more valuable than hers.

Outside the window, fashionable Mayfair disappeared. Soon they approached Islington.

By the time the coach clipped up the path leading to the stately Wynchester home, panic raced through Chloe's blood. She had never disappointed her family before. She had always completed every mission.

Until today, when a wild duke followed her home.

She exited first, on shaky legs. Tommy came next. They inched closer to each other before edging toward their house.

The Duke of Faircliffe alighted from his carriage in time to see Chloe's brother Graham race along the edge of the roof, leap sideways from the topmost gable to the cupola over the first-floor balcony, and perform an elegant forward flip to land in perfect silence on the grass below.

Lawrence's eyes widened in astonishment.

Graham swiped a hand over his flyaway black curls. "Why is *he* here?"

The duke straightened in obvious affront. "I might expect a modicum of respect."

"You might not, pup," Tommy scolded in perfect Great-Aunt Wynchester cadence. "You might be a duke, but this is our home, and it's up to us who we allow in it."

"Chloe," the duke said imperiously, "has informed me that—"

"You call her *Chloe*?" Graham's initial shock swiftly changed to speculation, and he sent her the sort of irritatingly knowing glance that only an elder brother could deliver.

She glared back at him mulishly.

"Er…Miss Wynchester, that is," Lawrence corrected himself, flustered enough to drop the haughtier-than-thou aristocratic veneer. "The point is, she's admitted a planned theft from my household, as well as possession of a certain vase that rightfully belongs to me."

Graham's smile disappeared. "You ruined our only collateral security?"

"I…" Chloe's eyes begged for him to understand. "I'm sorry, Graham."

Her brother did not look appeased. He looked betrayed and disappointed.

"She didn't ruin anything," Lawrence snapped. "It's not

'collateral security' if the person you're bargaining with doesn't know you have it or want it. Unlike your sister, *you* clearly have not mastered the art of debate."

Graham blinked, then visibly tried to mask another of his annoyingly knowing expressions. "The self-righteous duke leaps to defend his thief's honor. How interesting."

"*Graham...*" Chloe said in warning.

Before she could continue her threat, the front door to the house flew open and two more siblings strode outside.

Lawrence craned his head to watch with obvious interest, then outright confusion.

Elizabeth was relying less than usual on her cane—Chloe was delighted to see her sister's new stretches had eased some of her chronic pain—and Jacob sported a tricolored parrot on one shoulder.

"Ho there," Jacob called out. "What's this party?"

"Ho there," his parrot echoed, with a flap of its red, yellow, and blue wings.

At least, Chloe *assumed* the squawk had come from the parrot. One never knew, with Elizabeth close by.

"Keep that bird away from me, nephew," Tommy barked as Great-Aunt Wynchester. "There are no crackers in my reticule."

Lawrence's startled gaze went from Elizabeth's pale features to the golden bronze of Graham's skin to the rich brown of Jacob's. Belated realization dawned upon his patrician features.

"Oh!" he blurted out. "I didn't realize the Wynchesters weren't *real* siblings."

No other words could be a greater or more instantaneous call to arms.

"To the devil with you," Graham spat, fists clenching. "Nothing is more 'real' than our family."

Elizabeth's eyes flashed. "'Wynchester' is something you feel in your heart. Not something one must be born to."

"Someone like him has no heart," Jacob scoffed. "Peers needn't bother. Their 'lineage' matters more to them than actual persons."

"Arrogant nob," squawked the parrot.

Definitely Elizabeth.

Lawrence angled his head. "Well, actually—"

"Here he goes." Tommy gave a noisy sigh. "Prepare for two hours of His Grace pontificating in great detail how he's the expert on what makes a family and that we're wrong about everything we've lived in our own lives."

"I haven't time for that." Jacob tapped his chin. "But I do have a python and a Highland tiger I could feed him to."

"And an ill-tempered hedgehog," squawked his parrot.

"I have cable for tightropes," Graham offered. "I could string it across the roof like a spiderweb, and tie him to the—"

"Not every situation calls for a trapeze stunt and a rose clutched between your teeth," Elizabeth hissed.

"Then you're not doing it right," Graham whispered back.

Lawrence turned to Tommy in frustration. "Can you not control your nieces and nephews for one moment?"

Elizabeth let out an unladylike snort.

Jacob grinned at Chloe. "He really doesn't know?"

She shook her head. "He hasn't a blessed clue."

"I can't wait." Graham rubbed his hands. "This will be amazing."

Tommy smoothed a white tendril. "Just say the word."

The others turned to Chloe.

"Why are they all looking at you?" Lawrence demanded. His eyes widened. "You're their *leader*?"

"We're all leaders," she said firmly. "We are a family and a team."

"But, yes," Elizabeth piped up, "she's the leader-est leader."

Her words enveloped Chloe like a warm embrace. This family was where she belonged.

"Oh, come along, then," she said with a sigh. "Shall we go inside? Marjorie must be wondering what the fuss is about."

"If she's glanced out her studio window," Jacob said. "I doubt she noticed Graham's daring descent."

"'Daring Descent!'" Graham perked up. "I like it. Someone should inform the scandal columns."

Lawrence visibly wrapped himself in ducal gentlemanliness and offered Elizabeth his arm. "Would you like help back into the house?"

"No," she said flatly. "The handle of my cane hides a knife. If you come closer, I'll use it."

Chagrined, he turned awkwardly toward Tommy.

"I don't need you, either." She ran up to Elizabeth's side. "If you come closer, I'll hit you with the book I stole from your library."

"You stole a *book*?" He stalked forward. "I need that back!"

"See?" Jacob grinned at Graham. "We still have collateral security."

"Wynchesters always win," squawked the parrot.

The Duke of Faircliffe was the last to enter the house.

Chloe led them to the dining room, pausing only to murmur instructions for tea to a passing maid.

Once they were settled, Lawrence looked up and down the long mahogany table, then back to Chloe. "This room could seat two dozen. How many of you *are* there, really?"

"Enough," she replied indifferently, knowing the non-answer would vex him.

At the moment there were three persons on either edge of the long table: Jacob, Chloe, and Lawrence to one side, and Tommy, Elizabeth, and Graham on the other.

"Explain yourselves," the duke commanded. "Start at the beginning."

Chloe would definitely not be doing that. "You'll call off the Runners?"

Jacob startled. "Runners?"

"*Bow Street* Runners?" squawked his parrot.

"Faircliffe believed his missing vase to be stolen," Chloe explained. "It is not. It's upstairs. Call off the Runners and we'll negotiate an exchange. Do we have an agreement?"

Lawrence studied her as though he were just now seeing her properly.

"No Runners," he agreed slowly. "But no truce until I have all of the facts *and* the vase."

"No truce until you return our painting," Jacob added.

The duke inclined his head.

Graham leaned back. "Your father sold us our painting nineteen years ago, a few weeks after Bean fostered us. They'd met in some gentlemen's club with low enough standards to welcome a minor baron from a small foreign principality...as well as dissolute gamblers like your father, who was always on the hunt for a new wager to repay the last one he'd lost."

Lawrence's jaw flexed, but he did not argue. The picture Graham painted wasn't pretty, but it was accurate.

"From time to time, when the duke's pockets were to let, he'd try to sell us another painting, but we weren't interested."

"We had no need to purchase art," Elizabeth added. "By then, Marjorie was producing works worthy of a museum, and her tutors claimed there was little more they could teach her."

Tommy jumped in. "Ten months ago, she and I were in the parlor discussing an upcoming exhibition. Your father was visiting at the time and became quite agitated. He asked for *Puck & Family* back. Bean refused. The duke came back the next day to propose a temporary trade using collateral security. Bean refused again. There was some sort of disturbance in the barn—"

"Never let a hawk near your pet squirrels," Jacob murmured.

"—and when it was over, the painting and your father were both gone." Tommy pointed a liver-spotted finger at Lawrence's cravat. "He *stole* it from us."

"A duke would never *steal*," Lawrence mumbled. But the pallor in his cheeks indicated he was not at all convinced his father could be held to any such standard.

Graham snorted. "Because of him, we came up with a half dozen new rules."

" 'Never trust nobility.' "

" 'Forge everything.' "

" 'Don't allow anything of value out of the family again, or trust anyone who isn't a Wynchester.' "

"Wait," the duke interrupted. " '*Forge everything*'?"

"I didn't fake my bellyache," Tommy assured him as Great-Aunt Wynchester. "Lemon cakes are no laughing matter. But everything else was a lie."

Chloe's gaze caught Lawrence's.

"Not *everything*," she murmured softly. "There were… moments."

Naked, sensual, tender moments. Her cheeks flushed.

His pupils dilated as if he, too, was assailed by memories of their moments of passion. Of their joined bodies, slick with sweat, surging together. But lovemaking did not mean he accepted her—or her family.

Nor was she certain her family could ever accept *him*. Lawrence was straitlaced and respectable, and her siblings were…Wynchesters.

"True enough. Faircliffe isn't so bad, for an arrogant pup." Tommy patted his arm, illustrating to the others that she found the duke mostly harmless. "Anyone who makes bonnets as preposterous as his can deal with a few surprises here and there."

The corners of Elizabeth's mouth twitched.

"Few surprises," squawked the parrot. "And perhaps a pail of water over the head for causing all this trouble when he could have simply *opened* the letters we sent to him, *accepted* the money we were willing to pay for the safe return of our heirloom, and then popped the painting into the hands of a capable footman with instructions to nip right over and return the bloody vase back home, neat as can be. And furthermore—"

Lawrence's head jerked back in shock. "Wait…that *isn't* the parrot talking?"

Graham and Jacob dissolved into laughter.

"Not as cork-brained as he looks," the parrot squawked. "Next he'll ask about Father Christmas."

Tommy gave a very Great-Aunt Wynchester cackle.

"Don't get your breeches twisted," Graham drawled. "Siblings tease each other all the time."

Yes, but Lawrence had never had a sibling. He wouldn't have any idea what to do with a family like theirs. Chloe braced herself for his wounded pride or ducal hauteur.

Instead, a disbelieving grin blossomed on Lawrence's face. He looked strangely…thrilled?

"A talking parrot." He gave a low chuckle. "That's brilliant. I could use a trick like that in the House of Lords."

"You already have," Elizabeth replied in her normal voice.

He gaped at her. "I…what?"

"I told you I visit Westminster," Chloe explained.

"Usually she drags me along," Tommy murmured. "Although *I* won't stuff myself into dusty attics."

"Last week *I* went with her," Elizabeth said. "Chloe wanted me to witness how well you performed after the night you'd practiced together—"

He shot Chloe a startled look. "You told her about that?"

"You ought to be grateful for it," Elizabeth said. "When your peers veered from the topic, that's how we brought the chaos back to the script. Chloe would tell me what to say or what to ask—"

"And Elizabeth would do it in whatever voice I asked of her—"

"You should have seen the look on Rosbotham's face when his disembodied voice inquired about St. Marylebone Rectory—"

By now Lawrence was laughing right along with them. "Can I employ you?"

"Sorry, I'm busy that night." Elizabeth stifled a yawn. "Perhaps you should have been nicer."

"I'll rent you a parrot," Jacob offered. "Thirty quid an hour. Sixty if it talks."

"At those prices, you ought to rent me a python and throw in the Highland tiger for free."

Chloe gazed at the Duke of Faircliffe exchanging silly banter with her siblings in bemusement.

If he had truly felt a crime had taken place, he *could* have sent the Runners or made a claim to a magistrate. Instead, he'd piled into a carriage and come here hoping for an audience, and now he was at her dinner table, elbow to elbow with her siblings.

Arguing the merits of releasing ill-tempered hedgehogs inside Westminster.

Chloe knew better than to think this meant her family would receive invitations to his gala, but it felt bigger than a simple truce.

Perhaps Lawrence had muscled in to burn things down, but he had dropped the haughty armor once he realized her family was not the enemy. He was talking and laughing with her siblings as though they were...friends.

Despite his initial reaction, Lawrence now appeared to accept her siblings as they were. He might still say the wrong things, but that wasn't a new quirk. He'd had a long history of awkwardness before meeting any Wynchesters. In fact, they'd designed their ruse to exploit his naïve earnestness.

She shifted uncomfortably in her seat. Now that he knew, would Lawrence still want her in his life?

⟨⟩

26

*H*idden behind Lawrence's laughter was visceral, burning embarrassment.

Contrary to his imagination, the "poor, pitiable orphans" lived in obvious luxury. The old baron may have failed to provide dowries for his adoptive daughters, but—regardless of individual poverty—the Wynchester clan was far from shabby-genteel.

Had he felt sorry for them for not living in fashionable Mayfair, scrunched in with titled, important neighbors? The Vanderbean property's lush garden was larger than Grosvenor Square. Their marvelous three-story home was as spacious as an entire terrace row of town houses like his.

Despite its ample size, their home's classic architecture was ordinary on the outside...and full of splendor inside. White plaster ceilings with gilded floral friezes. Marble fireplaces carved in neoclassical patterns that matched the fanciful trim around doorways and the decorative lunettes on the ceilings.

Great-Aunt Wynchester was right to criticize Lawrence's woeful carpets. Every detail of the Wynchester home was well thought-out and gorgeous.

The walls were hung with silk: this room the soothing

green-blue of the sea; that room a deep and sumptuous rose; others ornamented with dazzling stucco. Intricate gilded candlestands rested on elegant marble pillars. Tempting Chippendale settees and armchairs abounded with plush silk-upholstered cushions. Lawrence trembled with mortification.

Good God, had he really explained the concept of *spoons* to Chloe?

His palms went clammy. He wanted to sink through the tasteful emerald-and-gold Kidderminster carpet that had been woven specifically to echo and complement the ceiling pattern overhead. His stomach twisted harder.

He had been trying to save her from embarrassment, and in return she had shamed him to his very bones.

He hurt. He was angry at himself that he let himself *be* hurt.

Lawrence had wanted their connection to be more than physical. It was true for him, and he had needed it to be true for her, too.

But what right did he have to feel betrayed in matters of love? *He* was the one who had been planning to propose to someone else. He had thought so little of Chloe and so much of himself that he had accepted farcical assertions of ignorance as obvious fact.

Of course she needed his help, he'd told himself. Didn't everyone?

No, Chloe did not.

He might have known the truth sooner if he had not compounded his father's mistakes by cutting himself off from the "undesirable element" in the name of protecting his reputation. In doing so, he had behaved just as reprehensibly as his father.

The Wynchesters would not have had to resort to trickery if Lawrence had been willing to listen.

He was listening now. Despite his and Chloe's inauspicious

beginning, despite all of his prejudices and arrogant assumptions, she had come to be as essential as art. Whenever they were apart, he longed for the moment he would see her face again.

If his heart was now in the hands of someone who didn't want it, well, that was his own bloody fault. He had *dreamed* of a family like the Wynchesters. Of course they would rally together and defend each other from all evils. Starting with the actions of Faircliffe dukes.

It was time to take responsibility for his past actions and forge a better future.

Lawrence cleared his throat. "I apologize for my father's shameful behavior. And for my own. I should not have ignored your attempts at outreach. As much as I would like to say I didn't register my failures to acknowledge you publicly, the truth is I did so on purpose. I *did* think myself above you, and I *did* instruct my household to reject any calls or correspondence, based solely on your name and status. I was wrong. I am sorry. I don't expect you to forgive me."

The Wynchesters exchanged meaningful glances.

"To be honest," Jacob said, "we wouldn't expect a duke *not* to act superior."

Elizabeth patted her cane.

Lawrence remembered there was a knife hidden inside.

"I'm glad you disappointed yourself, and you deserve to feel that way," Elizabeth said. "I am pleased you've realized your mistakes."

"More than realizations," he said. "I've changed, hopefully for the better. I hope you can give me a chance to prove my remorse is real."

Graham sent a sideways glance toward Chloe. "I assume we'd be tarred and feathered if we did not."

Chloe's cheeks flushed pink, but she held her brother's eyes.

"Consider this your good-faith second chance." Jacob's dark gaze pinned Lawrence. "Don't make a hash of it."

Lawrence coughed. "I'll try my best."

He could not stifle a thrill at the idea of having an opportunity to be near a family like this. To be close to Chloe. To have a second chance with her.

"Oh, good." Great-Aunt Wynchester rubbed her hands together as a pair of footmen carried heavy silver trays into the dining room. "Tea at last."

Lawrence's stomach turned at the prospect. At this point he would have to gag some down out of politeness. He hoped there was an extra tureen or two of sugar to make it more palatable.

The footmen set the trays in the center of the table. One was piled high with meat pasties. The other bore a jug of lemonade, a carafe of coffee, and what looked like a decanter of fine port.

Neither tray held a teapot.

He swung his startled gaze toward Chloe.

She batted her eyelashes at him innocently. "Don't follow the rules. *Create* them."

"That's the Wynchester way," Elizabeth agreed, and reached for the port.

"I begin to think you might all be secretly related after all," Lawrence grumbled, but he helped himself to lemonade.

"We wouldn't keep it a secret," Jacob assured him.

"We keep *other* secrets," Great-Aunt Wynchester agreed.

Her nieces and nephews tried to hide their chuckles.

Lawrence cast a suspicious gaze about the table. "No..."

They were not nieces and nephews. They were orphans of disparate parentage. Which meant none of them was related to the old woman seated across from him.

He narrowed his eyes at her. "Are you even a Wynchester?"

"I told you he would start to suspect," Chloe crowed.

"He got partway there," Graham admitted grudgingly.

Jacob waved a hand. "Go on, Tommy. Help him out."

Who was Tommy? Lawrence glanced over his shoulders, but no other siblings had entered the room.

"Oh, all right." Great-Aunt Wynchester set down her meat pasty with an aggrieved sigh, reached her liver-spotted hands up to her thin white hair... and pulled it off her head.

Lawrence dropped his fork with a clatter. "What in the..."

She ran her fingers through a shock of short brown hair, then pulled a stoppered glass bottle from her reticule. After dousing her serviette with some sort of fragrant oil, she swiped the wet cloth down one side of her face.

The age spots and wrinkles smudged onto the linen.

"You're...not..." His voice failed him.

Great-Aunt Wynchester added more drops of oil from her vial and proceeded to erase every trace of age from her face, neck, and hands.

A lad of perhaps five and twenty years grinned cheekily back at him.

Lawrence could not breathe. Had he thought discovering "poor orphans" living in luxury to be humiliating? There was no brash, clueless Great-Aunt Wynchester. It was just another lie his self-important, unfounded assumptions had let him believe without question.

"Tommy?" he said hoarsely.

"Thomasina," the lad said, and Lawrence revised his opinion yet again.

Not a lad but a young woman. With sharp cheekbones, a stylish male coiffure, and laughing brown eyes.

"But you can call me Tommy," she said. "Everyone who knows me does."

He gaped at her. "I can't believe my eyes."

"Wigs and cosmetics," she explained. "It's a bother to keep long hair pinned up against one's head, so the practical thing was to lop it off."

"Also it's easier to sneak into the reporters' gallery as a man," Elizabeth murmured.

Belatedly, Lawrence remembered Great-Aunt Wynchester saying she'd never stuff herself into a dusty attic. He now realized why: she didn't have to.

"Absolutely," Tommy agreed. "Being a man is the best part."

"I want to die," Lawrence mumbled into his palms.

"You gammoned yourself," Jacob pointed out. "The ruse would never have worked if you didn't have such abysmal preconceived notions about the elderly and us."

Tommy nodded. "You believed me to be frail and help-less, so I was. You believed Wynchesters to be ill-mannered, embarrassing bumpkins, so we were. What say you to that, impertinent pup?"

"God save me." He sank deeper into his plush, expertly carved chair. "I let you call me that in front of witnesses."

She patted his hand. "Never underestimate an old lady."

Ears burning, he lifted his face from his hands. "You let me ply you with compliments and fish for family stories about Chloe."

"All lies," Tommy agreed cheerfully.

"Except for the meat pies," Chloe added.

"Now that Faircliffe knows, what are we to do?" Graham asked. "Is this the end of Great-Aunt Wynchester?"

"Never!" Elizabeth protested. "Great-Aunt Wynchester is my favorite sprightly old bird."

"Pah, sprightly grandmother types have untimely deaths all the time." Tommy's eyes widened. "Have Chloe tell you about the horrible collection of German fairy tales at the reading circle. At least I was unmasked by a duke rather than pecked to pieces by crows."

"Crows are very intelligent," Jacob said. "I've trained mine to do dozens of tricks."

"Are they assassin crows?" Graham asked politely.

Jacob considered. "Not yet."

"Then they have nothing to do with Great-Aunt Wynchester's delicate constitution. Only one thing does." Graham turned to Lawrence. "Well, Your Grace? Can you keep a wee family secret?"

Five bright gazes fixed in Lawrence's direction.

Warmth filled his chest. They were trusting him with a secret—trusting his word that he would keep it—because *Chloe* trusted him. Treating him like family, if only for this moment.

"I suppose," he said as casually as he could. "Great-Aunt Wynchester is safe to continue terrorizing the streets of London."

"Huzzah!" Thomasina tossed her cosmetic-covered serviette into the air.

Chloe's smile melted Lawrence's insides.

She was sensational. Her siblings were astonishing and awe-inspiring. They accepted one another for who and how they were, disguises and strange pets and all.

Despite Chloe only being able to trace her history back to a basket discarded on an orphanage's steps, she had a huge, loving family that anyone would yearn to be part of. Irreverent, always laughing. The sort that would stand up for one another at any cost.

Despite being able to trace *his* lineage back eight generations to the first Duke of Faircliffe, Lawrence had...

Nothing.

A clatter in the corridor caused everyone's attention to swing to the doorway.

"It's Marjorie!" Tommy said in delight.

"Come and sit with us," Jacob called.

Marjorie did not leave the doorway.

"Who is this?" she asked, her voice loud and her eyes directed toward Graham.

"I'm the Duke of Faircliffe," Lawrence responded, presuming she meant him.

She didn't react.

Chloe waved in his direction. "That's the Duke of Faircliffe."

Hadn't he just said so?

Marjorie's eyes lit up. "We have our painting?"

"Not yet," Elizabeth said. "Help us torture him until he agrees to hand it over."

"I like torture," Marjorie said cheerfully, then took the seat farthest from Jacob. "I dislike birds at the dinner table."

"I forgot about Sir Galahad." Jacob dashed from the room with the bird still on his shoulder, only to return seconds later, parrot-free.

Marjorie wrinkled her nose at Lawrence. "She said you were handsome."

Chloe closed her eyes. "Marjorie, this is not the moment."

"Er . . ." The back of Lawrence's neck heated up. "Sorry to disappoint."

Marjorie considered him. "You're *very* handsome. If I painted portraits, I would paint yours."

He wasn't certain what to do with this information. "Why don't you paint people?"

"I prefer landscapes. What do *you* paint?"

"Marjorie," Graham interrupted gently. "Not everyone lives and breathes art."

"Lawrence does," Chloe said.

Jacob wiggled his brows. "*Lawrence* does, does he?"

"Er, Faircliffe," Chloe corrected quickly. "His Grace. Who has our painting. I hope."

That got their attention. All their eyes turned to him at once.

Elizabeth tapped her fingers on her sword stick. "*Do* you have it?"

"I do," he admitted. "Why are there two copies?"

"Who knows? We only care about *ours*." Chloe's eyes were fierce. "It's a piece of Bean and an intrinsic part of who we are. *Puck & Family* is *us*."

All six siblings touched their fingertips to their hearts, then raised them to the sky.

How Lawrence yearned to be part of such a tight-knit, caring group. To know what it was like to care for someone so much and be an integral piece of something bigger than oneself. To love unconditionally and be loved unconditionally in return.

"Well?" Great-Aunt—or, rather, Tommy prodded. "Will you return our painting?"

He certainly couldn't hold on to something that meant that much to them. Particularly when it was an object that no longer belonged to him.

Lawrence nodded tightly. "I shall."

They erupted in cheers and began talking over each other at once.

He watched them make plans amongst themselves in silence, as if he were a distant observer in a lonely theatre box gazing wistfully down at a fantasy world below.

When he handed over the painting, that would be it. The Wynchesters wouldn't need him anymore.

They had never been interested in him from the start.

27

As soon as Lawrence returned home, he hurried to the library. This was where he'd brought all of the artwork his wastrel father hadn't managed to lose over a whist table. Or, apparently, sold off to his friends.

The majority of the paintings on the walls had come from the country seat. The rest had hung throughout the town house. They had even found a handful of forgotten paintings tucked away behind a sideboard in his father's study. Lawrence had wondered why.

He now supposed that his father had removed them from the walls because he intended to sell them. The selections made sense: the rejected paintings had unusual subjects for an aristocratic household. Besides, if Father happened to have a near duplicate of the same painting, why bother to keep both?

Which begged the question: Where *was* the duplicate? Neither Lawrence nor the staff had come across any additional artwork, or it would be displayed here on the library walls.

He thought back to the night of his father's accident. Father was impulsive and reckless in all things. Apparently, the duke had been fleeing the scene of a crime, having just stolen a painting from the Wynchesters. He'd driven himself in a curricle that did not survive the crash.

A broken axle had thrown Father to the street, where one of the horses kicked his stomach and his leg. Lawrence was eating supper alone in the dining room when the front door banged open and the corridor filled with heavy footsteps and panicked voices.

That was when Lawrence glimpsed the painting. It would not have registered, had Father not seemed more concerned about its safety than the state of his fractured limb. Lawrence summoned a surgeon to inspect the injured leg. Father seemed fine. Once his leg was splinted, he took the framed painting into his study and did not emerge for hours.

By the third morning the old man could barely speak. He was drowsy and nauseated, and his limbs had swollen alarmingly. The sore leg was not the gravest concern after all. When the horse kicked Father's midsection, organs began to fail inside. There was nothing the surgeon could do. That night, Father was gone.

The painting must still be in his study.

Lawrence strode from the library to investigate at once.

The study had been dusted and swept but otherwise it was still the way Father had left it. A pile of journals here, a deck of cards there, a stoppered bottle of brandy next to an empty glass. The bare shelf where the cherub vase had once stood. Nothing on the walls.

He turned in a circle. Father had taken the painting without permission. He would have hidden it from view. Perhaps even removed the canvas from its frame.

Lawrence would find it.

Blood rushing in his ears, he lit every candle and sconce in the room. He was no longer willing to live beneath his father's shadow.

He flung open drawers, yanked tables aside, tossed papers about. The study was not a shrine. He could tear down the walls with his bare hands if he wished.

But he didn't have to.

Lawrence pulled up short and sent a considering glance toward the escritoire.

Years earlier he had glimpsed one of his father's hiding places on one of his many childhood visits. Lawrence had sat unnoticed in the corner, attempting to be close to a father who would rather find his pleasures anywhere but at home.

This had to be it. He moved the old duke's chair out of the way and dropped to the worn floor beneath the large walnut desk.

It had been handcrafted specifically for Father. There was a writing shelf that rolled out just above one's knees, and behind that a narrow compartment only six inches wide, sealed with a hidden sliding lock.

With searching fingers, Lawrence pushed the moving parts until the lock disengaged. A narrow door swung open. A handful of papers fell to the floor, followed by a rolled canvas tied with twine.

He had found it!

His heart pounded as he collected the fallen objects and withdrew from beneath the desk. He placed them all on the mahogany surface.

Painting first.

He untied the twine and unrolled the canvas. It looked exactly like the one he'd given to Miss York. Almost exactly. There were a few subtle differences—so subtle, Lawrence might never have noticed them had he not spent every spare moment of his time in the library, studying its remaining works of art. He tied the canvas up in a neat scroll once more and reached for the topmost parchment. It was a letter.

Any guilt he felt over reading his father's correspondence had disappeared eight months before, when Lawrence inherited the dukedom and the extent of his father's debts came to light. He hoped these weren't more debts waiting to be repaid.

He scanned the letter's contents in growing horror.

Your Grace,

Where are the papers of provenance? You said I would have them within three weeks, and it has been two years. I would not have made a fuss, but Albus Roth has made a name for himself in artistic circles. I may one day wish to sell "The Three Witches of Macbeth" at a profit, and will not be able to do so without the appropriate documentation. I implore you to surrender those papers at once.

Mr. John Wagner
Ribblesdale

Lawrence's fingers trembled. Mr. Wagner could not possess *The Three Witches of* Macbeth. The framed canvas was hanging on the library wall.

Where are the papers of provenance?

Lawrence pushed the rest of the letters aside and picked up one of the documents. Documents of provenance for *Titus Andronicus*. He grabbed another. Provenance for *Robin Goodfellow in the Forest with Fairies*. He reached for the next. *The Three Witches of* Macbeth.

That blackguard! Lawrence's father hadn't sold redundant pieces of art. His father had been selling *forgeries*.

That was why the paintings had been hidden behind the sideboard and the papers of provenance were tucked away in a secret drawer. His flesh went cold. He stared down at the letter.

Lawrence had never heard of a Mr. John Wagner.

Ribblesdale was more than two hundred miles away.

Likely that was by design. Father would not have chosen buyers with the means to make his life uncomfortable were the deception uncovered. That he'd involved Baron Vanderbean must have been an act of desperation.

Or was it? Nineteen years ago, the baron had just arrived in England. He was reclusive and eccentric, and, as Lawrence vaguely recalled, the gossips assumed the baron would soon return to Balcovia.

That he had made a home here in London instead would have initially been a blow to Father's plans, but once it was clear Vanderbean was not fussed in the least about pesky details like provenance, it was no wonder that Father had tried to take advantage of him again and again.

Until Albus Roth hosted his first public exhibition, and the paintings turned important overnight. Each piece of art became evidence of a crime. Father would have been desperate to switch the forgery for the original before the Wynchesters uncovered his deception.

Not just the Wynchesters . . . *all* of the innocent people the duke had swindled.

Lawrence scrubbed his face with his hands. The first thing he needed to do was get the papers—and the real paintings—to their rightful owners.

And hope a sincere apology would make up for years of deception.

28

⚜

*C*hloe curled up in her favorite window seat with a copy of *Evelina*, but her mind was far from the reading circle. Lawrence had said he would return their painting, but days had passed with no sign of him. It was impossible to concentrate on fiction when reality was so uncertain.

With a crackle of iron wheels on gravel, a coach came to a rest in front of her house.

She pressed her fingertips to the window. It was Lawrence!

He fed a bit of carrot to Elderberry and Mango, then cupped his hand over his eyes and turned his face up toward the house as if scanning windows in search of Chloe. Lawrence combed his fingers through his hair. It was immediately ruffled again by the wind. He straightened his cravat and smoothed his lapels and waistcoat.

Chloe smiled. She had touched those lapels, unbuttoned that waistcoat. She couldn't wait to touch them again.

She marked her page with a pink silk ribbon and dashed to meet him.

As she stepped into the sunlight, he glanced up and saw her. His wide smile lit his blue eyes with desire and sent a jolt of answering electricity streaking along her skin.

"Did you bring our painting?" she asked.

He held out his arms. "Yes."

"In that case..." She launched herself into his embrace.

His body was warm, the contours of his muscles familiar. She lay her cheek against him and breathed in the smell of his skin. His swift heartbeat kept time with hers.

The clock ticked too quickly for them both.

She peered up at him. "I didn't know you were coming."

His eyes twinkled. "I wanted to see what it felt like to appear on your doorstep unannounced. Should I have brought a false Great-Uncle?"

"Tommy would have been excellent in the role. If you think you found her convincing as Great-Aunt Wynchester..."

He grimaced. "Don't tell me she could take one stroll down my Hall of Portraits and make herself up like the sixth Duke of Faircliffe."

"All right." Chloe batted her eyelashes. "I won't tell you."

He groaned. "She's probably already done so."

"And worse," Chloe promised, then pantomimed sewing her lips closed.

"What about you?" His smile was warm, his gaze indulgent. One could easily imagine herself adored. "What were you doing when I arrived?"

"Reading in my favorite nook."

He retrieved a package from the interior of his coach. "I would love to see your nook."

She pointed. "I would love to see *that*."

"In that case..." He offered her his arm. "Shall we?"

She was tempted to snatch the canvas out of his other hand and sprint into the house to spread the word. Walking the twenty feet up the path at a sedate pace would surely be the death of her.

The moment they crossed the threshold, she called out to her siblings.

Most were in the dining room enjoying a midafternoon repast. The others arrived within the space of a breath.

Lawrence handed Chloe a canvas secured with twine.

She untied the knot and unrolled the canvas on a clear section of the table.

Everyone crowded around to see themselves dancing with Puck once again. A crow of delight filled the room.

"It *is* our portrait," Marjorie pronounced, assuaging the last of their doubts. If a single brushstroke had been out of place, she would have noticed at once.

"And technically"—Lawrence pressed his lips together in a grimace, then pushed on—"a forgery."

"What?" Six startled faces turned to his.

"You were right when you said my father was a wastrel who would sell anything to cover his gambling debts." Lawrence winced. "Or at least *claim* he'd sold it. He knew better than to peddle a false Rembrandt, so he chose an unknown new artist named Albus Roth."

"I adore Albus Roth," said Marjorie. "He had his first major exhibition last year."

Tommy nodded. "That's what we were talking about the night . . . your father . . ."

"No wonder he seemed agitated. His grand scheme was unraveling right before his eyes." Lawrence handed Chloe a folded document. "Here are the papers of provenance that should have been yours all along—as well as the real painting. The canvas you had on the wall was the false one. I owe you all an enormous apology."

The siblings exchanged glances.

"The one we've had on the wall all these years *is* the real one to us," Elizabeth said. "You can have the original back if you like."

"At a significantly higher price," Jacob added.

"No, thank you." Lawrence sighed. "I won't be in a position to purchase art for a very long time."

Chloe looked at her siblings. "Shall I give him back his vase?"

"Oh, I don't know." Graham lifted the document of provenance by the corner. "Shouldn't we deliver this evidence to the Bow Street Runners?"

Lawrence's cheeks paled.

Tommy and Graham snorted with laughter.

"I delivered all of the originals to the proper owners," Lawrence said in a rush. "I sent papers of provenance as well as a personal apology for my father's 'confusion'—"

"They're teasing," Chloe assured him. "Your father was wrong and so were you, so they haven't yet forgiven you...but your secret is safe with us."

Elizabeth scooped up the canvas. "Who's going to help return Puck to his place of honor?"

"Me!" the siblings cried in unison, then clattered up the stairs, leaving Chloe and Lawrence alone in the dining room.

"Come on, then." She walked past the stairs. "I brought your vase over here."

Before she could hand it to him, he rushed over to the mantel and lifted the glass angel reverently, as though the empty vase meant as much to him as the *Puck & Family* portrait meant to the Wynchesters.

Perhaps it did.

"I thought my father would never part with this." His voice was rough with emotion. "It seems there was much about the duke that I did not know. I am glad to have this back."

"As am I." She clasped her hands behind her back. "Now that we both have what we want, I suppose there's nothing to keep you here."

"Isn't there?" He returned the vase to the side table with

extra care, then turned back to face her. "There's nowhere I'd rather be than with you."

Before she could form a coherent reply, he cupped her face in his hands and kissed her.

She ran her palms up his sides, over his shoulders. Not just feeling him, but savoring the hard planes of his body, finding it familiar and wondrous all at once. He could leave now if he wanted. But what he wanted was her. And she could never have too much of him.

His body felt perfect pressed against her. Big and strong in the best possible way. His heat comforting, his embrace protective.

It was almost enough to make her believe he thought her just as worthy of his attentions as the debutantes and heiresses of the haut ton.

But she didn't want almost.

She wanted the real thing.

Her brother Jacob burst into the sitting room wearing two oversized leather gloves, a full-body leather apron, and a worried expression.

She and Lawrence sprang apart.

Jacob peered around them. "Have you seen Hydra?"

"Is that the python?" she asked, still trying to catch her breath.

"No, Hydra is a hamster." He paused. "Why? Have you seen a python?"

"I have not seen a python. Should we be looking for a python?"

He waved a gloved hand. "No, no. It's only Hydra who's gone missing."

"Have you asked Tiglet?" Lawrence suggested.

Jacob glared at him. "Tiglet is well trained and well fed. Tiglet would *never*..."

But he began edging toward the door.

"If all you're missing is a hamster," Chloe inquired, "why are you wearing protective armor?"

"Oh, this." He flapped his oversized gloves dismissively at his leather apron. "I've a few new creatures to train, and the first lesson is teaching the beasts not to bite."

Lawrence's brow furrowed. "Is it working?"

"Not yet," Jacob said, his cheerful confidence undaunted. "Don't be surprised if this is my ensemble for the next few days."

With that, he vanished down the corridor.

Lawrence looked at Chloe. "How certain are you that there's no python on the loose?"

"Eighty percent," she assured him, and sank into a plush chair. "Maybe closer to sixty-five."

He glanced beneath the chair across from her before settling gingerly on the cushion. "Do you have extra leather gloves I could borrow?"

"Only silk. Leather makes it difficult to palm things."

At his startled expression, she could not contain a laugh. In a million years she would never have predicted that she would one day freely admit her skill at nicking things to the Duke of Faircliffe.

He sat upright. "Show me."

Oh, why not? She pulled a sovereign from one of her pockets. Gold flashed as she flipped it between her fingers, over, under, back again, over, under...

"Goodness—it's gone!" She showed Lawrence her empty hands.

"Where did it go?" he demanded.

She lifted a shoulder. "Nowhere."

With a snap of her fingers, there was the coin again, its worn edges flipping over her knuckles in a metallic blur.

The duke was kneeling before her in seconds. "Teach me."

She snapped her fingers again, and the old sovereign disappeared. "Do you have your own coin?"

He narrowed his eyes. "Is this a swindle where you take it from me if I say yes?"

She batted her eyelashes. "Find out."

He fished in his pocket and pulled out a shilling. "Will this do?"

The thin silver coin lay in the center of his palm.

She waved her hand slowly over the top of his as if sensing the shilling's spiritual emanations, then wrinkled her face in confusion.

His eyes flicked to hers.

Ha! That was all the time she needed. Chloe flung herself back onto her cushion and picked up her book. "I thought you said you had a shilling."

"It *is* a shilling. It's—" A sound of baffled consternation choked in his throat. "I felt nothing! The shilling was there, and now it's gone."

"That's how it used to feel every time I had money: Poof! Gone again."

His eyes were still wide. "But how did you *do* it?"

She sat back up, unable to hide her grin. "It would be irresponsible of me to teach you that trick. I'll show you a different one. Have you another shilling?"

He crossed his arms over his wide chest. "Not for you."

"Good," she said with a laugh. "You're learning."

She touched his face and kissed him. When she pulled her hand away, his shilling was once again in her palm.

"Watch this." She adjusted the muscles of her hand so that the shilling caught right in the center of her palm. "It's delicate," she warned him. "If your fingers are loose enough to appear natural, the slightest bump could dislodge your coin."

She turned her hand over so the palm faced downward.

"It doesn't look like you're hiding anything," he said in awe. "Just a woman holding out her hand to be kissed."

She arched a brow. "Then kiss it."

He did.

When he leaned back, she turned over her palm. It now contained his shilling and the handkerchief she'd just nicked from his lapel.

He burst out laughing. "All right, braggart. Let me try."

She tucked his handkerchief into her bodice and handed him back his shilling.

He spent the next ten minutes repeatedly picking it up from the floor, then finally chucked it over his shoulder with an aggrieved sigh. "There. It disappeared."

Chloe wiped away tears of silent laughter. "Don't lose hope. All skills worth mastering require practice."

He looked aggrieved. "How long did it take you?"

"Days to hide a coin reliably," she admitted. "I started with buttons scavenged along the Thames. I had smaller hands then, but buttons come in all sorts of weights and sizes, just as coins do, so it was good practice. Later, Tommy would hide buttons in her bed or on her person and I would have to nick them without her noticing to win the game."

"Tommy was with you back then?"

"Tommy has been with me for as long as I can remember." Thank heavens for it. "Her cot was next to mine at the orphanage. There weren't many places to hide things, since we had no true possessions, but Tommy was resourceful and made me work for every button."

"Did you flip them the way you did with the coin?"

"No." Chloe made the sovereign fly through her fingers, then vanish again. "That came later, once I had coins to practice with."

His brow creased. "I didn't know orphanages trusted their charges with actual money."

"They don't," she said flatly. "I stole them from the pockets of rich passersby too busy being important to notice a hungry urchin by their side."

She expected him to judge her harshly for her crimes. He would have been one of the wealthy nobs. If an entire rookery was an eyesore to the ton, a skinny eight-year-old girl would have been just another blemish on their great city. Refuse spoiling the view until the street sweepers came to brush it out of sight.

"I don't blame you," he said. "There's no force more powerful than desperation."

A moment of silence stretched between them.

She let out a slow breath.

"It was farthings at first." Chloe gave a lopsided smile she doubted reached her eyes. "I didn't want to take *much*— not enough to be missed, but enough to make a difference to me. Limiting my bounty also made it more of a game. If I accidentally nicked a coin of greater value, I had to find some way to put it back. Soon I could tell the denomination with the barest brush of my finger. I no longer made mistakes. It wasn't a game anymore."

"What was it?"

"Survival." Ironic, since thievery was punishable by execution.

Those farthings and halfpennies kept the pangs of hunger at bay not just for her and Tommy but for several other children in the orphanage with protruding ribs and empty bellies. How she'd dreamed of one day becoming a lady of quality with a reticule full of gold! The first thing she'd buy with her riches was a meat pie for every hungry mouth.

"It was so little," she said. "But I did it anyway. It was the best I could do."

"I imagine it was everything," he replied. "You see yourself as powerless, but you were powerful. Then and now."

"Invisible," she corrected. "You have a storied family, and roots."

"I may be a tree, but you're the wind. Strong enough to shake the dead leaves from my branches, to carry pollen to the spring flowers. Air is invisible but essential." He met her eyes. "Without air, I can't breathe."

Chloe swallowed hard. She could think of nothing to say in response to such a statement. Her heart was beating so fast, it felt like a single roll of thunder rather than separate beats. Perhaps it wasn't thunder at all but the rumble of an earthquake before the volcano erupted, changing the world around it forever.

She'd felt like that once before. Twenty years ago next summer.

"Do you know how I met Bean? He drove past the orphanage in a flashy racing phaeton, looking smart and rich and fashionable. *Everybody* looked at him. It was impossible not to." She wiggled her brows. "Then he tied the carriage outside St. Giles's church and disappeared inside like a proper fool."

Lawrence groaned. "Please tell me you did not steal his phaeton."

"Of *course* I did." She straightened her spine with mock indignation. "Who abandons a racing carriage in a rookery?"

He covered his face with his hand. "How old were you? Could you drive?"

"Ten, and I'd never led horses in my life. Or even been *inside* of a carriage, as far as I knew. It took three tries to climb up into that phaeton. Its wheels were as tall as I was. The high perch felt like sitting on a throne on top of the world. I was dying to take it for a ride. The reins were still tied to a post, so I slipped back down to grab them. Before I could, Bean's hand trapped my wrist like a vise."

Lawrence's face blanched. "Did the baron threaten you with the magistrate?"

"The opposite. He drove me to the Puss & Goose and bought me a hot meal so ample, I couldn't finish it. And then he gave me this." The sovereign flashed between her fingers. "He told me to spend it on whatever I wanted, and when I needed another, just to ask."

"You didn't spend it?"

Her lungs caught in remembrance. "I couldn't. It was the first time I'd held a coin I hadn't had to steal first. The first time I possessed money of my own, free and clear."

"What did you do?"

"Nothing." She laughed and made the coin vanish. "I slid the coin into a hidden bag here, next to my heart." She tapped her chest. "I saw Bean again the following week outside the church. This time with a coach and a driver."

"Did he ask you what you did with the coin?"

"I expected him to, but he did not. Later he told me that was because it was now my money, not his, and he no longer had any business in the matter." Her throat pricked with heat. "He was always saying things like that. Treating us like people, letting us be in control of our own lives."

"Did he give you another coin?"

She shook her head. "He made me an offer. He said he had always wanted to be a father. His house was as big as a castle, full of silence and empty rooms. If I thought being a pretend daughter might suit me, I was welcome to pick any room I wished and make it my own. There would be fresh food and hot baths and clean clothes to wear. I'd have pin money that would be mine alone, no questions asked. And if I found I didn't like it, I was free to leave."

"It must have sounded like heaven," Lawrence admitted. "No wonder you said yes."

She stared at him. "I did not say yes. I would be the first child he fostered. It all sounded too good to be true. Possibly sordid."

"Then...how...?" he stammered.

"I did not fully trust Bean, but I *knew* the orphanage was horrid. I would have starved if I hadn't picked pockets, and there were others who faced fates worse than that. Sometimes risk is the only path to reward. If Bean *was* a good man—or at least better than the orphanage—my best friend deserved the same opportunity." A half smile curved her lips at the memory, and her throat grew thick. "The next time I saw him, I said, 'Only if Tommy comes with me.'"

29

*L*awrence gazed at Chloe and imagined her as a little girl whose love for a friend was so strong, she'd rather starve together than live a life of comfort without her.

There was no need to imagine. Chloe was still that woman today.

All of the Wynchesters had mettle.

Lawrence did not know the story of how they'd all found each other, but he had no doubt "Not without Tommy" had led to "Not without Jacob" and then to "Not without Marjorie" and so on, the bond becoming even more unbreakable with every new link in the chain.

Their love was too big to fit in a single heart. They had no choice but to share it with each other.

"You seem happy here," he said. "All of your siblings do."

And why not? They had a large, beautiful house with a large, beautiful garden. Staff, several carriages, apparently a menagerie of carnivorous beasts...

"We're very happy." Her joy lit her face. "I wouldn't trade this life for anything."

Or for anyone. Like him. He could scarcely blame her. If he'd been a Wynchester instead of a duke, he'd rather live happy and free than titled and constrained.

A union with Lawrence would be the opposite of comfortable. He could not *afford* to wed a bride who was anything short of fantastically wealthy—not without their home crumbling down about their children's ears.

He needed things Chloe could not provide, and she needed a man he couldn't be. No matter how much he might wish to. A wise man would walk away before both of their hearts broke.

Yet all Lawrence wanted was to stay. To belong to Chloe, and for her to belong to him. To have these idyllic moments be his real life, not a temporary reprieve from harsh reality. To not have his duties be so in conflict with his heart.

"Chloe says you want to paint."

He jerked up his head to see the smallest Wynchester hovering just outside the doorway. Marjorie's wisp of a frame was in shadow, but her green eyes were luminous. For such a slight woman, her voice was impressively loud.

"Er…" he replied.

She didn't blink. "I made you a studio. It's on the left, next to mine. You can use anything you find there."

Her pronouncement made, she vanished from the corridor before Lawrence could compose some way to decline gracefully.

"I don't paint." His hands felt strangely clammy. "I've never held a brush or stretched a canvas. I don't know how. Why would she…?"

Chloe looked at him quizzically. "Because that's what Wynchesters do. Well, once they've decided to keep someone."

His mouth went dry. "What did you say?"

"Marjorie wants to make you an honorary Wynchester."

His chest tightened with fierce yearning.

"One can become an honorary Wynchester?" he stammered.

Her eyes laughed at him. "We're all honorary Wynchesters.

But don't get your hopes up. Marjorie might have forgiven you, but it won't be easy to win the others' trust."

Fair enough. Lawrence nodded his understanding. After how he had treated the family, he deserved to be mistrusted. All he could do now was prove what kind of man he intended to be.

Chloe pushed to her feet. "Shall we?"

He didn't move. Nervousness crawled along his skin. "Shall we visit the art studio your sister made for the duke she wants to adopt like a stray puppy?"

She patted his shoulder. "You do such a marvelous job rephrasing things that I've either just said or already know about."

His face flushed. "It's a nervous habit. I summarize facts whenever I don't know what to say. Like now, for instance."

She looked hurt. "Marjorie and I won't judge you. We're not Almack's or Parliament. You can go in alone if you like and toss every one of your creations into a fire before you leave."

Could he? Would he?

Art had always been the great "if." If he hadn't been heir to a dukedom, he'd have been a painter. If the family fortune were intact, painting would be his first hobby.

But if he tried and failed, he would have no dreams left.

"I have something for you as well," Chloe said, then hesitated. "I wasn't certain when I should give it to you, or whether I even would. But perhaps now is the time."

"Is it a python?" he said hopefully. "I've heard those can swallow men whole."

"It is not a python." She produced a small rectangle of paper seemingly from midair. "It's a calling card."

He took it in both hands. The text contained only two words: "Jack Smith."

He tried to make sense of it. "Who is Jack Smith?"

"*You* are, if it makes it better."

Something in her eyes indicated she understood his reluctance as well as he did. Both he and Chloe longed to be recognized and appreciated for who they were, not for what they portrayed themselves to be.

"Things are always less complicated for Jane Brown than they are for Chloe Wynchester," she continued. "If it all goes horribly awry, I tuck her back into my basket as though the incident never occurred. After all, it wasn't *I* who embarrassed myself horribly. It was Jane Brown, who cannot hurt me because she doesn't exist." She bit her lip. "Sometimes being someone else is the easiest way to be yourself."

He gazed at the card in his hands. He supposed Jack Smith would have no problem exposing himself as a talentless fool in front of the woman he most wished to impress.

But then again, neither should Lawrence Gosling, eighth Duke of Faircliffe. He might have been raised to be anxious and lonely and overthink himself into knots, but he was not a coward.

He slid the card into his waistcoat pocket. "All right. But I'll go as Lawrence."

"Would you like me to join you as your muse and model?" She gave him a saucy wink. "Perhaps the inspiration for a lewd portrait?"

She wasn't serious ... was she? This idea sounded better by the second.

He ran behind her up the stairs to the third floor, where Chloe led him to a small room on the left. He stared in wonder.

Generous windows with curtains tied open filled the well-appointed interior with sunlight. Five easels with stretched canvases stood at inviting angles. There were tables with paints and rags and turpentine, an artfully arranged collection of objects to serve as the subject of a still life, and a plush green chaise longue, empty but for its cushions.

Chloe sat in the center and affected an artful pose. "Perfect for a very serious portrait of a very serious woman. Should I hold a bouquet of flowers? Or perhaps the loaf of bread?"

Lawrence felt giddy, as though he were up in this attic as his childhood self and had just received more than he had ever hoped for on his birthday. This studio was every bit the equal of professional studios used by portrait artists—and Marjorie had prepared it as a gift for him.

He had no way to repay her other than to enjoy every moment.

"I'll start by attempting to paint a still life," he decided, and turned to the blank canvas.

He hadn't the least idea how to mix paints, but Marjorie had already done so for him. There were half a dozen colors in little jars on a long table, next to a collection of palettes and a wide variety of brushes.

He chose a brush at random, then a palette, then yellow as his first color. Marjorie had placed a ceramic jug in the center of the scene. Lawrence would start there.

Chloe leaned back on the chaise longue to watch.

Over the next hour he dragged all five easels over to the arrangement for the still life to capture some semblance of what he saw. None of his efforts was recognizable as the artful display before him.

Yet he'd never had more fun in his life.

He scrubbed the paint from his fingers, then reached to pull Chloe into a kiss. Her mouth opened beneath his, welcoming him, granting him another wish. Every bit of the joy bursting within him was her fault. She dragged him from where he was most comfortable and set him free, again and again. His first attempts were dreadful, but it didn't matter as long as he was doing what he loved.

And he *was* doing what he loved. Standing here, kissing Chloe, holding her as though they would never need to part. The thought was unbearable. He loved her more than paint. More than his library. More than anything yet to be invented. He was not ready to let her go.

He might never be ready.

When he started to lead her toward the chaise longue, she placed her hand on his chest to stop him. Color came to her cheeks.

"Not here," she murmured. "My siblings are all around us."

"You're right." He glanced about appraisingly. "I need my own studio, posthaste."

She grinned at him shyly. "You like your gift?"

"I adore my gift." He ducked his head to give her another kiss. What he adored was Chloe. "Come home with me. There will be no siblings there."

She wrapped her arms about his neck. "Oh? Then what might you have to entertain me?"

"A bed." He let her see the passion in his eyes and hoped the love there didn't shine through, too. She already held all of the power. "And perhaps something else you might like."

She wiggled her brows and placed her hand in his. "Show me."

30

❦

Chloe and Lawrence stumbled through his bedchamber door in each other's arms. The blue-and-gold room was dominated by a large canopy bed in the center. She couldn't wait to make use of it. Now that her family had begun to accept him, there was no use hiding how much she desired him.

"I have an idea," she told him.

"So do I." He waggled his eyebrows meaningfully. "Many, many naked ideas."

"Then allow me to offer some motivation to go with them." She flashed a gold guinea between her fingers, then placed it in his palm.

His brow lined in confusion. "What's this?"

"Your second lesson." She grinned at him. "Make it disappear, and you can make an item of my clothing disappear."

He brightened. "This is my favorite lesson."

"And if I steal it from you"—she kissed the tip of his nose, then revealed that the guinea was out of his palm and into her own—"I may remove an item of *your* clothing."

"This is a very unfair game," he scolded her. "I accept the terms."

She unbuttoned his tailcoat and tossed it aside. His sleeves billowed out into a delicious state of undress. "Your turn."

He placed the coin in the center of his palm and pressed it in deep. When he turned his hand upside down, the guinea remained hidden for the space of a breath, then tumbled to the floor.

"I'll allow it," she said magnanimously. "Just this once."

"Shift," he said without hesitation.

She smacked his chest. "I can't take off my shift without first removing my gown and my stays."

"Your rules," he replied innocently. "I'm just playing by them."

She had invented this game, and she would show him just how well she played it. Rather than remove her own clothing, she arched her brow. His cravat fell to the carpet.

His mouth dropped. "When did you remove— How could—"

"Pick again." She ran a finger down the front of his waistcoat and slipped the guinea inside the pocket. When she splayed her fingers across the muscled planes of his chest, she could feel his heart pounding beneath her palm.

"Gown," he said, his voice a velvet purr. "Definitely gown."

She turned around and let him untie the laces until the thin sarcenet slid from her shoulders and down to her ankles. Gooseflesh tickled lightly up her arms. He pressed light kisses to her nape, from the top of her spine down her bare skin, until he was stopped by the collar of her shift. Her breasts tightened, and her head lolled to one side in pleasure. Only when he lifted his lips did she step out of the pool of periwinkle twill.

"My turn." She beckoned him closer to the canopy bed.

"It's not your turn," he protested. "I have the guinea. You put it in my pocket."

"Did I?" She held up the gold coin. "Boots, please."

He yanked off his Hessian boots at speed, then snatched the guinea from her hands. "My turn."

As before, he placed the coin in the center of his palm with almost comical concentration, then gently, ever so carefully, turned his hand upside down.

The guinea clattered to the floor.

"Boots," he commanded.

Before she could chide him for failing to properly conceal the coin—or bend over to remove her boots herself—Lawrence was on his knees between her legs, untying the laces himself.

Ostensibly untying the laces.

While his hands were making slow work of untying her half boots, his mouth pressed lazy, suggestive kisses through the thin linen of her shift to her bare hips and thighs beneath. Her pulse leapt as if to meet him there, at the place where his sinful mouth met her heated flesh. She gripped one of the canopy posts for balance. His onslaught of decadent kisses caused her eyes to flutter closed.

When at last he rose to his feet with his hand at chest level, she was too dazed with pleasure to understand the strange gesture he was making.

"Stays," he said, his voice husky.

It was then that she realized he'd fumbled the guinea on purpose so that he would be the one to pick it up and have the advantage of two turns in a row.

"Very good," she said in appreciation, and turned her derrière toward his groin. The hard length of him pressed against her, potent and promising. She could not wait to feel him between her legs, without any layers to separate them.

As he loosened her stays and slid them over her hips, he peppered slow kisses from beneath her ear, down the curve of her neck, to her shoulder. She slipped the coin from him without him noticing, and almost lost control of it herself when his open mouth brushed the side of her breast, so close to her peaked nipples.

She kicked the whalebone stays aside with her stockinged toes and held up the guinea, her words almost too breathy to be understood. "Waistcoat."

With a suggestive, knowing smile, he unbuttoned the fastenings and shrugged off the embroidered blue silk, then held out his hand for the coin.

She placed the guinea in his palm.

He arranged the coin as best he could, tensing his fingers this way and that to try to form a better hold and never quite succeeding. She gave a loud hiccup and burst out laughing. He sent her a quelling look, which only made her hiccup again. He turned over his hand.

The coin didn't fall.

He glanced up at her, wide-eyed.

She held up the guinea between two fingers. "Shirt, please."

"What—? How—?" He flipped over his empty hand and glowered at his traitorous palm. "You *hiccuped* it from me?"

With an unrepentant grin, she tugged his linen shirt free from his waistband. Ever so slowly, she pushed the hem up over the flat planes of his stomach, pressing a soft kiss to each muscle in turn until at last he pulled the rest over his head and flung it out of sight.

He took the coin from her and placed it back in his palm, turning sideways to ensure it remained out of her reach for the length of his trick. It lasted several seconds this time before tumbling free.

"*Shift,*" he demanded with obvious pleasure. "Allow me."

He knelt before her again, this time lowering his head all the way to her hem. Torturously, he kissed each inch of bare skin he exposed as he tugged the thin fabric higher and higher.

When he reached the juncture between her legs, his mouth lingered there.

She grasped the bedpost to keep from falling over and

parted her trembling legs to give his mouth full access. He licked and swirled, nibbled and teased. Her knees could barely keep her upright as the pressure built higher and higher.

Without pausing his erotic kiss, his hands continued higher to reach her breasts. She all but pressed them into his palms, greedy for every wicked sensation he wrested from her. His fingers teased her taut nipples while his tongue danced at her core until she was gasping for breath.

"*Trousers*," she panted.

He lifted his mouth only slightly from between her legs. "Do you have the coin?"

"Who cares about the deuced coin?"

"Capital point." He swung her into his arms and tossed her atop the bed, then removed his trousers and climbed in beside her.

She wrapped her fingers about his shaft, reveling in its thickness and heat. He shuddered as she stroked him, as though struck helpless by her touch. But he did not allow her to wield power over him for long.

He gripped her hips, turning so that he was on his back and she was seated astride him.

Her pulse quickened with anticipation. "What are you doing?"

"Teaching you a trick I think you'll like." He positioned her atop his shaft longways, allowing the hard ridge to glide slickly between her legs until her mind had no coherent thought besides *More, more, more*.

"Please..."

In answer, he allowed the tip of his shaft to penetrate her, just a bit, then a little bit more. As her body stretched to accommodate him, he lowered his thumb to her sensitive nub and began to stroke lightly.

A jolt of pleasure flashed through her, and she sank a little lower onto his shaft. She could not stand the teasing, longing to have all of him within her.

Without ceasing his thumb's expert ministrations, he leaned up and took one of her nipples into his talented mouth, suckling possessively.

"*Ohhh.*" Suddenly she was fully seated on his shaft, tilting her hips into his touch, arching her back to press her breasts to his mouth.

There was no holding back now, no patience, no teasing, just an uninhibited coupling toward mutual pleasure. She gave, she took, she demanded, she surrendered. He gripped her hips as she rode him, finding a rhythm that drove them higher and higher. The pressure building was too big, too much, too—

She cried out his name and he caught it with a kiss, his own hips pumping even faster.

As soon as her tremors subsided, he jerked his shaft free, spilling his seed to one side. With shaking arms, he pulled her close and cradled her to his chest. She smiled drowsily against him. His heartbeat pounded fast and strong, just like hers.

She cuddled against him, closing her eyes as he pressed little kisses to the top of her hair. Was it any wonder she loved him? She could curl against him like this for the rest of the week, for the rest of the year, for the rest of her life. Perhaps he wanted it, too.

"You're lucky," she grumbled. "You wake up every morning in bed with you."

She could sense, rather than see, his grin.

"So could you," he murmured into her hair. "Stay the night."

A damp chill feathered across her bare skin. She had *never* spent a night away from home. Not since the day she'd returned to the orphanage to find another needy child tucked asleep in her bed. They had replaced her after only a couple of hours. What would an entire night do?

Her breath came too quickly. "I can't."

"You could." He smoothed a stray hair back from her forehead. "A brand-new day dress and night rail await you on a special shelf in my wardrobe, in case I ever trap you in my arms for an entire night."

"That's very presumptuous of you," she mumbled.

"And expensive," he agreed. "I had to sell a painting, but if I can keep you a little longer, it will have been worth it."

She lifted her head. "You sold a painting?"

He nodded. "I had intended to replenish the larder, but then I thought to myself, 'What if I made love to Chloe all night instead?' I hope you like porridge for breakfast."

"I hate porridge for breakfast."

She burrowed into his warmth, pulse racing. What if she could make love to Lawrence all night? What if she could wake up in the morning not replaced at all but still held fast in his embrace? What if this was the first night of many?

"All right," she whispered, despite the fear. "I'll stay."

31

⟨⟩

*C*hloe could not repress a grin as she set out across Grosvenor Square, arms swinging jauntily at her sides. The sun was dim and the wind was sharp, but nothing could squelch this new spring in her step.

She'd spent the night with Lawrence. In his bed. In his *arms*. She hadn't expected to be able to sleep, but she'd lain her cheek against his steady heartbeat, and the next thing she knew, it was morning.

Chloe had sent a note home to Tommy saying, *Don't worry—I'm with Faircliffe*. Tommy's response had read simply, *I know. Graham told me*.

Chloe's cheeks heated. There would be no keeping *this* secret.

Perhaps it needn't be a secret for long. Not only was Chloe wearing a gown Lawrence had purchased for her, she was also walking across the square to the reading circle from his house. She had left by the rear door so as not to give the gossips fodder, but people would notice if this became a habit.

Was Lawrence thinking about courting her? Or at least thinking again about whether they might suit after all?

She tried to push such thoughts out of her mind, at least

for now. For the next few hours the reading circle deserved her attention.

This time was different. She was no longer lurking. Gone was her aggressively forgettable attire.

Chloe looked like a lady.

If she was overlooked like this, it would be because no amount of finery could make unremarkable Chloe Wynchester anything but ordinary. She infused her posture with confidence.

No more hiding in a shadow of her own making. The person whose acceptance she needed to earn was her own. She was Miss Chloe Bloody Wynchester. She wasn't inferior to anyone, no matter what their birth. She did impossible things all the time. Of course she could succeed at *this*.

She strode up the familiar path to the Yorks' front door. When the butler opened it wide, she offered not a calling card but a sunny smile.

"How do you do, Mr. Underwood?"

"Very well." He blinked, taken aback at being greeted by name, particularly when he likely could not recall hers.

Chloe slipped past him and took several steps down the corridor toward the parlor before a different obstacle blocked her passage.

"Miss Wynchester." The syllables dripped like poison from Mrs. York's curled lip. "I hope you don't think you are welcome here."

Ah. Respectable Mrs. York would not be appeased by a *How do you do* and a smile. When Philippa had lost Lawrence, Chloe had lost her usefulness.

She held her ground. She was visible; that was step one. Mrs. York might sneer down her nose at the Wynchester family, but she remembered Chloe's name and face.

"Thank you," Chloe said, and meant it. "That means more to me than you could know."

Mrs. York blinked. "Er...what?"

Philippa floated into the corridor in a cloud of delicate lace. "Mother, what are you...Oh, Chloe, there you are. Come on in. We're waiting for a few more guests before we get started."

Visible. Remembered. Recognized.

Wanted.

"I'd be happy to." Chloe started forward.

Mrs. York's arm flashed out to block her.

"Mother, desist at once." Philippa's voice was cold. "If you want me to consider reentering the marriage mart, you will unhand my friend."

Friend. The word made Chloe dizzy. Or perhaps that was due to being defended rather than dismissed.

"If your acquaintance in any way harms my daughter's chances..." Mrs. York hissed beneath her breath. "Mind yourself. Or I will pay you back in kind."

But she lowered her arm and allowed Chloe to hurry past.

Upon reaching the noisy parlor, she paused inside the doorway to catch her breath. Her tense muscles began to relax.

She liked the reading circle. No, she *adored* the reading circle.

During the previous weeks, they'd all been the heroines they read about. They'd fought invading armies or escaped crumbling abbeys or won the handsome prince. They argued over the parts they liked best and least. Wouldn't it have been better if this? Or more logical if that? *If I were Emily St. Aubert, how I would have felt and what I would have done was...*

Those were Chloe's favorite moments. It made Chloe think that if young ladies with family titles could imagine themselves as ordinary people in popular novels, surely some of them could imagine life from her perspective. It made her think that instead of pretending this was her group of friends, perhaps she could *really* belong.

"Next month," Philippa was saying, "we'll need a new book. Who's next on the list to choose?"

Immediate chaos broke out as ladies vied against each other, complaining that it had been months since they last chose, and they were positively brimming with suggestions on what everyone else should read.

A voice cut through the din. "Miss Wynchester hasn't had a turn."

All eyes swung toward Chloe in unison. *Seen. Remembered. Recognized.* Her cheeks flamed with heat.

Lady Eunice was the one who had spoken. She was the daughter of a marquess.

"All right," Philippa agreed. "Chloe, your turn. Bring your selection next week so we can all note the title. Where on earth is Gracie?"

"Her tardiness gets worse with every passing week," groused another young woman. "If she hadn't been waltzing with rakish scoundrels all night..."

"Inconsiderate hen," said another. "Some of us want to talk about books."

"Let's start without her," someone else suggested. "The rest of us are here."

The rest of us. Chloe was part of an "us." Her limbs lightened with joy.

"Did you hear the Duke of Faircliffe is on the market again?" whispered one young lady to another.

Chloe froze and pretended every iota of her being wasn't trying desperately to overhear.

"Now that he's available," said the young lady's friend, "I, for one, will send as many sultry looks over my fan at Almack's as it takes for him to notice me."

"Do that," said another. "I'm going to sneak into his theatre box at the next performance. I needn't even swoon into his arms. My presence will be enough to stake my claim."

"Diabolical," murmured her friend, impressed.

At the moment the only woman who held his attention was Chloe. Her chest fluttered. She still couldn't believe she'd spent the night in his arms. And that he'd invited her to do it again tonight.

Gracie rushed through the open door out of breath, her cheeks chapped from the wind. "I'm here, I'm here!"

"*Finally*," called one of her friends. "The book bacchanalia can begin."

"All right, ladies." Philippa clapped her hands together. "Please take your chairs. It's time for *Evelina*."

Everyone scrambled for the best seats—where there was more light, or next to a bosom friend. Chloe hurried to the one in the corner, the one Lawrence had found for her because it was out of the range of the Yorks' many decorative mirrors.

Gracie reached the chair when Chloe was still two yards away.

She paused, indecisive. Tossing a magistrate's daughter out of an armchair would not help her to be accepted by the group.

"Gracie," Philippa said. "Not there. That's Chloe's chair. If you'd arrive on time once in a while, you could claim a different one for yourself. Go sit by Lady Eunice so we can begin."

That's Chloe's chair.

Her head swam.

Chloe's chair.

"Apologies," Gracie giggled, and rushed off to join Lady Eunice.

Chloe sank into her chair with weak knees. Never had the mahogany seemed so sturdy, the velvet so soft and welcoming, the view so perfect. This was *her* chair. Her place. Her personal slice of "us."

Her head swam at the new sensations.

"Who's going to Mrs. Ipsley's tonight?" Gracie asked, as if she had not heard Philippa call the reading circle to order.

Everyone began speaking at once. It seemed Mrs. Ipsley was hosting "just a small gathering" to which everyone who was anyone had apparently been invited.

"We're all going," Florentia crowed in delight. "I should have known."

Chloe hugged herself as if she didn't care.

"I'm not." It was a small voice, but she had found one. "I wasn't invited."

"What?" Lady Eunice pressed a hand to her bosom as if in genuine shock that Mrs. Ipsley could make such an omission. "Your invitation must have been lost."

"It wasn't lost," Chloe mumbled. "It was never coming. I'm a Wynchester."

"Bah," Gracie said. "The older generation might care about such things—"

"Patronesses..." Philippa agreed. "My mother..."

"—but *we* obviously do not," Gracie finished. "It's 1817, for heaven's sake. We're modern women."

Lady Eunice nodded. "I'll call on Mrs. Ipsley as soon as I leave here. Your invitation will be on your mantel by the time you arrive home."

Florentia smiled wickedly. "A party isn't a party without the entire Ladies of Lusty Literature Book Coven."

"We haven't a *name*," Philippa protested in mock horror.

It was too late. The company had already dissolved into raucous laughter, bandying about improper title after improper title until references to lust and book bacchanalia seemed pious in comparison.

Chloe's cheeks hurt from grinning at the antics of all her...friends? Perhaps next time she wouldn't have to try so hard to avoid seats facing looking glasses. She suspected all she would see was joy reflecting back at her.

She leaned forward and leapt into the competition for who could invent the most scandalous group name.

32

Lawrence could not calm his nerves. His pacing would have worn holes in his carpets if he still had any.

Spending an entire night with Chloe had been more than he'd dreamed it would be. Perfect. Magical. A terrible idea.

No matter how much he yearned to, he couldn't keep her. His duty was to his title, not his heart. He should not let himself forget it again.

Even if she was everything he wanted.

To clear his head, he raced Elderberry down Rotten Row. On the way home, he passed Gunter's Tea Shop.

A row of carriages lined Berkeley Square. Some of the passengers still perched in their open conveyances. Smart waiters dashed back and forth between the shop and their customers, taking and delivering orders. On a fine, sunny day like today, Gunter's was second only to Almack's in amassing the greatest number of fashionable people. If he hoped to find an heiress with a dowry capable of saving his ancestral estate, he ought to start there.

Lawrence tied Elderberry to a post.

Leaves crunched just behind him.

"Faircliffe," said the Marquess of Rosbotham with far more joviality than their superficial acquaintance warranted.

"I hear your courtship with that York chit spoiled like month-old cream."

So the word was out.

Lawrence clenched his fingers. Until he settled his finances, he could not afford to alienate any member of the ton and risk his standing.

"No promises were made, nor hearts broken," he replied evenly. "Her business is her own, as is mine."

"Oh, come now," Rosbotham chuckled. "Her mother claims the girl was the one to walk away, but we both know that family would have toppled a king for a chance at a dukedom. What's wrong with the chit? You can tell me the truth."

"The truth," said Lawrence, each clipped syllable frosty with unconcealed disdain, "is that Miss York is an exceptional young woman of intelligence and good breeding who would make any discerning gentleman a lucky groom indeed."

"'Intelligent.'" Rosbotham made a moue and gave an exaggerated shiver. "Say no more."

With a wink, he sauntered off to the next clump of fashionable customers awaiting their ices.

Lawrence ground his teeth in frustration. There was nothing wrong with Philippa York. Not only had Lawrence meant every word, it had been a compliment. "Intelligent females" were no plague to be avoided at all costs. Cleverness and resourcefulness were traits Lawrence particularly admired.

It was why he loved Chloe. His chest ached.

He adored being able to talk with her about anything and everything. Chloe didn't just incite his passions; she made him *think*. Nothing could be more attractive.

One of the waiters jogged up to Lawrence to take his order, then sprinted off to the next customer.

It was the Earl of Southerby, who had not hidden his interest in Chloe.

Lawrence clenched his jaw.

The earl grinned at him. "Couldn't help but notice your fascination with artwork at that soirée the other night. What is it the Yorks have? A Van Eyes?"

"Van Eyck," Lawrence corrected. "And no. It was a van der Weyden."

Southerby gave a snort of jovial self-deprecation. "It could have been a van der Prinny Himself and I wouldn't have known any better. How do you keep it straight?"

"I visit exhibitions," Lawrence said. "They have helpful little plaques next to each work of art."

"Do they?" The earl chuckled. "I've a wretched eye for art. Are you a practitioner?"

"No," Lawrence replied in haste. But that was only part of the truth. "Not until recently."

Southerby made a face. "I'm horrid at art. Once, on a whim, I hired an art tutor." He gave a conspiratorial grin. "I've never laughed harder in all my life than at the mess I made with paints. Of course, that was nothing compared to the time I fell through the ice at the Thames Frost Fair. What did I know? It was my first time ice-skating."

Lawrence stared at him in consternation.

Could it really be that easy? To do whatever one was driven to do, even if you ended up hurt or embarrassed? To let your worst failures one day be an amusing anecdote?

Or was that Southerby's privilege as a wealthy, titled rake? Unlike Lawrence, the raffish earl didn't *need* society's approval. His coin and his charm made up for any short-comings.

"God save me." Southerby shot a nervous look over Lawrence's shoulder. "Here come two patronesses and the Overton woman. She's determined I should fall in love with her daughter. Or at least the chit's dowry. Run while you still can."

Lawrence couldn't run. He needed to land an amenable heiress. When one's pockets were empty, one's social status was the most valuable currency to have.

The earl darted off before they arrived.

"Why, Your Grace," cooed Mrs. Overton. "What flavor are *you* dying to taste?"

Chloe Wynchester's quim was the wrong answer, so Lawrence replied, "Burnt filbert, Mrs. Overton. And you?"

"Maple," replied Mrs. Overton. She nudged her child forward. "My daughter prefers pistachio."

Miss Overton was no doubt a fine young lady, but Lawrence was nearly twice her age and very much not interested. He was also, however, not in a position to lose favor with the powerful patronesses. Almack's was known as a marriage mart for a reason. He could save his dukedom if they helped him make the right match.

Lady Castlereagh's lips pursed.

Mrs. Overton followed her distant gaze, then yanked her offspring closer to her side.

"What is it?" asked her daughter.

"*Wynchesters*," said Lady Jersey with scorn. "In a barouche."

He tensed as the sound of carriage wheels rolled behind him.

"Don't worry," Lady Castlereagh assured him, misreading his discomfort. "Those creatures won't come over here. They wouldn't dare."

Lawrence's hackles rose. To the haughty patronesses, even a casual interaction with a family as unconventional as Chloe's was enough to damage one's reputation. A penniless duke in want of a large dowry was obliged to care very much about the consequences of his actions.

Lawrence's primary concern, however, was how the onlookers would treat the Wynchesters.

The barouche halted at the corner of the square nearest

Gunter's pineapple sign. First out of the carriage was Elizabeth, who stepped to one side and leaned on a splendidly crafted cane—presumably hiding a lethal blade—as a footman reached up to help the next passenger.

This was a slender, pretty young lady Lawrence had never seen before in his life...until he realized it was Tommy in a debutante-pastel gown and a wig of golden ringlets.

Last came Chloe, her cheeks flushed and her hair perfectly curled and her delectable body clothed in the sapphire walking dress Lawrence had given her that morning. His heart thumped. He could stare at her for hours, days, a lifetime. She was a vision far more beautiful than any painting.

The Wynchesters had not yet spied him standing across the street in the shade with some of the most powerful women in London. Instead, they nipped into Gunter's Tea Shop with bright chatter and happy faces.

"Wretched how they gad about as though they were the baron's heirs," said Lady Jersey.

Lady Castlereagh shuddered. "My husband's solicitor had it from a colleague that the estate was wholly entailed to the son, besides a few tokens for the orphans. No dowries for any of them."

The orphans. Lawrence ground his teeth in disgust. As though children's parentage were their defining feature!

Mrs. Overton tugged on her daughter's hand and gave Lawrence an aggressively encouraging smile. "My daughter is the very epitome of breeding and taste."

The epitome of breeding and taste looked as though she'd rather sink through the grass and disappear than endure her mother's unsubtle matchmaking.

The door to the tea shop swung open and out strode Elizabeth, Tommy, and Chloe in turn. They linked arms before crossing the street, glancing ahead as though to scout the best spot to wait for their ices.

Chloe's eyes met his at once.

Someone else might think the slight pause in her step was due to an obstruction in the road. Lawrence knew it was because she'd seen him—and whom he was standing with. At Chloe's pause, Tommy and Elizabeth followed their sister's gaze.

"They're not... They cannot be looking *our way*," said Lady Castlereagh.

Lady Jersey glared down her nose. "It's His Grace who has caught their eye. Everyone knows that Wynchester girl has been angling for him—not that she'll have any success."

His muscles tensed. When he'd first agreed to owe Chloe a favor, an invitation to his gala wasn't much of a sacrifice. He'd planned to be married to Miss York by then and no longer in need of the patronesses' good favor. He could afford an act of charity.

But it wasn't an act anymore. His love for Chloe was very, very real, and his social and financial straits more precarious than ever. If he defended the Wynchesters, his standing would instantly and permanently fall.

"Are they walking toward us?" Mrs. Overton whispered. "Tell me they're not."

"Of course they shan't," Lady Castlereagh said with satisfaction. "Could you imagine?"

Lawrence could indeed imagine. Those three young ladies mattered far more than the opinions of gossipy matrons. He might not be able to offer Chloe everything he might wish, but neither could he allow her to be slandered.

Come what may.

"The Wynchesters," he said coldly, "are the epitome of..."

What were they the epitome of? Certainly not breeding and grace. These siblings were more likely to rob Almack's than to simper in it.

"...excitement, cleverness, and wit," he finished, lifting his nose to its coldest angle. "I, for one, prefer the frank conversation of women unashamed to be who they are over the petty gossip of ladies who build themselves up by tearing others down."

There was no going back.

33

Late the following afternoon, Chloe strode through Green Park toward Hatchards. It was an unrelentingly dreary day, full of dirt and fog and overcast skies, but there was a spring in Chloe's step as she leapt nimbly around the growing puddles.

She was off to decide on her first reading circle recommendation, which was cause enough for celebration. On top of such good fortune, Lawrence was to meet her at the bookshop—ostensibly to gauge the price of a few volumes in his collection, but actually, as he had told her over breakfast in bed, because he'd miss her.

Her bosom swelled as she once again failed to keep a sappy grin from taking over her face. He missed her. They'd spent the night together for the second time in as many days, and she'd returned home only four hours earlier. But he missed her.

She missed him, too. The more time they spent together, the more impossible it became to be apart.

A little voice inside her asked: *Must* they stay apart? Didn't this mean he'd had a change of heart about the importance of a perfect reputation? Might he think Chloe his ideal match?

Yesterday, when she'd spied Lawrence outside Gunter's,

she'd expected him to pretend not to see her. He had been chatting with the fashionable and the powerful. Just because Chloe wasn't allowed at Almack's did not mean she couldn't recognize the women in charge of deciding which individuals were welcome.

No Wynchesters, of course. Lawrence could lose his subscription for fraternizing with her.

But he had strolled over to where she stood with her sisters and eaten his ice cream with them beneath a tree as though it were perfectly unexceptional for a duke to publicly acknowledge an association with her scandalous family before dozens of high-society witnesses.

What if it could be? What if it *was*? She had not allowed herself to dream about a life with him because she had not believed it possible until yesterday.

"Pardon us, miss." Two well-dressed lads exchanged speculative glances, then stepped in front of her to block her path. "You wouldn't be a Wynchester, would you?"

"Er..." Chloe blinked at them. She was barely used to being recognized at the reading circle. Being stopped on the street by strangers was a new experience entirely. "Yes, I am a Wynchester."

"But are you *the* Wynchester?" The lad consulted a square of paper in his hand. "*Chloe* Wynchester?"

A prickle of unease danced on the back of her neck. She wished Elizabeth were here with her sword stick. It had come in handy on more than one mission. Chloe tightened her pelisse about her sapphire walking dress. She should not have worn it two days in a row, but she adored it more than any other gown in her wardrobe. *Lawrence* had purchased it for her.

She didn't need a sword stick. She could deal with two wealthy brats. How did they know her name?

"Yes," she said cautiously. "I'm Chloe Wynchester."

The lads burst out laughing.

"How could you tell without a face?" demanded the one on the left.

"It's the same dress," answered his friend, "wrapped around a blank canvas."

"Nothing there at all," agreed the first, and they stumbled off in chortles of laughter.

"W-wait," called Chloe, spinning toward their retreating forms. "Why did you want to know?"

They paused to face her, eyes shining with mirth.

"Oh, haven't you seen?" said one.

His friend elbowed him in the side. "Give her yours."

"I want mine, now that we've seen her." The lad pushed his friend forward. "Give her yours."

After some jostling, one of them finally stepped forward, a rectangle of paper fluttering in his outstretched hand.

Chloe took it from him with trembling fingers.

"It's a penny caricature," his friend explained helpfully. "They're all over town. I think it's a Cruikshank."

The first lad doffed him on the cap. "It's a Rowlandson, you bufflehead."

"Looks like a Cruikshank to me." His friend pulled out his own copy and ran a dirty finger round the edges. "Where's the signature?"

Chloe didn't give a fig about the signature.

The caricature was of *her*.

The illustration was of yesterday. The scene outside Gunter's. The famous pineapple sign was blowing in the wind above a trio of fashionable ladies pointing and laughing at a man and a woman on the opposite side of the sketch. The ladies were patronesses of Almack's. Their features had been exaggerated, which only served to make them more recognizable.

The gentleman was Lawrence. He was down on one knee, in the mud, offering up armfuls of flavored ices with a theatrical expression of infatuation.

The woman was Chloe. Wearing the same wonderful, beautiful sapphire walking dress she had on now.

In the caricature, her face was not making a comical expression. Chloe's face did not have *any* expression, because the artist had neglected to sketch her visage. She was just a generic woman shape, with nothing inside.

The caption read:

A fall from grace! The Duke of F— falls
for the most forgettable face of all.

Chloe crumpled the cartoon in her fist. She kept crumpling until it was a hard little ball, just like the heart shriveling in her chest.

This was what it meant to be seen with Lawrence publicly. Ridicule for her and ridicule for him. She would be seen not as a person with thoughts and feelings but as an object of scorn, no more memorable than a puff of air, remarkable only in her ability to attract no one's eye but Lawrence's.

Her vision swimming, Chloe faced ahead and forced her boots to keep walking. It was a caricature, not the end of the world. Who cared what two silly boys found amusing?

But every storefront seemed to have the day's caricatures pasted to their windows. Her beloved duke, portrayed as a clownish buffoon. Herself, a vague outline with nothing of worth inside.

She walked faster, head down to ignore the empty shell of herself reflecting back at her again and again. Her crossed arms were cold, her legs leaden, but she kept moving, moving, moving, her stinging eyes on the pavement before her.

Just as she reached the safety of the bookshop, she glimpsed Lawrence up ahead, striding toward her.

His eyes were on a slip of paper in his hand, which he balled in his fist and threw aside, only to snatch another from a passing windowsill and crumple it with the same fury.

It was the caricature; of course it was.

And the butt of the joke was not boring, irrelevant Chloe Wynchester but the addlepated duke who had publicly doted on someone so unworthy.

Ha ha, can you imagine? What a horse's arse! Chloe Wynchester, of all pitiable creatures. He might as well have brought ices to a stick of wood. Bound to have more personality, and a better chance of being allowed into Almack's. Ha ha, what a fool!

The toes of her boots stopped inches from the toes of his.

His eyes met hers. "They—"

"I already saw it." The words felt like pebbles in her throat. "By now, all of London has seen it. It'll be reprinted in the scandal columns by morning."

Her face flamed at the thought of her brother Graham turning to that page as he ate his toast.

Chloe swallowed hard. "I suppose you lost your voucher."

The anger in his blue eyes made him look like he wanted to crumple all of London into a ball and toss it into the fire.

"I don't give a damn about my Almack's voucher."

But of course he did. He had to. Almack's Assembly Rooms was more than stale bread and weak ratafia. It was status. It was acceptance. It was power.

Anyone would resent her for snatching opportunities from his fingertips.

"Today it's Almack's," she said. "Tomorrow it's a political ally, and the day after that—"

He tensed when she said "political ally," and she remembered Philippa and her father.

"Ah," Chloe said. "I've *already* cost you a political ally. You claim you don't care about Almack's, but Westminster is your life. You would put nothing above Parliament. Where does that leave us?"

He didn't meet her gaze. "I realize that recent actions may have implied—"

That they had a future.

"There was never going to be an 'us,' was there?" she said, her voice hollow. "I'm fine enough to invite into bed—even well enough to share ices with—but nothing more. A passing fancy until you find a woman you *would* marry. Someone even more perfect than Philippa."

Someone completely unlike Chloe Wynchester.

"*Yes*," he burst out. "That's exactly what I intend to do, because it's the only thing I *can* do. I've a duty to uphold. Responsibilities. I *must* wed an heiress. My father left the dukedom destitute. With the loss of a year's crops, I've no income and nothing left to sell. I could never marry you."

Lawrence had not changed his mind about her. The duke simply wasn't ready to stop playing with his toy.

"I'm trying to think of a discreet arrangement," he said. "Public appearances may invite ridicule, but if we're out of sight, we'll be out of mind. If no one sees us together—"

She stumbled backward. *This* was his happy ever after?

"Never let the people who matter learn you cavort with a Wynchester, you mean?" Her voice shook, but she pressed on. "*You* will be out in society. Routs, dinner parties, Westminster. I would be your secret? Some chit you won't acknowledge in front of witnesses, lest caricaturists mock you again? A clandestine mistress tucked in a trunk with the bonnets until it's time to play? Or kept up in the attic, peering down from a peephole?"

A tendon flexed in his neck. "I didn't say 'mistress.'"

"Too much of a commitment?" she said hollowly. "I notice you didn't deny the rest."

Had she thought nothing could hurt her as much as that silly caricature? Being laughed at by all of England was not nearly as mortifying as realizing the most romantic moments in her life had filled Lawrence with shame.

"When I stole your carriage, you were terrified that passionless 'compromise' would lead to marriage. But it wasn't compromise that scared you at all. It was the thought of being caught with a Wynchester. You even lamented, 'Why couldn't it have been Honoria?'"

Because Lawrence believed Bean's legitimate daughter Honoria existed... and was an heiress. Even then, it had not been about the person but the money. Lawrence would have lowered himself to marry Honoria Wynchester for the right price. Chloe would not sell herself so cheaply.

Her hands and legs trembled with hurt and mortification. "Over the past two months, you and I have been in dozens of increasingly compromising positions. You've considered marriage at none of them, because you've managed to keep your dirty secret. No one knows, so you needn't treat me like a *respectable* lady."

He desired her but wished he didn't. He was only biding his time until he found a debutante with duchess potential and a large dowry. He expected Chloe to understand.

Now she did.

She gave a mirthless laugh. "To you, Wynchesters are like writing plumes. We're to be used and discarded."

He shifted his weight. "I wasn't going to discard you."

"You were going to keep using me." She fought the

prickling in the back of her throat. "No, thank you, Your Grace. I'm not interested in discreet arrangements."

Chloe had wanted so much more. She had wanted the fairy tale. Her stomach roiled at her own naïveté. There would be no magical moment. Her love was not enough.

She did have money, although perhaps not as much as Philippa could offer. Bean's trust was meant to provide for *Chloe's* future, not to be handed over to a duke and spent all at once. Yet the sum might be enough to tempt him. But was it worth the cost to her pride?

"Chloe…"

Her lungs struggled. She wanted him to choose *her*, not her inheritance. She didn't want to be exchangeable for any other convenient heiress. She wanted to be loved for who she was. She wanted a husband who would be *proud* of her, not ashamed to be seen in her presence.

"What if I had money?" she asked in a small voice.

He winced. There it was. The expression he wore when he was about to explain some maddeningly basic concept he believed she failed to properly comprehend.

"It's not just money," he admitted. "I've spent years restoring my reputation and cannot throw that away on—"

Throw away.

He looked at her and thought *throw away.*

Just like her parents had done.

"Go to hell." The words were shards of glass, ripping her apart from the inside.

She feared he would argue. He was as skilled at debate as she was. For a passionate statesman like Lawrence, important causes were worth fighting for. If he said the right thing, fell at her feet with confessions of love, her resolve might crumble.

Instead, he inclined his head and said, "I'm sorry, Chloe."

Then turned and walked away.

That was it. She was not important enough to argue with. Not important enough to fight for. Not important enough to want her to stay.

She was a blank spot in a pretty dress, destined to be crumpled up and tossed away.

34

When dawn came, Chloe covered her aching eyes with her pillow. She would *not* cry over Lawrence. She *would not*. If he didn't want her, she didn't want *him*.

She'd repeated the mantra to herself all night in the hopes that she would believe it by morning. So far, it hadn't worked. Her throat still burned and the backs of her eyes pricked with unshed tears.

But she was strong. She'd lived through far worse than a broken heart. She would survive this, too.

If she ever convinced herself to rise from bed and face the day.

By noon a rumble in her stomach reminded her that her siblings would soon wonder what was happening. She hadn't gone down to breakfast. Hadn't emerged from the solitude of her bedchamber at all. If she wanted them to treat her like nothing was wrong, she was going to have to show her face.

She shoved on the first bland, shapeless gown her fingers touched and ran a listless hand over her hair. Good enough.

With trembling fingers, she forced herself to wrench open the door handle and step out into the corridor. A murmur of voices came to an abrupt stop.

"Chloe?"

She paused, her heart pounding. The sounds hadn't come from downstairs in the dining room but from the Planning Parlor, just a few feet down the corridor. Her knees weakened.

What if her siblings were talking about her? What if they were discussing the caricature? They would all have seen it by now. Graham's morning broadsheets were served right along with breakfast.

Her lungs begged for air. She hadn't been able to breathe since her encounter with Lawrence. Maybe she would never breathe properly again. How could she? She didn't have a nose or a mouth or a face, according to the rest of the world. She didn't have feelings or thoughts or a place in society.

No. She couldn't face her siblings. Their sympathy and kindness would break her.

Chest heaving, she dashed back through her bedroom door, closed it firmly behind her, and collapsed against it, her unsteady shoulders trembling against the immovable slab of wood. Blank, like her. Her heart hammered.

She stared at her wardrobe full of expensive, useless fripperies.

Silk and satin and lace and velvet. Earrings, feathers, tiaras, combs, pearls. Had she thought any of that changed who *she* was?

With Lawrence, she'd risked being Chloe. Sometimes fancy, sometimes frumpy, sometimes silly. She'd taken off the mask, hoping not to go unnoticed.

He'd wanted her to put it back on. Wanted to hide her away. No, *throw* her away. The real Chloe was worse than unremarkable; she was repellant. No amount of diamonds and curls could ameliorate the unfixable.

She didn't want any of it anymore.

Why couldn't she be enough just as she was? Why couldn't she be seen, and remembered, and wanted as Chloe?

Vision blurring, she yanked open the doors to her wardrobe and flung each treasured item onto a growing pile in the corner. Rubbish, all of it. She'd give it away. It was past time to stop believing in fairy tales.

Her door swung open and Tommy burst in, her eyes wide and her expression stricken.

"*Go*," Chloe croaked. "I can't…"

Tommy rushed to her and wrapped her in her arms.

"Don't you dare be kind to me." Chloe stood as still as she was able, every bone brittle. "If I look at you, I'll cry."

"Then cry," Tommy said, and the crack in her voice indicated *she* was already crying. She might not know the details, but she knew Chloe was in pain, and that was enough to hurt her, too.

Chloe hugged her sister hard, burying her wet face in Tommy's neck. Maybe she *had* started crying first. Maybe she'd been crying this whole time and hadn't realized it.

"I'll kill him," Tommy choked out.

"Can't make a silk purse from a sow's ear," Chloe mumbled.

Tommy yanked Chloe out of her arms, her fingers digging into Chloe's shoulders so she could glare straight into her face.

"You are *not* a sow's ear. You are the cleverest, kindest, most compassionate person I know. You were born beautiful, inside and out. The happiest day of my life was when we became sisters. You're the sun in my sky, Chloe Wynchester. Nothing glitters without you."

"She's the sun in *my* sky," came Graham's gruff voice from somewhere behind them.

Elizabeth pushed past him to wrap her arms about Chloe and Tommy both. "No, mine."

A scrambling of feet indicated Jacob and Marjorie had joined the fray, jostling with Graham to be the next to join the embrace around Chloe.

"You're perfect just as you are," Jacob said.

Marjorie found Chloe's hand and squeezed.

"You're the reason we're a family," Graham said fiercely.

Tommy hugged Chloe harder and whispered, "You make all of us sparkle."

35

⏝

*L*awrence sat on the edge of his bed and buried his face in his hands.

Publicly standing up for Chloe had only made things worse. He'd hurt her, not helped her. It was the last thing he'd meant to do. He loved her, even if he couldn't offer what they both wanted.

It had taken forever to realize *she* was the lucky one.

He'd been raised to believe everyone shared the same ambitions: an important name, an important title, a heritage, and entailed land. All those things were a privilege. Yet, if he could make any childhood wish come true, it would be to feel that he belonged, not just be another cold link in a dutiful chain of dukes. He'd wanted a large, boisterous, loving family.

A family like the Wynchesters.

He still wanted that, but there was one thing he yearned for even more. He wanted to belong to Chloe. To be worthy of her. He didn't just want to prove to Chloe that her needs mattered. He wanted her to know *she* mattered. That he loved her more than words could convey.

But what could he do about it?

His situation hadn't changed, and he'd only made hers worse.

He thought back to that moment at Gunter's—the moment that had changed everything. And then he remembered what had happened right before the conversation with the patronesses.

Southerby.

The earl had flabbergasted Lawrence with his easy admission of his flaws and complete lack of embarrassment. Southerby would rather try and fail—even try and fail and become an object of mockery—than never to try at all.

Could Lawrence do any less?

He rose to his feet. If he truly loved Chloe, then nothing else mattered. The best ducal reputation in the world meant nothing without her. She was everything. Come what may, they could face anything as long as they stood together.

But first he needed to talk to his servants. Lawrence's life would not be the only one impacted by the decision he wanted to make.

He hurried from his bedchamber and called an impromptu meeting in the parlor, next to the hat trunk. He looked around at Hastings, his butler. Peggy and Dinah, the maids. Mrs. Root, his housekeeper. Jackson, his footman. Mrs. Elkins, the cook. Lawrence had come to think of them less like servants and more like family.

"How is your niece's baby?" Mrs. Elkins asked Mrs. Root.

Mrs. Root's eyes shone. "Betsy and little Kenneth are hale and hearty. You should see the darling little scrunched-up faces he makes. His father is absolutely in love." She turned to Lawrence. "When do you intend to start your family, Your Grace?"

He cleared his throat. "That is actually why I've summoned you all to this meeting. I would like to ask for Chloe Wynchester's hand in marriage."

Dinah blinked. "Shouldn't you be saying this to Miss Wynchester?"

Lawrence met each of their eyes. "She has no dowry." The words tumbled from his lips like lead weights. "If we wed, I will not be able to afford this town house. I don't know how long I will be able to afford to pay you. Perhaps only a month or two. I will of course be writing effusive letters of recommendation." He paused. "Or...I can resume my hunt for an heiress."

Hastings reared back in surprise. "Give up Miss Wynchester, Your Grace?"

"And your chance at love?" Mrs. Root echoed, appalled. "Didn't you hear anything I've been saying about the meaning of family?"

"Mrs. Root and I have watched over you for decades," Hastings said, "waiting for the moment you would finally find happiness."

Mrs. Elkins's eyes were kind. "There are thousands of kitchens, Your Grace. But there is only one Miss Wynchester. Finding a new position will be well worth it, if it means you're finally happy and loved."

Peggy and Dinah nodded.

"What are you still doing here?" Jackson said gruffly. "Don't you have a lady's heart to win?"

"Thank you." Lawrence's throat was so thick, the words were barely intelligible. "I'll...I'll do whatever it takes to keep all of you close for as long as I can."

Swiftly, he strode to his study. At his escritoire he withdrew ink, parchment, wax. He would not force himself back into Chloe's life, but he would do his best to show her how much he needed her in his.

His plume scratched across the foolscap in fits and starts as he contemplated each word and phrase. If it took a hundred crumpled drafts to get there, so be it. He had one chance to get this right. To prove how much she meant to him, without a shadow of a doubt.

If she accepted his plea to accompany him to the opera, others would see her presence as a public proposal.

Chloe would know it was so much more than that. His private box was a window into his soul. An invitation was a declaration of love. Lawrence would be welcoming her into his world, just as she had done for him.

And if she did not accept...

Lawrence would have only himself to blame for a life without love.

36

The sun was setting when Chloe stopped her driver in front of St. Giles's church, at the same post where she'd first met Bean. It seemed fitting.

The woman in charge of the Women's Employment Charity rushed out to greet her.

"Thank you so much, Miss Wynchester." She pressed a hand to her chest. "Your donation will aid countless parishioners to obtain posts and receive wages. This will change so many lives."

Chloe was happy to help. She'd kept a few of her plainest clothes for the future adventures of Jane Brown, but the majority were inside the trunks several volunteers were now hauling into the church.

Trunks delivered, she turned back toward her carriage.

A little boy of perhaps six years of age stood awestruck in front of it, staring upward, eyes wide.

His shoes were too small for his feet. The tips had been cut away to allow his toes to protrude. His threadbare shirt and trousers hung large on his narrow frame, as though he was meant to grow into them. She doubted the tattered material would last until summer.

Chloe bent to one knee before him, mindless of the grime

now seeping through her skirt. She could afford new clothes. This boy could not.

She reached into an inner pocket and handed him a simple drawstring bag.

He shook his head. "Wot do I want wiv a girl's purse?"

Ah. He wasn't a pickpocket, like her. Not yet, anyway.

"There's a gold sovereign inside." The one Bean had given her here, at this very spot. "And warm red mittens."

The latter proved the more convincing. He snatched the bag from her hand as if afraid she would change her mind, and raced into one of the many dilapidated homes without a backward glance.

Chloe pushed to her feet and swiped the dirt from her knee. The mittens now had a new home, with an owner who would appreciate them.

As to the coin... who knew? Perhaps it would purchase a new pair of shoes. Or perhaps a decade from now a young man would pass the sovereign along to another child in need.

She felt lighter on the road back to Islington. The wardrobes in her bedchamber were no longer bursting at the seams. Rather, they contained the items Chloe actually wished to wear. There was something for every eventuality: a neighborhood assembly here, a clandestine raid there.

She didn't need the Duke of Faircliffe or the world of the ton. Let them disparage her and discard her if they wished. She was done allowing herself to be hurt.

As she walked up her front path, she pasted a carefree expression on her face for her siblings' sake. She might not be happy yet, but she *would* be. She did not want them to worry about her... or, worse, to pity her.

Graham and Elizabeth were seated at the dining table when Chloe summoned the courage to walk into the room. They smiled at her as if they, too, were pretending today had been a normal day like any other. But the newspapers were there on the table.

"I'm so sorry, Chloe." Elizabeth's words were gentle. "We want you to be happy, and we don't know how to make it so. If you want to set fire to everything, we support you. If you're in love with Faircliffe, we support that, too."

"He's going in the Thames either way," Graham warned. "But I'll fish him back out if you love him."

Tommy and Marjorie walked in and took seats close to Chloe.

"What are we talking about?" Tommy asked.

"He Who Does Not Deserve Our Sister," Graham answered.

"And who shall never be mentioned again," Elizabeth added.

The butler appeared in the doorway.

"Delivery." Randall held up a silver tray. "For Miss Chloe from the Duke of Faircliffe."

"He Who Shall Never Be Mentioned, Except by Our Butler," Graham amended.

"I'll take it." Chloe accepted the folded parchment with unsteady fingers. "Is his footman awaiting a response?"

Randall shook his head. "No, miss. The letter arrived some hours ago while you were out."

Her siblings exchanged glances, then stood up from the table as one.

"We'll give you privacy," Elizabeth murmured.

Tommy's eyes met Chloe's. "I'm right upstairs if you need me."

Chloe nodded gratefully. She waited until her siblings' voices faded, then slid a shaking finger beneath the fold of parchment to break its seal. Was this a rebuke for having up-ended Lawrence's life for a deuced painting? After their last encounter, what was left to say?

Something strange was inside the folded letter. An oddly

shaped flat disc, rather like a piece to a jigsaw. She tilted it into her hand.

It was an ivory ticket for the Duke of Faircliffe's private box at the theatre.

My dearest Miss Chloe Wynchester,

Tonight at eight, the King's Theatre will present "Don Giovanni." It is one of my favorite Italian operas, and I would love to share the experience with you.

If you are free this evening, it would be my great honor for you to join me in my private box.

I would be delighted to escort you personally, and would also be happy to send round my coach if you prefer.

If you have other plans, or are uninterested in continuing our association, I shall understand.

Your servant,
Faircliffe

Chloe's fingers trembled so much, she had to read the message in its entirety three times before making sense of it.

He was inviting her to sit with him in the most public private theatre box in all of London. Every unmarried young lady on the hunt for a husband dreamed of preening in that box, to the envy of all.

Welcoming Chloe into those hallowed seats was not a small apology but the biggest way to tell those who had dared laugh at her to go to the devil. He was staking an unapologetic claim to the caricaturist, the patronesses, the lads on the street, hundreds of witnesses, and thousands of gossips.

She pressed the letter to her chest and tried to breathe.

This wasn't just an opera. This was Lawrence saying *I see you* and *I'll make certain everyone else does, too.*

He was choosing her over everything else. A symbolic statement this blatant meant marriage—in name, in deed, and in public—if she wished to accept it. Her pulse raced beneath her trembling hands.

The next step was up to her.

She stood and looked about the empty dining room that had been so full of siblings moments before. Accepting this invitation meant choosing Lawrence above all else, too. It would mean leaving her safe, happy-go-lucky, loving family and stepping into a world that undoubtedly would contain all new caricatures mocking her and the man she loved on the morrow.

Could she do it? *Dare* she do it?

She glanced at the clock. Scarcely an hour remained before the opera was set to begin. If Chloe meant to have a future built on love, the time to act was now.

And a Wynchester never said no to adventure.

She hurried to her wardrobes. If she was going to go through with this, she would do it right. A duchess would be memorable; she would speak her mind, she would stick out, and she would stand up for herself and everyone else who could not advocate for themselves.

And if she was wrong about Lawrence, wrong about what this invitation meant, wrong about how things would turn out if she risked all of herself so publicly...

...she would do it anyway.

By now the theatre was beginning to fill with spectators. Chloe dressed as quickly and as carefully as she was able. Lawrence would already be perched high up in his lonely tower, waiting to see if there would be any answer to his overture.

As she made the trip to the theatre, Chloe's knees shook and her heart banged against her constricted chest.

This was no rehearsal, like those she and her siblings acted out before embarking on something wild and new.

She did not have Jacob and Graham flanking her, or Elizabeth with her sword stick, or Tommy as their indomitable Great-Aunt Wynchester.

Chloe would have to do this by herself, *for* herself.

She swept into the King's Theatre with her chin held high. She knew the architectural plan by memory after countless visits with Bean and later with Marjorie. The Faircliffe box had been infamous even back then. The old duke had been the owner, but it was his young son who spent every performance there alone, his eyes never straying from the stage.

Tonight, Chloe came for Lawrence, but had come as herself. She was no highborn lady bred to be a living copy of the latest Parisian fashion plate. She was Chloe Wynchester, whose tastes were far more eclectic.

She was wearing her favorite slippers, her favorite stockings, her favorite shift, her favorite gown, and her favorite shawl. These were also her favorite earrings, her favorite necklace, her favorite bonnet, her favorite brooch. That none of it matched did not matter in the least. These items were comfortable and bright and unmissable. They made her happy.

If the caricaturists made light of her ensemble, she would just wear it again.

This time, everyone would remember her.

Was Lawrence ready for such a statement? She did not know. But accepting her meant accepting *all* of her. She was tired of hiding behind pseudonyms and bland clothing. She was ready to be Chloe.

Even if it meant going home alone, at least she would have been brave enough to ignore the laughter and be herself.

It was a quarter to eight when she reached the private boxes. All of the chandeliers were lit. Her arrival would be visible to every spectator in the house.

She strode into the Faircliffe box as though she belonged there.

Lawrence was waiting. His eyes widened when he saw her. And then a slow, disbelieving smile curved his lips until his dimple shone.

"You wore my bonnet." He was grinning now, the arrogant beast.

"I have questionable taste," she informed him pertly.

There was no need to tell him that if her theme was "All of My Favorite Things," she had no choice but to wear his bonnet.

Flashes of light sparkled in the audience as opera glasses tilted in their direction. Their words would not be overheard, but every thread and every gesture would be gossip fodder for weeks on end.

"I was foolish," he said. "I reacted out of fear and a misplaced sense of duty."

She raised her brows. "Can duty be misplaced?"

"I didn't think so." His words were slow but certain. "Now I know better."

"You're still a duke," she reminded him. "You still have a hall of portraits of all the dukes who came before you, and you still enjoy a reputation of being just like them. Don't throw it away on me unless you're certain. Think carefully and go after what you really want."

"I did. I am. I want it all." His crystal-blue gaze did not leave hers. "I want you."

"You want to go back to how things were?"

"No. I want to go with you into *our* future, hand in hand." He took a deep breath. "I'm sorry I lashed out at you. I let others' opinions outweigh my own."

"You have a dukedom to consider," she murmured. "Your future heirs."

"That's right," he agreed. "I should have been thinking of them. I know what it is like to grow up lonely, ignored by my father, with the expectations of generations hanging over me. And you know what it's like to be loved. To be happy. To accept and be accepted, to have fun, to be a team. Which is the better legacy?"

She cleared her throat. "My answer will be biased."

"As it should be." His lips twisted. "I valued my sterling reputation above all other concerns. I thought society's definition of the perfect bride, the perfect marriage, should be my definition, too. But people change. Look at you, for example."

She tensed, expecting the sudden turnabout of his words to cause her neck and face to turn mottled. Look at Chloe, a carousel of colors, a hotchpotch of styles all rolled into one.

But she did not blush. She was proud of herself. She'd *chosen* to come here, chosen to do this.

And he was choosing her back. Here, now, where everyone could see.

"We wouldn't have met if you hadn't tried to steal that painting and accidentally abducted me instead." He stepped closer. "Your ulterior motive was the best thing that could have happened to me."

"The best thing that could have happened to *us*," she corrected. "You were trying so hard to fit someone else's ideals that you didn't realize you were already perfect just as you are. You don't need to fit some ancestral mold to be worthy. You have always been that, right from the start."

"I want to be a duke I can be proud of. To do that, I need to be the sort of father my children would want. And that means choosing love first."

Perhaps her cheeks would flush after all. "Love?"

He sank to one knee. "I love you, Chloe Wynchester." He held out his hand. "I don't need something you can give me. I need *you*. Marry me. You already have my heart. Will you take the rest of me for the rest of our lives, too?"

Chloe dropped to her knees as well and placed her hands in his. "Only if you take all of me, too."

"It would be my pleasure." She could feel him grin wickedly as he pulled her into his arms. "I love you so much. Let me spend the rest of our lives proving how ardently."

"And I love you, which is why I feel I should warn you"—she tilted her mouth to his ear—"our heads are below the barrier. No one can see us. They'll think you're stealing a kiss."

"Then they'll be right," he said, and covered her mouth with his.

They didn't glimpse the stage again until intermission.

37

The following morning, Lawrence reclined on a chaise longue with Chloe in what the Wynchester family aptly referred to as the Sibling Salon. There was a Wynchester sibling draped across every surface. He wished he counted as part of the family and tried to console himself with the victory of them being willing to share Chloe.

At the moment, his bride-to-be was nestled against his chest with her eyes rapidly devouring the book in her hands. It was to be her chosen title for next month's reading circle meeting—maybe. There was a small mountain of bound volumes next to the chaise longue, vying for the honor. Lawrence suspected there were many more nights before the fire just like this in their future.

Graham was also reading on the sofa opposite. Instead of novels, his cushions were piled high with broadsheets. Every now and again, his throat would make a sound very close to a giggle, and he would jerk up from his newspaper, eyes sparkling, only for Chloe to warn, "Do *not* tell me," without looking up from the book in her hand.

Marjorie had filled every table with random objects for her still lifes but apparently had not decided their final form.

She flitted from table to table, adding fruit, removing flowers, rearranging ceramic vessels. There was no easel in sight, although she wore a smock over her gown and a tiny smudge of aquamarine paint on one cheek.

Jacob sat in the center of a large carpet, surrounded by five slinky ferrets and a thick parapet made of rolled blankets. He had successfully convinced one of the ferrets to leap through a wooden hoop in exchange for a bit of cabbage, although Lawrence could not fathom what nefarious purpose acrobatic ferrets might serve.

Elizabeth sat at the pianoforte, idly plinking familiar melodies and reproducing uncanny imitations of other siblings' voices, both male and female. Occasionally a rousing chorus would come not from Elizabeth's mouth but rather from one of Jacob's ferrets or a clump of Marjorie's grapes.

Tommy perched on the edge of a striped armchair, decked out in something she referred to as Early Yorkshire Governess. Every now and then she would say a phrase and Elizabeth would correct the accent until Tommy tired of repeating, "And now on to lesson two, if you please, children," and would dash off only to return in another costume entirely. So far tonight, she had also been a sailor, a dockworker, and a fishwife— "fish spinster," according to Chloe.

Lawrence supposed the Wynchesters must have a thousand such private jests. He couldn't wait to learn them all.

Jacob had offered to loan him a wooden hoop and a spare ferret, but Lawrence had courteously declined. He had no idea what to do with a circus-trained weasel, but he did know what he wanted to do with Chloe: hold her close for the rest of their lives.

It was likely the only thing they would ever be able to do. Lawrence did not have the funds to shower her with the expensive jewels and exotic holidays that he wished he could give her.

He kissed the top of her head.

She tilted her face up toward him with a smile. "How am I so lucky to win the handsome prince?"

"*I'm* the fortunate one," he reminded her. "You're the one saddled with an extraordinarily dashing prince with appallingly light pockets. I might not be able to offer the life you deserve, but I can promise one thing: we might be poor, but we'll be happy."

Graham glanced up from his newspapers.

Tommy cleared her throat.

Elizabeth stopped playing the pianoforte.

One of Jacob's ferrets escaped its rolled-cotton fence.

"Er..." Chloe set down her book and sat upright to face Lawrence. "How is it possible that you have not fully comprehended just how wealthy Bean was?"

Lawrence frowned. "The *baron* was wealthy. That doesn't mean *you* are. He didn't even provide you a dowry. You said so yourself."

"Can I tell him?" Tommy begged.

Graham shrugged. "He's a Wynchester now. Why not?"

Lawrence's chest thudded at the words. "I'm... an honorary Wynchester?"

"Not honorary," Jacob corrected. "You're a full-blood Wynchester."

Elizabeth tapped Lawrence's foot with her cane. "As long as *we* accept you, the sole requirement to be a Wynchester is to *want* to be with all your heart."

"I want that almost more than I've ever wanted anything," he admitted, pulse racing. Did they really...? Was he really...? "Is there some sort of ceremony?"

Chloe's eyes laughed up at him. "We already decided to include you. Just accept."

"I accept!" His spirits soared. He'd wished to belong to her for so long, it didn't yet seem real. "But your face earlier...is there something else you're not telling me?"

"Well..." She bit her lip.

"Chloe has twelve thousand pounds," Tommy blurted in a passable Yorkshire accent.

Lawrence could not parse the syllables. "She has what?"

"Well, it's more than that by now." Chloe plucked at a hem. "My bequest was twelve thousand, but Bean had given me a substantial sum when I first became a Wynchester. What I haven't spent on fashion, I invested in the five percents. It keeps growing."

"Why did you spend any of it on fripperies?" Elizabeth scolded her. "You know Bean wanted you to save your coin and use the family money for—"

"You have thousands of pounds *and* family money lying about?" Lawrence gaped at Chloe.

"We all do," Tommy put in with a shrug.

"Not the house," Elizabeth explained. "The gossips are right about the property belonging to the new baron."

Graham rustled his broadsheets. "We must console ourselves with our 'pittance,' as the papers say."

"'*Pittance*'?" The word wheezed out of Lawrence's throat.

With twelve thousand pounds, they could pay debts, make conservative investments—like with Lord Southerby—and save most of the rest. He and Chloe might not be able to build palaces to rival Carlton House, but they and the entailed estate would be *fine*.

It was more than he had dreamed.

Tommy bounced on her chair, governess persona forgotten. "Can we give him our wedding gift?"

"We're not married yet," Chloe pointed out. "The three weeks of banns haven't been read."

"It sounds as though we can afford a license to skip that step," Lawrence said weakly.

"Come." Elizabeth tapped the floor with her sword stick. "Follow me."

The siblings fell into step behind her like a well-practiced parade.

When they headed for the stairs, Lawrence narrowed his eyes at the next landing. "Is it art supplies? Has Marjorie fashioned me another studio?"

"No studio." Jacob's ferret nibbled his hair. "Just boxes."

"*Shh*," hissed the others. "Spoilsport!"

Elizabeth flung open the door to a small room beyond the landing. "*Et voilà!*"

Lawrence blinked. It was indeed a closet stuffed with nondescript wooden crates.

"Thank you," he said politely. "What is it?"

Tommy grinned at him. "Your housekeeper gave us your ledgers. These crates contain all of the books and paintings you've had to sell to make ends meet since you started helping Chloe. Your ugly carpets are just behind."

He started. "Mrs. *Root* handed over my private ledgers?"

"Oh, all right, I sneaked in and took them." Tommy plucked a ring of keys from a hook on the wall and tossed the jangling set to Lawrence. "You can have these back."

He gaped at her. "You have my housekeeper's *keys*?"

"Of course not!" Graham brushed this away with great offense. "We made our own."

"We also made *you* our own." Chloe gave him a saucy grin. "Lawrence Gosling, eighth Duke of Faircliffe, seventh Wynchester in Crime."

He covered his face with his hand. "I cannot believe you incorrigible wretches duplicated Mrs. Root's keys."

"No reneging," Elizabeth informed him cheerfully. "Once a Wynchester, always a Wynchester."

"In fact"—Graham turned to face him—"now you can join in our adventures!"

Jacob's face lit up with enthusiasm. "How are you with controlling birds of prey?"

"Do not give our new sibling a pet hawk," Tommy said firmly.

"Or teach him the call," Chloe added.

Jacob lifted a hand to his mouth and let out a horrific gurgling noise.

Seconds later a rhythmic tapping rattled the closest window.

"That's Hippogriff." Jacob's chest expanded with pride. "I'll introduce you in a moment."

"Tomorrow will be soon enough," Chloe informed her brother, then turned loving eyes to Lawrence. "Weren't you about to whisk me off for an evening in your crumbling castle, Handsome Pauper?"

"Why, yes." He pulled her into his arms at once. "That's exactly what I want to do."

And so he did.

EPILOGUE

꧁꧂

14 June, 1817
Faircliffe Town House

*C*hloe swirled in her husband's arms in the center of a grand ballroom, filled with lights and people and music. By any standard, the Gosling-Wynchesters' end-of-season gala was a splendid crush, if perhaps not precisely the sort her husband's ancestors might have envisioned.

For one thing, the jewel of tonight's rout was not the orchestra and the dancing but rather the once-private library now open to guests. A hundred people were on the dance floor, but dozens milled about the renovated library, settling into a plush sofa to thumb through the pages of an intriguing book, or admiring the angelic vase on its pedestal of honor or the artwork upon the walls.

Thanks to Marjorie's tutelage, Lawrence had even hung one of his own paintings: a landscape featuring Elderberry and Mango.

He and Chloe split their sets evenly: one to dance, one to mingle with guests, and back again. It was the best kind of exhausting. She had never smiled so much in her life. Her cheeks ached from laughter, her feet were numb from dancing, and her throat was sore from delightful conversations with so many friends, old and new.

Chloe tilted her mouth toward her husband's ear as they waltzed.

"Is the Leader of the House of Commons fighting with Lady Quarrington over marzipan?"

"Your brother has Tiglet stuffed in his waistcoat," Lawrence whispered back. "We can unleash him if necessary."

Chloe grinned back at him.

At first she had worried that it would be a struggle for him to learn to rule society rather than allow society to rule him, but her spirited duke had been more than a match for the challenge.

As for her fear that she would never be memorable enough to be bon ton, Chloe had discovered that their prejudices were irrelevant. She didn't need their approbation. The Duchess of Faircliffe did—and wore—what she wished. Hadn't they seen the caricatures?

She and her husband had gleefully accumulated their own circle of powerful people: some peers, some from the fashionable world, some thinkers, some poets. A few statesmen and agitators. A smattering of artists. And every single member of Chloe's reading circle, a few of whom appeared to have brought Chloe's book recommendation with them to the gala: Pierre Choderlos de Laclos's shocking *Les Liaisons dangereuses*.

Over the last weeks of Parliament, she and Lawrence had worked day and night disseminating pamphlets, participating in charities, parsing research, rewriting proposals for parliamentary acts, and putting together planned remarks and incisive questions to fashion a series of watertight speeches. He had been magnificent.

"After this," her husband murmured, "it will be heaven to do absolutely nothing for a while."

"Oh, I don't know." Chloe trailed the tip of her finger up his lapel and wiggled her brows suggestively. "I'm sure we can think of something."

He caught her hand and brought it to his lips. "How soon can we leave this party?"

"It's *our* party. Of course we can disappear if we like." She glanced over her shoulder. "Let me speak to my sister first. She's been standing next to the refreshment table for half an hour, and hasn't eaten a single thing."

"*Tommy?* Stoically resisting the allure of fresh lemon cakes?" Lawrence let go of Chloe's hand with obvious reluctance. "Perhaps she has a fever."

"Or something," Chloe agreed.

It took more time than she liked to weave through the well-wishers to the refreshment table, but when she arrived, her sister still had not changed position.

Tommy stood in shadow two paces from the dish of meat pies, her face half-obscured by a profusion of false curls.

"Eat one," said Chloe.

Tommy blinked at her. "Eat one what?"

"Whatever you like. This table is covered with all of your favorites." Chloe gestured at the towers of lemon cakes and meat pies.

Tommy looked startled to discover the treats in front of her. Chloe hid a smile.

"Hmm." She linked arms with Tommy and lowered her voice. "Miss Philippa York is here tonight."

Tommy's gaze flew back across the room. "I know."

Chloe tilted her head. "She looks nice."

"She's beautiful," Tommy corrected. "She's always beautiful. The cerulean trim beneath her bodice really brings out the blue of her eyes."

"Mm-hm," said Chloe. "And she's no longer spoken for. Unbetrothed and completely free."

Tommy swallowed. "I know."

"You could attend the reading circle as Tommy now, instead of Great-Aunt Wynchester," Chloe suggested. "I could formally 'introduce' you."

Tommy shook her head. "I can't."

"Or," Chloe said, "you could just...*talk* to her."

"I *can't*." But Tommy's gaze was locked on Philippa.

"Of course you can," Chloe said. "You're a Wynchester, and Wynchesters can do anything."

Tommy took a nervous breath. "Even this?"

"Even this," Chloe promised. "Just do three impossible things: walk over to her, introduce yourself, and smile. It could mark the beginning of a wonderful adventure."

Tommy straightened her shoulders. "No Wynchester can resist adventure."

"That's right." Chloe let go of her sister's arm.

"Wish me luck," Tommy whispered.

Then she straightened her wig and strode toward Philippa.

Don't miss Tommy and Philippa's story in *The Perks of Loving a Wallflower*, available fall 2021.

ABOUT THE AUTHOR

Erica Ridley is a *New York Times* and *USA Today* bestselling author of historical romance novels. When not reading or writing romances, Erica can be found riding camels in Africa, zip lining through rain forests in Costa Rica, or getting hopelessly lost in the middle of Budapest. She loves to hear from readers.

You can learn more at:
EricaRidley.com
Twitter @EricaRidley
Facebook.com/EricaRidley
Instagram @EricaRidley

*Looking for more historical romances?
Get swept away by handsome rogues and clever
ladies from Forever!*

HOW TO CATCH A DUKE
by Grace Burrowes

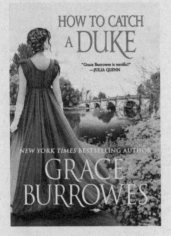

Miss Abigail Abbott needs to disappear—permanently—and the only person she trusts to help is Lord Stephen Wentworth, heir to the Duke of Walden. Stephen is brilliant, charming, and absolutely ruthless. So ruthless that he proposes marriage to keep Abigail safe. But when she accepts his courtship of convenience, they discover intimate moments that they don't want to end. But can Stephen convince Abigail that their arrangement is more than a sham and that his love is real?

THE TRUTH ABOUT DUKES
by Grace Burrowes

Lady Constance Wentworth never has a daring thought (that she admits aloud) and never comes close to courting scandal...as far as anybody knows. Robert Rothmere is a scandal poised to explode. Unless he wants to end up locked away in a madhouse (again) by his enemies, he needs to marry a perfectly proper, deadly-dull duchess, immediately—but little does he know that the delightful lady he has in mind is hiding scandalous secrets of her own.

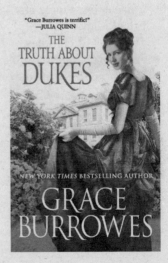

THE DUKE HEIST
by Erica Ridley

When the only father Chloe Wynchester's ever known makes a dying wish for his adopted family to recover a missing painting, she's the one her siblings turn to for stealing it back. No one expects that in doing so, she'll also abduct a handsome duke. Lawrence Gosling, the Duke of Faircliffe, is shocked to find himself in a runaway carriage driven by a beautiful woman. But if handing over the painting means sacrificing his family's legacy, will he follow his plan—or true love?

A ROGUE TO REMEMBER
by Emily Sullivan

After five Seasons of turning down every marriage proposal, Lottie Carlisle's uncle has declared she must choose a husband, or he'll find one for her. Only Lottie has her own agenda—namely ruining herself and then posing as a widow in the countryside. But when Alec Gresham, the seasoned spy who broke Lottie's heart, appears at her doorstep to escort her home, it seems her best-laid plans appear to have been for naught...And it soon becomes clear that the feelings between them are far from buried.

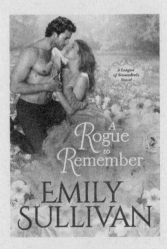

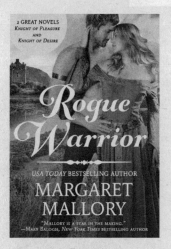

ROGUE WARRIOR (2-IN-1-EDITION)
by Margaret Mallory

Enjoy the first two books in the steamy medieval romance series All the King's Men! In *Knight of Desire*, warrior William FitzAlan and Lady Catherine Rayburn must learn to trust each other to save their lives and the love growing between them. In *Knight of Pleasure*, the charming Sir Stephen Carleton captures the heart of expert swordswoman Lady Isobel Hume, but he must prove his love when a threat leads Isobel into mortal danger.

ANY ROGUE WILL DO
by Bethany Bennett

For exactly one Season, Lady Charlotte Wentworth played the biddable female the *ton* expected—and all it got her was Society's mockery and derision. Now she's determined to take charge of her own future. So when an unwanted suitor tries to manipulate her into an engagement, she has a plan. He can't claim to be her fiancé if she's engaged to someone else. Even if it means asking for help from the last man she would ever marry.

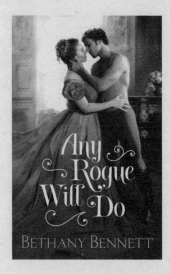